THE LEGEND OF THE
DOGMAN

David C.

Posthumus

2 /25

DAVID C. POSTHUMUS

The Legend of the Dogman
by David C. Posthumus

Copyright © **2022, David C. Posthumus**
Published by Timber Ghost Press
Printed in the United States of America
Edited by: C.R. Langille
Cover Art and Design by: Greg Chapman
Interior Design by: Firedrake Designs

Print ISBN: 978-1-7365867-3-0
Ebook ISBN: 978-1-7365867-2-3
Library of Congress Control Number: 2021948020

www.TimberGhostPress.com

CONTENTS

To Steve Cook, disc jockey at WTCM Traverse City, Michigan, for imagining the legend of Northern Michigan's Dogman and bringing it to life through song.

To my grandfather, Donald E. Allen ("Bapa"), for playing the song for us all around the kitchen table at the farm when we were kids and instilling in us a love for the Great Outdoors and all things spooky.

To my brother, Brad, my sister, Courtney, my nephew, Landon, my mother, Sydney, and my dear friend, Patrick Swanson, for being the first readers of The Legend of the Dogman manuscript.

To my cousin and best friend, Russell T. VanTol, for being the bravest of us all. Rest in peace, my brother. I will miss you for the rest of my life.

And to my incredible wife, Emily, for her nearly endless patience and support throughout the entire Dogman project; not to mention all my other projects. I love you.

Thank you,

David C. Posthumus
Wednesday, September 22, 2021
Belmont, Michigan

THE LEGEND OF THE DOGMAN

PART I

DAWNING

"This is the time to fear
Cause in this decade
The seventh year is here
And somewhere in
The Northwoods darkness
A creature walks upright
And the best advice you may ever get
Is don't go out at night."
—Steve Cook

"Who's afraid of the big bad wolf?
The big bad wolf, the big bad wolf
Who's afraid of the big bad wolf?
Tra-la-la-la-la!"
—Fiddler Pig and Fifer Pig

CHAPTER 1

Sunday, April 29, 2017
Near Marion, Michigan

The McGregor family went mushrooming every spring. It was a family tradition that stretched back to when Joe McGregor was a boy growing up in scenic Northern Michigan. Every year in late April and May, Joe and his father would spend a few hours together out in the woods each evening hunting for the elusive and delicious morel, one of the most prized and expensive wild mushrooms you can find. Morels are conical in shape with long hollow caps with a ridged and spongy look, almost like a honeycomb.

Sometimes on the weekends, Joe and his dad would spend an entire day outside, walking the trails and combing the woods, their eyes glued to the ground in search of the camouflaged fungi that blended in so well with the leaves, pine needles, and dead grass of the previous autumn. The rush of excitement when you spotted one and the thrill of victory as you reached down to pick it just never got old. Those times Joe spent in the Northwoods in the springtime with his father were some of his fondest childhood memories.

Morels are common in Michigan, growing in every county in the state, and mushroom hunting is a popular spring hobby. Plus, it's a great way to get some exercise and enjoy the great outdoors. Most morel hunters are tight-lipped about their favorite spots, but the majestic mixed pine and hardwood forests of Michigan's northern Lower Peninsula are prime locations for wild mushrooms.

One of the McGregor family's favorite spots was a densely wooded area of state land north of the small village of Marion in Osceola County. It sits between the Clam River to the north and the Middle Branch River to the south, both classic trout streams and tributaries of the mighty Muskegon River, the second largest river in the state.

Joe McGregor, along with his wife Lindsay and their five-year-old daughter Lily, had left their home in Cadillac around nine that morning after a hearty breakfast. Joe had packed their mesh bags, a wicker basket for Lily, and a picnic lunch packed securely away in the trunk. After a half-hour drive, they parked their car on the shoulder of an isolated dusty backroad, retrieved their gear, and headed off into the woods. It was a chilly sunny day, but they were happy to be spending some quality time together in the forest.

Just after one, the McGregors finished their lunch of sandwiches, baby carrots, apple slices, and potato chips. Joe and Lindsay shared a bottle of cold and refreshing iced tea while Lily happily slurped her chocolate milk. Lily was thrilled to the gills when Daddy surprised her by pulling out three big pieces of the cheesecake Mommy had made that week. They emerged from the little red and white cooler as if by magic, neatly arranged on a plastic plate and covered with Saran Wrap.

As the McGregors hiked back into the woods to continue

their hunt, Joe took stock of their haul so far for the day. It had been a productive one: Joe's white mesh bag contained at least fifty morels, while Lindsay, who had a great eye for mushrooms, bagged at least eighty. Even Lily had stopped daydreaming and playing to find eleven morels, which now bounced around merrily in her basket as they walked.

They reached the spot where they had left off before lunch and got back down to business. Joe and Lindsey walked slowly in opposite directions, their eyes scanning the ground in front of them, while Lily quietly hummed a tune and walked over to examine a particularly neat-looking tree stump.

What the McGregors didn't realize that crisp spring afternoon was that while they were out hunting for morels, there was something else out there lurking among the tangled trees and ferns; something dark, something menacing, something evil.

And that something was hunting *them.*

Joe was on fire; it seemed like he was finding a morel everywhere he looked. His father had always told him that where you found one, there was sure to be another; like they grew in pairs or something, a bit of folk-wisdom, the veracity of which Joe doubted but pondered briefly.

And there was another one!

He knelt down and cut the stem at ground level with his pocketknife and set it in his bag. This one had been peeking out from the blanket of dead leaves covering the ground around the trunk of a gigantic maple tree. Scanning the ground around it, another mushroom came into focus not ten feet from where Joe had cut the first one. It suddenly popped out of the background of leaves like one of those weird visual puzzles you stare into until you see a three-dimensional image in them. Or so they said. Joe was never very good at those damn things. While Joe was off to the east of the trail in a little gully, Lindsay was west of the main trail, up on a rise dotted with elm trees. She too was having great luck that day—the morel god of the Northwoods was surely smiling down upon her. As she bent down to pick another mushroom, she spotted two more. Lindsay smiled and nodded happily as she dropped them into her mesh bag, which was bursting, nearly overflowing with over a hundred morels.

Worth their weight in gold, she thought, patting her bag. *But what would go good with them for dinner tonight? Fish? Chicken? Definitely some wild leeks on the side.*

Lindsay continued contemplating the evening's meal as she walked, scanning the ground, a contented grin on her face. She enjoyed her status as the best mushroom hunter in the family; it was a spot of pride and also fueled some friendly competition between her and Joe. She chuckled, wondering how he was faring, knowing that he would never match her haul that day. Lindsay was about a hundred yards away from Joe, and Lily was between them, still walking and humming along the trail. The McGregors had hunted morels at that spot many times before, and they all knew the routine, so splitting up was no big deal... at least not until that fateful afternoon late in April.

It got Lindsay first.

It happened so fast that she never even knew what hit her. The thread of her life was cut so quickly and so cleanly that she was dead before she even hit the ground. She had just found a morel in the leaves at the base of a particularly bushy old elm tree with a thick trunk and had knelt down on one knee to pick it.

That's when it struck from behind the old elm with a blow so savage and powerful that it took Lindsay's head clean off. It bounced off the bed of dead leaves like an underinflated basketball, making a muffled *thuck* sound before rolling several feet to the south and coming to rest right beside a large morel.

Joe was next.

He was really concentrating, focused, homed in on the task at hand, his eyes glued to the ground in front of him, scanning back and forth like a speed reader on crack. He met his end roughly ten minutes after his wife's sudden death. But unfortunately for Joe, he saw his killer.

A dark figure suddenly appeared from behind a maple tree directly in front of him. Joe looked up, an expression of dumb surprise on his face, not knowing or believing what he was seeing. They were eye-to-eye for a split second before the thing dug into Joe's stomach, opening it up like a surgeon with a scalpel while simultaneously tearing out his throat with its teeth. Hot blood jetted from the gaping wound in Joe's neck, splashing against the trunk of the maple and pooling on the leaves beneath him. He didn't even have time to scream.

All the while, Lily skipped along the trail through the woods, clutching her wicker basket tightly in her little hands. She was singing "Let's Go Fly a Kite" from *Mary Poppins,* swaying along cheerfully with the movement and momentum of the song.

No one knows exactly what happened to Lily McGregor that day. All I know is that she and her mother and father were never seen or heard from again.

CHAPTER 2

Sunday, April 29, 2017
LeRoy, Michigan

Jack Allen had just turned 33 in mid-April. His wife Claire had thrown him a party at home, just the two of them with their three-year-old daughter, Melanie. There was a card, a few presents, a small vanilla cake with blue frosting and multicolored sprinkles. Melanie especially was floored when they lit the single candle in the center of the cake, and she and Mommy sang, "Happy Birthday." The grin never left Melanie's face, her eyes beaming, her shoulders hunched up like her whole body was contributing to the sweet smile. Gone were the days when Jack and Claire would have gone out partying to celebrate his special day, staying out late and sleeping off hangovers the following day. But Jack was content with his quieter life now, with being a husband and a father.

The Allen family lived in a white two-story farmhouse with a green corrugated-metal roof on 16 Mile Road. The farmhouse was situated in a small village in Northern Michigan called LeRoy, a sleepy little one-horse town in

Osceola County. LeRoy began as a lumber town. Settlers first came to the area in the 1860s and 1870s because of the abundance of rich white pine, cedar, and mixed hardwood forests. Lumber companies bought up large tracts of land, coveting the "green gold" so prevalent in the area, and the Grand Rapids and Indiana Railroad built tracks to transport the lumber. The excellent soil attracted farmers, and many descendants of the first farmers still lived and farmed in the LeRoy community.

As the population grew, retail merchants and other businesses came to the area. By the 1880s, there were some thirty businesses and several churches, a hardware store, a general store, a community hall, a hotel, restaurants, saloons, and a school serving the community. In 1884 the *LeRoy Independent* newspaper was founded. Like other lumber towns, LeRoy suffered from the boom-and-bust cycle, and the population steadily declined throughout the twentieth century. By 2017 LeRoy was home to about 250 people, mostly farming families and people who made a living with their hands.

Jack didn't quite fit this mold, but he loved LeRoy nonetheless. Jack was an assistant professor at Ferris State University in Big Rapids, about a half-hour drive south. Ferris State wasn't a huge university—there were just under fifteen thousand students enrolled there—or the most prestigious but teaching allowed Jack and his family to live where they wanted to. Jack taught courses in anthropology and Native American studies; things like cultural anthropology, anthropology of religion, native peoples and cultures of North America, and Native American spirituality.

Jack's wife, Claire, had a degree in psychology from Central Michigan University. She had a nice thing going— some comfy office space and a small but loyal patient base in nearby Cadillac—but had decided to take time off when

Melanie was born in 2014. She figured she could go back to it when Melanie was in school. Plus, Jack's assistant professor salary was enough for the time being. In fact, they were doing better than fine: they were happy.

They lived on a beautiful stretch of land Jack had inherited from his father, who had inherited it from his father. The Allens had lived in LeRoy for generations and were among the first white settlers in the area in the 1860s. The farmhouse, which everyone just called "the farm," was visible from 16 Mile Road, nestled atop a little hill with an old crippled windmill standing just east of the house. The entryway from the road was guarded by two old Carolina poplar trees on either side, bent and gnarled and reaching for each other. The driveway went up toward the carport then curled around a slight incline, with the front door of the farm facing north, away from 16 Mile.

If you continued down the driveway to the east, you'd descend a gentle slope—not much of a hill, really—and come to a great ancient red barn with a slightly rusted corrugated tin roof. The barn sat about fifty yards northeast of the farm like a hunched old man in a red-and-black-checked hunting jacket, groaning and creaking with age. It was functional, though: Jack had a workbench set up and kept a bunch of tools and supplies in there, using it for various projects and tinkering around. Jack and Claire did their best to keep up with the barn in terms of maintenance, although they didn't use it or rely on it in the same way Jack's father and grandfather had back in the 1900s when the lower level housed a tractor and other farming equipment and the ground floor functioned as a horse barn. These days the barn was mainly used for storage, but it held a special place in Jack's heart, on account of all the memories he associated with it.

He had grown up with it. Really that old red barn was a

family heirloom, a precious piece of Jack's identity and heritage, even though the wood was rotting away in some places and the roof was getting rusty.

The farm and barn were on the southeast corner of the Allen family property. The rest of the property consisted of a sprawling three-hundred-acre web of trails, woods, fields, and swamps, all with a little babbling clear-watered creek that meandered through it from northeast to southwest, which everyone called the "Crick." White pine-mixed hardwood forest dominated the landscape, with scattered blotches of marsh and swampland throughout. A large cedar swamp loomed darkly on the land like an irregular shadow. The Crick was officially known as the Rose Lake Outlet, a shallow little creek that drained Rose Lake, a natural inland lake about a mile south and west of the Allen property.

This natural wonderland in the Northwoods of Michigan was the magical playground of Jack's childhood: where he learned to love the outdoors; to hunt and fish; where he connected most with his father, his brother, and his cousins; and where, as a boy, he learned how to have fun, and later, how to be a man. This land was part of Jack, and it had also started to become part of Claire Greene, as she had been known when he first met her at a house party at Central Michigan in 2003. Claire also loved the quiet life they shared together out in the country in LeRoy, nestled in among the pines, and they intended to raise their daughter up to love and appreciate it too.

Every evening, weather permitting, Jack went for a long walk on the trails, timing it so he could catch the sunset over the trees in the lane leading up to the barn and get back to the farm just as dusk was turning to the dark of night. He loved the quiet stillness of twilight in the woods, just the gentle whisper of the breeze swaying in the tops of the scrub pines and caressing the ferns and tall grasses. He and Claire used to take both morning and evening strolls together, but since Melanie was born, it had become a bit of a scheduling issue, so more often than not Jack hiked by himself in the evenings. He didn't mind, though; it gave him some time alone in the woods to reflect on the day and enjoy the peaceful natural beauty. He always felt alive and energized when he was out in the woods.

That evening toward the end of April, it was a crisp forty-five degrees outside with a slight wind coming down from the northwest. By then, the spring thaw had more or less broken the last remnants of winter's chill hold on the landscape, but it was still wet and spongy, with frost visible on the grass in the cool mornings and crisp evenings. Sunset this time of year in Northern Michigan hit at about 8:30, so Jack threw a jacket on, laced up his hiking boots, and hit the trails by about 7:45.

He left the farm and headed west along a trail that took him past a stand of tall, straight red pines in neat little rows, looking a bit like tin soldiers marching off toward the north. The compacted dirt of the trail felt good beneath his boots as he breathed in the chill evening air through his nose, seeing the steam from his breath in front of him as he exhaled. Without thinking, he ran a hand through his mop of light brown hair and smiled, happy to be outside and grateful to be alive.

The trail veered north as he passed a majestic old maple tree on his right that must have been at least a hundred years old. It was a kindly, fat old tree, and Jack had fond memories of it growing up. That old maple tree seemed to mark the boundary between the tame, controllable, ordered realm of human civilization and the chaotic, unpredictable realm of wild nature. Jack always felt like he was bravely setting out into the unknown when he crossed over this magical threshold into the beyond, an intrepid explorer entering a mysterious wild land where most men feared to tread. He smiled at the thought as he glanced toward the unforgiving terrain of what he and his cousins had always called "the Sahara" when they were boys. It was a slightly sloping rocky area that dipped down to the west and acted as a natural windbreak, collecting sand, dirt, and dust, hence its name.

As he passed by the Sahara, the trail opened up and was straddled on either side by grassy sandy plains and ferns in the foreground with stands of dense pines and spruces in the background.

Jack's breathing was smooth and steady as he came to the clearing where the deeper woods began: a muddy trail leading across a stone bridge over the Crick and into the thick dark woods beyond it. The sour scent of wet decaying leaves was in the air, mingling with the aroma of pines and ferns. The trail was more overgrown here, and the dense forest seemed to collapse inward, reaching out and surrounding you so that you couldn't see the sky clearly once you entered.

Usually, Jack would have continued on at this point over the stone bridge and into the deep woods, the murky marshland on either side of the trail, his great-uncle Rob's old deer blind deteriorating a couple hundred yards up on the left where the trail forked. But that night in late April, Jack felt something strange that made him decide to turn east and head back home. He felt something, no doubt, but later, he thought he may have *heard* something as well

All of a sudden, Jack had an uneasy feeling that hit him like a bolt of lightning and stopped him dead in his tracks. He had just reached the shadowy entrance to the deep woods before the stone bridge. Jack was struck, seemingly out of the blue, by a strong memory of his father, Stephen, the man who had taught Jack everything he knew about the outdoors, about responsibility, honor, and life; a man Jack had worshipped and shared a close and loving relationship with.

The memory, of Jack looking deeply into his father's weathered stubbly face, was abstract and fleeting but powerful, so much so that Jack swore he could actually *smell* his father. That familiar scent that was a mix of Old Spice aftershave and Winston cigarettes. He closed his eyes and could actually *see* the checked red and black flannel jacket his father always wore. The memory and the scent it left hanging in the air, imagined or not sent a wave of emotion shuddering through Jack's body, and his eyes went misty. He squeezed them shut as his hand instinctively shot up and wiped the corners of his eyes, breathing in a gasping, wavering breath.

Goddamn, he thought. *I haven't thought about Dad in months, maybe years. What a shitty son I am. I miss him. When I get home I'll have to give Mom a call and—*

Just then, a noise up ahead in the thick woods along the dim trail beyond the stone bridge startled Jack out of his reverie. He looked up, following the sound with his eyes, a little spooked. It had sounded like something moving stealthily through the undergrowth, like leaves and branches gently brushing against some form. It was maybe fifty yards away down the trail. Jack stared ahead breathlessly, silent and unmoving. Tense seconds ticked by as Jack waited. When he didn't hear anything again he shook his head and sighed.

God, what am I so scared of? he thought, a little embarrassed. *I'm jumpy as hell tonight. It was probably just a deer, maybe a turkey or a coyote. I should just get home, pour myself a little drink, and—*

At that moment, a gray squirrel crashed through the brush thirty yards from Jack, scampering frantically from the left side of the trail to the right. Jack nearly jumped out of his skin, gasping, his heart pounding in his chest.

"*Dammit!*" he cried, kicking dirt toward the squirrel with his boot as he recovered from his fright.

He chuckled to himself, shaking his head in nervous amusement as he turned and headed east along the trail into a shallow draw, the swamp on his left and a thick stand of scrub pines just off to his right. The shadows were growing, and darkness was coming on fast, a thought that made him put a little extra zip in his step after his alarming run-in with the squirrel on that strange, spooky evening.

As Jack hiked down the trail, veering slightly to the north toward the swamp, an eerie feeling overtook him... like he was being *watched*... or *followed*. He glanced over his shoulder into the misty tree line, where the landscape dipped fifty yards back into the marshes, and the Crick ran down through a narrow ravine. He squinted into the gloomy tangle of undergrowth and bare skinny tree trunks but saw nothing. Yet the unnerving feeling that something was watching him, following his every move, remained, actually growing stronger as he emerged into the clearing by his uncle's deer blind, a veritable fortress built into a massive oak tree where four trails met.

His pace quickened into a brisk walk (*a very brisk walk; a fast shuffling walk*), and his heartbeat picked up as well, matching the pace of his gait. He made a sharp right turn and headed south down the trail known as "the Lane." The Lane was a straight and narrow trail with thick scotch pines on either side that opened up into a rye field on the left after a hundred yards or so, eventually leading up to the great red barn sitting atop the hill like a sentry, a symbol of home and hearth.

Dusk was settling in now. Jack's visibility was waning but not that ghastly feeling of being watched and shadowed that made the hair on his arms and the back of his neck prickle up and made his whole body tingle. He occasionally stole a frightened look back over his shoulder, but it was too dark now to see much of anything. Jack was breathing heavily now, loudly humming a tune he had heard on the radio earlier that day, thinking this would make him safer and make things seem more normal and less scary.

Suddenly he heard a rustling in the dark behind him, not more than twenty-five yards away.

That was it.

Jack broke into an all-out sprint then, his frightened eyes fixed straight ahead as his arms pumped up and down furiously. He could just make out the end of the lane in the fading glow of dusk, where the rows of pines ended, and it opened up onto the rye field. He was twenty yards away from the clearing... ten yards... five yards. His heart slammed wildly in his chest, and a burning stitch developed in his side as he gasped for breath.

He passed the clearing at a dead sprint and kept going, not stopping to look back. Jack raced up the hill toward the barn on a grassy two-track path, tall grass swaying in the light breeze on either side of him. A floodlight was on above the large double doors of the barn's lower level. At that moment, as he reached the barn and was suddenly bathed in that circle of glorious protecting light thrown by the halogen bulb above the barn door, Jack had never been more grateful for anything in all his life.

He whirled around, hands on his hips, breathing heavily, sweating, his head bobbing up and down and chest heaving with each breath. He surveyed the trail behind him in the near darkness.

Of course, there was nothing.

He could just barely make out some dark, vague shapes down in the lane, but it was impossible to tell what they were from where he was standing, breathless and distressed. He told himself they were just trees or bushes, and he was probably right. He also told himself that he was crazy: a big crazy scaredy-cat, to be exact.

Jack breathed out deeply, turned, and timidly walked up the stone steps embedded in the hillside southeast of the barn. Switching off the barn lights and dragging the main double doors closed for the night, he trudged up the gentle slope on the gravel driveway toward the old farmhouse, exhausted and embarrassed by how he had gotten so spooked. Already his rational mind was working to explain away what he had felt and heard on the trails.

A deer, a turkey, a coyote, a cougar, maybe even a bear. Hell, maybe it was just another squirrel, you big wuss! Any of those things are all easily explainable and not that out of the ordinary. A little scary, maybe, but perfectly normal in these parts, his mind explained away anxiously to him. *If it wasn't your senses playing tricks on you—which it probably was—then it was just some ordinary animal going for a stroll in the woods at dusk, same as you were.*

But deep down, Jack knew the feeling he had experienced was real. First, the poignant memory of his father, then the creepy feeling that he was being watched, and finally, the certainty that he was being followed. He *had* heard that noise in the lane, hadn't he? These thoughts were running through his head as he settled into bed that night, kissing Claire softly on the forehead before rolling over onto his side and closing his tired eyes.

As he slept that night, his brain was already hard at work rationalizing his experience, forgetting and moving past it, filing it away in the "Unlikely or Impossible" folder. By the time he awoke, the memory of his walk in the woods the night before was already fading like darkness at sunrise.

Jack awoke the next day with a fuzzy head and a dry sour mouth. He had sunk a few bourbon and sodas on ice the night before while watching TV to take his mind off things after his strange hike around the trails. It was seven A.M., and the sun was beginning to peak over the eastern horizon, spreading its orange-yellow glow across the landscape. Jack yawned, a guttural moan escaping from his throat as he rubbed his forehead, sitting hunched over on the side of the bed.

He stumbled to the bathroom, lurching like Frankenstein's monster, and relieved himself. Glancing in the mirror, he thought he kind of *looked* like Frankenstein's monster, a thought that made him wince and shake his head. Fumbling in the medicine cabinet, he popped two ibuprofens into his mouth and swallowed them down with a splash of water from the sink.

Jack took a shower and was toweling off as he padded back to his bedroom where Claire was sitting up in bed, the covers drawn up just above her breasts.

"Morning, dear," Jack said, grabbing a pair of boxer briefs from a dresser drawer.

He smiled as he stepped into the boxer briefs and pulled them up.

"Good morning," Claire yawned, her eyes at half-mast, still heavy with sleep.

Even at this early hour—maybe *especially* at this early hour—Claire was beautiful. A real natural beauty, her straight dark-brown hair cascading over her shoulders, her hazel eyes kind and mesmerizing to behold, the shape of her face and features symmetrical and proportioned, and lips that could draw you in with everything from a voluptuous, confidant come-on smile to a conspiratorial knowing smirk or a candid, merry toothy grin. Claire had all this and more; much more. Looking over at her at that moment, a warm surge of love and devotion overpowered him.

"I love you, baby," Jack sighed, shaking his head in a gesture of total surrender.

Claire cocked her head to one side and exhaled, grinning as her eyebrow rose slightly in an expression that said, *Now, what do you want?*

"I love you too, Jack," she said, her smile widening. "But if you really loved me, you'd make me something for breakfast."

Jack pulled on a pair of dark-wash blue jeans and a Led Zeppelin t-shirt and walked barefoot down the hallway to the kitchen.

"And a cup of coffee, please!" he heard Claire call after him, giggling a bit after she said it.

Jack shuffled into the kitchen, a nice cozy kitchen, nothing too fancy. There were two ways to access the kitchen: one through the hallway past the bathroom near the front door, the other through the wooden saloon-style doors adjacent to the living room. A lot of good family time was spent around the kitchen table, an antique round oak table Jack had inherited from his mother and father. The view out the two picture windows on either corner of the table was magnificent. The window on the west side of the house looked out toward the windmill and barn and down the hill to the rye field, while the window facing north peered out into the three-season porch before cascading down the hill into the scotch pines and brush. This particular morning the sun was bathing everything in a beautiful golden radiance that brought a smile to Jack's face.

It's going to be a good day, he thought as he opened the fridge and pulled out a carton of eggs.

Pivoting on one foot, he turned and swung the fridge door closed with his hip, making his way over to the countertop. Setting the eggs down on the Formica, he bent down and retrieved a frying pan from the cabinet below. He placed it on the range and fired up one of the back burners on the stovetop. He turned the heat down to medium and coated the pan with cooking spray. Jack then got to work cracking eggs into the frying pan. They sizzled as the mucousy whites spread in all directions, uniting into one great pool.

Gotta make sure I get those final exams written, he thought, his mind turning to the tasks on his work to-do list for the week. He filled a tall glass with cold water from the sink and slammed it, hoping it would ease his aching head. *Then the study guides. Then I need to email them to the students* and *remind them about the final and my exam policy... can't believe I need to remind them about the fucking final exam.* He sighed and shook his head.

Jack reached into the cupboard above the countertop and came down with a glass jar filled with ground coffee and got coffee brewing.

Next he fished a loaf of wheat bread off the top of the refrigerator chewing on his tongue as he thought more about business, his eyes fixed on where the wall met the white textured ceiling but not really looking at it. He laid three pieces of toast out in the toaster oven, cranking the knob to the right, bringing the toaster oven to life like a glowing furnace. It began to click rhythmically.

It's alive! It's ALIVE! he thought, his eyes widening in mock excitement, a crazy amused grin touching his lips. *What's with all the Frankenstein references today?*

Just then, Melanie came bursting into the kitchen through the saloon-style doors.

"Daddy! Daddy!" Melanie cried excitedly in her high musical voice, making her way around the countertop to where Jack was standing in the nook between the sink and the oven.

"Good morning, sweetheart!" Jack smiled, happy to see her.

He picked her up in a warm hug, and they embraced for a few seconds before Jack kissed her on the cheek and put her back down.

"*Guess what,* Daddy?" Melanie said, a look of excited intrigue on her sweet face.

"What, sweetie?" Jack gasped, a tone of mock suspense in his voice.

"I just went pee on the potty, and now I'm wearing my new princess panties *AND* this *bee-you-tea-full* dress," she said proudly, curtsying before twirling in her dress with little sailboats on it.

"Oh wow, way to go, Mel!" Jack said, genuinely impressed. "And my oh my, what a lovely dress you're wearing! It really twirls well."

"Thank you, Daddy," Melanie nodded with a serious look on her face, sounding more like a teenager than a three-year-old.

She's a three-nager, Jack thought. *Dear God, help us.*

Jack heard the bathroom door down the hallway to the left open, and Claire strolled into the kitchen, reaching down to give Melanie a good-morning hug.

"How'd you sleep, baby girl?" she asked, reaching to help Melanie up into her booster seat at the table.

"*No,* I can do it *myself,*" Melanie said stubbornly, hands on her hips, drawing out the last syllable for effect.

Claire glanced over at Jack, and they shared an amused look while Melanie climbed up into her seat. Just then, the coffeemaker began to huff and puff, spitting out air noisily like a backfiring old Ford, signaling the end of its daily routine. Jack handed Claire a Michigan State Spartans coffee mug from the cupboard, and she poured herself a tall cup of steaming black coffee, adding a splash of milk from the gallon in the fridge. Walking back to the table, she scooted a chair up to it and sat down, cupping her hot mug with both hands and breathing in the steam and aroma of the magic black drink.

Jack sauntered over to the table, a green sippy cup filled with water in one hand and a bowl of Honey Nut Cheerios in the other. He placed these offerings in front of Melanie at the table and backed away placatingly.

"Here's your cereal, my love," he said as Melanie dug in.

"Thank you, Daddy," she said with a mouthful of Cheerios.

Melanie *loved* cereal.

Jack grabbed a spatula and flipped the eggs in the frying pan before pouring himself a cup of coffee. He set it aside by the sink when the toaster oven dinged and scooped the toast out onto a plate and buttered it. Arranging plates with two eggs and wheat toast, he handed a plate to Claire before retrieving his coffee and scooting up to the kitchen table. Melanie took care of the third piece of toast, drizzled with a bit of honey from the lazy Susan.

As Jack took his first bite of eggs and toast, washing it down with a healthy gulp of coffee, he looked from Claire to Melanie and nodded his head, feeling a profound sense of thankfulness.

Claire had just left with Melanie to go grocery shopping in Cadillac, which was about a thirty-minute drive from the farmhouse. They did a lot of their shopping in Cadillac, a charming little town of just over ten thousand people that had nice grocery stores, department stores, restaurants, a movie theater, and a mall. In a pinch, the Allens might pick up some essentials at the Village Market in LeRoy or the Dighton Store in Dighton, but you paid an arm and a leg at those places, and the quality wasn't as good as what you'd get in Cadillac.

Meanwhile, Jack pulled on a checked wool shirt and sat on the little bench on the three-season porch, slipping into his work shoes. He grabbed his to-go mug of coffee, his brown leather messenger bag, and his cellphone. He pulled the front door closed behind him as he stepped out onto the patio and into the late April sunshine, shielding his eyes instinctively with his hand as he looked up at the blue cloudless sky. Jack locked the door behind him and walked gingerly down to the little parking nook between some apple trees to the east and an old pear tree to the west. He whistled as he walked, smiling and feeling good.

Jack climbed into his black 2013 Chevy Blazer and fired up the engine. Turning west onto 16 Mile Road, he drove at a leisurely pace. This was the last full week of classes at Ferris State before the end of the spring semester and summer break.

Jack was relieved and excited to get the semester wrapped up. He had some research to finish up this summer: a book project on the culture and history of the People of the Three Fires, the three main Native American Tribes in Michigan, the Ojibwe, Ottawa, and Potawatomie. For a college professor on a two/three teaching load, meaning he taught two courses in the fall and three in the spring, summer was the best time to get research done. Sometimes it seemed like it was the *only* time he could get any research done. Jack liked teaching okay, but he really got into academia because of the research. He *loved* the research; it was a passion that drove him.

Jack was a cultural anthropologist, which meant he

studied the culture, history, and language of a people other than his own. His main area of interest was religion and ritual: how and why religion motivated people and influenced identity at the group and individual level.

He typically lectured on Tuesdays and Thursdays, which gave him Mondays, Wednesdays, and Fridays to attend meetings, hold office hours, write exams, grade assignments and exams, correct papers, and, if he had any time left over, get some research done. That day he had to write exams for his three courses that spring: cultural anthropology, native peoples and cultures of North America, and linguistic anthropology. He also had to compile study guides for his lower-level courses.

Jack's older brother, Brad, had invited him to lunch that afternoon with a few of their friends. Brad Allen owned a small construction business called Allen and Co. Construction that got a lot of regional business and kept him very busy. Brad was three years older than Jack, a big hardworking man's man with a gentle soul and a big heart. In terms of their temperaments and professions, Jack and Brad couldn't have been more different: Brad labored outside with his hands, played varsity football and basketball in high school, and never missed a Detroit Lions football game; Jack worked in a musty book-filled university office, usually had his nose in a book, and played guitar and sang in several rock bands since he was in high school. Though they were opposites in many ways, that didn't seem to matter much to them; they had always shared a deep love and respect for each other, each appreciating the other's complementary strengths and interests. That being said, Jack and Brad had several things in common, the most prominent being a love for the Northwoods, devotion to family and friends, big hearts, quick smiles, and hearty laughs.

Brad and his crew were building a new home for the

Thompson family in Rose Lake Forest in LeRoy, a scenic housing development with lakefront access not two miles down the road from the farm. Jack hoped to finish up his work for the morning and make it over to the site to check it out before heading to a late lunch with the crew around two P.M… which is exactly what he did. His work went well with only minimal interruptions and emails to field, and by noon, he was wrapping things up and heading out the door. He stopped in the faculty lounge on his way out to refill his thermos with hot coffee.

Jack headed up the highway toward the Thompson's house. He sipped delicately at his coffee, listening to a Beatles song on the local rock radio station, drumming his fingers on the steering wheel and singing along. Before long, he pulled onto the gravel private drive.

It was a gray ranch-style house with an attached two-car garage set back into a hill that had been partially leveled the previous spring to make space to lay a foundation and pour a basement. Brad's construction company subcontracted with other local and regional companies to do the concrete work and the plumbing and electricity, but aside from that, Brad and his crew of three employees had done the bulk of the construction on the new home, which had been a sweeping success thus far.

Jack pulled off to the side of the temporary gravel driveway, put the Blazer in park, and turned off the ignition. Grabbing his coffee, he got out and headed for the front door.

Things are right on schedule around here, he thought, climbing the stairs of the front porch. He knew because this new project was all Brad seemed to talk about lately. *At this rate, the Thompsons should be able to move in by the end of June or early July.* Jack knocked before letting himself in.

"Afternoon, Jackoff!" Jack's friend and Brad's employee, Sam Patterson, said with a shit-eating grin on his face.

At six-foot-tall and one hundred and sixty pounds, Sam was thin but wiry-strong, not much fat on him to speak of. He had shaggy blonde hair that came down over his ears and blue eyes that made women look twice when he walked into a room. Sam had a good sense of humor and sharp wit, an all-around likable guy. He was a good and loyal friend to both Jack and Brad: they'd known him forever, and he'd been working with Brad for almost five years now. He was reliable and hard-working, honest too. Brad and Jack first met Sam while attending Pine River High School back in the late 1990s; they were all proud to be Pine River Bucks. They were pretty tight and liked to joke and harass each other a bit to make things interesting.

"Morning, Samantha!" Jack retorted, returning Sam's comical bravado and grin. There was a mischievous sparkle in his eye. "How are the cabinets coming along?"

"Fine, just fine," Sam said, shaking Jack's hand. "This place is really coming together nicely, wouldn'tcha say?"

"I was just thinking the same thing myself," Jack smiled, nodding. "At this rate, you should be finished up by late June, don't you think?"

"Yes, sir, I think that sounds about right."

"Little Brother!" Brad lumbered into the room and put his big affable arm around Jack's shoulders, squeezing him a bit too hard for Jack's liking, not that he would have admitted it.

"Hey, Brad," Jack smiled, giving him a healthy squeeze back. "This place is really coming along. Looks great!"

"Thanks, yeah I know! I'm super pumped about it," Brad grinned. "How about a tour?"

Brad took Jack through the house room by room with Sam not far behind, showing him everything and explaining all the details about how it had come together, challenges they'd faced, and how they'd overcome them. Jack was impressed, and Brad was beaming with pride.

After the tour, they were all standing around in the kitchen.

"Well, who's hungry?" Brad asked.

"I could eat," Sam said.

Brad grinned. "Well, fuckos, let's get cleaned up real quick and then head out." They chuckled, and Jack took a healthy slug of his coffee.

It was almost two P.M. Sam went outside to clean up with the hose, while Brad and Jack went to get Leslie, who was working in the guest bathroom. Brad headed down the hall toward the guest bathroom with Jack shuffling along behind him, his stomach beginning to growl. The light was on, and he could hear music playing, drifting lazily out of a Sony boombox on top of the sink. It was country, sounded like George Strait. Listening, Jack recognized the song as "Desperately." He liked the song.

Good old King George, Jack thought as he came into the doorway of the guest bathroom.

Leslie Patterson was on a stepladder in the corner of the room, laying and grouting tile above the shower surround they installed the week before. She was about five-foot-eight, slender but shapely, with auburn hair that had a hint of curl to it that fell onto her shoulders in a carefree way. Leslie had deep, dark-brown eyes that you could easily get lost in, like staring into a mandala. On the job site, she dressed practically, typically wearing jeans and a t-shirt or maybe a flannel or sweatshirt if it was chilly. She looked good in tight jeans, but out on the town on a Friday or Saturday night, she'd knock your socks off, take your breath away, turn heads when she walked into a room, and capture and hold the attention of the single men and some of the married ones too. Leslie had a certain undeniable grace and an aura, a presence or magnetism, that made it seem like she could do anything she wanted to and *with* whomever she wanted to. When she turned on the charm and did herself up for a night out, she was irresistible and unstoppable and she *knew* it. But the coolest thing about Leslie was that she rarely let that knowledge go to her head. She was a kind and generous person who everyone liked to be around. An energy-giver, as Jack's mom used to say.

Now here she was, balancing effortlessly on a stepladder facing the wall, her back to the door, concentrating as she applied and shaped a groove of light gray grout above the guest shower with a touch and finesse that came from years of experience and can only be described as masterful, like an artform, really. She didn't notice when Brad and Jack came into the doorway.

"Les," Brad called, almost in a whisper.

"*Oh* my *GOD!*" Leslie gasped, jumping. She reached for the wall for balance. "You scared the shit out of me, Brad! Oh, hey, Jackass." More often than not, Les and Sam referred to Jack affectionately as "Jackass" or "Jackoff." Leslie giggled, slightly embarrassed, shaking her head as she recovered from her surprise.

"A little jumpy today, are we?" Jack teased, rolling his eyes with vaudeville sarcasm.

"I guess so," Leslie laughed. "You know I just get so focused on what I'm doing, I totally zone out and forget about the rest of the world."

"I think maybe you should switch to decaf," Brad cracked a wiseass grin on his face. "But anyway, we're all getting Pibbs for lunch. You in?"

"Yeah, for sure," Leslie replied, turning back to her work. "Just give me a sec to finish this row."

Mr. Pibbs was the best restaurant in the small village of LeRoy. Hell, it was the *only* restaurant, aside from Travelers Bar and Grill, which was more or less across the street from Pibbs. Jack, Brad, and their merry crew ate lunch together regularly, maybe once a week, alternating between Pibbs and Travelers. Occasionally they'd get adventurous and drive the extra ten or fifteen minutes to Mineral Springs Pub and Grill in Tustin.

That Monday afternoon in late April, they all rode to lunch together in Jack's Blazer, as they often did. Jack noticed some clouds coming in from the west threatening rain as they took a right off Mackinaw Trail into the Pibbs parking lot, next door to the LeRoy Village Market grocery store. The doors of the Blazer swung open in unison, and everyone hopped out. Sam and Brad lit cigarettes and plopped down on the bench outside of Pibbs as Jack held the door for the others who filed in.

"Wherever you like," croaked a large waitress, motioning with her head toward the dining area.

"Thanks, Barb," Leslie nodded.

They maneuvered over to a corner table by the window looking out at Mackinaw Trail, the main drag through downtown LeRoy, if you could even call it that. "Don't blink, or you might miss it" could've been LeRoy's motto.

Jack sighed as he sat down and scooched into the round wooden table. Just then, the bell dinged as the front door opened, and Brad and Sam shuffled inside. They looked around, made eye contact with Jack, then headed over to the table.

They were all seated when Barb came by with menus and took their drink order. They all ordered coffee and water.

Pibbs was busy this afternoon. They had caught the lunch rush head-on, and there was a lot of coming and going, conversation and laughter.

A few minutes later, they had ordered their lunches and were sipping on their drinks, chatting like the old friends they were. Brad was the brains of the operation, the supportive leader; Sam was the prankster and jokester, and Leslie was the saucy sarcastic firebrand. Jack fit in as the leader's endearing kid brother, "the professor," as they sometimes called him. They were all quite happy with their roles, the roles they were born to play, in fact.

It was a late lunch, and they were already hungry, so by the time the food came fifteen minutes later, they were ravenous. The conversation came to an abrupt halt once Barb put the plates down on the tablecloth. Occasionally one of them made a comment or cracked a joke in between mouthfuls, but the grub definitely took priority over the gab.

Jack was homing in on the last corner of his turkey club sandwich when the bell above the door dinged again. In walked Ben Williams wearing bib overalls and a flannel shirt. He was a local farmer who everyone in town seemed to like. Ben had a concerned look on his face, which usually wore a happy-go-lucky grin. Under his arm was a stack of papers of some kind. Ben noticed Brad, Jack, and the crew, raising his chin in a gesture of greeting.

"Afternoon, Ben," Brad called, a look of concern in his eyes. "Everything alright?"

"Hey, Brad," Ben mumbled, making his way around tables and chairs over to their spot by the window. "Afternoon, Leslie. Sam. Jack." Ben touched the bill of his baseball cap as he greeted the table.

"What you got there, Ben?" Sam asked, eyeing the sheaf of papers under his arm.

"Well, Katie's dog Lyra went missing two days ago," Ben said, exhibiting the papers he was carrying. They were missing posters with a picture of a cute dog, a brown and black mutt with tan-colored eyebrows.

"Oh, Ben, I'm so sorry to hear that!" Leslie said with a tightlipped frown on her face. "I know how much she means to Katie. She's a sweet pup."

"Yeah, she's awfully upset about it, ya know?" Ben continued, visibly upset himself. "So I'm trying to spread the word around town and posting some of these fliers around, ya see. Would y'all do me a favor and keep an eye out for her?"

"Oh, yeah, of course, Ben," everyone at the table agreed, nodding.

"Hey, you know, I'm sure she'll turn up" Brad said. "Probably just went off after a deer or something—"

"Maybe she's shacked up with Bateman's Doberman," Sam joked, trying to lighten the mood. "That dog's always sniffin around the ladies... *literally.*"

Ben looked at Sam severely, that troubled look still on his face.

"I hope you boys are right," he said doubtfully. "It's not like her to run off for so long, ya know? Anyway, Katie's pretty tore up about it, so please let me know right away if you see her."

"Yeah, of course," Jack said, shaking his hand firmly. "Hope everything works out alright."

"Thanks, Jack," Ben nodded, touching the brim of his hat again. He looked from Jack to Brad to Sam and then to Leslie, then he turned and headed back the way he came. Even his gait was heavy with worry. He stopped at the counter up front, an ancient cash register perched on top of it, and spoke to Barb and another waitress, nodding, that same worried look still etched on his face, before heading back out the door.

"Poor Katie," Leslie murmured. She had finished her chicken caesar wrap and was now staring blankly out the window. The Williams were neighbors of Leslie's growing up, so she knew them well.

"Yeah, I'm sure it'll work out alright," Sam said, stuffing a french fry blotted with ketchup in his mouth.

"Yeah, I hope so," Leslie sighed, still gazing out the window, lost in thought.

The foursome finished their meals and gulped the last of their beverages. It was Leslie's turn to buy, so she headed up to the counter to settle up with Barb as the others made their way to the door. Brad and Sam went out first to indulge in after-lunch smokes. When they were finished, they all piled into Jack's Blazer and took off down Mackinaw Trail back to the Thompsons' house in Rose Lake Forest.

CHAPTER 3

Saturday, May 6, 2017
LeRoy, Michigan

Finals week had just come to an end, and Jack took the weekend off to relax and spend time with Claire and Melanie. He had a mountain of grading to do before he could submit his final grades for the semester, but he wasn't going to worry about that now. He was happy to be done with teaching for the summer and excited to get going on his research again. It was a drizzly gray spring morning in Northern Michigan, and everything smelled fresh and clean. The Northwoods were coming alive again after their long cold winter hibernation.

They had just finished breakfast. Mel had gone off to play Disney princesses with Claire in the living room, a "game" she *always* wanted to play and one that Jack and Claire were ungodly tired of. But it was Claire's turn this morning, so Jack was sitting at the kitchen table drinking a cup of coffee and catching up on the local news on his cellphone. Jack liked a website called *News Beat* for all kinds of local stories out of places like Reed City, Big Rapids, Cadillac, Evart, and

Manistee. Checking out the local news was a weekly ritual for Jack, and oftentimes, the stories he read were uproariously funny, seeing as they were usually *very* local; *very ethnographic,* as an Estonian linguist colleague of Jack's would say.

The stories today were pretty funny, in a morbid sort of way. They were also just plain odd. Jack chuckled at the typo in the title of the first story he clicked on.

From bigrapidsnews.com via *News Beat,* May 6, 2017:

REED CITY CHICKEN FARMER LOSES CHICKENS IN GRISTLY MASSACRE

REED CITY – A Reed City poultryman, Ned Blevins, filed a report with the Osceola County Sheriff's Department yesterday claiming seventy-six of his one hundred and thirty chickens were slaughtered in what appears to be a sick prank. Osceola County Sheriff John Dearborn investigated and corroborated Mr. Blevins's story. "The scene was disturbing, to say the least," Dearborn said in a phone interview. "Seventy-six innocent chickens all torn up for no apparent reason. It's a real shame. Now either this is some prank or there was a wild animal that got in there, maybe a cougar or a coyote, possibly a bear. In any case my officers and I are investigating and if it turns out to be some malicious criminal act, rest assured we will find the culprit and bring him... or her to justice."

Jack giggled in spite of himself as he read the gripping account of poultryman Ned Blevins and the great "gristly" Reed City chicken massacre of 2017. The next article he clicked on was about a horse-ranch venture just outside of Buckley.

From *Cadillac News* via *News Beat,* May 6, 2017:

BUCKLEY RANCH REPORTS HORSES MISSING, FOUR DEAD

BUCKLEY – Faye and Leo Martin, the owners and operators of the Lucky Seven Ranch in Buckley, reported that during the night of Thursday, May 4, someone broke into their stables and killed four of their horses, two American quarter horses, an Arabian, and a Morgan. Two thoroughbreds are also currently missing. "There's a slight chance that this was an animal attack, but it seems unlikely," Leo Martin said in an email exchange with *Cadillac News.* "The assailant got in through a stable window, but it was pretty high up for an animal to have gotten to it." The Martins are asking for prayers and any information regarding the two thoroughbreds still missing.

Jack shrugged his shoulders and made a face that said, "Don't look at me; I don't know anything about it!" *People are sick,* he thought, sipping his coffee and clicking on the next story.

From manisteenews.com via *News Beat*, May 6, 2017:

MANISTEE FARMER REPORTS COWS SLAUGHTERED

MANISTEE – A Manistee farmer, Robert Wiley, reported that last week someone broke into his cattle pen and killed several head of cattle. Ten dairy cows were discovered on Wednesday morning with their throats cut. Another four were found dead with no apparent injuries.

The last story Jack read that morning was more serious and troubling, a real mystery.

From *Cadillac News* via *News Beat*, May 6, 2017:

MCGREGOR FAMILY OF CADILLAC STILL MISSING

CADILLAC – Cadillac native Joe McGregor and his wife Lindsay and daughter Lily have been missing since Sunday, April 29. They left allegedly for a hike around nine A.M. and have not been seen since. McGregor's mother, June McGregor, told *Cadillac News* that her son and his family liked to hunt for morel mushrooms during the spring and may have gotten lost or injured while doing so. McGregor, like many Northern Michigan mushrooming enthusiasts, rarely shared the location of his favorite spots, even with his mother, so she is unsure of where they may have gone. A manhunt is currently under way, and June McGregor asks that if anyone has information pertaining to the whereabouts of her son, daughter-in-law, and granddaughter, that they please contact her directly or *Cadillac News*. Mrs. McGregor is offering a reward for any information that leads to the discovery of her son and his family's whereabouts.

Melanie walked into the kitchen wearing a flowing yellow gown, just like the one worn by Belle in the animated Disney classic *Beauty and the Beast*.

"Daddy, Daddy!"

Jack smiled and locked his cellphone. "Yeah, sweetheart?"

"You have to come in here now and be the Beast," she said with a very serious look on her face. She spun around, admiring the way her dress twirled and headed toward the living room.

"Okay, I'm coming, Belle," Jack said in his best Beast growl.

He stood up and followed his daughter into the living room to play.

Leslie Patterson had some shopping that she needed to do in Cadillac that Saturday. She got an early start, eating a quick light breakfast of buttered toast with honey, fruit with a healthy dollop of plain Greek yogurt, and coffee. She was in the car and pulling out of her driveway by 9:30 A.M.

Leslie had just passed the Village Market and Mr. Pibbs and was coming up over the hill where the speed limit jumps back up to fifty-five.

That's when she saw the dog.

It was a small black and brown shape on the side of the road, a few feet off the shoulder, clearly dead.

Leslie's heart skipped a beat as she thought back to their

lunch at Pibbs at the end of April, when Ben Williams had come in looking sad and worried with the missing posters for his daughter Katie's dog, Lyra. The Williams's place was just a mile up the road.

Oh no, Leslie bit her bottom lip. *Lyra must have been hit by a car. Katie's going to be crushed.*

She turned around in the next driveway and drove back to the spot, pulling over onto the shoulder just north of the carcass, lying there stiff as a board. Leslie left her car running and cautiously walked up to the furry lump on the side of the road. She was envisioning Katie's reaction when Ben broke the bad news, playing out the scenario in her head, hoping to find ways to lessen the impact and make it easier for Katie, the sweet little girl who used to be her neighbor. Leslie remembered when the Williams family first got Lyra several years ago, how happy and proud Katie had been. It was *her* dog, *her* responsibility, the first real responsibility she had taken on.

When she reached the lifeless shape, she drew in a sharp breath. Her reaction at first was one of surprise, shock really, but that quickly turned to one of disgust and horror, which transitioned into hot anger, and finally settled into a deep sadness. It was Lyra, all right, and she was stiff and dead, but it didn't look like she had been hit by a car. It looked like she had been purposefully killed by some sick psychopath, disemboweled and horribly mutilated. What was left of her was hardly recognizable.

Leslie stood there on the side of Mackinaw Trail and sobbed silently, covering her mouth with her hand, heaving with emotion.

Then she went back to her car, got her cellphone out of her purse, and dialed Ben's home number. Leslie gathered herself for a tough emotionally-draining conversation. She closed her eyes, fighting back a fresh flood of tears, and said a brief silent prayer for Katie Williams, who was about to get some terrible news.

It was oppressively hot and humid, sweltering like the Cambodian jungle. The midafternoon sun was relentless, scorching down on him, simultaneously baking and suffocating him. He was sweating and uncomfortable in his long-sleeved camouflage jungle fatigues, but he didn't dare move. They were out there; he could *hear* them; he could *feel* them. They were close, but he didn't dare look up to sneak a glance and risk being seen. He was in an exceedingly dangerous situation, separated from the rest of his unit, a lone soldier trapped behind enemy lines. He was deathly afraid that his position had been compromised and that the enemy would be on him in no time, swooping down on him mercilessly like the flying monkeys in *The Wizard of Oz*. And if that happened, well… then it would all be over.

He and his comrades had been patrolling the area in single file, silent as a tomb. They stayed off the trails and kept close to the edge of the woods where the underbrush was thicker and the cover better.

Suddenly, out of nowhere, the enemy appeared, flying around a curve in the trail not a hundred and fifty yards ahead of them. There were three of them, cruising fast in a military-spec off-road vehicle, which was now heading straight for him. The moment he saw them, he had hit the deck, dropping down flat on the ground about ten yards from the edge of the clearing. Apparently, the other two soldiers in his unit had sprinted toward the woods where they could either escape or find better cover and hunker down, but he had been so blindsided by the sudden appearance of the enemy that he had panicked. And now here he was, separated from the rest of his unit with the enemy heavily-armed and bearing down on him.

Time was running out.

As he lay there on the soft bed of russet-colored pine needles, head down and motionless, his heart pounding in his chest, he feared that this just might be his death bed; his last hurrah; last dance; the final curtain. Had he been seen? Surely the enemy had seen his comrades duck and run for cover, but had they seen him drop down? As various fatalistic scenarios played out in his head, each one bloodier and more alarming than the one before, a rogue bead of sweat slowly began to trickle down his nose, producing a glaring itch that just had to be scratched. It was undeniable, unavoidable. He scrunched his nose in an effort to shake the insufferable runner free, but to no avail. It was then that he made a decision: he would wipe the sweat from his nose and get a quick look at the enemy's position, then make a snap life-or-death decision on how to proceed. Fight or flight: does he go out in a blaze of glory, guns drawn, or make a desperate dash for cover in the thicker growth and pines and hope for the best?

Okay, he thought, closing his eyes and taking a deep breath. *Here we go. One, two, THREE!*

He reached up with his right hand and wiped the offending bead of sweat from his nose while simultaneously lifting his head up from his prone position.

What he saw made his eyes widen in hopeless terror; his jaw dropped to his chest, and he could feel the adrenaline start to pump faster and harder in his veins.

They had seen him, all right, and they were close now—too close. The military-issue light-utility vehicle was within fifty yards of him now and closing in fast. Two enemy soldiers were standing on the rails, one on either side of the vehicle. One of them was pointing ahead, directly at his position. This one motioned and said something to the driver, who nodded. As the lone soldier lying on the ground watched in horror, the driver made eye contact with him, and as he did so, a twisted snarl of a grin spread across his face.

It was now or never; do or die.

In the blink of an eye the soldier sprang from his prone position. His first two or three steps were long, loping strides as he got his feet under him and began to pick up speed. His heart was already pounding in his chest and pushing up into his throat as he cut the distance to the edge of the woods in half. Out of the corner of his eye he saw the two enemies who had been standing leap off the vehicle and hit the ground running. The sounds of the approaching engine and the thundering of their boots on the ground filled him with dread.

As he reached the edge of the clearing, shots rang out in a rapid-fire burst that strafed the ground to his right and left, sending puffs of dirt and grass into the air and missing him by mere inches. Breathless, he crossed over the edge and made it into the woods, sprinting hard as bullets rained down on him, whizzing past and slamming into the pines all around him. Now it was a footrace, and he felt for the first time that maybe he had a chance. He weaved in between trees with an effortless grace he never knew he possessed, his arms pumping, breath coming in deep, churning gasps. The rounds continued to zip past him, tearing up the earth and hitting the trees with deep, gut-wrenching *THUNK*s that made his stomach crawl.

The shrub swamp was only fifty yards east of his current position. His only chance—an exceedingly slim one, he knew —was to make it there; get past the bracken, ferns, and shrubs guarding the edge of the soupy marshland; and launch himself headlong into the squelchy wetlands and submerge there undetected. Despite the persistent doubts filling his head, he pushed on at a dead sprint.

He had no idea where the enemy was or if they were even still in pursuit. Then he heard the rapid-fire *POP!-POP!-POP!* of their guns and felt the deadly projectiles whiz past his head, dangerously close this time, and he knew they were still coming.

That's when he made his fatal mistake.

Arms still pumping, the edge of the swamp in sight now, he turned his head and stole a quick glance over his left shoulder.

That's when the toe of his boot struck a downed tree branch, sending him sprawling headlong about six feet through the air, arms flailing wildly, a look of dumb surprise and utter dejection on his face. He crash-landed painfully in a crumpled, writhing heap, gasping for air as the wind was knocked out of him.

He rolled over with a groan and, looking down, realized he had punctured his left leg on a jagged, broken stick that was still embedded in his thigh. His eyes widened in panic as he reached down and pulled the stick out of his leg with one quick jerk. Bright fireworks of pain exploded in his head as blood oozed from the puncture wound in his thigh through the fresh, jagged tear in his jungle fatigues.

Thinking fast, he rolled back over onto his stomach and pushed himself up, hobbling on one leg, wincing in pain, as he limped as fast as he could toward the swamp.

But it was too late.

The edge of the swamp was only ten yards ahead of him when it happened.

He heard a dry, sickening *POP!* that reverberated feverishly in his head. At the same time, he felt the thunderous impact of a slug that tore through his back and came out through his chest, ejecting a thick wad of pink, frothy blood and mucus and leaving behind a gory exit wound about the size of a silver dollar just above his left nipple. The force of the blast spun him around and knocked him to the ground, mere feet from the swamp's edge.

Faintly, he heard the voices of the enemy as they approached, guns drawn to claim their prey. Lying on his back and looking up peacefully at the clear blue sky, his body was racked by a sudden violent cough. He gagged and began to choke pitifully on his own foamy blood, which was now flowing freely from his mouth and nose, as well as the gaping wounds in his chest and thigh. A delirious, demented grin washed over his face. As his vision faded, he expired there on a bed of dead leaves and pine needles at the edge of the shrub swamp, a bed which had indeed turned out to be his death bed.

The two enemy soldiers approached the body cautiously, guns drawn, one from each side in a pincer movement. Within moments, they were standing over the corpse, around which a few black flies buzzed obnoxiously.

"Got you, fucker," one of the enemy soldiers said gleefully, nudging the body with the toe of his boot.

The corpse's eyes suddenly popped open.

"Yeah, fuck you, Brad," Jack said, grinning.

His older brother Brad laughed and offered Jack a hand and helped him to his feet.

Luckily for the twelve-year-old Jack, the bullet that killed him was actually a paintball, and the gore that had bloodied his camo jacket was just red paint. The enemies who had hunted him down like a wild animal and blown him away in cold blood (or cold paint, rather) were his older brother Brad and his older cousins, Pat and Jay. Jack's comrades were his cousins, too, and the best friends he would ever have, at least until he met Claire several years later. Ever since they were little, they were inseparable; the Three Musketeers. Russ, the younger brother of Pat and the eldest of the younger-cousin triad, and Rick, Jay's younger brother and the youngest of the six male cousins in the Allen family. All six boys were tight, but the younger three, Jack, Russ, and Rick, were especially close, a holy trinity, as were the older three, Brad, Pat, and Jay.

It was the summer of 1997, and they had been playing an exhilarating round of a competitive game of their own invention, which they had named, simply enough, "the Game." The Game was kind of like a hybrid between hide-and-seek and bloody murder, but instead of getting tagged by the seekers/murderers, you got shot with paintball guns. Oh, and the seekers/murderers, who always happened to be the three older cousins, rode around on an old red golf cart with a white molded-plastic top, smoking cigarettes and always ready to open up with their semi-automatic paintball guns in an epic drive-by shooting. This golf cart was no off-road vehicle by any stretch of the imagination. Still, the Allen cousins treated it as such, habitually pushing it far beyond its limits in every conceivable way. Over the years, that golf cart had taken a beating: it had been flipped over at high speeds on multiple occasions and even survived a head-on collision with the flagpole in front of the farm in a botched Nerf drive-by.

A typical round of the Game went something like this: Jack, Russ, and Rick went full-on commando, donning camouflage from head to toe, sometimes even painting their faces with the Government Issue Camouflage Compact Kits they had scored from General Jim's Surplus in Clare. With their canteens and long-range military standard walkie-talkies they would head out on foot onto the trails and into the woods, usually around ten or so in the morning. Sometimes they packed jerky or sandwiches or other snacks in army surplus knapsacks to keep them going throughout the day, as a single round of the Game could easily last eight hours or more. The older cousins would wait at the farm, which was the home base, for an agreed-upon length of time, usually around fifteen minutes. Then they would pile into the old red golf cart, and the game—or the hunt—would officially begin.

The field of play was the entire breadth of the Allen family property. It was three hundred acres of majestic Northern Michigan woodlands, a veritable natural playground crisscrossed with trails and a creek, dense woods juxtaposed with open tallgrass fields, and marshes that seamlessly flowed into murky swamps.

Given only fifteen minutes initially to disappear like ghosts into the wilds of the Northwoods, the younger cousins—let's call them the hiders, rather than the murder victims—typically set out at a dead run, racing the clock to get into a good, well-covered position before the older and faster seekers hit the trail. Everything was run like a military operation, carefully modeled on—and just as dramatic and exciting as—the classic action and war films they had grown up watching, like the Rambo movies, *The Rock*, and particularly Oliver Stone's 1986 classic *Platoon*. Incidentally, Jack's mom would have killed him if she had known he had watched *Platoon* at the tender age of eight, but the joke was on her; he had seen it over at Russ's house under the watchful eye of his aunt and uncle, and it just so happened that Russ's mother was Jack's mom's identical twin!

The object of the Game was first and foremost to survive, to avoid being caught (or shot, if you want to get literal about it). Secondly, the goal was for the hiders to make it back to home base (the farm) and ring the old dinner bell on the front porch. If they could do that without being captured by the dreaded seekers or peppered with paintballs, then victory would be theirs, and oh how sweet it would be. There was one proviso: the hiders had to stay on the move; they couldn't just bed down in one well-hidden and fortified position for more than fifteen minutes or so at a time, otherwise it gave them a decidedly unfair advantage. Besides, that would have made the Game less exciting and death-defying.

When they first invented and started playing the Game, the hiders were young and stupid, cannon fodder for the older boys who mercilessly and gleefully pelted them with stinging paintballs, oftentimes at close range. But as they got older—and digested more war movies and battlefield tactics—the hiders got pretty damn good. They developed effective strategies and established a series of secret hidden bases scattered across the landscape that gave them the upper hand in the epic struggle that was the Game. Eventually, Jack, Russ, and Rick reached an apex where they were rarely caught—or shot—by the seekers; they could easily reach the farm and ring that splendid victory bell at will. But that wasn't too exciting, and the easy victories became a bit hollow, so they began to stay out in the woods, more or less constantly on the move, even beginning to seek out confrontation with the dreaded enemy. As time went on, the hiders seemed to do less hiding and more reconnaissance, patrolling more or less out in the open, recklessly daring the seekers to find them and give chase.

Perhaps that was how and why Jack found himself in his current predicament, separated from Russ and Rick and dead for the rest of the round, hit in the back by a well-aimed shot from his older brother Brad's paintball gun.

According to the official rules of the Game if you got shot you had to stay where you were for the remainder of the round. You were out—caught, found, dead; choose your analogy—and could not participate again in any way until the current round was finished. Sometimes this meant you had to wait around for quite a while.

So Jack stood at the edge of the swamp and watched as Brad and Jay headed back through the birches and maples toward the trail where Pat was waiting on the golf cart. Jack wiped the red paint off his jacket as best he could and examined his left thigh. He actually *had* fallen on a stick when he tripped over the branch, and it had put a hole in his pants, not to mention his leg, but it wasn't too bad, just a minor puncture wound. He'd live. Sometimes you had to sacrifice your body while playing the Game.

The mosquitoes and black flies were bad as usual in the Northwoods, a thick cloud of them buzzing incessantly around his head. Occasionally Jack swatted at them, spastically shooing them away from his face with both hands while cursing. Luckily the cousins always doused themselves with bug spray ("bug dope," as their grandpa always called it, the good kind, too, with DEET) as an essential part of their pre-Game ritual. So the bugs were there but more of an annoyance than a real threat in terms of biting. But without the bug spray, those deer flies would take a chunk out of your skin the size of a pencil eraser and make you bleed—at least that's how it felt to Jack—and you'd end up as one big talking mosquito bite, itchy, red, and puffy. Once you came down around the white pine trail and crossed the stone bridge over the Crick, you entered into the dense woods, and that's when the bugs got thick, a massive buzzing cloud that could suffocate you if you didn't keep moving; they'd literally eat you alive.

After twenty minutes or so, Jack was getting bored. He looked out across the swamp, dipping down to the south and extending for about five hundred yards from where he stood. It was beautiful, but there was always something dark and ominous about it, something kind of menacing. This particular area was what he and the cousins referred to as the "Bogs": a marshy wetland with shallow standing water (they characterized it as "soupy") and emergent vegetation—what they called "marsh grasses": mostly cattails, sedges, bulrushes, and pondlilies. The emergent marsh gradually flowed into a shrub swamp, dominated by tag alders, willow, and various wetland shrubs and woody plants that could reach up to about fifteen feet tall. The shrub swamp was a transitional zone between the marsh and the humid cedar swamp, primarily fed by groundwater and dominated by northern white-cedar. This species of cedar is relatively short and forms a dense, low canopy; a tangle of fallen, leaning, bent, and misshapen trees mixed with vines, sedges, ferns, and mosses. The soil—the soggy, spongy bed of the cedar swamp—was of ancient, well-decomposed organic material. A thick layer of moss topped the wet earth here and there like a dark green mattress topper with a tint of luminescent yellow. The sunlight penetration to the ground was poor, giving the cedar swamp a dark, mysterious appearance that added to its enigmatic allure.

The Bogs were the least explored and least traversed area of the Allen property—and hence the most mysterious. In the spring, seasonal flooding made the Bogs impassable in many places. Still, in the late summer and fall, when the water was low, a brave and persistent explorer—or soldier—could trek through most of it. However, a good many shoes and boots were known to have been sucked clean off unsuspecting stockinged feet, some of them lost forever in the depths of the squelchy black mud, sacrificial offerings given unwillingly to the great swamp god of the Northwoods. There was also an old family story about an entire rowboat that was swallowed whole in the deepest recesses of the Bogs back in the early 1900s, never to be seen again. In recent years the Bogs had become a central hub for Jack, Russ, and

Rick when they played the Game, a well-protected spot off the beaten trail where they would hole up periodically and strategize or have a quick snack.

Standing on the edge of the Bogs, Jack sighed, his shoulders slouched. He was getting impatient just standing around fighting off bugs, and he began to wish his comrades would hurry up and get shot already so they could reset and start a new round. He took a few gulps from the canteen hooked to his OD green GI Pistol Belt, another gem purchased at General Jim's.

As he looked out past the marshes, Jack saw a painted turtle perched on a rotting log, peering down into the standing marsh water with a curious, sleepy look in its eyes. A red-bellied woodpecker tapped a steady beat on a nearby cedar tree.

Then Jack looked further, beyond the turtle and the woodpecker, toward the dark cedar swamp in the distance. He could just make out the dense web of trees and shrubs that marked the transition from the shrub swamp to the cedar swamp. The smoky, hazy green of the lush moss blanketing the ground clashed with the twisted, leaning cedar trees that grew above it, like gnarled bony fingers reaching for the sky. The Bogs always reminded Jack of Dagobah, the planet in Star Wars where Luke Skywalker learned the ways of the Force and trained with the great Jedi Master Yoda. As Jack began to go down a Star Wars rabbit hole, something out there at the edge of the cedar swamp caught his attention.

Something moved.

But what was it?

Jack squinted to get a better look.

Beside a tall, straight cedar about a hundred yards away, Jack saw a figure standing at the edge of the swamp. It was a dark presence, and it immediately gave Jack the creeps; his skin crawled, and his hair lifted. He couldn't see the whole figure, as it was partially hidden behind the tree, but it was tall, very tall, and it seemed to be looking right at Jack with a pair of glowing amber eyes like concentrated fire or reflected sunlight.

This strange figure chilled his blood.

It looked like a man wearing dark clothes, like the navy blue or brown coveralls that a mechanic might wear, and a floppy hat of some kind. Yet, it also reminded him of some kind of animal. It was covered in coarse dark fur and had pointy ears.

But he couldn't be sure about the details at this distance. In any case, the thought of a man standing out there in the swamp looking at him made Jack's heart pump like mad and sent adrenaline coursing through his body.

As he looked out at the mysterious, menacing figure, his eyes wide, mouth agape, it slowly retreated back behind the cedar tree and out of sight.

Jack's whole body tensed.

He started grinding his teeth as he squinted in a desperate attempt to locate the figure again... but it was nowhere to be seen. Wasting no time, he spun on his heels and took off at a dead sprint back toward the trail that twisted through the birches and maples, breathing hard, the sour taste of fear filling his mouth.

Jack didn't dare look back as he raced through the trees, his heart and arms pumping fast in unison.

Dear God, what the fuck was that what the fuck was that what the FUCK!?

His head was spinning as he attempted to make sense of what he had seen. His boots pounded on the dead leaves beneath his feet, and he weaved in and out of the trees again with that rare grace he wasn't aware he possessed. His steps were like the notes in a well-crafted symphony, melody and harmony weaving together just right in the moment.

Up ahead, he could just begin to make out the trail, winding lazily through the part of the property they all called the "Birches," a slightly dark, densely forested part of the trails. As he scanned the trails at a dead sprint, his heart leaped for joy, and he nearly burst into tears. The golf cart was still there!

Thank you, Jesus! Oh, thank you, God!

He burst out from the edge of the woods and continued on toward the trail. Brad, Pat, and Jay were sitting on the golf cart smoking cigarettes. Brad's eyes widened when he saw Jack racing toward them.

"There's… a…" Jack stammered breathlessly as he reached the golf cart. "There's… a… MAN…. back there!" He looped his arm around one of the bars of the golf cart's roll cage and fell into it, leaning against it for support as he tried to catch his breath.

"THERE!" he stammered, pointing out toward the woods he had just emerged from.

He scoured the trees, checking for the first time to see if he had been followed. The image of that figure just standing there in the swamp staring at him made him feel sick. He looked back at the other three.

They were frozen, speechless. Brad and Pat had cigarettes clamped between their teeth, unmoving, while Jay held his still and rather daintily in his right hand. They looked at Jack.

Then all three of them burst out laughing.

They resumed smoking their cigarettes, and Jack's mouth dropped open, a desperate deflated look washing over him.

"Guys, I swear!" he pleaded. "Brad, I saw this thing, this figure out there in the swamp. I don't know if it was a guy or an animal or what, but it was just standing there behind a tree looking right at me! Brad, I swear!"

"Shut the fuck up," Pat said good-naturedly. "You know how your eyes can play tricks on you back here. There's no way there's anyone back there in the swamp."

"Yeah," Brad agreed. "If anything, maybe it was a bear. You know they see black bears back here sometimes." As he shared this bit of wisdom, which everyone already knew, his eyebrows raised, and his tone was lofty and proud.

"Yeah," Jay chimed in. "Coulda been a bear. Hell, maybe it was Russ!"

They all chuckled at this, pleased with themselves and their vast wit and wisdom.

"It wasn't Russ!" Jack nearly screamed, a look of sheer exasperation on his face. His breathing was under control now, and as his pulse slowed his rational mind began to reassert its control over him, offering up more logical—not to mention less frightening—explanations of what he had seen—or what he *thought* he had seen. "Well fuck you guys, then," Jack said, a wry smile breaking out on his face. "Maybe I just got a little too excited back there. Maybe I was a bit sleepy."

He took the canteen from his belt, twisted off the cap, and took a long slug. The water was warm, but it was wet and good. He swallowed it down with a loud satisfied sigh. He glanced back toward the swamp, invisible now through the scattered birches and pines.

"Well, take me with you guys at least then," he said, holstering his canteen on his army belt. "I'm tired after my sprint from the boogieman." He smiled, knowing it was going to take a while to live this one down, even though every single one of them had similar hair-raising experiences alone in those woods. It was very true that your mind played tricks on you out here, he thought. Sometimes you'd see things that weren't there or hear phantom sounds that couldn't be explained. Your brain suggested things and made them seem real, like the images moving across the screen at a movie theater.

"Well, come on then, pussy," Pat grinned, pulling Jack out of his thoughts. "Wouldn't want you to shit yourself out here in fright."

They all laughed and ditched their cigarette butts under a rock on the side of the trail. Jack climbed onto one of the rear seats next to Brad, and they took off down the trail in search of Russ and Rick.

For better or for worse, the memory of Jack's frightening experience that day in the swamp faded quickly, slipping from his consciousness as easily as a nightmare slips away in the bright light of morning, gone before you have your first sip of coffee. That memory sank down deep into Jack's subconscious, like the old rowboat that was eaten whole by the Bogs in the early twentieth century. But unlike the boat, which was never seen again, Jack's memory of the lone figure in the swamp would emerge and come to life again years later.

The first two weeks of May that year were rainy: drizzly, cold, and dreary. Jack, Claire, and Melanie hunkered down and laid low at the farm, playing a lot of board games and doing puzzles. Melanie was taking a dance class in Cadillac, which she absolutely loved. Claire spent her spare time reading; she loved fantasy novels but also kept up to date on the current psychology literature.

These were happy times for the Allens, despite the spring cabin fever.

Jack spent a lot of time working on his current research

project. He often worked from home in the small study on the second floor where he had a desk, a comfy chair, a computer with two monitors, and a bookshelf stuffed with some essential volumes. Jack also went into the office on campus two or three times a week, depending on what he was doing. He had finished up his grading for the semester earlier in the month and submitted his final grades, a tremendous excitement and relief flooding through him as he clicked submit.

Jack usually took a day or two off after final grades were submitted and the long grueling semester was officially over. He did this out of sheer exhaustion because he needed a break and to clear his head and get into research mode. Jack loved learning about Native American cultures and loved spending time with the elders and medicine men who had become his close friends. They brought a lot of joy into his life, and he knew that it was mutual, which made him very happy and grateful.

When Jack was really interested in something, like his research, he tended to throw himself into it—*obsessed* might be a better word for it, which is how Claire often characterized it. He'd been like that ever since he was a kid. He went on kicks, totally engrossing himself in something, some topic or activity, obsessing over it, usually for several weeks to several months at a time. Then he would lose interest, sometimes gradually, other times more abruptly, and eventually move on to the next thing. Some of Jack's obsessions included writing; reading novels; music; playing guitar; various rock bands (mainly a predictable cycle of the Beatles, Led Zeppelin, and Neil Young); and Native American culture, history, and spirituality. In any case, when Jack was in the throes of a kick (*obsession*) he threw his entire being into it with gusto and reckless abandon.

You might say Jack was working his way into a kick at the

moment with his research, which was so refreshing and inspiring to him after a long spring semester of teaching, endless emails, boring meetings, and bureaucratic bullshit. Those first few weeks in May, he was working some late nights, really getting into a writing groove. It made him feel terrific, like he was accomplishing something, but he also felt guilty about neglecting some of his duties in other areas of life.

Like all things, it was a give and take: you can't be exceptional at all things all the time, he told himself. It's impossible. Life is full of tough decisions, and sacrifices must be made. Academics and scholars—and those two things aren't always the same—often have to temporarily and periodically sacrifice their other roles as partners, parents, sons, daughters, brothers, sisters, friends, etc. in order to produce things. This is probably true of all professions, but Jack knew the academic world best, and he was a case in point.

At the moment, Jack felt like he was neglecting his family just a bit while he was riding the research train. And besides, he told himself, he would make it up to Claire and Mel when the project was finished. When the book was published, it would make things better for all of them.

And it would.

And *he* would.

The flexibility of the academic life meant that he really would be able to take time after the project was finished to focus completely on his wife and daughter. Maybe they'd go on a vacation. And he knew Claire understood that. And he loved her for it.

Wednesday, May 17, was another cold and gray day. Jack had spent the entire day at his campus office in Big Rapids, getting there just after eight A.M. and not leaving until he ran home for dinner around six o'clock.

Melanie was in rare form that night, cracking everyone up at the table, telling them about her dream the night before. She had been flying through the sky with a bunch of whales eating pancakes, and in the middle of her telling, she broke down into an uncontrollable fit of giggles.

"Daddy?" she said, looking over at Jack, her head slightly cocked to one side.

"Yeah, sweetheart?"

"I love you," she said.

"Aww, I love you too, Mel," Jack said, feeling happy. He tousled her hair.

Melanie went back to her pizza and carrots as Claire and Jack shared a loving amused glance across the table as they held hands.

Jack put Melanie down for the night just after seven, reading her two books and singing her a song before giving her a hug and a kiss on the cheek.

"Goodnight, my sweet girl," Jack whispered, blowing Melanie a kiss.

"Goodnight, Daddy. I love you."

"I love you too. See you first thing tomorrow morning," Jack gently pulled Melanie's bedroom door shut as he glided out of the room.

Jack walked down the stairs and came into the living room, where Claire was curled up on the couch with a glass of red wine and a paperback book. He went to her, stooping down to give her a kiss on the head and to gently rub her back and shoulders.

"I gotta get a few things finished up at the office," he said. "I shouldn't be too long."

Claire looked up at him from her book.

"Okay, dear," she yawned. "Want me to wait up for you?"

"No, no, don't wait up. Get some sleep if you're tired. Love you." He kissed her on the cheek.

Jack headed into the kitchen and then out onto the screened-in porch. He laced up his shoes, got into the Blazer, and headed off to campus for the second time that day.

Jack spent a good hour finishing up a draft of a chapter on nineteenth-century Ottawa ceremonial life. It was just a draft, but it was a solid one, and Jack was pleased with it.

By nine-thirty, he was tired, his eyes were bleary, and he was at a good stopping point. He made a note to remember where he left off and what he needed to do the next day, and then he headed out, locking his office door behind him. As he walked through the parking lot to the Blazer, he glanced toward the west and saw the sun going down, just a small faintly-glowing orb on the edge of the horizon. It was not quite dusk.

After an uneventful thirty-minute drive, Jack was heading east on 16 Mile Road toward the farm. There was a red sedan in front of him, an older woman with shiny white hair and thick glasses was driving, and she was going slower than a sloth in a footrace. There was no one else on the road.

Jack was getting ready to pass her when suddenly her turn signal came on. As they limped along the undulating road, they came to the junction of 16 Mile and Forest Trail, the road that led into Rose Lake Forest where Brad was building the Thompson home. It was getting dark now; dusk had settled in on that cold May evening and nearly transitioned to full darkness. As Jack slowed down, nearly coming to a complete stop, the red sedan turned right onto Forest Trail.

When he looked back up at the road, something caught his eye in the field to his left, just north of 16 Mile.

At first, he thought it was a man.

It was past dusk now, that brief period when the world was an inky post-twilight shadowland, and maybe his eyes were playing tricks on him, he thought. It was like a dark shadow of a man, or maybe it was wearing a dark suit of some kind, but it didn't move quite like a man. It was hard to make out at about fifty yards away, but it was somehow taller and ganglier than a man, and it seemed to be hunched forward a bit, like it was prone, waiting to pounce.

"What the *fuck...?*" Jack trailed off aloud as he squinted out the windshield, brows furrowed.

Just then, whatever it was in that field north of 16 Mile Road seemed to spook. It looked up suddenly, and Jack gasped when he saw two amber-colored eyes, glowing like a jack-o-lantern, boring a hole through him from the side of the road. Jack froze, gawking in disbelief, and a sudden sense of fear and excitement flashed through his body.

At that moment, lights flashed in the rearview mirror, temporarily blinding Jack, and an old red Ford Ranger came sputtering up about a half-mile behind him. Jack was crawling along 16 Mile trying to get another look at that thing in the field, squinting hard and shielding his eyes, flipping his rearview mirror down to avoid the Ranger's headlights. His eyes darted here and there looking for that man—or beast or whatever it was—he had just seen only moments ago.

But it was gone.

Vanished without a trace.

It's early to see bear around here, he thought, accelerating. *Could have been a man with colored lenses on his sunglasses,* he mused, mulling over the possibilities in his mind and unconsciously trying to find a believable solution that didn't shake his convictions too much. There had to be some reasonable explanation.

Yeah, I bet that was it, he thought, taking a left into his driveway, slinking between the giant reaching twin Carolina poplar trees. *My headlights must have made them light up and glow like that when he looked up.*

His encounter that night was still on his mind as Jack brushed his teeth and got ready for bed. He decided he would investigate the next morning and see if there were any tracks or evidence left behind at the scene. If it had been a bear, it would've left tracks. This conviction and plan of action made Jack feel better, less uncertain and edgy after the experience had left him a little unnerved despite himself.

Later that night, Jack crawled into bed with Claire, who was still up reading. He kissed her on the cheek, and they chatted about the day, holding hands again. Later, they made love, softly and quietly, before giving in to the seductive siren call of sleep.

But just as Jack began to doze off, a thought struck him and began to nag at him.

It could've been a bear, or possibly a man, sure, he thought. *But either way, where the fuck did it go? It just seemed to disappear after that truck pulled up, vanished into thin air, but I only lost sight of it for a few seconds. It must have been fast, whatever the fuck it was.*

With this thought, Jack shivered and fell into a light, fitful sleep just after midnight.

Jack's alarm went off at seven A.M. He fumbled for the snooze button, still half asleep, groaning softly. He rolled over and put his arm around Claire, who was also stirring, and the two of them drifted back off for a few precious minutes until the alarm buzzed again, filling their room with its noxious sound.

Jack shaved, showered, and dressed. Entering the kitchen, he saw Melanie at the table in her booster seat, huddled over a bowl of Cheerios. Claire was at the table as well, sipping a cup of coffee and eating toast.

"Daddy!" Melanie cried, looking up from her bowl with milk dripping down her chin.

"Good morning, my beautiful girl," Jack smiled, kissing her on the top of her head and rustling her hair. "Morning, dear," he said to Claire, pecking her lightly on the cheek.

"Morning," Claire said, looking up at Jack.

Jack poured himself a bowl of Cheerios and a cup of coffee. They sat at the kitchen table, eating and chatting about the day. Melanie had dance class that afternoon, and she was very excited about it, telling Jack all about her dance instructor Kara.

Jack finished his cereal and rinsed out his dishes in the kitchen sink. He filled his to-go mug to the brim with piping hot coffee and grabbed the lunch he had made for himself the night before out of the fridge. He hugged and kissed Melanie and Claire on his way out the door.

He hopped into the Blazer and as soon as the door slammed shut behind him, his mind focused on what he had seen the night before. He would stop and check out the area for tracks or any other sign he could find.

Jack took a right out of the driveway and headed west. Within a couple minutes, he was coming up to the three-way junction where Forest Trail meets 16 Mile. Jack turned left onto Forest Trail and pulled off onto the shoulder. As he got out of his SUV, a sudden wave of nerves hit him.

Why the hell do I have butterflies right now? he thought, swinging the driver's side door closed behind him.

The sun was up, glazing the landscape with an orange glow. It was a crisp morning; the air smelled good and fresh. Jack peered over toward the field across the street, thinking for a moment that he might see something there again. He meandered up to the shoulder of 16 Mile, looked both ways, and crossed the street at a trot.

It was Beckett's property. Jack and his family had known

the Becketts for generations and had always been on good terms with them. They were good solid countryfolk, as honest as the day is long, as they say. Even if old Dave Beckett saw him snooping around, he wouldn't think anything of it.

Now Jack was on the north side of the road, shuffling through the gravel shoulder toward the grass and foliage ahead, dewy and glinting in the morning sunlight. He trudged through a dip just north of the road, coming back up in the taller grass, his shoes wet with dew. He reached the spot where he had seen the figure the night before, his eyes glued to the ground as if he were tracking a deer the way his father had taught him to when he was a boy.

At first, he didn't see anything.

But then he noticed some depressions in the undergrowth where the grass had been recently trampled and flattened. No clear tracks, though, but Jack followed the signs farther to the north and east.

That's when he first saw the tracks in the dry sandy soil where the crabgrass was thin and balding.

They were clearly boot tracks, heading east. Jack sighed and chuckled to himself, relieved that it was nothing to worry about.

Probably Old Man Beckett going out for an evening stroll, he reasoned.

But then some vexing questions popped up in his head, like the fact that Dave Beckett was much shorter than the figure he'd seen last night and certainly not spry enough to up and disappear the way it did, whatever it was.

No, no, no, Jack thought, getting irritated with himself. *Now, this is silly. I'm making something out of nothing here. A mountain out of a molehill. The light was bad, and he seemed to be crouching down like he was looking for something. That must have thrown off my perspective and made him seem taller. I was looking up at him from the other side of the road after all. My eyes could have been playing tricks on me. Appearances can be deceiving, especially at night, and I was dead tired after a long day at the office.*

But what about those eyes?

Colored lenses on sunglasses, like I said last night. Maybe shooting glasses! Yeah, that must have been it! Lots of shooting glasses have those polarized orange lenses, Jack thought, pleased with himself now. *And the boot tracks here prove it. This was nothing to get all spooked about. Just Old Man Beckett going for an evening stroll.*

Jack was shaking his head and smiling, rolling his eyes at himself, when his cellphone rang, causing him to jump. He answered the phone as he turned and headed back toward the Blazer. It was Claire with a logistics question about Melanie's dance class later.

Jack felt much better as he got back into his SUV and drove down 16 Mile to Mackinaw Trail. With the mystery solved, all was right in the world again.

But if he had followed those boot tracks twenty yards further east he would have noticed another set of tracks stalking them.

The second set of tracks was decidedly canine and unusually large, with long claw marks jutting out from the toe pads, piercing the sandy soil.

If Jack had followed the tracks even further east and slightly north, he would have seen where they ended: in a thick clump of trees about fifty yards north of 16 Mile Road.

If he had investigated further, he would have found blood and lots of it, sticky and black in the matted dewy weeds.

It was mid-May, and the weather was warming and drying up. Summer was in the air in Northern Michigan, and everything was alive and green. It was Thursday, and Jack and Claire were especially excited. They had arranged for a babysitter that night to watch Melanie while they (*wait for it*) were GOING OUT WITH FRIENDS! Cue the fireworks and the marching band.

It was a rare and elusive thing these days when Jack and Claire got to go out on the town together and/or with other adults. Planning for something like this was a bit like having a lucky penny. You believe in it until it doesn't work. It was like an amazing dream that you never get to finish because you get woken up just before the best part, and the bubble is forever burst, and you wake up unsatisfied and kinda pissed. You feel cheated.

Well, this was one of those times. Jack had his fingers crossed all day that nothing would come up (*babysitter canceled, Melanie got sick, Claire got sick, Claire got tired, Melanie woke up and wouldn't stop crying so we had to rush home and soothe her until she calmed down, other family emergency, etc.*) that would stop this night in its tracks before it ever even happened. He was actively *willing* it to happen, giving off positive energy in every direction and to anyone he could. Jack wanted—no, needed—this to happen because when Jack and Claire went out, got away from the kid, had a few drinks, some good food and conversation, looked each other in the eye a bit, those old sparks tended to fly again, which meant fireworks later when they got home: bright explosions of colored lights, loud booming blasts, and an orgasmic feeling of euphoria.

That Thursday night, they had planned to go out to dinner with Sam and his wife Tonya and Leslie and her boyfriend, Matt. Jack and Claire loved going out with this crew, so Jack was doubly hoping against hope that their evening plans would not be derailed.

As evening approached and Jack was copy editing the next chapter in his book project, he glanced at the time at the bottom right corner of his computer screen.

Almost four o'clock and still no bad news! No eagles of doom have landed, he thought. *I must not think of it. I must not think of it. I must not—*

Just then, his cellphone rang. Jack froze.

—Shit! Who's this? Jack thought, his eyes bulging with concern as he pulled his phone from his pocket.

"Hey, babe," Claire purred on the other end.

"Baaaaby," Jack said, elongating the word suggestively. "We still on for tonight?" Jack's voice trailed off while simultaneously raising in pitch.

Claire laughed. "Yeah, so far, so good," she said in a tone of collusion. "Erin will be here at eight, and then we'll head out." There was a brief moment of silence on the other end. "And I'm really looking forward to getting out with you," she said, that enticing purr back in her voice.

"Mmmmm," Jack purred back. "Well, I'm looking forward to *making* out with you." He realized how dorky it sounded as he said it.

Claire laughed again, and as she did, Jack envisioned the smile on her face. When she laughed, she became dangerously beautiful. It had been easy for Jack to fall in love with her.

And it didn't hurt that she looked really good in a pair of tight jeans.

"Okay, well, see you later," Claire said.

"I'll be home before five," Jack said. "Love you, baby."

Jack hung up the phone, clenched his fists, squeezed his eyes shut, and hissed *yessssss* out loud like a horny snake. He spun around, suddenly light on his feet, and went back to work, grinning like an idiot.

———————

It was after dinner now, and Melanie had just taken a bath. She was in her pajamas, sitting with Mommy on the couch, getting her hair combed, and having a bedtime snack of pretzels with peanut butter. She was watching *Dora the Explorer*. Melanie *loved Dora the Explorer*. Melanie ALWAYS watched *Dora the Explorer*. But damn, was Melanie sweet. And cute. And lovable. And talented. And smart. Jack was head over heels for her. He loved both of his girls so much and felt like the luckiest man on earth to have them in his life, two of the most amazing people he had ever known.

After her snack, Jack brushed Melanie's teeth and put her to bed, reading her two stories and singing her one song, as usual. He kissed her on the forehead and gave her a long hug.

"I love you, girl," he whispered. "Sleep tight, and I'll see you first thing tomorrow morning."

"I love *you*," Melanie said, emphasizing the last word in a silly way. "Night, Daddy."

Jack pulled the door closed behind him as he left Melanie's room. He poked his head in their bathroom and watched Claire get ready for a minute. She was wearing nice jeans and a black short-sleeve top with lacey trim. She was beautiful.

Claire turned and saw him looking in at her.

"Hey, you," she smiled seductively. "I'll be ready to go in ten minutes or so. Erin should be here any minute."

"Mmmm you look amazing, babe," Jack grinned, shaking his head. "Looking forward to hanging out with you."

"Me too," Claire looked into Jack's eyes. "Now get outta here so I can get ready."

Erin, the babysitter, showed up a few minutes late, which had begun to really freak Jack out, who feared the worst, but all wasn't lost, and it was just a case of better late than never. It was really happening! Claire and Jack were almost to Travelers Bar and Grill on Mackinaw Trail to meet their adult friends out on the town for a drink, some appetizers maybe, and some good conversation. They were both glowing. Jack was giddy.

Travelers was an interesting place. A good word to describe it would be local. Or maybe ethnographic, to use an anthropological term. *Very* ethnographic. All the locals from LeRoy came to Travelers for food, drinks, and fun just about every Thursday, Friday, and Saturday night. People came from Tustin and Dighton too, and usually there were weekenders and folks just passing through. It was packed during the summertime when folks from the city stayed at their summer homes and cottages and cabins "up north," as Michiganders called it. Any given Thursday, Friday, or Saturday might end up a wild night at Travelers. The food was okay, but the beer was cold, and the drinks were strong and tall.

They had a *blast* that night. Claire and Jack were loving each other, laughing, and joking. They were happy to be out with their friends and celebrating a precious night of freedom.

Later, Jack would think back and remember that night as one of the last nights of true honest fun and enjoyment before the obsession and fear really took hold and changed everything.

But that was later.

That Thursday night in May at Travelers was magic. That night was wild.

Claire and Jack were both hungover Friday morning, moving a little slow. The night before at Travelers, Claire, Leslie, and Tonya had split a few bottles of red wine and Jack shared a few pitchers of beer with Sam and Matt.

Then Matt had bought the first round of shots. Tequila. He had just gotten back from a business trip to Mexico and was all enthused about tequila.

After round two, Jack and Sam decided they really liked Matt. They were both pretty protective of Leslie, whom they'd known since high school and treated more or less like a sister... well, maybe a stepsister you occasionally had confusing licentious thoughts about. In any case, Leslie and Matt had been dating off and on for a few years now but things had started getting serious within the last six months or so. Matt seemed to be a good guy. He was funny, and really cracked Jack and Sam up about his adventures south of the border.

Claire usually didn't do shots, but that night she was in her element, so visibly happy and carefree that she really did seem to be glowing in the soft yellow bar lights. Leslie egged her on, and Claire ended up doing two tequila shots with everyone before throwing in the towel and switching to water. Her face was a bit flushed, and she was enjoying herself, smiling and laughing.

Around eleven she leaned in toward Jack, putting her hand on his upper thigh, and whispered, "We should get out of here before too long." She gently pecked his earlobe after she said it and squeezed his thigh , her hand moving up toward his crotch.

"Oh yeah?" Jack challenged, his eyebrows raised.

Sam and Matt had been observing this little interaction from afar as it unfolded.

"You guys can't leave yet!" Matt said.

"Yeah, the night is young!" Sam added.

They looked at each other. "One more round!" they shouted merrily, eyeing Claire and Jack. "Come on, it's Thirsty Thursday!"

Everyone agreed and had one more rambunctious round before winding down around midnight. In the parking lot, they were all giggling and joking, Leslie and Claire were especially bubbly that night. They all said their goodbyes and headed off into the night, which had cooled down a bit, leaving a thin fog draped over the ground like a blanket of ghostly gray snow.

Jack paid Erin for her services. Melanie hadn't made a peep all night.

Man, this night is going perfectly! Jack thought, giddy with anticipation.

He grew even more excited when he opened the door to their bedroom.

The lamp on the nightstand was on low, casting a circle of warm golden light onto the bed. Claire was laying across the comforter, her head propped up on the pillows. She was wearing a pair of sexy lacy black panties… and nothing else. Her long legs and cute soft feet curled out in front of her seductively. Her firm and perky breasts called to Jack, yearning for attention, and she had one of them in her hand, gently massaging it.

Jack almost tore his clothes getting them off. Within a few seconds, he was on her and they were kissing, tasting, sucking, grinding their bodies together in such rhythm that they seemed to be one organism. Soon, he was inside her, and the world seemed to fade. They were both lost so deeply in the rhythm, the sounds, the smells, the hot wet passion that still burned inside between them, uniting them.

When it was over, they lay quietly side by side on the bed, breathing heavily and contentedly. Before long, they were both asleep, spooning and exhausted under the sheets.

Osceola County Sheriff John Dearborn and his deputy Sam McCleary responded to a call from a hysterical Mrs. Barbara Beckett. Barb was crying, saying her husband Dave never came home on the night of Wednesday, May 16. He had gone out for his usual evening stroll around the Beckett property, leaving about 8:15 P.M., and she hadn't seen him since. It was now Friday afternoon. She had called all of Dave's usual haunts, Travelers, Mineral Springs Bar and Grill, and his drinking buddy Chuck, but no one had seen or heard from him since Wednesday. That's when she decided to send her son and grandson out on a little reconnaissance mission to investigate, to walk the trails and comb the woods to see if they could find any sign of Old Man Beckett. They set out on their quest Friday morning.

"Sh-Sh-Sh-Sheriff," Mrs. Beckett blubbered, brave yet pitiful at the same time. "They found a b-b-body." She hitched in a shuddery breath. "They said it's hard to say for sure if it's Dave. He was tore up pretty bad… " There was a deafening ominous pause. "But he's wearing one of Dave's boots!" She blurted, bursting into tears. "Oh, dear *God!*" she wailed.

Now Sheriff Dearborn and Deputy McCleary were at the scene: the field across 16 Mile Road near its junction with Forest Trail. They had found tracks: boot tracks that were suddenly joined and shadowed by animal tracks, large canine prints that seemed to be stalking the boot tracks. Following the prints east, they came to a thick cluster of trees about fifty yards north of 16 Mile Road.

The boot tracks abruptly ended there in a macabre scene of gore that neither man was prepared for. When he saw it, Deputy McCleary gagged and had to turn away and take a walk.

Sticky black blood was splashed all over the ground and some of the trees. When Dearborn approached the body, he felt spongy clots give sickeningly beneath his boots. The body was unrecognizable.

The head was gone.

They would later find it lodged between two branches fifteen feet up in a nearby pine tree. Below the jagged stump of neck was a grotesque mess: there was little left in the way of clothing—a bit of a right sleeve, one leg of a pair of Levis; there was little left of a body too—the chest and stomach had been opened, most of the corpse consumed, gnawed to the bone like a juicy Thanksgiving turkey. The leftover raw meat and exposed tendons made Dearborn cringe. Red-black blood had pooled and congealed in the open stomach cavity, creating a reflective surface, a grisly mirror that was too much even for Sheriff Dearborn. When he inadvertently caught a glimpse of his reflection in the coagulated blood, he heaved and threw up his lunch.

One leg was missing below the knee, but on the other leg was a boot, the same kind worn by Dave Beckett, just as Barbara Beckett had said. They were able to positively identify him as Old Man Beckett when they found his severed head fifteen minutes later, a gruesome cherry on top of this morbid surprise.

Later that evening, Sheriff Dearborn was brushing his teeth and getting ready for bed. As he flipped off the bathroom light and darkness flooded the room, the horrific image of his own face reflected in the mirror of Dave Beckett's congealed blood flashed into his head.

He gasped and covered his eyes with his hands.

Word spread like wildfire about the gruesome death of Dave Beckett and everyone in town was talking about it in hushed tones of fear and disbelief. The Allens struggled with the loss of a dear family friend—the Allens and the Becketts had known each other for generations. Claire brought a casserole over to the family and sat at the kitchen table sipping tea while Barb Beckett struggled to find the words to express herself and the sudden jarring loss of her husband of twenty-eight years. Barb made a valiant effort to describe the void left in her heart, but she was unsuccessful. She was empty. Claire went to her and hugged her. Her face pale, her eyes vacant and tired, Barb's head slumped onto Claire's shoulder.

The police ruled it a freak animal attack, although the culprit was never apprehended. At the funeral, Jack held Claire's hand tight as they lowered the casket into the ground. The people gathered sang "Abide With Me" as the Beckett children embraced their sobbing mother.

Filled with emotion, Jack's mind raced. A Pandora's box had been irrevocably opened by the unnerving events of the last few months. The weird news reports, the strange experiences and sounds in the woods, the unmistakable feeling of being watched and followed, the dark shape, and those haunting glowing eyes in the Beckett's field. Jack was especially unnerved by the fact that he had nearly stumbled upon Old Man Beckett's body himself that morning when he was tracking the boot prints. Jack shuddered at the thought, his eyes fixed on the shiny casket as it was laid to rest in the earth.

He was also deeply disturbed by the nagging thought that whatever had killed Dave Beckett could have easily killed him too. Those eyes had seen him, after all, and now, as Jack closed his eyes for the closing prayer, those eerie amber orbs came alive in his mind's eye, blazing on the back of his eyelids like great fiery beacons signaling grave danger.

Jack couldn't take his mind off it.

What the hell is going on around here?

That night Jack and Claire held each other in bed and cried themselves to sleep.

It was the last week of May. Jack laced up his hiking boots for his evening hike around the trails. The bugs were starting to get bad; big hungry mosquitoes and deer flies out cruising for a bite. Jack sprayed himself with bug spray before trotting out the door and heading northwest down the trail toward the great maple border between the realm of order and civilized human society and wild, untamed nature and chaos.

It was a cool, overcast evening, with temperatures dropping down into the low fifties. Jack walked at a brisk pace, admiring the scenery as dusk descended and the light retreated. A pair of gray squirrels jabbered at each other, running in wild looping circles on the trail ahead of him. They scattered when he got closer. Jack spotted a red-tailed hawk perched in a treetop in a cluster of beech trees off to the east.

Despite the tragic loss of Dave Beckett, things were good. Jack was happy—as happy as a guy could expect to be anyway. Claire and Mel seemed to be happy too. Although work tried to rear its ugly head in his mind, he pushed those thoughts away and enjoyed the early-evening woods. The breeze whistled in the pines, causing them to sway gently back and forth like the crowd at a folk concert.

As he rounded the white pine, weaving north where the trail curves up and the windblown sand gathers into a shallow gully, he saw three whitetail deer nibbling out in the field. He stopped to admire the graceful creatures, a doe and two fawns, the latter with their heads bent low to the ground, munching away. Jack watched them for a minute or two with a sense of grateful admiration. Then, as he continued on down the trail, the doe noticed him and sprang away through the field to the east, her fawns following clumsily behind. They disappeared through the thicket of trees that marked the boundary between the tall-grass field and the area Jack and his brother and cousins called the "Moors." They named it after the most prominent landscape feature in Sir Arthur Conan Doyle's classic Sherlock Holmes tale, *The Hound of the Baskervilles.* Even though the "moors" on the Allen property shared little with actual moorland, aside from the rolling open hills and low-growing grasses and shrubs.

Jack recalled how as youngsters they would pile into his grandfather's old red golf cart and head out to the north side of the Moors where the trail was like a flat semicircular racetrack. They'd pick up as much speed there as possible, then fly down the big hill along the property line, laughing and yipping hysterically like lunatic hyenas. It was almost like a rollercoaster, only a lot more dangerous, and your stomach definitely dropped and gave you that sinking feeling as you plunged over the top of the hill, spitting dirt and dust up into the air behind you.

If their parents had known what they were up to, they'd have all gotten the spanking to end all spankings. They'd probably have their golf-cart privileges revoked as well, not that they could've sat on it anyway with their asses being so sore from the spankings, but they didn't care. What Mom and Dad didn't know wouldn't hurt them. They'd race down that hill at breakneck speed, the poor old golf cart bumping and groaning, wishing it was still primly ferrying golfers along smooth paved cart paths and well-manicured fairways rather than being repurposed as an off-road dragster by a bunch of wild, irreverent kids.

Jack smiled again as the childhood memories faded back into the misty past.

He continued on down the sandy trail toward the stone bridge, which marked the beginning of a section of dense woods. His boots clicked on the bridge, the Crick below running clear and shallow over its sandy bed. Dense dark woods loomed on either side of the trail, and the black flies thickened into a buzzing cloud. The bug spray did its job, though, and Jack continued on unfettered by the swarming insects.

If you left the trail and followed the Crick along its meandering course westward, you'd eventually come to a little horseshoe bend. There, the woods transitioned into a murky cedar swamp, where a footbridge crossed the Crick. It was there Jack and his cousins built a tipi when they were in their early teens.

They spent a lot of time in the tipi growing up. They used to hike back there, leaving the trail and trudging through the deep woods, ducking under the branches of pines and elms, and finally arriving at their little fort. They dug secret compartments in the ground where they stashed some candles, a lighter, and a flashlight in a Ziplock baggie. Jack and his cousins would go out to the tipi at all hours of the day and night and light a small fire, chat and joke, burp and fart, and sometimes sneak a few nips off a bottle of Julius Kessler whiskey, stolen from Jack's father, who always drank Kessler's.

If you followed the Crick even farther toward the west, you'd eventually come to the remains of what Jack and his father called the "Trappers' Shack": an old log cabin up on a flat-topped rise north of the Crick where two grizzled old fur trappers had lived in the late 1800s. This wasn't on the Allen's property, but Jack and his father had hiked there once or twice when Jack was younger. Later, Jack had taken Russ and Rick to the spot, where they reverently explored the rotten remnants of the old pine logs and wood planks of the shack and what was left of an old wood-burning stove, now mostly buried in leaves and brush. They felt like archaeologists excavating an ancient human habitation, and it was magical. Jack didn't know it at the time, but those two seasoned trappers just up and disappeared in the early fall of 1897; vanished without a trace, and no one ever saw or heard from them again.

Seventy yards or so up the trail past the stone bridge on the left side, an old deer blind stood where his great-uncle Rob used to hunt deer. As he reached the blind, he veered left at a fork in the trail, heading northeast to an area they called "Cherry Ridge," named after the stands of cherry trees there. As he passed Cherry Ridge at a brisk pace, off aways to his left was a dark foreboding cedar swamp. This part of the property was called the "Back Forty," and a rusted barbed wire fence marking the Allen property line extended along the length of the trail here, just a few feet off to the east.

Walking north along the Back Forty, the trail rises slightly and veers to the west. It was getting dark now; the tip of the dying sun was just barely visible on the western horizon. Jack looked off toward the scattered pines to the north as he followed the trail west toward another deer blind. This one was somewhat of a legendary spot among the Allen clan: called the "Big Stump," more deer had been taken from this blind than from any other on the property. Every deer season, the boys vied for a chance to sit at the Big Stump and try their luck at landing a monster buck.

As Jack approached the blind from the east, memories of his father flooded his consciousness. Although the blind looked different now than it had when he last sat there with his father (now it was a modern two-story atrocity with carpeted floors, rolling chairs, and a propane heater), he could still envision in his mind's eye what it had looked like then, and the special times he had shared there with him. The memory brought stinging tears to his eyes.

Jack's father, Stephen Edward Allen, was a late baby boomer, born in the early winter of 1952. His father, Robert James Allen Jr., had been a combat engineer in World War II and had liberated the Buchenwald and Dachau Nazi concentration camps in April 1945. Stephen grew up with his three sisters in the old farmhouse on 16 Mile Road that Jack and his family now called home. That old house seemed to be a living entity unto itself, whose bricks and wood and roots were intimately intertwined with the generations of the Allen family.

Stephen, or Steve as he was known to his friends and family, was a quiet, serious man, honest and hardworking, who made the most of what he had, carving out a living with his two hands. He worked his entire adult life at the Holmes Sawmill in Tustin, running a board edger from eight A.M. to five P.M. He'd pull into the driveway in his old red Ford F-150 every weeknight at half-past five, covered from head to toe in sawdust, smelling like pine sap, sweat, and cigarettes. He'd usually drink a cold beer and smoke a Winston cigarette on the front porch, then grab a quick shower before supper. He worked hard to provide for his wife, Mary, and his two children, Bradley Robert, born in 1982, and John Henry, born in 1985. The doctors had told Steve and Mary they wouldn't be able to have children, but Steve was an optimist, so he and Mary just kept on trying.

Steve had an older sister, Lara, who also happened to have two boys, Pat and Russ. Miraculously, Steve's younger brother Reed also had two boys, Jay and Rick. Grandma and Grandpa couldn't have been prouder: six grandkids, all born within seven years of each other; the eldest, Pat, born in 1980, and the youngest, Rick, born in 1987. The cousins grew up like kings of the castle, with the entire Northwoods as their own personal playground. They were extremely close.

For as long as Jack could remember, his father had been his teacher, mentor, and role model, and they shared a slightly formal yet warm relationship. Steve and Mary loved spending time with their boys outdoors. In the summer, the Allens would go camping, and Steve would take the boys fishing and hunting for small game. In the fall, they hunted whitetail deer with bow and arrow and rifle. During the long Northern Michigan winters, they would snowshoe and cross-country ski. Afterward Mary would fix up mugs of steaming hot chocolate topped with little marshmallows that they'd happily sip together as they watched the news or a show on their old television set. Steve taught Brad and Jack how to survive in the woods and live off the land, but he also passed on a deep and abiding love for the outdoors that stayed with his children throughout their lives.

It was late fall in 1997, a year that had been strange in many ways. Jack had turned twelve in April, and Jack's father had seemed tense and irritable since about that time, which was out of character for him. It made Jack and his older brother Brad uneasy. Peculiarly, Steve hadn't mentioned hunting all year and even seemed resistant to the idea when Jack finally brought it up at the dinner table one evening in October. This was exceedingly odd, as hunting was one of their favorite pastimes and something they cherished doing together every year. But Jack was persistent, and Steve's excuse that he had too much going on at the mill this year seemed hollow and strange to Jack. Eventually, Steve relented and agreed to take him out.

It was a Saturday evening, November 17, 1997. Jack and his dad quietly trudged out to their deer blind in their hunting gear: insulated camouflage coveralls with hunter orange vests and hats. Jack had his bolt-action, military surplus hunting rifle slung over his shoulder, while his father had the butt of his Winchester Model 94 .30-30 nestled in the crook of his right arm, the barrel pointing up and over his left shoulder toward the orange autumn sky. It was a beautiful clear day, the mid-November air was crisp, and the faint scent of burning leaves teased their nostrils like a long-forgotten memory.

That afternoon they were sitting at the "Big Stump," near the northeast corner of the Allen property. Over the years the Allens had great luck at the Big Stump, and Jack himself had already shot two nice bucks while sitting there: a ten-point monster in 1995 with a bow and a respectable six-pointer the following year with his trusty rifle.

But it wasn't the deer or the blind or the cold that made this particular evening out hunting with his dad stick in Jack's mind, even many years later. He had hunted with his dad on similar occasions many times—maybe a hundred times—throughout his life. No, it was what happened at dusk that night that Jack couldn't shake, the way his father had reacted, tensed, breathless, wide-eyed. He had never seen him that way before. Although he was never sure of just what had happened, of what they had seen that night, it had left an indelible impression on Jack that stuck with him for the rest of his life.

As dusk set in around 5:15 that fateful night, they were both exhilarated. They had been sitting in the blind on uncomfortable hunting stools since about three that afternoon, keeping warm by sipping coffee and hot chocolate out of their old stainless-steel thermoses. Quietly munching on beef jerky, they hadn't seen much of anything the entire day, but often the most action occurred at twilight, when the crepuscular whitetail was most active, so they were hoping for the best. On top of that, Jack was tired and cold, anxious to head back to the farm and warm up before dinner. But as the light slowly faded and darkness descended, enveloping the ghostly landscape like a dense fog, both Jack and his father were restless on their feet, squinting silently as they scanned the tallgrass field in front of them for any shadows or signs of movement.

That was when Steve Allen's breath suddenly caught in his chest like he had swallowed a bug.

It made Jack start too, and looking over at his father, he noticed him tense up, his features hardening in the darkening shadows of dusk.

"What is it, Dad?" Jack hissed, his voice barely a whisper and quaking ever so slightly.

When Steve didn't respond, a slight wave of fear washed over Jack. He tried to follow his dad's line of sight, straight south, down toward the base of an old majestic cherry tree that stood tall and thick, watching over the tallgrass field like a faithful sentinel.

At first Jack didn't see anything out of the ordinary, just what appeared to be dark lifeless shadows within shadows; intermingled grays and blacks faintly outlined on the landscape.

Was it a deer? The thought suddenly flashed in his head, the most obvious explanation that had somehow escaped him up until that anxious moment. He breathed an audible sigh of relief at the mere thought of it.

But then one of the shadows moved.

And as it did, it became clear to Jack that this was no deer. He was frozen with fear, his breath coming in shaky shallow gasps, his chest heaving. The shadow crept along the edge of the tallgrass field on all fours, silent as a mouse, stealthy as a cat... or perhaps a wolf. Wild thoughts flooded Jack's mind as he stared wide-eyed at the enigma in the field, not a hundred yards away from the deer blind in which he and his father stood, silent and still. He had never really seen anything in the woods he couldn't identify until he laid eyes on this creature. Maybe it was the encroaching darkness playing tricks on him.

Jack's heart was pounding in his chest as he glanced over at his father, who was still squinting in concentration, his focus dialed in on the silhouette in the tallgrass field. Jack turned his gaze back to the shape in the field, which appeared to be coming toward them. He noticed that his palms were sweaty in his gloves, and he glanced to his left, where his rifle stood propped against the tree stump that was the foundation of the deer blind.

In the eerie glow of the moon, as Jack and his father looked on, the creature rose up slowly and sinuously onto its hind legs. Jack's eyes bulged with growing fascination and horror, not believing what they were seeing.

It was almost manlike, tall, lean, and muscular. But, whatever it was, the sight sent a chill down Jack's spine.

His trance was broken when his father suddenly reached for his Winchester. Shouldering it, he took aim, but the creature must have heard or felt the movement because it spooked and dropped back down onto all fours as Steve fired off a shot that was deafening in the cold stillness of the night. He cocked the rifle and quickly fired off another round, the acrid smell of gun smoke filling the blind. They both looked out anxiously toward the tree by the field, but the creature was nowhere to be seen; vanished, it seemed, into the encroaching darkness. The silence that filled the blind was as deafening as the gunshots moments before, despite the ringing in Jack's ears and the waning smell of gun powder in his nostrils that reminded him of fireworks on the Fourth of July.

"What *was* that, Dad?" Jack asked again, a breathless wonder in his voice.

"Not sure, son," Steve Allen replied quietly, almost under his breath. He turned to Jack and put his right index finger to his lips, calling for silence, as he continued to monitor the situation out in the tallgrass field. For some reason, this ominous gesture frightened Jack nearly as much as the shadowy figure they had just seen at the edge of the field.

Jack and his father stood in silence for another five minutes or so, scanning the area for any signs of life or movement. The darkness thickened around them until it was nearly pitch black.

"Grab your rifle, Jack," Steve whispered, shattering the uneasy silence.

Jack did as he was told. He was scared and confused and could tell his dad meant business. Jack's father also kept his rifle close as he fished out a flashlight from his coat pocket.

"We'll come back for the rest of the gear later," he said, moving quietly toward the exit. "Stay behind me but stay close. Keep your eyes open, gun ready."

As silently as possible, Steve pushed the pine boughs aside that served as a door to the blind. In single file, the two hunters carefully made their way over to the cherry tree at the edge of the tallgrass field, their rifles at the ready, each step bringing them excruciatingly closer to the location of the mysterious sighting. Steve, in the lead, had his Winchester cocked and pointed at the tree where the creature had *stood*. The light was nearly gone now, aside from the eerie glow of the moon.

Jack's heart pounded as they approached the tree, not fifty yards away now. The ground crunched beneath his hunting boots, already hardened by the cold early winter weather. Reaching the tree, Steve held up his right hand, and they came to a sudden silent halt. Jack's breath was heaving in his chest as he goggled at the tree in front of them, his breath barely visible in the incandescent moonlight.

That's when his father suddenly switched on the flashlight and thundered around the base of the tree, his Winchester shouldered and ready to fire.

Something leaped out from behind the tree, its soft yellow eyes gleaming wide in the flashlight's beam. Jack screamed, nearly jumping out of his skin, and raised his rifle to shoot.

"It's okay, Jack, don't shoot!" his father yelled from a few yards away. "It's just a deer." He said, breathing heavily, and wiped the sweat from his brow with the back of his hand. "Just a deer."

Steve and Jack searched the area for a blood trail, but there was none to be found. They were both uneasy and on edge after the evening's events, so after a few minutes, they headed back to the blind, retrieved their thermoses and the rest of their gear, and headed back to Steve's pickup, parked on the Back Forty trail northeast of the blind. Jack noticed his father was a bit nervous, glancing back over his shoulder and scrutinizing every shadow, keeping his rifle cocked and close at hand.

The short drive back to the farmhouse was uncomfortable, even paranoid, with his father saying very little.

"Must have been a bear, son," he finally said, but Jack sensed that his father didn't really believe that. He looked like he had seen a ghost, and there was a definite sense of worry, perhaps even fear, which weighed heavily on him as he spoke. "Or maybe a bobcat. You just never know what you'll come across in these woods sometimes," he said. "Especially at night." When he said that, he glanced over at his son in the passenger seat and their eyes locked. There was a haunted look in Steve's eyes, eyes which at that moment seemed somehow darker than usual.

Jack was very happy to finally get inside and warm up in the safety of his home. He never mentioned the strange happenings of that evening to his mother, who was reading a magazine and sipping tea on the couch in the living room when he came in. His father stayed outside for a good half hour after returning home, smoking cigarettes and watching the trail leading toward the dark woods.

Back in the present, Jack stood on the trail beside the Big Stump deer blind as the memory of that night in 1997 withered. It gave Jack an uneasy feeling like there was more to remember, another part of the story that was still buried in his subconscious.

As you stood looking south from the Big Stump you'd see the open tallgrass field and the cherry tree where Jack and his father had seen that strange apparition in the moonlight nearly twenty years ago.

Jack took the long way around this evening, heading straight east from the Big Stump along a dark trail in an area called the "Birches." The light was all but gone now, the shadows dancing in the twilight before full darkness enveloped the landscape.

Jack walked at a brisk pace; power walking, you might say. He was now working up a sweat and getting into a good breathing rhythm. As he weaved along the dusky trail through the Birches, he came to a familiar bend where he and his cousins used to leave the trail and cut through the birches and maples, heading south toward the edge of the swamp. They had a nice spot there that became a secret headquarters of sorts when they played in the woods as kids. The trees were too dense and the darkness too thick to see the spot from the trail, and besides, it was a good seventy-five yards off the beaten path. That night something made Jack stop there for a moment.

He couldn't put his finger on it, but he sensed there was something about that place at the edge of the swamp, something that made the hair on his arms stand up and the skin there to tighten into gooseflesh. Whatever it was, it sent a cold shiver down his spine.

Just then, he heard a strange sound back there in the dense birches and maples. It was deep; way back there, maybe coming from the swamp.

But what was it? It sounded like a low grunt, some kind of guttural cough. He heard it again, three times in rapid-fire succession this time. It sounded like it was getting closer.

What the hell was that? Jack thought, eyes wide. *A bear? A cougar? Hopefully not either of tho—*

There it was again, three times in a row, louder, closer. Three coughing grunts.

Jack turned on his heels and took off down the trail at a jog. He decided he wasn't going to wait around to see what this strange, threatening sound was. Not tonight anyway. He flicked on his headlamp, showering the trail and trees in front of him with a bright white light. Luckily he knew the trails like the back of his hand, but he didn't want to risk tripping over a downed branch and twisting an ankle or something, certainly not when there might be some animal behind him.

You just never know what you'll come across in these woods sometimes, he thought, trying to remember where he had heard that bit of wisdom.

He pushed on at a decent clip, pounding over the wood bridge over the Crick on the east side of the property.

Turning sharply to the west, he continued down a trail that was tunnel-like, with dogwood trees and tall raspberry bushes on either side that seemed to reach in toward you, forming a semicircular tangle of growth above him.

Jack shot a glance to his right, looking out across the Crick into the Birches. The beam from his headlamp bounced with his strides, and he figured the light would hopefully spook whatever it was he had heard back there. He didn't see anything, which eased his mind, but visibility wasn't great either, so he kept up his pace, jogging fast around the bend in the trail to the south. This straight trail was called the "Lane." It was a hundred yards long or so and flanked on either side by stands of tall scotch pines, which the Allens periodically harvested.

As Jack progressed down the Lane, he saw the big red barn up on the hill to the west. An uplifting wave of relief washed over him at the familiar sight, and he slowed his pace a bit, thinking he was safe, in the clear.

That's when he heard the howl.

It was scratchy and guttural and loud.

He jumped as cold shockwaves surged through him. It must have been a few hundred yards away, possibly back near the trail through the birches where he had heard those odd grunts mere minutes before.

"What the FUCK?!" he yelled. *You never hear wolves around here!*

Jack sprinted the rest of the way up the hill toward the barn. When he came to the rock stairway embedded in the side of the hill, he took the steps two or three at a time.

Jack was on the gravel driveway now. The old windmill and farmhouse were directly in front of him, not more than fifty yards away. The floodlights on the barn and the windmill were welcome sights after his harrowing trek through the woods that night.

Breathless, Jack reached the concrete slab that was the front porch of the farm. He slumped, hands on his knees, and gasped for breath. Jack turned toward the barn—toward the trail—and squinted out into the darkness, unsure of what he was looking for. Perhaps a bear, a cougar... probably a wolf.

However, nothing was there.

Jack sat down on the wooden bench on the front porch and spent the next half hour or so keeping an uneasy watch, much like his father had done nearly twenty years ago after their strange encounter hunting at the Big Stump.

CHAPTER 4

INTERLUDE: CAR TROUBLE

Monday, May 29, 2017
Near Manton, Michigan

Sarah Hansen was having a bad day, and it was about to get worse.

That morning she burned her finger on the frying pan while cooking breakfast. In the time it took to run her throbbing finger under cold tap water, the toast had burned to a black crisp. Then, on her way to work, she realized she left her thermos of coffee at home. This realization came just before the cruise control on her car mysteriously stopped working as she drove south on U.S. 131.

"Shit." She pushed the cruise button off and on again to no effect.

She drove down from her home in Manton to Cadillac, where she worked as a real estate agent, about a fifteen- or twenty-minute drive, depending on traffic and weather. Once she got to work that fateful Monday, things didn't improve. In fact, they got worse.

Around noon Sarah discovered she had lost a sizable sale to a rival realtor. And not just any rival realtor: adding salt to the wound, she had lost the sale to an old enemy of hers from high school, Cindy Rogers. The same Cindy Rogers who had taken her spot in glee club *and* stolen her eleventh-grade boyfriend, Max.

That bitch! she thought, sitting at her desk, taking a big sip of coffee.

"FUT!" she cursed. The coffee was scalding hot and burned her mouth, causing her tongue to swell.

When things didn't improve after lunch Sarah decided to pack it in and go home early. She was going to curl up on the couch, have a few drinks, watch some bad television, and lick her wounds.

She left the office just after three o'clock. After only a few miles on the highway, heading north on 131, she noticed the gas light had come on; when, she knew not.

"You've gotta be kidding me!" Sarah whined, flabbergasted and dejected.

She saw a sign for a gas station at the next exit and pulled off the highway. Taking a left at the stop sign, she headed west on East 30 Road toward an empty rural scene straight out of a slasher movie. She could almost hear the banjos dueling. There was no sign of life anywhere.

It was only fitting on that day that the gas station she pulled off for was closed. In fact, it looked like it had been closed since about 1963. The windows were boarded up and graffiti covered the pumps. To finish the scene, an occasional tumbleweed drifted listlessly by on the breeze. She scowled and exhaled furiously, cursing the day, cursing her luck, her teeth clenched, feeling like she was about to scream with rage. Her hands gripped the wheel in white-knuckled fury as she slowed to a stop in front of the abandoned service station.

Then Sarah took a deep breath, exhaled through pursed lips, and closed her eyes. She glanced at the fuel gauge: it was getting precariously low now, but she decided to follow the road for a few more miles west to see if there were any other gas stations closer to town.

She figured, worst-case scenario, she'd have to double back and get on the highway and hit a gas station farther up the road. But come to think of it, she didn't know of any off-hand for at least a few more miles heading north on 131. And besides, what she really wanted was a Snickers ice cream bar. She figured she had earned it after the day from hell she was having.

What Sarah Hansen didn't realize was that her hell was actually just beginning.

Sarah Hansen pulled out of the vacant parking lot, lonely as a crypt, and headed west on East 30 Road toward its junction with Old U.S. 131. As she spluttered along, almost on fumes, Sarah noticed that there was less and less to look at alongside the road, just trees and overgrowth on either side of her. No homes, farms, businesses, or civilization to speak of.

Just then, her car made a strange wheezing sound. She glanced down at the fuel gauge.

When her eyes came back up to the road, she saw the deer standing there, a look in its eyes as vacant as the parking lot of the ghost-town service station down the road.

Sarah gasped and swerved to the right, audibly clipping the deer's tail. The car skidded and fishtailed as it careened off the asphalt onto the gravel shoulder before hitting the ditch and rolling twice down a shallow ravine overgrown with foliage. When her car rolled, Sarah's forehead smashed into the steering wheel.

Everything went black.

Now she was unconscious, buckled snugly in her Toyota Camry, bleeding from a gash on her cheek caused by flying glass when the driver's side window shattered. But other than the cut, she was miraculously unharmed. The car had come to rest upright, smashed and immobilized on bent rims and blown tires. But after its dramatic double axel, it landed in just such a way that it was completely invisible to the naked eye from the road. The only evidence of Sarah's accident was a bit of burned rubber leading off the road and into the shoulder. The car itself seemed to be consumed by the tall grass and thick shrubs and trees down in the ravine on the side of the road. It was hidden near the edge of a clearing where the deeper woods began, dark, hazy, and ominous. When the dust cleared, a stifling silence fell like the curtains after a dramatic scene in a Broadway production.

The first thing Sarah knew when she came to was pain.

She had a horrible pounding headache that gave her a sickly feeling in her stomach. She raised her head, and pain shot down her neck and into her back, her head throbbing, dried blood cracking on her face.

Sarah reached down and unbuckled her seat belt, which had undoubtedly saved her life. She fumbled for the door handle. Amazingly, despite the crushed sardine can that her car now was, the door opened easily but with a loud squeal. She moved slightly and vomited, hacking and dry heaving out the door of her Camry.

She half crawled, half fell out of the car, hanging on the best she could to consciousness.

That's when she realized it was dark. There were no streetlights on this lonely country road that she could make out, but admittedly at the moment, her sight was patchy with black spots of blind pain. She tried to raise herself up onto her knees and realized that her legs were not broken; the only good thing that had happened to her that day. She felt like crying but bit her lower lip in grim determination instead. Sarah staggered up to her feet and stumbled before she crawled up the embankment to the side of the road, searching desperately for lights or a car passing by. She had no sense of what time it was.

Sarah made it to the gravel shoulder and began to trudge along the road back toward the highway, a pitiful, miserable limping sight under the thin moonlight. After a hundred yards or so, when it was getting harder to walk, and she still hadn't seen any sign of life, she began to panic.

That was when she heard it: a sound in the ditch on the left side of the road, like something was walking down there, following her.

Sarah snapped her head around, causing a jolt of pain to shoot down her neck and into her back, and searched the ditch for the source of the sound.

Then she saw the eyes: two glistening amber orbs not more than thirty feet away from her. They were coming toward her.

Sarah screamed, a desperate, dry cry of terror and panic. She tried to run but tripped over a stone on the shoulder, which sent her sprawling painfully into the ditch north of the road.

She didn't get a good look at it in the dim moonlight but felt a sudden piercing warmth in her abdomen as razor claws slashed four deep gashes across her stomach. Freshets of blood gouted up into the night air and pooled in her lap as she lay motionless in the dirt. She reached down instinctively and felt her gutted intestines, warm and wet in her pale shaking hands. Sarah was in shock, her mouth opening and closing involuntarily as if she were trying to say something.

Then her throat was torn out, and a sickening gurgling croak oozed from her mouth as she expired on the side of the road, eyes wide, staring blankly up at the night sky.

PART II

AWAKENING

CHAPTER 5

Sunday, June 17, 2017
LeRoy, Michigan

The first half of June had been uneventful as the Northwoods and the Allen family transitioned from spring into summer.

Jack's nephew Logan was moving into his first apartment in Big Rapids and was looking for dishes—dinnerware, Claire had corrected him. Actually, Logan was looking for anything he could get his hands on for cheap (i.e., free), whether it be old furniture, boxes, silverware, lamps, you name it. Since Jack and Claire doted on Logan, the only son of Claire's only sister, Rachel, they decided to help out.

The big red barn at the farm was home to an endless assortment of stuff that Logan might find potentially useful, so they had him over one Saturday afternoon to scrounge through the dusty barn and see if there was anything he wanted to have. After a few hours, he had left with two truckloads full of odds and ends to furnish his new apartment. He was tickled pink about his score and thanked Jack and Claire. They just smiled and nodded. They were happy to help, but they were also happy to get rid of some of the junk that had been accumulating and gathering dust in the barn for years.

Wearing a grin from ear to ear, Logan pulled out of the driveway heading west on 16 Mile Road. He tooted the horn good-naturedly as Jack and Claire waved goodbye.

Jack was surprised to get a call from Logan the very next day. It was just after ten A.M.

"Uncle Jack? It's me, Logan."

"Hey, buddy, how are you?"

"Fine, fine," Logan said, "Hey, remember when I was over at your place getting stuff for my new apartment?"

"You mean yesterday?" Jack said, stifling a chuckle. "Yeah, I remember."

"Well, thanks again for helping me out like that. I really appreciate it. But…" Logan trailed off. "I was really hoping to get some dishes, you know, like plates and bowls and cups and stuff?"

"Like dinnerware, you mean?" Jack glanced over at Claire with a goofy smile.

"Yeah, like dinnerware!" Logan said. "I must have totally forgotten about it yesterday when I was over. You don't happen to have any extra dinnerware laying around anywhere, do you?"

Jack could sense his nephew's shy, awkward assertiveness through the phone.

"Well, you know, what, Logan?" Jack began. "We never poked around in the loft yesterday, but I think we have a nice dinnerware set that Grandma used to use before she moved into her condo and downsized. I guess I forgot about it when you were over."

"Oh, that's great!" Logan said.

"I'll head down there in a few minutes here and dig it out

and you can swing by tonight or next week sometime to pick it up. Sound good?"

"That'd be great, Uncle Jack! Thanks a ton!"

"No problem, Logan. You take care now, and say hi to your mom for us."

"Will do! See you soon!"

Jack hung up the phone and smiled over at Claire, who sat at the kitchen table sipping a cup of coffee and reading the newspaper.

"We forgot to give him the *dinnerware*," Jack said in mock sarcasm, shrugging his shoulders, palms up.

"Oh, heavens!" Claire giggled. "We can't have that!"

It was a clear, breezy day in June. The sun was shining, the days were beginning to get longer, and the nights were still crisp as the wheel of the seasons was just beginning to shift toward summer in northern Michigan.

I love this time of year, Jack thought as he strode down the gravel drive toward the barn.

Coming to the large red double doors, Jack reached for the padlock—which was never actually locked—and unlatched the barn doors. Jack returned the padlock to the loop, leaving the hasp loose. Then he swung the doors open wide and stepped up into the familiar entry space of the barn.

The barn smelled musty, like old decaying hay and wood— a somewhat sour, earthy smell that stuck in your nostrils but wasn't altogether unpleasant. Sunlight streaked in through gaps in the wallboards, illuminating cascades of flowing dust particles that appeared to dance, suspended eerily in midair. They seemed to know something, to have a story to tell of years long past, perhaps of secrets and memories that were locked in the well-worn boards and sawdust of the old barn. Between the sunlight coming in from the doors and the eerie light streaming through the wallboards, the barn was well lit.

Standing in the main entryway, between two ten-foot-long two-by-ten planks positioned on the floor that served as a two-track where Jack and his father would pull up their cars to change the oil, Jack glanced up at the loft in the northwest corner of the barn. It was a small hayloft, about forty feet by twenty feet, with an old wooden ladder leaning against the wall for entry.

Just seeing the old loft filled Jack's head with memories of his childhood. He and his cousins had turned the loft into their "secret" fort when they were younger, maybe nine or ten. They had spent many hours playing up there with their toy guns, spying on their girl cousins or the grownups, who kindly played along, and generally sharing magical childhood times together. Then later, in their teen years, they had used the loft for more clandestine endeavors, stashing dirty magazines there and sneaking up to the loft for a beer or two or talk about sex and girls. By their twenties, Jack and his cousins had grown away from the loft, as childhood and all its magic gradually and tragically faded into memory.

Jack sighed aloud as a sharp pang of sadness for lost innocence, and youth struck him. Swallowing the lump in his throat, he walked over to the ladder leading up to the loft.

I bet no one's been up here for ten, maybe fifteen years, Jack thought, reaching for the ladder with both hands.

He gripped the ladder firmly and shook it a bit, testing its integrity. It seemed to be strong and sturdy, so Jack tentatively stepped onto the bottom rung with his right foot. He put a bit of weight on it. It held, so he put all his weight on it. No problems, so Jack made his way to the second rung and repeated his cautious integrity checks. Soon, Jack stepped off the ladder onto the floorboards of the loft.

The musty, dank smell of mildew and rot was stronger there, and Jack had the creepy feeling that he was breathing air that hadn't been breathed in over a decade. He wondered what all might be up there. After his father left in 2007, his mother had moved into a condo in Cadillac. Jack remembered moving some boxes up into the loft at that time, including the dinnerware set he was presently seeking.

So, it's been ten years, he thought, thinking not only of the last time he had set foot in the loft but also remembering his father's sudden departure.

Again, Jack sighed aloud and swallowed the growing lump in his throat, squeezing his eyes tightly shut against the tears that were threatening. He cleared his throat and shook his head, suddenly remembering why he was up in the loft in the first place.

Now, where did I put that stuff? He scanned the hay and other detritus on the floor along the walls.

There were several boxes stacked along the northeast corner of the loft, each labeled in black marker. His eyes lit upon a familiar box with the word *DISHES* scrawled on its side in his mother's hand.

"Dinnerware—ha!" he laughed as he approached the box.

He knelt down and blew the accumulated dust off the top of it. Reaching down with both hands, he moved the box slightly away from the wall so he could get a better grip on it to pick it up.

That's when Jack noticed his father's old wooden trunk, tucked away neatly behind the stacked boxes.

After his father left, his mother had told him that the trunk was full of old papers and bills. *Your father was a bit of a pack rat, after all,* she had told him, a nervous smile on her face. Jack hadn't thought anything of it at the time and had lugged the trunk up to the loft along with the boxes and other odds and ends his mother was discarding. Jack had completely forgotten about the trunk; it hadn't crossed his mind once in ten years. Now, as he crouched down on the creaky loft floor, frozen in place, staring the ornate woodwork and tarnished golden latch secured with a dusty old combination lock, the trunk seemed to be alive, to call out to him as if it had a story to tell.

His heart started beating faster, and he noticed the hair rising on the back of his neck. His mouth was dry, and he licked his lips, which were twitching slightly. His fingers danced up and down in waves of anticipation, like a gunfighter's milliseconds before drawing his pistol in a gunfight.

He slid the box of dishes over to one side and sidled up next to the trunk. Taking the combination lock in his left hand, he noticed that his palms were sweaty. Wishing himself luck, he tried the lock, pulling the outer case down and away from the shackle.

Nothing. It held fast.

Quickly he tried 2—3—1, the area code in LeRoy. Holding his breath, he tried the lock again.

Nothing.

"Fuck!" he shouted, slamming his fist on the floorboards, sending a puff of dust into the air.

Looking down at the combination dial, he felt helpless, nearly ready to give up or just smash the lock with a crowbar or a shovel.

Just then, Jack closed his eyes and breathed deeply, spinning the dial absent-mindedly. The familiar musty smell of the barn and the loft filled his nostrils. He opened his eyes and glanced up at the wall above him. An ancient yellowed poster of the great Denver Broncos quarterback, John Elway, hung there. Elway had been one of Jack's favorite football players throughout the 80s and 90s. The poster was covered in cobwebs, and the corners were curled, and yet amazingly it was still intact and hanging there, looking down at Jack as if it had been meant to be. Elway's arm was cocked back, ready to throw a deep bomb for a touchdown, no doubt, and as Jack reminisced, smiling and suddenly light-hearted, he noticed Elway's jersey.

"Lucky number seven." Jack shrugged his shoulders.

Holding the lock in his left hand, he spun the dial with his right, entering in the combination 7—7—7. He pulled down on the outer case, and, miraculously, it came free of the shackle with a satisfying click.

Holding the opened lock in his hand, Jack just crouched there for a moment, mystified.

Holy shit, it worked!

He shook himself back into the present moment and lifted the lock from the trunk latch, setting it off to one side on the floor. Lifting the hasp free of the loop, he opened the trunk lid, which had last been opened by his father at least ten years ago. A musty dank smell of mildew, dust, and old paper filled Jack's nostrils. Butterflies fluttered in his stomach and for some reason, it seemed almost like a religious experience to him, like he was opening the Ark of the Covenant. Jack peered down into the box of the trunk, wide-eyed and breathless.

His first thought was: *These aren't bills,* remembering what his mother had told him ten years before about the contents of the trunk. A shudder ran through him.

What the hell is this stuff?

Stacks of old papers, some of them held together with rusty paperclips or staples, some handwritten, some typed, some photocopies, newspaper clippings, a few maps, some of them marked and circled with red ink. Jack also noticed a few stacks of paper tucked away in manila folders. The common thread that tied them together was the ubiquitous thin layer of dust covering them. With a confused but curious look on his face, Jack reached into the trunk and pulled a stack of papers off the top.

It appeared to be a journal entry of sorts, written by his great-great-grandfather Edward James Allen. Jack read the title aloud: "My Experiences in the Garland Swamp, Wexford County, Michigan, June 1887, by Edward J. Allen." Biting his lower lip and thinking for a second, he stood up and plopped down in a dusty old wicker chair perched in the corner of the loft.

He flipped through the pages, held together by a paperclip, and his eyes fixed on something that drew his attention: *"...the creature emerged... eyes of amber fire..."*

Jack's heart nearly stopped as his brain made the connection between those ominous words on the page and his own strange experiences over the past few months, particularly the glowing eyes he had seen in the Beckett's field.

As Jack began reading, transfixed and silently mouthing the words as he went along, he found himself sucked right into the vivid tale his ancestor wove.

Monday, June 6, 1887
Wexford County, Michigan

It was a cool summer morning in early June. The sun began to creep up over the horizon at about six A.M., a little shy at first but coming on strong by a quarter past the hour, bathing the northwest Michigan landscape in a dull yellow-orange glow. The tops of the pines and hemlocks of the lush forest began to burn with an amber radiance, like embers blown back into life after the chill damp of the dark night.

As the sun rose, the hardened and weathered men of the logging camp rose with it, groggily rubbing the sleep from their eyes as they emerged from their tents and shelters, shaking out their sleeping rolls and drawing deeply from their canteens. Some slept in the bunkhouse, a log cabin built of pine with rough board floors and a tarpaper roof held down with saplings. Small campfires burst into life as cast-iron skillets and coffee pots moved like shadows in the early morning silence. The smell of bacon, skillet bread, and coffee filled the air as some of the grizzled mossbacks—as loggers were often called in those days—stumbled down to the bank of the majestic Manistee River to wash up or fetch water. Edward James Allen was among them.

At 35, Jim, as everyone called him, was still a force to be reckoned with. Logging had kept him strong and sharp. His hands were massive and calloused, his arms like tree trunks and his grip like iron shackles. Yet he was fair and honest, humble too, his smile quick and warm. Jim Allen was well-liked and respected by his peers.

By half-past six, the men were eating and slurping coffee from tin cups, grunting and conversing in low tones. The camp consisted of 26 loggers, two cooks, and a camp boss or foreman, who also kept the books. As the men finished their breakfast, some flicked dregs from their cups, while others lit pipes or hand-rolled cigarettes, smoking quietly in the cool morning sunlight. Some ambled over to the outhouse for their morning constitutional.

This ritual was followed by the next: packing up the necessary gear and supplies for the day's work. As the men got to it, the foreman, a plump, educated man named Lewis, weaved through the camp shouting, "We're moving out in ten minutes! Prep your gear and meet at the privy!"

He didn't need to remind them. Everyone knew the drill. This crew had worked together for a long time, and by now it ran like a well-oiled machine, efficiently harvesting the white, red, and jack pine that fueled the booming Michigan lumber industry, especially the white pines, some of which were 200 years old, as many feet high, and five or six feet in diameter. Logging was a lucrative business in Northern Michigan. In fact, by 1880, Michigan was producing as much lumber as the next three states combined.

But to Jim it was a job, a job he liked, mind you, mostly because it kept him out in the wilderness where he felt both alive and at peace.

By seven A.M., the line of weather-beaten men, horses, and mules began to move steadily across the landscape, following the course of the Manistee River northeast into the wilderness. The clean cold river water babbled and glistened in the early morning sun, a dark blue-black mirror reflecting the green pines along its banks. The men and pack animals were loaded down with axes, hatchets, crosscut saws, drawknives, hunting knives, rifles, shotguns, canteens, and packs.

Thirty minutes later, the men reached their destination. They found themselves in a broad stand of towering pines about a half-mile south of the river where they had been cutting the week before. As the crew set to work chopping, sawing, and felling, they filled the air with sawdust and the scent of fresh pine sap. The foreman strolled over to where Jim and his pal Dave Vandenberg were tag-teaming a particularly massive white pine with a two-man felling saw.

"Allen!" Lewis barked.

"Yes, sir?" Allen replied, looking up from his work and mopping his brow with a handkerchief.

Lewis said, "Take a detail of ten men and head northeast toward the Garland Swamp." He swatted wildly at a black fly that buzzed around his head, then spat tobacco juice over his left shoulder, wiping his mouth with his shirt sleeve. "We left some logs up thataway that need to be floated downriver to port in Manistee. Not too many. Bring some horses and a sled along and be back by noon."

"Yes, sir." Allen straightened up from the crouched position he was in.

Jim and Dave recruited nine other men, making eleven total, including Jim, the leader of this happy little expedition. With a two-horse team dragging a sled, the men set out northeast for the Garland Swamp.

The day was turning out to be a beautiful one, cool and breezy, and the men felt good as they trudged along, despite the ubiquitous black flies and mosquitoes. A logger named Johnson and his friend Ellis whistled a tune that caught on the breeze and brought a smile to Allen's face. They were all in a playful mood as they reached the outskirts of the Garland Swamp, murky and foreboding like a mysterious old haunted mansion at dusk.

As the men studied the swamp from its edge, searching for the trail their crew had followed the week before, one of the men suddenly gasped.

"Would you look at that?" he stammered, a sense of awe in his voice.

"What *is* that?" asked Dave Vandenberg, squinting.

"Looks like a dog... but it's too big for a dog," Johnson pondered. "Maybe a wolf?"

"Well, I don't know 'bout you boys," Ellis grinned. "But I'm gonna find out!" His eyebrows rose as he said it, and there was a glimmer of mischief in his eyes.

"Wait for me, asshole," Johnson laughed as he cocked his Winchester and started after Ellis, who was already walking —or stalking—toward the unwitting animal, not a hundred yards away in a clearing at the edge of the swamp.

The other men followed suit, forming a perimeter while two men each took the far sides in a pincer-like maneuver, creating a surround like they were flushing birds out of the tall grass. But try as they may, they couldn't keep up with Ellis and Johnson, who were practically sprinting toward the unidentified creature in the clearing.

As the two men got closer, the animal noticed them and started to retreat eastward in a bounding, four-legged trot. It didn't seem like it was in much of a hurry, which gave Vandenberg and Williams time to catch up and block its path, playfully chasing it back toward its original position in the clearing at the edge of the swamp. As far as they could tell, the creature was quite large with matted brownish-gray fur and pointy canine ears outlined with bushy fur.

As the creature neared the clearing, Ellis and Johnson came within forty feet of it and got a better look.

For the first time, a sudden fear shot through Ellis. It struck him to the core and turned his heart deathly cold, causing the hair on the back of his neck to stand up and the skin on his arms to turn to gooseflesh. He stopped dead in his tracks as the beast retreated further into the swamp.

Johnson was laughing as he continued the pursuit.

"Maybe we should just let it go, Johnson," Ellis said, a look of cold dread in his eyes, like he had just seen a ghost.

"Aw, come on, ya girl," Johnson crowed. "I just saw it scamper into that hollow log not thirty yards into the swamp."

By then, the rest of the eleven-man crew had arrived on the scene. They stood in a rough crescent shape with Ellis and Johnson in the center.

"What the hell *was* that?" asked Williams, catching his breath.

"I don't know," smiled Johnson. He handed his Winchester to Allen and snapped off a four-foot pine bow from a nearby tree. Shaving off its branches with his pocketknife, he grinned, his eyes wide and bright. "But I'm gonna go over there and find out!"

He glanced impishly at Ellis, whose face was pale, eyes sunken.

"YEE-HAW!" Johnson suddenly screamed as he took off at a fast walk into the swamp, causing Ellis to nearly jump out of his skin.

The others looked at one another, not knowing what to do.

"Well," sighed Jim. "Let's humor him just this once before we get on with our mission."

The men nodded, grunting in affirmation, and set off into the swamp after the stick-wielding Johnson.

When they caught up with Johnson, he was already peeking in one end of the hollow log.

"He's in here, boys!" he cawed gleefully.

He took his stick and poked around blindly inside the log.

That was when they heard it, a sound that froze their blood and made their eyes bulge in base terror—a sound they would hear in their nightmares that would wake them up in a cold, shuddering sweat. A sound they would all spend the rest of their lives trying to forget.

It wasn't exactly a scream, and it wasn't exactly a howl. It was more like an unearthly demonic cross between a horrific guttural bellow and the howl or growl of an angry canine.

But what they saw next was even more frightening than that terrible scream.

As the men stood there, frozen with their breath caught in their throats, the creature emerged from the other end of the hollow log, grunting and growling ferociously in between loud wheezing breaths, its humped spine heaving up and down. The men watched in silent open-mouthed terror, utterly turned to stone, as the beast reared up on its muscular hind legs and slowly—deliberately—*stood upright*.

It was at least seven feet tall, with enormous paws and long, razor-sharp claws that looked like they could tear through flesh like the teeth of a crosscut saw tear through soft pine. Its snout was full of equally sharp teeth, which it bared and gnashed. Drool oozed from the creature's savage mouth, which curled in an angry snarl that looked like a ghastly smile. Its eyes were amber fire, burning into the souls of each and every man present.

Some of the men let out airy choking screams that came from the darkest recesses of their souls, screams they didn't know they could produce. A few of the loggers turned and ran in terror as Johnson, frozen to the spot in fear, wet himself, shaking violently as the stick he carried fell to the ground. The creature was no more than twenty feet from him, growling and wheezing, bearing its teeth as it glared at Johnson. On two legs, it lurched forward, taking a step toward him, then another, still another, coming within ten feet of the terrified lumberjack. Johnson had broken out in a shaking sweat and appeared to be either weeping or hyperventilating or both, his eyes popping out of his head.

Just then, Jim regained his wits. He raised the Winchester and took aim at the creature, shaking like a leaf as he drew a bead on its hairy visage.

He fired.

Once.

Twice.

By the third shot he was quaking so badly he thought he might hit Johnson.

The beast roared in a fury and shot an icy yellow-orange glare in Allen's direction, imprinting on him a look Jim could never erase from his memory, a look which kept him up at night.

In a flash, it darted off on all fours deeper into the misty swamp and was soon out of sight. Jim never knew if he hit the creature or not. He didn't see any blood, but he wasn't sticking around to investigate either.

Allen and Vandenberg gathered up the petrified Johnson, and the eleven-man detail, now brandishing their weapons and peering over their shoulders, beat a hasty retreat back to the main camp they had left that morning. No one said a word on the trek back.

Those eleven men packed up their belongings and turned in their resignations that very day. Most of them left town that night and were never heard from again in those parts. The foreman was astounded and confused but mostly angry.

"Those goddamn sons of bitches leavin' me high and dry!" he grumbled.

As for Jim, after that day near the Garland Swamp in early June of 1887, he never quite did enjoy the wilderness again. He never felt safe or at peace again in the Northwoods and avoided them as best he could, especially at night. He and his family stayed in LeRoy in Osceola County, about fifty miles or so from that logging camp on the Manistee River, but he quit logging for good that day and took a job as a carpenter.

Jim Allen spent the rest of his days trying to forget what he had seen that fateful day, those amber eyes in the swamp that had bored a hole straight through him and would never leave him in peace again.

Jack sat in stunned silence, eyes wide, mouth open, barely able to breathe, let alone move, as he finished reading his great-great-grandfather's account of his experiences. It was just over 120 years ago to the day.

His brain worked fast and furious, synapses firing rapidly, making connections between his family's past, all the strange things he had himself experienced. Jack sifted through all the hazy memories from his childhood, the clues he had not understood or investigated at the time, and the connections he had failed to make.

Until now.

A dawning of deep dreadful understanding washed over him like a demonic baptism.

The awakening had begun.

CHAPTER 6

Saturday, June 24, 2017
LeRoy, Michigan

I t's fair to say Jack's life changed after he read the 1887
Garland Swamp account written by his great-great-
grandfather, Edward James "Jim" Allen. Whether it had
changed for better or worse was still up in the air, but it was
leaning toward worse.

Jack couldn't take his mind off the unexpected discovery
of his father's mysterious trunk. An irresistible Pandora's
box, he vowed to explore and read through the contents of
the old trunk as soon as he possibly could. He was especially
struck by the ominous description of the eyes, eyes that he
himself had seen.

An overwhelming obsession began to take hold of Jack.
He spent all his time thinking about the wolf-like creature
with the blazing amber eyes. He needed to know more,
needed to know *everything,* and so he found himself spending
a lot of time up in the loft digging through his father's
wooden trunk.

It was beginning to affect his life in unforeseen and

negative ways, both at home and at work. His unrelenting quest to understand the contents of the trunk overshadowed and took the place of his scholarly work. For the first time in his life, he was listless and unfocused at the office and couldn't bring himself to care about his book project. Everything and everyone began to seem like obstacles in the way of his quest. The quality of his work began to slip, and his students, colleagues, and friends started to notice.

He was also slacking at home, both as a father and as a husband. He made less time for Melanie, and although it broke his heart, he made excuses to avoid spending time with her. Spending less time with Melanie meant more time to focus on his new research. His precious goddamn research. He sensed that Melanie was feeling the disconnect but was unable to comprehend or express it. And Claire sensed that something was going on, too, although she didn't yet know about the trunk or what Jack was up to. But she had come to a decision to confront him about it when the time was right.

That Saturday afternoon, June 24, he had bailed on going into Cadillac with Claire and Melanie. It was a rainy overcast day, so they planned to go to the children's museum for an hour or two and then grab some lunch on their way home.

"Please, Daddy?" Melanie had pleaded. Both she and Claire had expectant looks on their faces.

Jack had hesitated. Claire knew the answer as soon as he dropped his eyes from his daughter's eager glance. Claire sighed angrily and shot Jack a dirty disappointed look before turning away from him.

"Oh, you know, honey," he began, regret creeping into his voice. "I have a lot of work I need to finish up," he lied, ashamed of himself as soon as the words left his mouth.

The hope in Melanie's face turned to disappointment and her shoulders slouched. Jack really hated himself at that moment. He also hated the creature for enchanting him and putting him in this regrettable situation in the first place.

"Oh, okaaaaaaay," Melanie pouted, her shoulders drooping even lower.

As she and Claire got into the Camry, Jack went over to her window. Claire rolled it down, and Jack poked his head in and kissed Melanie on the cheek.

"I'm sorry, babe," he said, suddenly feeling like he might cry. He bit his lip and squinted his eyes against the emotions welling up inside him. "I promise I'll make it up to you soon. Okay?"

"Okay, Daddy," Melanie said.

"I love you very much." He gave her one last kiss on the cheek and patted her gently on the head.

He smiled up at Claire in the driver's seat, and she smiled back, only semi-coolly.

He watched them pull out of the driveway and waved as they accelerated west on 16 Mile Road, headed for an afternoon in Cadillac.

The June rain smelled crisp and good as Jack made his way to the barn. Everything was green and lush, weighed down with life-giving water. His heart was weighed down too. He hated disappointing his daughter (not to mention his wife), but he told himself that it was for their safety—and his —that he find out as much as possible about the mysterious events. Jack ran his hand through his damp hair to get it off his face before unlatching and sliding open the red and white barn doors. Within a few moments, he had mounted the ladder and was on his way up to the dusty loft, which smelled especially damp and musty that day due to the rain.

The week before, he had moved the old wicker chair closer to the trunk, so now he could dig through its contents while seated comfortably. Leafing through the stacks of brittle paper, he mumbled the titles of each to himself until he came across something that sounded especially interesting. He wasn't going through things in any systematic way. First, he had to get his bearings, to get his head around things, and try to get an idea of the big picture before he went through and inventoried all the finer details.

As he combed through the contents of the trunk, his guilt gave way to an odd mixture of giddy excitement and fearful apprehension.

Before long, he came across something that grabbed his attention. It was a typed account of events involving a dairy farmer named Stillwell who lived near Tustin, not far from the Allens' farm. In fact, it was just down the road a ways. This realization sent a jarring shudder through Jack's body, and he exhaled loudly, shaking his head uneasily. This bunch of papers was held together by a rusted orange-brown staple punched into the upper left-hand corner. However, what really drew Jack's attention to it was the note scribbled at the top of the first page in faded blue ink.

In his father's scrawling, nearly illegible hand, it read: "Report of an interview with Alvin Stillwell. Conducted by Daniel E. Allen on August 22, 1957." His eyebrows furrowed in thought. He seemed to look through the pages clutched in his hands. Daniel Allen was Jack's grandfather. Did he know about all this too?

Jack began to read the typed account from the beginning.

Throughout June and July 1957, several incidents occurred involving a dairy farmer near Tustin named Alvin Stillwell. In early June, he had gone out to assay his cow herd and found a prize-winning heifer dead. Not only was the cow dead, it was badly mutilated, her stomach slit clean down the middle as if by a surgical instrument, her half-eaten, dark-red-kidney-bean colored intestines splayed out in the early morning sunshine. Stillwell supposed it was a coyote or perhaps a lone wolf ranging farther south than was typical. Maybe a cougar or a bobcat. That would have been the sad end to the story if it had been an isolated incident.

Instead, the attacks continued into July. Next, was a bull named Billy in mid-June. Then two bulls and another heifer in the same night later that month. Stillwell left his two cattle dogs out in the pen the very next night, which seemed to solve the problem until the morning of July 6.

Stillwell woke up that morning around seven A.M. to blood-curdling screams coming from the pen. He fell out of bed, throwing on his bathrobe and an old pair of work boots. Grabbing his trusty 12-gauge shotgun off the rack by the door, Stillwell raced as fast as his boots would take him to the scene, feeding shells into his weapon as he went.

What he saw when he got there shook him to the core.

His ten-year-old daughter Lisa was hunched over something, sobbing uncontrollably, her head in her hands. As he got closer, he realized she was crying over the stiff, lifeless body of their family pet, Izzy, an Australian Cattle Dog. Izzy's throat had been torn out, and one eye was missing, her gray-black fur a mottled sticky mess of dried reddish-brown blood. Lisa was in hysterics, shaking and sobbing, petting the unresponsive carcass, crooning pitifully between shuddering wet sobs.

"IZZY! IZZY! You're gonna be okay, girl. You're gonna be okay!"

Stillwell fought back his own strong urge to cry—or scream with rage. He knelt down and gently took Lisa in his arms.

"It's okay, honey," he murmured, biting his lower lip to keep it from quivering and squeezing his eyes shut tightly as the stubborn tears came. "Why don't you go inside and have Momma get you a cup of milk. I'll take care of Izzy now."

As Lisa stammered away toward the house, as if she was sleepwalking, her body still shaking and shuddering from the shock, Stillwell rose and gripped the shotgun. He scanned the pen in search of Dodger, the other family pet.

It didn't take him long to find him.

His breath caught in his throat and his stomach lurched when he saw it. Dodger, or what was left of him, was twisted and mangled *into* the barbed wire fence that surrounded the cattle pen on the north side. His insides were exposed, he was missing a foreleg, and something had smashed his skull in on one side. Stillwell turned away, pale and nauseous, afraid he might throw up at any moment.

This hadn't been done by some coyote or wolf. He doubted even a cougar was capable of such atrocious precision. Maybe a bear, he thought, but even that was doubtful. Stillwell decided then and there that he had to find out for himself what—or who—was to blame for the killings.

After he had soothed and consoled his shaken family (and himself with a stiff whiskey), Stillwell buried the family's faithful canine companions under the old sugar maple in the front yard. Then he made a plan to catch the son of a bitch responsible for these heinous acts, whether man or beast.

Around eight P.M the next night, he kissed his wife and daughter, filled a thermos full of coffee, and shouldered his 12 gauge on the way out the door. Propped up on a stool in the hay loft of the barn, Stillwell waited for sundown. He had a clear view of the pen and gate from here through a loose slat on the north side of the hay loft. Sipping coffee from the thermos-lid cup, he waited, the shotgun propped up against the wall next to him and loaded with slugs.

Stillwell waited… and waited… *and waited.* The moon was almost full, bathing the landscape in a blue-white effervescent glow. Glancing at his watch, he yawned. It was getting on midnight now, and still no sign of anything suspicious. At one point, he fell into a light doze, his head gently nodding forward so that his chin almost touched his chest before he startled awake with a quick intake of breath. Shaking the drowsiness from his head, he flicked the meager remains of his last cup of coffee onto the loft floor before pouring himself a fresh cup.

Stay awake, you fool, he thought to himself. *You might miss it altogether if you keep nodding off.*

After two more cups of coffee, the time was just before two A.M.

That's when Stillwell looked up from his beverage and peered out through the opening in the loft toward the north entrance of the cattle pen, dimly lit up by a spotlight he had installed last season.

There it was.

He breathed in, slowly at first, unsure of what he was seeing. He squinted through the dark shadows cast by the pale moonlight at the figure approaching the gate. It was large. An animal of some kind, sauntering up to the cattle pen on all fours.

Was it a dog? It was big for a dog. Maybe a wolf? It looked canine, for sure, not feline. Could it be a black bear, the black ghost of the woods? Stillwell was uncertain, but the creature was nearing the circle of light cast by the spotlight, which would give him a better view. He raised his shotgun, resting the barrel on a cross board, and waited as the beast crept nearer and nearer.

Finally, it reached the halo of light beneath the spotlight at the closed gate. From Stillwell's vantage point he could tell it was definitely not a bear. It was either a large dog or a wolf. Wolves were rare this far south, but they did occasionally make their way down into the Lower Peninsula.

This canine had brownish-gray fur, a long snout, and pointy ears.

As Stillwell looked on, a bit puzzled, something happened that made his heart begin to pound like a bass drum and seem to rise into his throat, choking off his breath.

The thing down there, dimly illuminated by the spotlight, rose up steadily onto two legs! As it reached its full height, it uttered a series of heaving, coughing sounds, like it was growling or clearing its throat.

A light sweat broke out on Stillwell's forehead, glistening as he stared down at the creature, trying to make sense of it all. He felt confused, more than anything, but deep down, he also recognized a dull fear that began to spread like an infection.

He put his cheek to the stock of the shotgun, closing his left eye as he took aim.

Rest the pumpkin on top of the fence. Rest the pumpkin on top of the fence, he thought to himself, repeating the mantra his grandfather told him when he taught him how to shoot many years ago.

He drew a bead on the creature, now less than a few feet from the gate of the cattle pen. Stillwell was a good shot, according to all accounts, but he was shaking a bit as a blank dread rose up in him. He exhaled and squeezed the trigger.

The shotgun barked and kicked back into his shoulder causing his ears to ring as the smoke cleared. He shook his head a bit from the burst and looked frantically down toward the gate. He hadn't heard any sound, no yelp or cry to speak of.

His line of vision cleared, and he caught a glimpse of something that made his skin crawl.

The thing was still down there, right where it had been by the gate, unmoved by the blast from Stillwell's 12 gauge. It was still up on its hindlegs, deep, heaving breaths shuddering rhythmically through its body.

It was looking up at Stillwell.

Yes, no doubt, it was leering up at him in his hiding place in the hay loft, the light of the spotlight reflecting off its amber eyes. It seemed to be sneering or grinning at him.

Stillwell startled, gasping for breath, and for one terrifying moment, their eyes were locked in a hypnotic staring contest. He seemed frozen, unable to move, an evil spell cast upon him by the mysterious, malevolent creature below.

He came to, then, and fired off another shot with his 12 gauge. This time the creature bawled, a deep scratchy barking sound that sent shivers down Stillwell's spine. He fired again, and finally, the animal backed away from the gate, collapsing back onto all fours and bounding off into the hazy summer night, leaving only the image of those amber eyes shining up at Stillwell, burned into his memory forever.

Aside from the shaking, Stillwell didn't move for quite some time; in fact, he barely breathed. He was scared shitless, and this was a man who didn't scare easily. He waited until first sunlight, keeping an eye on the edge of the woods adjacent to the cattle pen, afraid to go down there in the dark to investigate. When he finally did, it was early morning, and he found nothing of interest, no blood or fur, just large canine prints in the sandy soil leading up to the gate. The prints matched the ones he had found at the scenes of the previous incidents: impossibly large with long talon-like claw prints extending from the pads.

Dog? Wolf? Whatever it was, Stillwell didn't want to encounter it again. He was spooked to the bone.

He never did see the creature again. He hired some help to keep an eye on things at the farm, and the very next day, he and his family went house hunting for a place in town, away from the dark dusky woods and the memory of those glinting eyes in the moonlight.

———

As Jack read the last page of Stillwell's frightful account, a loose piece of yellowed paper that had been tucked up in the corner of the stapled pages fell to the hay-strewn floor of the loft. It was a newspaper clipping from that same year, 1957.

From the *Cadillac Evening News*, September 22, 1957 (page 4):

GIANT DOG ATTACKS PROMINENT CADILLAC CHURCH

On Wednesday, September 18, Reverend Leonard Ellis of the First Cadillac Lutheran Church reported to police what he thought to be vandalism or an attempted burglary. When the police arrived on the scene to investigate, what they found surprised everyone involved. The deep gashes in the old church door first noticed by Reverend Ellis were actually made by the claws of a massive dog, according to the official report filed by the Cadillac Police Department. The most shocking part of all is that this dog would have had to stand seven-foot-four-inches tall. "I was mostly confused and shocked at first," explained Reverend Ellis. "But now I think I'm just plain scared. I sure wouldn't want to run into something like that on my way to church early on a Sunday morning." Be sure to check out the *Cadillac Evening News* for updates on this unusual case as it unfolds.

———

Sitting on the wicker chair in the loft, Jack just shook his head after reading the article. He couldn't believe what he was seeing.

Could all of this really be connected? Could this thing really exist?

Keeping things from his wife ate him up inside, but Jack wasn't ready to talk to her about this yet. He was afraid she'd think him insane; that said, he still needed some time to himself to process all that he had learned since discovering his father's trunk in the loft. So even though it pissed Claire off, Jack decided to have a night to drink beer and think things over. It was a Thursday night, and after he got Mel to bed, he kissed Claire on the top of the head, hopped in his Blazer, and headed down to Travelers.

It was busy for a Thursday night, but then again, Travelers was always busy during the peak summer months. Lots of city folks from out of town were passing through or staying at their summer homes. Jack sauntered toward the bar, scanning the crowd, but he didn't see anyone he really knew.

Good, he thought. *I don't feel much like talking.*

He spied an empty stool at the bar, walked over, and slid onto it, a half-hearted smile on his tired face as he pulled up to the bar. To his right was a young couple, drinking and nuzzling in hushed tones, whispering sweet nothings in each other's ears. To his left was a gnarled older man in dirty overalls, maybe sixty-five or seventy, who Jack had seen around once or twice. Crawford was his name if memory served.

"Hey, Jack," the bartender said as he walked over. His name was John, and he had tended bar at Travelers for years. "What'll it be tonight?"

"Hey, John," Jack nodded. "How 'bout a tall Miller on draft? Thanks."

"You got it," John replied, grabbing a tall beer mug from a plastic dish rack behind the bar. He turned to the taps opposite the bar and drew the beer, tall, golden, and effervescent. He placed a small white paper napkin on the bar in front of Jack and plopped the cold beer down on it.

"Better leave it open for me tonight, John," Jack said, casually saluting the barkeep as he brought the mug to his lips. He took a long pull, and it felt good going down. *"Ahhh,"* he sighed in satisfaction, setting his beer down on the napkin and wiping his lips with the back of his hand.

He glanced around at the other people at the bar.

They all look so carefree, he thought to himself. *And here I am worried about the fuckin boogeyman. Some kind of fuckin monster or werewolf or some shit.*

Just then, as Jack scanned the Thursday night crowd at Travelers, his eyes met the eyes of Crawford, the older gentleman sitting next to him at the bar. Sipping his beer, Jack smiled and nodded, and Crawford did likewise, but Jack noticed something in his eyes, like a dark shadow was cast over him too. The thought left his mind as quickly as it had come, and Jack turned back to his beer and his thoughts.

So, let's get caught up here, sports fans. First, I had that weird feeling out hiking in the woods, like I was being watched, or tailed. Either way, it was damned strange and more than a little spooky. Then there was the Williams' dog that went missing and turned up dead. But I guess dead isn't the best word for it. More like horribly murdered and mutilated by some homicidal maniac. Then there was that thing I saw in the field at dusk while I was driving home from the office.

The memory of that chilling close encounter suddenly came back to Jack with brutal force and sent a shuddery chill down his spine. His whole body tensed as he realized the seriousness of it, just how close he had been to it... to the beast. His eyes burned with a laser focus as he swigged down some more beer.

Those eyes! Those amber fucking eyes! And of course there's the killing of Dave Beckett. And now I find this trunk of Dad's in the loft, locked and hidden away, gathering dust, and it's like all this research he did. All these stories he collected about strange shit happening to people around here: the creature in the Garland Swamp, the creature that haunted the old Stillwell dairy farm. Could it be the same kind of creature that's terrorizing LeRoy now? Could it be the same creature? No way. No fuckin way. That's impossible... isn't it? All these accounts and interviews that Dad collected CONFIRM this crazy shit that's been happening! It's like Dad knew about all this. Wait a sec, he absolutely knew!

That's when he felt another set of eyes on him. He turned to his left and saw Crawford glancing over at him, a look of concern and reluctance on his face.

"Some spooky things been hap'nin round here lately, no?" Crawford said in a quiet tone with a knowing look in his squinting eyes. His bushy white eyebrows looked like fat furry caterpillars.

"What do you mean?" Jack asked.

"Seems like there's some strange things going on this year, and when I sees the look on your face, I sees a man who's got sump'in on his mind. Care to talk it over?"

"Uh, sure, yeah, I guess," Jack replied, confused. He leaned in a bit closer to the older man. "Thanks."

"Not here," Crawford hissed. "I s'pose I'm gonna head outside and have me a cigarette," he said, louder this time. "Why don't you come keep me company, son?"

With that, Crawford stood up from his barstool with a grimace and slowly and unsteadily shuffled toward the door. Jack, energized but still slightly confused, polished off the rest of his beer, then stood and followed the old man outside.

They stood outside near the corner of the building, far

enough away from the entrance so no one could hear them. It was a cool night for June, with a pleasant breeze, and the sun was just going down over the western horizon. Crawford pulled a pack of Winstons from the pocket of his overalls and lit one up, inhaling deeply before blowing a long stream of smoke from his nostrils. Jack caught a whiff of the cigarette smoke, along with a healthy dose of booze on the man's breath.

"I can always tell a man who's seen it," he said, looking down at the ground and flicking the ash from his cigarette. "It's sump'in round the eyes, sump'in dark. It changes a man."

He looked up then and squinted into Jack's eyes, taking another long drag off the Winston.

"I suspect you saw it on my face in there too just then, didn'tcha?"

Jack remembered the darkness he had noticed in Crawford's eyes when he had glanced over at him in the bar. Like an empty hole on a moonless night. The realization struck him hard.

Jack said, "You know, now that you mention it, I did notice something." He nodded his head, the acrid smell of cigarette smoke hanging in the air.

"Ya see, a lot of us old-timers know about it… but it's not something we usually like to talk about, not with just any old fool anyways. It ain't right… It ain't right… But when I saw you in there tonight, I could just sense it, ya know? I could sense it was on your mind, don't ask me how, and then when I saw your face, I just *knew*. Hell, I can't explain it, and that's what makes it so damned hard to talk about. I can't explain *any* of it! None of us can. But we sure can tell when someone's had their doors opened up a bit too wide, ya know? We can tell when someone's seen it. Sure as shit. It leaves a mark, ya know."

Mark of the beast, Jack thought.

Crawford sighed and smoked in silence. Jack shuffled his feet. He was nervous but also exhilarated. And not a little scared.

"But what *is* it?" Jack asked, his voice betraying the desperate confusion he felt.

"What *is* it?" Crawford said sharply, glaring over at Jack. "What *is* it?" He dropped his cigarette in the dirt and smeared it out with his boot. "Well, that's the question now, ain't it? I s'pose no one knows for sure…Well, maybe not *no one. Somebody* must know, I suspect, but it sure as shit ain't me. I dunno, what'd it look like to you, son?" The sharpness in his voice had softened now, and the way he asked this last question was like a little boy comparing notes about the monster under his bed.

"Jesus, I don't know," Jack said, looking up at the sky.

It was dusk now, quiet and peaceful. Jack realized he had never really described it in words, and he was suddenly frightened that saying it out loud might make it all the more real or maybe attract or invoke it. But this was his best chance to learn something about it, so he continued, feeling his way with his words.

"It was tall, muscular, with brownish-gray fur."

"*Yes, yes…*" Crawford said, his eyes ablaze, willing Jack to continue.

"It was like a *dog.* Or a wolf, maybe, but it also wasn't like that. It was also…" Jack chose his words carefully, trying to paint the vivid picture of the creature in his mind for Crawford. "It was also like a *man.*"

"*Yes,* by God, it is," Crawford said breathlessly, with almost religious fervor in his voice, the fire still blazing in his green eyes. "That's what some of the old-timers used to call it, ya know. They called it the *Dogman.*" He said this in a hushed, reverent tone, looking around in a frightened, paranoid way.

"Dogman?" Jack hissed, breathless, the hair on his arms and neck standing straight up. It seemed as though his entire body had turned to gooseflesh in an instant. *That's it,* he thought. *That's exactly what it is. And Dad knew about it.*

"Its *eyes,*" Jack said, flexing his diaphragm to ward off a shudder.

"YESSSS!" Crawford breathed. "The yellow eyes. Or were they orange? I s'pose I haven't seen it for many years now."

"And it walks on *two legs,* like a man."

"Yes," Crawford said, that hushed reverence apparent in his voice again. "Well, I'll be damned, son, you sure know a lot about it, don'tcha?" He pulled another Winston out of the pack with his teeth and lit it, drawing deeply. "Ya know 'bout the cycle?"

"The cycle?" Jack repeated a confused look on his face.

"That's right, the cycle. That's what the old-time locals used to call it anyways, the cycle. S'posedly this thing, this creature—this *Dogman*—*only* comes around every seventh year. Now I know, I know, sounds crazy, don't it?" He shook his head. "But they all swear by it, and if you think about it, you'll see it's true. These sightings, these encounters, these *MURDERS...*" He stopped for a second, breathless. He closed his eyes to regain his composure and breathed in deeply, exhaling loudly through pursed lips. He took another drag from his cigarette and continued. "These things seem to cluster at certain times, every seventh year. '77, '87, '97." He paused. His eyes found Jack's. "'07... That's the cycle, or so they say."

Crawford was still looking at Jack, whose mouth was slightly open. He looked like you could have knocked him over with a feather. He was speechless, his eyes glazed over in shock and disbelief.

"Did ya ever hear 'bout what happened in Sigma in '87?" Crawford asked, one bushy eyebrow raised inquisitively.

"No, no, I haven't—" Jack said.

"Well, let me paint a picture for ya, son."

Sigma was a typical small town in Northern Michigan, smack dab in the center of Kalkaska County. According to the 1980 U.S. Census, Sigma was home to 330 people, and the folks who lived there, Sigmans, as they called themselves, preferred that it stay that size. Not really growing nor shrinking, Sigma was just there. Things tended to move slowly in Sigma, and that's just how the locals liked it.

It was kind of off the beaten track, about twenty-five miles from nowhere, as the townsfolk used to joke. Outsiders were looked at askance. As in many other towns like it, the locals were suspicious of city folk, and on occasion, they were even known to be a bit standoffish with them, letting down the veil of Midwest nice and revealing the sharp fangs underneath. But that was okay because it seemed like the only people from out of town were on their way to somewhere else, and in a hurry, I might add. Michiganders from bigger cities like Detroit or Grand Rapids—hell, even from *Big* Rapids—might have made jokes about Sigma, but Sigmans didn't care. Those city folks didn't know what they were missing. Didn't know much at all, if you ask me.

The year 1987 started out just like every other year; that is to say, slow and quiet.

Until the summer came along.

It all started during the first week of June.

Once nighttime came people started hearing things. Strange things. Odd sounds they couldn't quite explain but couldn't forget neither. Multiple Sigmans from separate locations swore up and down they heard something walking around outside their windows at night.

But that wasn't the worst of it.

No sir, the scratching was far worse. Whatever it was lurking out there in the Northwoods darkness was scratching up and down on the windows.

Some of the old-timers had heard of the legend of the Dogmen. Maybe some of them had even seen one. Some of the youngsters had heard those stories too, but these small Northern Michigan towns keep their cards close to their chest. They mind their own business and keep their secrets to themselves, as any self-respecting person would, if you ask me.

Still, during the daylight hours some of the hotblooded youngsters laughed and joked about the Dogmen roaming round, but nobody joked about it after the sun went down. Everybody seemed to get real serious once dusk rolled around. They all had this empty, haunted look in their eyes, like scared little children left alone in a haunted house. Yep, nobody in Sigma joked much after sundown that June. Nobody slept much neither.

Things escalated throughout June. Pets and livestock came up missing. Some were found later, or what was left of them, frightfully mutilated and torn up. People's barns were getting torn up too. Old Farmer Ben's tractor was miraculously dragged a good twenty feet and then flipped over, seemingly of its own accord, and heavy pieces of farm equipment were somehow tossed around like ragdolls. Bags of feed were ripped apart and scattered in all directions. Random smears of red blood and black gore were painted helter-skelter on barn walls, looking like some insane, demonic ritual.

Then one night, one of the heavy reinforced wooden double doors of the hardware store was torn clear off its hinges, and a set of four deep scratches were etched into it like calligraphy from hell.

By mid-June, everyone in Sigma was scared shitless, not to mention severely sleep-deprived. Some, the smart ones, left then and there, or at least sent their kids away to stay with relatives far away from that place. They all thought they were going crazy, some kind of collective hallucination. But I'll be damned if it wasn't a pack of blood-thirsty Dogmen that appeared—*materialized*—out of the murky depths of the Northwoods and descended on that unsuspecting town and all its inhabitants.

And that's when the telephones went dead.

The eerie sounds continued each night, but now they were accompanied by other, even more terrible and gut-wrenching sounds that coalesced into an infernal, grisly symphony that would make your hair stand up and your skin crawl. Horrific grunts and screams... and howls that would chill the blood in your veins and send shivers down your spine. The macabre cacophony that filled the night was more than most could bear.

Some Sigmans packed their bags and left their homes unlocked, doors open, with their belongings still inside. Others fled in terror without even packing a bag, suppers left uneaten on the table. Still others—the very brave or the very stupid, I'm still not quite sure which—loaded guns and decided to make a stand.

But everybody who stayed there in Sigma stayed awake. Wide awake. What exactly happened in those last few days in June no one really knows for sure. There are no witnesses left to speak of. Was it a massacre? Did the Dogmen tear every last man, woman, and child in Sigma to shreds in a gory, unspeakable spectacle? If so, where are the bodies? Where are the bones? Did they all just pack up and leave? If so, where the hell did they go? And why haven't we heard from them since?

All we do know is that Sigma now stands as a ghost town

and that 330 souls seem to have vanished into thin air. All that remains are the empty houses and cabins, the ghostly shells left over from the tranquil life that Sigma's residents had known until that fateful summer in 1987, bleached by the sun like so many skeletons in the closet of the collective past.

But I know better, sure as shit I do. Somewhere in the Northwoods darkness... a creature walks upright. "And the best advice you may ever get," Crawford said, a frightened quiver in his voice. "Is don't go out at night."

Jack was shaken to the core, ashen-faced, wide-eyed, wrung out like a sponge, and utterly speechless.

"And these ain't isolated incidents, neither," Crawford continued, a ghastly look on his face. "That same summer over to Luther, not fifteen miles from here as the crow flies, they had an 'incident' too. Out at some cabin in the woods— prolly the summer place of some damned city slicker. They said it looked like an attempted break-in, but we all knew better. The police were called to the scene to take a look. Said sump'in tried to chew its way in around the doors. Said there were dog prints outside the window. They found claw marks on the door, too, *deep suckers,* just like at the hardware store in Sigma!"

Crawford was getting more and more animated as he spoke, not really looking *at* Jack anymore, but looking *through* him, with a chilling look in his eyes like a man possessed.

"And ten years before all that the Dogmen terrorized Bellaire! That was in the summer of 1977. I remember it like it was yesterday. All the folks up thataway said they heard the most awful screamin in the night out in the woods. The newspapers said it was a bobcat, maybe the wind, but I suspect no one really looked up there. There're a lot of wild cats up thataway, sure, but I ain't never come across no damned cougar that screams like a man!" He shook his head back and forth as he spoke, his index finger wagging a cynical rebuke.

"So this thing is all over the fuckin place—pardon my French—like it's terrorizin or hauntin all of goddamned Northern Michigan! And remember what I told you about the cycle? The seventh year?"

Jack nodded, his lips pursed, breathing hitched.

"Well, these same damn kinds of things been happenin every seventh year for as long as anyone can remember! Goin all the way back to the 1800s! Prolly even before that, if ya ask me. If you can get the old-timers to talk about it, any damned one of im in these parts knows about it! But they all have a way of forgettin, ya see. I can't quite put my finger on it, but it's there. Folks around here have a way of turnin their heads, of lookin the other way, ya know? Of forgettin tragedy and disaster and refusin to see the pattern or even discuss it. It's like some kind of damned collective amnesia or sump'in."

Crawford was frustrated, angry even, feeling helpless. He lit another Winston and continued on.

"Those of us who know about it are like some secret club or sump'in. We don't share it with outsiders much, but we know. Maybe we're afraid it'll hear us and come a callin. Maybe we're afraid of gettin sent to the loony bin if we start blabbering about it, ya know? I mean, come on, how *crazy* does it all sound when you say it out loud?" Crawford eyed Jack knowingly, that one bushy caterpillar eyebrow raised again.

There was an uneasy silence as Crawford puffed away on his Winston.

"My father," Jack began, thinking of the old trunk in the barn loft. "He knew about it too."

"Did he now?" Crawford asked, his eyes glinting. Jack

noticed a hint of derision in his voice. "Well, who was your father, then?"

"Steve Allen."

Crawford gasped and his breath caught in his throat, causing him to cough and hack on his cigarette. His eyes were wide and cautious as he flicked his cigarette butt onto the gravel. Jack could almost feel him clam up.

"Well, it's been nice talkin to ya, son," he said.

Jack was very confused.

"Wait, what?" he stammered. "What'd I say? Where're you going?"

Jack followed him for a few steps.

"Is there anything else I should know? Please! What can I do about all this?"

Crawford stopped and turned back toward Jack, a pale, fearful look on his face.

"Well, son," he said, a breathless quiver in his voice. "You just be careful, keep your eyes open, and don't be goin out at night none. That's the best advice I can give you, son. Don't go out at night. The seventh year is here. Now I really need to be goin. It's late."

With that, Crawford shuffled back into Travelers, paid his tab, and left without saying another word to Jack.

CHAPTER 7

INTERLUDE: THE DOG DAYS OF SUMMER

Monday, July 3, 2017
Manistee National Forest, Michigan

This camping trip is going to be the shit, thought Tyler Kowalski, one hand on the wheel of his old, electric-blue Ford Escort.

Tyler flew up M-37 North as fast as his rusty Escort could take him. Sitting next to him in the passenger seat was his current love interest, an absolutely bodacious blonde named Kelly Branowitz. He had met her in a macroeconomics course they had taken that spring at Michigan State University in East Lansing. Forced to work together on a group project, they hit it off. Sparks really flew later in the semester when they ran into each other one drunken Thirsty Thursday night at Mick's American Café, a dank, cement-basement of a college bar that always smelled like vomit and bleach, but more like vomit. Tyler bought Kelly a drink, which turned into two more. Later, as the house band ripped through "Livin' On A Prayer," everyone on the dancefloor drunkenly singing (or screaming) along, hands in the air, Tyler had slammed the rest of his pitcher of Miller Lite and went in for a kiss.

The kiss turned into two, and pretty soon, they were snogging in the back seat of a Yellow Cab. After being poured out onto the street in front of Kelly's place, they had continued their amorous activities upstairs. Long story short, they had been hooking up regularly ever since, and you know what? Tyler was actually really into her. He was beginning to have serious, adult thoughts about serious, adult things, not just sex, of course, but things like commitment and responsibility and monogamy.

Toward the end of the spring semester, they decided to go camping over the Fourth of July up in the Manistee National Forest, a beautiful spot in the northwestern Lower Peninsula with great hiking trails and plenty of secluded places for them to pitch a tent.

Tyler picked Kelly up at her family home. Thank God her folks weren't there! And now here they were, listening to, of all things, "Livin' On A Prayer," on the radio.

Tyler glanced over at Kelly and grinned an evil grin, reaching out and gently caressing her smooth, shapely thigh. Kelly was wearing cutoff jean shorts that left little to the imagination and a maroon halter top. She reached down and put her hand on his, drawing it up higher on her leg, an evil grin of her own emerging on her pretty face. Tyler's eyes bulged a bit, and he noticed something else beginning to bulge in his pants. Distracted by these developments, he accidentally swerved and had to jerk his hand away from Kelly's thigh and grab the wheel with both hands, his eyes wide and flustered.

Kelly laughed and stuck her tongue out at him playfully, that naughty smirk still on her face.

"Oh, you are going to *get it* as soon as we get there, babe," Tyler said, shaking his head in breathless anticipation.

"I hope so," Kelly replied, winking at Tyler and licking her lips suggestively.

She leaned back and propped her pretty little bare feet up on the dashboard, so he could see how her smooth legs went on for days.

"*Damn,* girl, you're going to get us in a wreck if you keep this up, looking so damn good!" he said.

"Just keep your eyes on the road, ya perv," she said, giggling a little, almost daring him not to keep looking at her.

Tyler just shook his head and sighed.

Tyler and Kelly arrived at the Manistee National Forest entrance gate at about noon. The sun was out, and puffy, white clouds dotted the sky. The temperature was a breezy seventy-six degrees, perfect for camping, hiking, and romping in the woods. The soil was sandy, and the mixed pine and hardwood forest was dense and breathtaking. Straight rows of red pine dominated the landscape, and both Tyler and Kelly were silent for once as they drove slowly along the scenic trails to their campsite near the Manistee River Trail along the east bank of the Manistee River.

They pulled up to their campsite, a beautiful little spot tucked in among the red pines overlooking a horseshoe bend in the river. The water was a dark, grayish-green color, and the sunlight reflected off it in some places, while in others, the mirrorlike surface of the water reflected the pines and hardwoods along the river's course.

The Escort huffed and squeaked to a halt in front of an old, green picnic table chained to a steel ring embedded in the ground. Next to it was a fire pit with a metal fire ring around it and an old cast-iron grate laid over the top.

The passenger door burst open, and Kelly stepped out, giggling as she surveyed the campsite.

"It's perfect! Let's pitch our tent right here on this nice flat space overlooking the river!" she said.

Kelly raced over to the spot, just north of the picnic table and firepit, and began to pick up sticks, clearing the space of debris. Meanwhile, Tyler made his way to the back of the car. He popped the trunk and grinned as he opened the large, red Coleman cooler he had packed. Tyler dug his hand into the stinging-cold ice and pulled out a cheap bottle of champagne. Closing the cooler, he fished out two tin camping mugs from his duffel bag and walked over to where Kelly was clearing twigs

He stood behind her in silence as he fiddled with the cork, concentrating, his tongue poking out of his mouth. Finally, he was able to get underneath it with his thumb enough to loosen it, and the cork shot into the air with a loud *POP*.

Kelly jumped a little and whirled around at the noise. A happy smile spread over her face, and she appeared genuinely touched by this romantic gesture. She watched as foam bubbled over the mouth of the bottle onto Tyler's hands as he poured two generous glasses into the tin cups. Setting the bottle down on the grass, Tyler handed Kelly a cup.

"To you, my beautiful summer flower," he said with a smile, raising his glass.

It was cheesy as hell, but it seemed to work.

She met his gaze and raised her glass, clinking it against his gently.

"To *us*," she said, smiling ear-to-ear. "This is going to be an *amazing* trip."

They both took long pulls from their cups, which immediately lightened their moods even more and brought a faint flush of rouge to Kelly's cheekbones. They were both feeling light and giddy, happy to be alive and happy to be together.

That afternoon, Tyler and Kelly pitched their Kelty tent,

staked down the rainfly, and moved in their sleeping bags and gear. They finished off the bottle of champagne as they worked, before moving on to beer and wine. By the time the tent was up and furnished, they were both merrily buzzed.

They had a passionate quickie from behind, on their knees in the tent, which happened with such sudden ferocity that their pants and underwear never made it completely off, dangling around their ankles throughout the sweaty encounter.

After, they packed some drinks in a daypack and went for a three-mile hike along the beautiful Manistee River Trail, holding hands and chatting while sipping their drinks. At one bend in the trail, when they came around the corner, and the summer sunlight reflected off the water and lit up Kelly's face and shimmering blonde hair just so, Tyler thought to himself, *Jesus, I think I'm in love with this girl.*

Tyler stood there frozen for a minute like a dummy, just gazing at her. She noticed and glided over to him. She leaned in and kissed him on the lips, moaning softly, her tongue snaking into his mouth and swirling around his. He moaned too, a deep, primal sound that came from the depths of his soul, kissing her back with every ounce of passion in him. She dug her fingers into the hair on the back of his head as his hands squeezed and felt her back, hips, and buttocks, pulling her into him, their torsos grinding together in an ancient, primitive dance. They ducked off of the trail and made love again on the leaves behind some pine trees, both of them reaching a screaming, shuddering climax at the same moment. When they were finished, they laid back against the soft earth, breathing heavily, the air filled with the aroma of dry leaves mingled with their love, their hands clasped together, blissfully exhausted and satisfied.

Tyler reached into the front pocket of his backpack and produced a long, thin joint that he had rolled for just such an occasion. Kelly sighed, a content, tired smile on her face, her fingers tracing gentle lines on her sexy, tanned stomach. Tyler flicked a BIC lighter and sparked the joint. He breathed the pungent smoke in deeply, down into his chest, and held it there as he passed it to Kelly. She took it with her thumb and forefinger and hit it a few times, her cheeks bulging like a chipmunk and her eyes widening as she coughed out a thick cloud of white, skunky smoke. Tyler smiled at her as she passed the joint back to him.

"Aww, Kel, you're such an amateur," he said, giggling, puffing on the joint. "It's cute, really it—"

Tyler froze.

He thought he had heard something out by the trail.

Tyler waited, not moving an inch, just listening intently, the joint held up to his mouth between his thumb and forefinger, lifeless except for the thin trail of curling smoke rising from the lit end.

Kelly looked up at him alarmed when suddenly his head jerked around toward the trail. Tyler had heard something, alright. He craned his neck to see, squinting through the pines, a sudden fear and dread washing over him.

What the fuck is that? he thought. His breath quickened and sweat popped out on his forehead.

He heard a rustling sound, faint at first, but growing louder, coming down the trail *toward them.* With growing alarm, he realized it was the sound of leaves crunching under feet... or maybe paws.

Just then, his eyes caught movement on the trail, not twenty yards away from them. It was brown, or maybe dark green, tall, lumbering on two legs, vaguely human in shape.

Oh, my Jesus, it's Bigfoot! Tyler thought for one delirious instant, his heart pounding so hard in his chest he could almost hear it.

That's when he recognized the park-ranger hat.

It was a dark olive-green color, perched atop the head of a female forest ranger in a khaki uniform spotted with patches and badges.

"Oh, SHIT!" Tyler groaned, frantically snuffing out the joint with his right hand while fanning the skunky-smelling smoke up and away from him and Kelly with his left.

He was burying the evidence with dirt and leaves, grateful that they had at least put all their clothes back on when the ranger called out from the trail.

"Good afternoon, folks," she called, a note of suspicion in her voice. "Everything alright back there?"

"Uh… yeah! Yeah, everything's fine here, thanks!" Tyler stammered, stumbling to his feet.

Kelly stayed put, seated on the ground. She smiled and nodded, trying not to look guilty.

"Ma'am?" the ranger said, addressing Kelly and peeking in for a better look.

"Yeah, we're fine, just fine, ma'am, thanks!" Kelly said, talking fast. "We just got a little, uh… tired on our hike and decided to take a break and sit down for a minute, but we're good now, thanks."

She smiled again and nodded as she stood up and brushed off her shorts. Tyler shouldered his daypack as he and Kelly moved toward the trail, his right foot planting where he had buried the joint.

They emerged from the pines onto the trail where the ranger stood, hands on her hips and head slightly cocked to one side. She was tall and brunette with an athletic build, a tomboy, no doubt, in her khaki forest-ranger uniform, but undeniably pretty.

"We're camping over by the trailhead tonight, ma'am," Tyler said with a forced smile. "This is our first time camping up here, and boy is it beautiful!"

He and Kelly looked at each other, nodding and laughing nervously.

"Where you from?" the forest ranger asked.

"Oh, we're students at Michigan State, ma'am," Kelly said. "Well, actually, I'm from Grand Rapids, and Tyler here is from Okemos."

"Yup," Tyler agreed, shoulders slouching a bit as he nodded, trying to look wholesome.

Suddenly the ranger's stern demeanor changed, and she shrugged.

"Okay, well, you two enjoy your time here," she said, tipping her hat as she started on past them down the trail. "Be sure not to leave any food unsecured around here. You never know what kinds of hungry animals might be lurking in these woods," she called over her shoulder.

"Yes, ma'am," they replied in unison.

"You bet," Tyler reiterated, giving the ranger an awkward thumbs up.

They looked at each other, wide-eyed, holding their breath. A smile began to slowly make its way across Tyler's face.

Then the ranger abruptly stopped in her tracks and spun around to face the startled couple.

"Oh, and there's one more thing," she said, her eyes fixed on them.

The smile on Tyler's face turned into a sniveling, pathetic frown as the ranger started back up the trail toward them. Kelly's heart was racing as she pondered how she would kill Tyler for bringing the weed. She tried to maintain the quasi-innocent smile on her face as the ranger came to within a few feet of them, her eyes still glued to them.

"Yes, ma'am?" Tyler whimpered.

"Apparently, there's a skunk that's been sprayin near here,

so it might be best if you folks stay on the trail," the ranger said with an absolute deadpan expression on her face.

With that, the ranger turned and headed back down the trail, a perceptible bounce in her step. Tyler and Kelly, for the second time this trip, were speechless, but Tyler swore he heard the ranger chuckling to herself as she passed out of sight.

Kelly punched Tyler on the arm as they made their way back to their campsite.

"You asshole!" she cried, half serious, half joking. "We could have been arrested! All because you had to get high!"

"Oh, come on," Tyler said. "No one forced you to hit it, and besides, we didn't get in trouble. The ranger knew, and she didn't even care!"

He was right, of course, but by then they were both flying high, buzzed from the drinks they had consumed and now floating on top of that from the pot.

After a while, Kelly let it go, and they more or less forgot about their run-in with the ranger. They started enjoying each other's company again and were even able to laugh a bit about the afternoon's encounter. In fact, once they started giggling, they found that they couldn't stop.

They were laughing and smiling as they rounded a bend in the trail and came to their campsite, just as they had left it. Tyler made his way over to his car, popped the trunk, and went digging through the cooler again, coming out with a beer, which he cracked and took a healthy pull from. His other hand emerged from the ice-and-water mixture with a package of Ball Park franks. Kelly poured herself a glass of merlot as Tyler fished out a pack of hotdog buns and two roasting forks from the trunk of his Escort. Apparently, their afternoon hike had given them both a bad case of the munchies.

Tyler gathered some kindling and built a fire with some

firewood they had picked up at a gas station, while Kelly sipped merlot out of a tin mug, relaxing on the picnic table. As the fire blazed, they skewered their wieners and slow-roasted them over the open fire. The hotdogs plumped nicely and began to turn a rosy red color. Tyler put his dog in a bun and pulled it off the roasting fork, hot juices running out of the holes left by the fork, looking like the fang marks left behind by a hungry vampire. Kelly got her dog in a bun, too, as Tyler produced packets of ketchup and mustard from his jeans pocket. The two of them sat together in silence on the picnic table, eating their hotdogs, drinking their beer and wine, and gazing out at the shiny, beautiful Manistee River, mesmerized and content. Because the fire-roasted hotdogs tasted so good to them at that moment, they each cooked up another.

They each had a few more drinks that night. Though they were coming down from their weed buzz, they had kept up with the liquids, so by seven o'clock, they were both pretty drunk. They put on some warmer clothes and wrapped up together in a Pendleton blanket that Tyler had packed, cuddling and chatting together. Occasionally they would lean in for a kiss of varying length and intensity, but mostly they were enjoying the woods, the river, and the conversation.

The pair watched the sunset over the river and the pines, beautiful hues of golden-orange shot through with wisps of pink and blue, embracing the horizon, the sun a small amber eye receding down into the underworld, losing its power as it fell.

By nine-thirty P.M. the sun was down, it was dusk, and the temperature had dropped to the low 60s. The glow of the moon illuminated the night, bathing the earth in ghostly silver shadows. Tyler and Kelly heard the call of a great horned owl faintly in the distance, the sound echoing for a moment before it was drowned out again by the crickets.

"It's a beautiful night, isn't it?" Tyler asked, nuzzling his nose into Kelly's neck under the blanket.

"Yes, it really is," she replied, her head resting under his chin.

They sat together, wrapped up in Tyler's Pendleton, peacefully listening to the crackling of the fire and watching it burn down to embers. Around ten o'clock, Kelly yawned.

"Oh, babe, I'm *so* tired," she sighed, her eyes heavy. "Wanna go to bed?"

"Yeah, I'm beat too," Tyler replied, scratching the back of his head.

At that moment, he thought about telling her he loved her. He really thought he did and that he should tell her. But the moment passed, and he missed his chance.

They stood up. Tyler pulled his headlamp on over his head and switched it on, shaking out the blanket as they meandered toward the tent. They thought of brushing their teeth, but they were both too exhausted and tipsy to bother. Kelly unzipped the tent flap, and they took off their shoes and crawled into the tent, one after the other. It was dark in there, but with the beam from Tyler's headlamp, they were able to find their pillows. Lying down on their sleeping pads, too tired even to bother with their sleeping bags, they snuggled together under the Pendleton, their arms wrapped around each other.

Tyler switched off his headlamp. They were both sound asleep within minutes.

It came in the night, around two A.M.

Kelly woke up first. A strange noise outside the tent had

startled her awake. She lifted her head a bit, still groggy, eyes squinting, before turning onto her side and closing her eyes again to go back to sleep.

That's when she really heard it, a sound that was something between a dry, hacking cough and the deep grunt of some wild animal. It was a sound that sent chills down her spine and made her heart pound. Her eyes shot open in the darkness, her breath caught in her throat, and a sickening fear and panic began to rise up in her.

She heard the sound again, closer this time, and also the faint sound of footsteps moving closer to the tent, the sound of leaves gently crunching under the weight of feet... or paws. She clenched her teeth, shaking uncontrollably, feeling like she might burst into tears. She nudged Tyler, who was fast asleep next to her.

"Tyler!" she hissed, but it came out more like a desperate scream. *"Tyler, wake up!"*

Tyler stirred and mumbled something inaudible. Kelly rolled over and elbowed him again, harder this time.

"Tyler, wake up! *Please!*" she pleaded, her heart pounding in her chest. "There's something out there!"

"What?" Tyler moaned, rubbing his eyes with the palms of his hands.

He sat up and looked at her, trying to focus his tired eyes.

"There's something outside," Kelly said, her eyes staring into Tyler's. She was trembling. "I heard—"

The cough/growl sound echoed outside the tent again, louder and closer still. Kelly gasped and jumped at the same time, grabbing onto Tyler's arms, gooseflesh breaking out all over her. Tyler heard it too, and it made the hair on his neck stand straight up.

"What the fuck was that?" he whispered.

They both heard footsteps then. Whatever was out there seemed to be circling the tent, no more than ten feet away. It got all the way around to the front of the tent, by the door, when it made that terrible noise again. Tyler and Kelly held each other in the tent, shuddering in terror, when they heard a scratching noise on the rainfly. It made a sickening zipping sound, like long nails or claws scraping slowly across taut nylon fabric.

Tyler got to his knees slowly as the thing moved past the door to the east side of the tent. They could hear its heavy, coarse breathing and its nimble steps as it stalked along the ground. In their buzzed state, they had left the air vents zipped up, so they couldn't see out. Tyler maneuvered over to the vent on the east side of the tent as silently as he could. He glanced back at Kelly, who was seated on her heels, silent and unmoving. The look on Tyler's face was a mix of fear and grim determination. His hand slowly reached out and grasped the air-vent zipper.

All of a sudden, he quickly unzipped the vent flap, up and over, so that the solid piece of fabric fell forward, hanging into the tent, revealing a half-circle window of netting that let in a trace of moonlight.

Tyler and Kelly were silent as a crypt, their eyes widening in abject terror, as their brains processed what their eyes saw.

Looking into the tent through the mesh window, no more than a few feet away, was a creature, unlike anything they had ever seen before. In the eerie glow of the moonlight, they could make out the upper body of a wolf or large dog. It was muscular yet bony, its shoulder blades and a slight hunchback visible in the dim light outside the tent. It had shaggy, dark fur and pointy, triangular ears sticking up on its head. Its snout protruded out, home to two rows of large, sharp teeth, glistening white in the moonlight. The cuspids must have been at least three or four inches long. Its mouth was open slightly, and it appeared to be grinning, a ghastly smirk on its face as it bared its teeth, its quivering, shiny gums curling up and over deadly fangs.

But the most terrifying sight of all was the creature's eyes.

Staring in at them through the mesh air vent were two large, yellow-orange eyes, glowing in the soft moonlight. The eyes caught them in their deadly, hypnotic gaze for a few moments before the creature unleashed an utterly indescribable shriek that shook the tent to its poles and made both Tyler and Kelly scream in terror.

"RUN!" Tyler shouted, eyes wide, scampering on his knees toward the tent door.

He managed to unzip the door, bursting out of the tent in his socks, Kelly not far behind him.

But Tyler's right foot caught on the lip of the tent as he bent down slightly to avoid the top of the rainfly.

That split second was all it took.

A giant paw with long, razor-sharp claws jutting out from gnarled pads whistled through the air with great speed and force. When it connected with the side of Tyler's face, it made a sickening crunching, thudding sound, like a heavy boot stomping on a watermelon. Tyler's right eye socket caved in instantly, and his cheekbone shattered, the claws etching deep, bloody tracks in the side of his face and taking his right eye out as they pulled back for another swipe.

At least he was unconscious when the thing fell upon him, tearing his limp body apart with teeth and claws, opening up his stomach under the ghostly moonlight.

Kelly was halfway to the car when she turned to look back. When she saw Tyler's mangled body on the ground and the creature hovering over it, she screamed a gut-wrenching shriek that cut through the night.

The beast stopped and looked up at Kelly, its eyes glinting in the moonlight. She screamed again, a hopeless, lunatic scream of desperation, as the beast stood up and lurched forward toward Kelly. That was when she first realized that it walked on two legs, lunging on muscular hind legs like a human or a bear. The thing growled at her, popping its teeth ferociously.

Kelly turned and ran for the car as fast as she could, crying and screaming. She made it to the car and wrenched on the driver's side door handle, the creature mere feet away and closing in quickly. The car door suddenly burst open, and she jumped inside, slamming it shut behind her and locking it, just as the creature reached the driver's side of the car. The thing slammed its paws hard against the window. The car shook violently, and the window gave a little, emitting a repulsive cracking sound. Kelly screamed in terror as the dog/man looked from the window to its paws, a hideous grin on its face, now covered in her slain boyfriend's blood and offal, a gooey string of blood and drool hanging from its snout.

Kelly frantically reached for the ignition to start the car and came back empty-handed.

Tyler had put the keys in the tent.

This crushing realization hit her slowly and deeply. Her head sunk down and rested on the steering wheel. She began to sob, sitting alone in the dark in her dead boyfriend's electric-blue Ford Escort at their camping site in the Manistee National Forest, as the creature stalked around the vehicle menacingly, its amber, unfeeling eyes peering in at her, waiting.

Manistee National Forest Ranger Kay Swanson had the Fourth of July off. She had spent it camping at Bear Lake with her husband, Tom, their two-year-old son, Brandon, and her parents.

The next day, Wednesday, July 5, started the same as most days. Kay had coffee and breakfast with Tom and Brandon, took a shower, and dressed for the day in her khaki uniform, fitting her park-ranger hat gently on her head.

She got into her Forest Service-issued Chevy Silverado and headed for the National Forest for her morning rounds.

Ranger Kay chuckled, remembering those two kids who had been smoking weed and how nervous she had made them when she played bad cop. She decided she'd pay them another visit this morning. Why not?

Even before she reached the campsite, a dreadful feeling came over her, a premonition that something was terribly wrong. As she pulled up to the campsite, the first thing she noticed was the car. It looked like it had been battered and smashed to pieces by a baseball bat or a crowbar or something. The windshield was covered in spider cracks, and the driver's side window was totally smashed in, jagged pieces of glass jutting out from the bottom of the window frame. And... what was that smeared all over the door?

Could it be? Blood? she thought to herself, not really believing what she was seeing.

She put the truck in park and opened the driver's side door. Her heart started to race as she cautiously stepped out of the truck. She walked toward the car, trying to peer around it to get a better view.

"Hello?" she called uncertainly. "Anyone there?"

That's when she heard the open door of the tent, flapping and snapping gently in the breeze.

She saw Tyler first, lying on his back near the tent. The right side of his face was missing, and all that remained was bloody, raw meat buzzing with black flies. His left eye was open and intact, staring up blankly at the sky. A glazed film had formed over it. His body was badly mangled, his stomach and chest torn up, and what was left of his blue jeans were ripped and matted with dried, black blood. It looked like scavengers had been feeding on the corpse.

Ranger Kay gasped for air, eyes wide, holding back a shrill scream that she feared would come at any moment. She would never forget that sight. It filled her with a horror so deep and suffocating that she would have nightmares about it for the rest of her life.

Then she turned to the right and saw Kelly's body in front of Tyler's Escort. Her hand shot to her mouth, and she screamed, drew in a hoarse breath, and screamed again.

Kelly's remains were scattered around the campsite. Her body, or what was left of it, was badly mangled, almost unrecognizable. Her stomach had been opened, and the remains of her entrails bulged out of a gaping, foot-long gash that extended from the top of her pubic arch to the bottom of her sternum. Some of her intestines had been dragged ten feet or so out of her body cavity and lay strewn about the gruesome scene, half-eaten. Her left leg was missing from the knee down, leaving a bloody stump of white bone reflecting the early morning sunlight. Her right arm was severed, lying limp and bloody by the firepit twenty feet away from the body, and three fingers were missing from her left hand. Kelly had been decapitated, and a bit of spinal cord was visible amidst the raw meat of her severed neck.

Ranger Kay screamed again, a dry, panicked scream, her eyes bulging out of their sockets, her heart pounding up into her throat. Instinctively, she turned toward her truck and took one lumbering, uncertain step forward.

She kicked and stumbled over something round and heavy with her right foot. Her eyes shot down toward the ground, and she let out a shuddering gasp as she came face to face with Kelly's severed head, its mouth open in a final, twisted scream of terror and agony, its eyes wide and flecked with dried blood, staring up pleadingly at Ranger Kay.

At that point, Ranger Kay realized she was going to vomit. She nearly reached the brush east of the campsite, stumbling and tripping over her own feet, before her breakfast of scrambled eggs and toast came up, splatting onto the grass with a sickening sound. She was sweating, utterly and completely afraid, petrified by the scene she had just witnessed. That's when another self-preserving wave of fear and panic struck her, hard and fast, like a freight train.

She wiped a string of drool from her mouth with her sleeve and whipped her head from side to side, surveying the area nervously. She thought the bear—or maybe cougar or wolf—that had done this could still be around and more dangerous than ever now that it had acquired a taste for human flesh and blood.

Without another thought, she sprinted toward her Silverado, terrified, sneaking hurried glances over her shoulder as she reached the truck and opened the door. She flung herself up into the driver's seat and slammed the door behind her, locking it.

This was probably the last thing these poor dead kids here did before it got them, she thought, shivering, noticing how dry her mouth was.

She reached down and picked up her CB radio receiver with a shaking hand and called to report the incident and get help.

Then she burst into tears.

Saturday, July 8, 2017
LeRoy, Michigan

E very summer since 1973 the village of LeRoy holds an
annual homecoming celebration called LeRoy
Razzasque Days. Taking place the second weekend of July,
the festival includes a kid's parade and games in the park; a
Junior Prince and Princess LeRoy drawing; a Grand Parade;
chicken barbeque; a huge striped refreshment tent; food
booths; an odd assortment of carnival rides; a softball
tournament; live music; and a raffle. LeRoy comes alive for
Razzasque Days every second weekend in July, and most
residents would agree it's always a rousing success—good for
LeRoy's morale and coffers.

The festival was held in a large park, basically just an
open grassy area east of Mackinaw Trail, between Henry's
Store and the Village Market. For the LeRoy Area Museum,
not to mention every restaurant, bar, hotel, grocery store, or
business of any kind in the village, Razzasque Days was the
busiest time of the year, bringing in more money in two days
than most of them saw in two months.

Razzasque Days always filled Jack Allen with a piercing nostalgia—the sights and smells smell of hotdogs, popcorn, cotton candy, barbeque, and elephant ears frying in hot grease mingled with the scent of sawdust and cigarette smoke; the sound of children laughing on the Tilt-A-Whirl, Helter Skelter, or Ferris Wheel or screaming on the pirate ship or in the funhouse; taking silly pictures in the photo booth; face-painting and balloon animals—it were all magical and could instantly transport him back to his childhood. He remembered going to Razzasque Days with his mother, father, brother, and sister every summer, and it was one of the most poignant and special of all his childhood memories. He had passed on his love for the festival to his daughter, Melanie, who was *VERY* excited to go this year and ride the Teacups and eat cotton candy and a corndog with mustard on it.

It was Saturday, and the Allen family was piled into the Blazer heading down Mackinaw Trail to the festival. Mel was *ecstatic,* and it made Jack and Claire smile. He reached for her hand and held it. He was happy, and for the first time in a long time, he was going to forget about all this crazy Dogman business, just like the rest of LeRoy always did, and just enjoy himself and his beautiful family and the Razzasque Days celebration.

Melanie was having a *fabulous* time. She went on the Teacups *three times,* ate junk food, tried a snow cone for the first time, *and* Jack won her a stuffed frog playing the Milk Bottle game. And that was all before lunchtime!

After lunch, Melanie got her face painted to look like a cheetah, and then a clown named Jo-Jo made her a cheetah balloon animal. Could this day get any better?!

Now she was lying on a blanket in a nice grassy spot in the shade, splitting an elephant ear with chocolate sauce with her mom and dad. What an epic day.

Jack and Claire had been holding hands nearly the entire day, smiling and laughing as they watched Melanie having so much fun. It was the closest and warmest they had felt toward each other since Jack discovered his father's trunk in the barn loft. Now, as Melanie stuffed her chocolate-covered face with fried dough, Jack leaned in and kissed Claire on the lips.

"You know I love you," he whispered, looking into her eyes. "I'm sorry I've been so off lately. It's been crazy, and maybe we should talk about it sometime."

"I'd like that."

He kissed her again. "No matter what, I'll never stop loving you. Never."

"I know," she said.

He smiled at her, and she smiled back at him, and for the first time in over a month, there was a spark there again. There was real love there between them; real love that wasn't complicated by some bullshit or bad feelings or questions or anxiety or fear, just real love.

Jack kissed her again and squeezed her hands in his. It was a hot sunny day in July.

"How about a cold beer from the 'adult beverage tent'?" he asked, making air quotes with his fingers.

"Mmmm, that sounds refreshing," she said with a smile.

"You're beautiful," he said, his eyes penetrating hers. "Stay right here."

Jack turned and walked off toward the adult beverage tent, whistling with his hands in his pockets like he was a kid again.

They had dinner that night at Brad's cabin on Rose Lake, a 370-acre natural inland lake in northwestern Osceola County. "The lake," as they all called it growing up, is only about a mile and a half southeast of the farm off of 16 Mile Road, and for as long as anyone could remember, the Allens had a lakefront lot with a little trailer on it where they would go swimming, play in the sand, fish, boat, and relax in the sun.

Brad built his cabin with his own two hands and just a little help from friends and family. It was two lots down from the Allen family lot. Brad lived with his girlfriend Nellie, a brunette who grew up in Grand Rapids and owned her own women's clothing and accessories boutique in Cadillac called, Bliss. Nellie also helped with the interior design of homes that Brad built or bought and flipped. They made a good pair, their quirks and edges fitting well together and complimenting each other.

Now they were all sitting at the patio table on Brad's back deck that looked out over the lake, which was a dull pewter under the evening sky, the surface so calm it looked like glass. The sun was just beginning to lose its power as the evening came on. They had just finished a lovely dinner prepared by Nellie and Brad and now chatted quietly. Claire, Nellie, and Melanie giggled about something Mel had said, and Jack and Brad stood up and walked down the steps to stand by the lake. Brad lit a cigarette.

The Allens had a great family weekend together: first Razzasque Days and then dinner with Brad and Nellie at the lake. Jack and Claire made love that night, feeling closer than they had in a long time. Afterward they both slept like the dead, exhausted yet satisfied.

Jack woke up the next morning with an irresistible urge to continue reading through the papers his father had collected in the trunk in the barn loft. He was rankled and confused by the way Crawford had reacted at Travelers that night when he had said who his father was.

What the hell was that all about? he thought.

He had a feeling, a premonition, that there just might be

an answer in his father's trunk in the barn loft. It freaked him out a bit, but it also excited him.

It was evening now, Sunday, July 9. Jack and Claire had just put Mel down together, and now Claire was curled up on the couch with a paperback, sipping on a glass of chilled rosé. It was just after seven o'clock. At that time in July the sun sets around 9:30 P.M., so Jack had a couple hours of light left. He decided to spend it up in the loft going through his father's papers, trying to make some sense of what had been going on lately.

"Hey, babe, I'm gonna head down to the barn for a bit. I got a project I'm working on."

It wasn't a lie.

"A project?" Claire looked up from her book. "What kind of project?"

He thought for a moment, then sighed and sat down next to her on the couch.

"When I was rooting around in the loft back in June," he began. "You remember? I was looking for that box of dishes —*dinnerware*—for Logan?"

Claire nodded and sipped at her wine.

"Well, I found something else up there that's been on my mind ever since." He wiped the corners of his mouth with his thumb and first finger. "It's this old wooden storage trunk of my dad's. You know it's been almost ten years now since he left, and I've been thinking about him a lot lately, so it was strange timing just randomly stumbling upon this trunk of his when I did. Anyway, it's full of all these papers and newspaper clippings and journals and stuff, *research,* you might say, and a lot of it has to do with my family history. I've been going through it over the last few weeks."

"Ah, so *that's* what you've been doing spending so much time in the barn lately," Claire nodded, a look of dawning realization on her face. "I thought you were just going crazy." She made a face at him then took his hand in hers.

"Yeah, it's funny you should say that, cuz I've been feeling like I'm going a little crazy lately." He looked at her. "I'm just really into this stuff right now, into reading about my family's history, the history of the area, the land up here... the *wildlife*." A barely perceptible shadow darkened his eyes momentarily like a cloud blocking the sun. "Maybe it's just my way of dealing with the anniversary of when he left, ya know?"

And as he said this, Jack thought that maybe it was true—maybe that was why he was suddenly so obsessed with figuring things out, with sketching the pattern and filling in the missing pieces. There were other reasons too, of course, but maybe part of it was his way of reconnecting with his father in some way. There was no doubt that the trunk in the loft had taken on some sort of life of its own for him; it was like a living, breathing being that glowed with its own undeniable energy and beckoned to him with a force that Jack couldn't resist; like his father was communicating with him through it, leading him on, trying to *tell* him something.

Claire put her arms around Jack's shoulders and squeezed him.

"I totally understand, babe." She kissed him on the cheek. "I'm glad you told me, and if you ever want to talk about it, I'm always here for you."

He leaned in and kissed her on the lips. He hadn't exactly lied to her, but he had also purposefully withheld some key information. Jack didn't want to scare her, and he didn't want her to think him crazy, like he really had gone off the deep end and belonged in the nuthouse. He needed to amass more evidence first and put all the pieces together in a way that made sense. What he needed was an airtight case that was convincing and undeniable, then he would come clean with Claire. Jack would tell her everything, from the beginning to the end, and then they'd find a way together to stop this thing, whatever it was. He also needed to get Brad and the cousins in on it too. They could help; hell, they might even know something about this that he didn't. He decided then and there that he needed to have a talk with them too.

"Thanks, babe," he said. "I don't know what I'd do without you." And he meant it.

Jack squeezed her hand gently, stood up, and walked out of the living room like a man on a mission.

Jack sat in the wicker chair in the corner of the loft, the trunk lid yawning open. He was sifting through stacks of paper his father had collected on the Dogman, tingling with excitement. It was hot up in the loft, and he was glistening with sweat, but he didn't care. He was hungry for information, thirsty for clues.

The first thing he saw that night was a loose piece of paper with the word "TRINITITE" printed at the top of it. It looked like it had been copied out of an encyclopedia or something. Jack's curiosity was piqued, and he read that trinitite is a jagged rock, like melted glass, left behind after a nuclear explosion. Specifically, trinitite is created when sand and dirt are swept up by the blast and instantly liquified by the heat. It's usually light green or red in color and is mildly radioactive but safe to handle. Aside from nuclear bomb test sites, trinitite has also been found in craters left by comets or meteoroids that make it through the earth's atmosphere and land on earth. When this happens, they are typically referred to as meteorites. Scrawled in Jack's father's hand at the top righthand corner of this enigmatic document was this cryptic note: *"From Wilmer Slow Bear."* Jack made a puzzled face, shrugged his shoulders, and returned the sheet of paper to the trunk.

Next, he pulled out a manila folder with a label stuck on

it. *"Incidents in 1937"* was written on the label in his father's chicken scratch in faded blue ink. Jack opened the folder and read through the typewritten pages with great interest and zeal.

———

The first account was of a sighting in Bowers Harbor, just north of Traverse City, in the summer of 1937. Henry Oakes was the captain of an eighty-foot-long two-masted schooner named *Neverland* that would sink in Lake Michigan in the winter of 1941. Oakes, along with his entire crew of fifteen men, went down with the ship and were never seen again.

But this was the summer of 1937. Oakes and his crew aboard *Neverland* were coming into port in Traverse City. They had been shipping lumber all over the Great Lakes region and had just sailed north from Chicago via Lake Michigan. Sailing up and around the Leelanau Peninsula, they had headed south into the Grand Traverse Bay. Spirits were high and some of the men were high on spirits as they had been on the water and away from their loved ones for some time.

Something odd happened as *Neverland* continued its trajectory south.

As they passed Bowers Harbor to the east several crew members reported seeing something strange that unnerved them, scared them outright, and these men were no spring chickens; they were tough, seasoned mariners who'd been around the block a time or two. Although Captain Oakes didn't see it himself, several of his men told him that day that they had seen a pack of wild dogs roaming Bowers Harbor as they passed it on their way into port. But these were no ordinary dogs.

They moved on their hindlegs and were massive, six or

seven feet tall and weighing at least three hundred pounds. They were menacing and aggressive. They were what the French fur traders of old would have called *loup garou* or *rougarou* 'werewolf', and Oakes's men would've known; many of them were descendants of those original French-Canadian fur trappers and voyageurs who came to the Great Lakes from Quebec.

When *Neverland* and its crew came in to dock in Traverse City, Captain Oakes went to the local authorities and reported what his crew members had seen at Bowers Harbor that day. The sheriff laughed in his face. Ultimately Oakes's story was never officially recorded because he hadn't personally seen the creatures and because it was known that several members of the crew had been intoxicated at the time.

The forgetting disease, Jack thought, as he finished the schooner captain's account.

He sighed and flipped the page to the next account from 1937.

Robert Fortney saw the creature in June of 1937. It was dawn on the morning of Saturday, June 5. Fortney was fishing on the Muskegon River near the small village of Paris, just north of Big Rapids. He had gotten an early start that morning, casting his bait into the glittering, russet-brown water before the summer sun drove the fish to cooler, deeper water. It was right around sunup, and he had already caught several nice ones: two brown trout, two steelhead, and one beautiful smallmouth bass, all of which were now drying off in the wicker creel at his feet.

Then something caught his eye coming out of the woods into the clearing not sixty yards to the north.

Very much like what Captain Oakes's crew had seen at Bowers Harbor that same summer, Robert Fortney saw a pack of wild dogs emerge from the deep woods along the banks of the Muskegon River. Like the Bowers Harbor "dogs," these creatures were large and muscular, covered with wild brown and black fur. Fortney noticed a peculiar smell, like something old and earthy, a smell that was somehow threatening and offensive.

When the pack of dogs started coming his way, Fortney picked up the rifle he carried with him and fired in their direction to scare them off. The dogs scattered and retreated back into the dark woods. Except one: the largest of them all, the alpha, the leader of the pack. Instead of running away, this beast actually rose up onto its hind legs and stared straight at Fortney, who was fast becoming highly agitated. But the malevolent glow of the beast's moonlike amber eyes had a hypnotic effect on the fisherman, who cocked his head and stared back into those menacing orbs, despite himself.

The creature began to approach the hapless fisherman, a fly caught in a spider's web. Now it was fifty yards away, still holding Fortney's gaze like a child holds a butterfly. Then it was forty yards away, stalking its prey slowly. When it was only twenty-five yards away, a fish suddenly jumped in the river. The splash brought Fortney out of his trance.

He shook his head and gasped, fear and panic eating away at him like gangrene. He shuddered as he raised and shouldered his rifle.

He took aim.

The creature was coming at him faster now, snarling ferociously and popping and gnashing its teeth.

It was fifteen yards away when Fortney fired.

The kick of the rifle and the sharp crack of its report temporarily stunned Fortney. When he regained his composure, the beast was nowhere to be found. He searched the area frantically, his head on a swivel. He guessed that it must have disappeared into the woods when he shot at it, but he couldn't be sure.

Fortney gathered his belongings as fast as he could and got the hell out of there.

He never did come back to that spot again, despite the enviable haul of fish he had taken out of the Muskegon River that Saturday morning in June of 1937.

Jack had come to the end of the papers in the manila folder labeled *"Incidents in 1937."* He shakily stuffed them back into the folder and returned it to his father's antique trunk. He checked his cell phone: it was 9:30 and just starting to get dark. There was a beautiful full moon that night.

Jack closed the trunk. He was freaked out and the wheels in his head were turning, more like doing figure eights. Jack stood and descended the ladder to the main floor of the barn and started walking toward the door. It was dark out now except for the light of the full July moon.

Suddenly he heard a noise on the gravel outside the barn.

He crouched and froze, his heart pounding. He could feel his pulse all the way up in his throat, and it was starting to run like an Olympic sprinter.

There was a tall shadow out there. Gravel stones skipped and danced softly on the driveway just outside the barn doors, scuffed by the feet—*or paws*—of whatever was out there. Jack set his jaw.

"Who's there?!" he called in as stern a voice as he could muster.

It stopped. Whatever it was out there stopped and listened.

Jack didn't move. His breath came in ragged, wheezy gasps.

"Jack?"

It was Claire. Her voice was soft, confused, but with a hint of amusement.

Jack's whole body went limp as he heaved a great sigh of relief. His shoulders sagged, and his legs felt like Jell-O as he walked over to the barn door. He peeked out, and Claire was standing there, a mischievous grin on her face.

CHAPTER 9

SUMMER: AUGUST 2017

Tuesday, August 8, 2017
LeRoy, Michigan

Jack was in the woods on his evening hike. It was a beautiful August night, and the sun was just beginning its descent in the west. He passed Cherry Ridge on his right and was walking by the cedar swamp on his left. The ferns on either side of the trail were nearly as tall as a man and so green they looked luminescent. Jack tried to get past the negative things he had been dealing with lately and move on; he just wanted to let it all go. But that night, a nagging, vague fear had welled up in him as soon as he crossed the white pine at the beginning of his hike. This undefined dread had intensified once he crossed the stone bridge over the crick, and now it was stifling. It even had a smell: an ominous, earthy musk like rotting leaves and wild, ancient things.

Dead things.

The odd scent was thick in the air, and it compounded Jack's fear and anxiety. And, oddly enough, Jack somehow faintly recognized that smell, like something out of a long-forgotten memory.

As he continued along, past the swamp, he found himself on the trail they all called the Back Forty, the barbed-wire fence marking the property line not far off to his left. The sun's power was waning, but it radiated with that golden-orange glow that makes sunsets in Northern Michigan so spectacular. Despite the portentous aroma in the air, he smiled at this, examining the way the evening sunlight danced playfully on the leaves of the trees, glistening and moving on them like a living organism. There was definitely something magical about the Northwoods in—

A twig snapped behind him.

Jack's head whirled around as a startled gasp escaped him.

Standing on the trail, not fifteen yards behind him, was a creature so terrible that Jack squeezed his eyes shut, praying this was a nightmare.

It was the creature his father had known about, and his father before him; the beast described by Crawford that terrorized the town of Sigma in 1987; the thing Jack had seen himself on multiple occasions growing up and more recently in the field off of 16 Mile Road. He had never seen it this close, and he feared he wouldn't live to tell about it.

It was tall and muscular, standing upright on sinewy hind legs and massive, claw-tipped paws. Its broad shoulders and bony back were hunched forward in an aggressive stance. Rough black fur covered its body, and its pointy ears stood erect atop its head. It was the source of the musky scent Jack had noticed, which was now overwhelming, making Jack feel woozy, almost sick, as if it was enchanting or hypnotizing him, drawing him in against his will. He stood in stunned silence, unable to breathe or move, his feet glued to the earth as if they were buried in quicksand. He stared helplessly into the face of the beast.

The Dogman.

Wrinkles creased the creature's low forehead, scant fur thickening as it approached the top of its skull. Its eyebrows were angular and threatening. A canine muzzle and jaws protruded out with twitching whiskers. Long, sharp teeth lined its mouth, and foamy drool dangled from it in ropelike strands. A leering grin was on its face, and it was snarling. Its snout was tipped with a wet black nose. Its cheeks were hollow and fleshy near its eyes, which blazed with a haunting amber glow.

It was the eyes that brought Jack out of his trance.

Suddenly his heart started beating again and seemed to burst into his throat. The beast let out an unearthly shriek that was a cross between a coughing, dry hack, a terrible human scream, and the howl of a wolf.

Jack turned and ran.

The beast dropped to all fours and gave chase.

It wasn't much of a contest. After a dead sprint that lasted less than a minute, Jack dared to look back. He turned his head, his arms and legs still pumping, and there was nothing there! He drew in a sharp breath of surprise, too confused to feel relief, and slowed to a stop. Jack searched the trail for any sign of the creature he had just seen. He began to wonder if his eyes had been playing tricks on him in the fading evening sunlight.

That's when it attacked.

It came at him from the side, from behind a shaggy pine tree, and Jack just barely caught a glimpse of a large black blur in his peripheral vision. It had happened so suddenly and with such force that Jack was already losing consciousness when the first blow struck him across his neck and left cheekbone, leaving a set of gaping gashes that burst with hot blood.

He was unconscious before he hit the ground, and the

beast, triumphant and mad in the August twilight, fell upon him with apelike fury.

Jack shot up in bed with a breathless gasp. He was drenched in a film of cold sweat and breathing heavily. He shook his head, shuddering and blinking wildly. His hand shot to his neck and left cheekbone, expecting to feel the flaccid white lips of the wounds opened there by the creature's claws and the warm sticky blood that had erupted from them.

But there was nothing.

It had all been a dream, a terrible, realistic nightmare, almost as if the beast was toying with him, taunting him. As Jack's heartbeat began to slow down to normal, he sighed and rubbed his eyes with both hands.

Jack got up and stumbled to the bathroom. He supported himself unsteadily with both hands on the sink, eyes shut, as he tried to shake the dream from his head.

He looked up, and in the mirror above the bathroom sink, he saw the *eyes.* Instead of his own, the luminous amber eyes of the beast peered back at him in the mirror's reflection. Jack nearly screamed and closed his eyes in frightened panic. When he cautiously opened them again, one at a time, the demonic eyes were gone, and he was looking at his own frightened, pale reflection.

He didn't sleep much the rest of that night. At one point, around four A.M., he fell into a fitful thin sleep that only lasted for twenty minutes or so. He sprang up in bed again with a shiver, gasping for breath, and he swore that for a brief, terrifying moment, he could smell that dreadful earthy musk, like rotten leaves and ancient death.

The obsession was beginning to take over his life. He felt like he had no control over it, and that scared him. After discovering his dad's trunk in the barn loft and his strange conversation with Crawford at Travelers, he decided he had to do some research of his own.

Scribbling a brief note to Claire that didn't give much away, Jack had left the house early on the morning of Sunday, August 13, driving fast through the misting rain up US-131 north to Traverse City. His grip on the wheel was overly tight as he tried to connect the pieces of the story that he still couldn't quite believe, mouthing the words silently as he thought through them.

The Dogman. Don't go out at night. Don't go out at night. The cycle. The seventh year is here the seventh year is here the seventh year is here.

He stared ahead without seeming to really see anything.

The drive took just over an hour, and he was relieved, or maybe exhilarated, as he pulled into the parking lot of the Traverse Area District Library, his windshield wipers squeaking rhythmically as they did their work. The TADL was by far the best library in Northern Michigan, but most importantly, it had complete runs of the *Cadillac Evening News* and the *Traverse City Record Eagle* in its archives, two of the oldest newspapers in the area, along with just about every other small-town newspaper ever printed in Northern Michigan.

He chatted distractedly for five minutes with Nancy Jones, the archivist, an attractive young woman no more than thirty or thirty-five years old. Nancy led him through the serpentine archives to a lone desk topped with an ancient and massive microfilm machine, like a rare dinosaur fossil, in a dusty corner of a large room with few windows. He sat down at the dusty wooden swivel chair in front of the desk, his hands gripping the arms of the chair as he squinted at the old machine, sizing it up as if he were going to do battle with it.

Jack's mouth watered, and his fingers tingled with anticipation as the archivist brought him the spools of microfilm he had requested. He inhaled deeply and licked his lips like a hungry man sitting down to a meal, his hands weaving together unconsciously as if in prayer.

"Why do you only want the rolls for the seventh years?" the archivist asked.

Jack's head turned toward Nancy.

"Hu-Huh?" he stammered, trying not to sound alarmed.

"The microfilm you requested," Nancy said matter-of-factly, holding up a spool. "1897, 1907, 1917, 1927, 1937. All seventh years. How come?"

Jack was stunned. He froze for an agonizing few seconds, and you could've knocked him over with a feather. He had to pull something out of his ass and quick.

"Oh, yeah, of course," he smiled, shaking his head in a shy, self-deprecating way. "Well, you see, I'm doing a research paper on Traverse City for my community college local history course. I want to get a general feel for what it was like to live here in the old days, and seven's my lucky number, so I thought checking out the seventh years would be as good a way as any to get a sample of what Traverse City life was like in the past."

He held his breath and shrugged, looking up at Nancy, that same shit-eating grin plastered stupidly on his face. A nervous second passed. Then another. On the inside, Jack sweated bullets waiting for Nancy to respond.

Say something! Anything!

"Oh," Nancy replied in a bored, falling tone. She snapped her gum and gave Jack a puzzled look. "Cool. Well, good luck with your paper." She walked toward the door leading out of the microfilm room. "Let me know if you need anything."

"I will," Jack nodded, relief flooding over him. "Thank you, Nancy."

Jesus, that was a close one, Jack thought as he pulled out the tray and put the microfilm roll for the year 1897 on the spindle, carefully threading it under the rollers and into the take-up reel. He fast-forwarded to the first image, pushed the tray back under the lens, and glanced expectantly at the yellowed cover page of the *Traverse City Record Eagle* newspaper on the viewing screen.

It didn't take him long to find some interesting stories.

Things had started out slowly and seemed normal enough in northwestern Michigan that winter, a pattern that would become familiar to Jack in his research. The early winter months saw few alarming incidents to report, none that Jack considered to fit the pattern anyway.

But things accelerated once the spring thaw hit Northern Michigan in late April.

The first suspicious incidents reported in 1897 involved pets, chickens, and livestock, another pervasive pattern Jack uncovered. Reports of this kind skyrocketed every seventh year, along with unsolved murder and missing-persons rates, according to the FBI's Uniform Crime Report, a disturbing trend that either the whole region was daftly unaware of or else foolishly and perilously overlooked. Was it a quiet denial? Or maybe an unconscious—or perhaps even conscious—forgetting during the nadir years of the cycle? This blind, seemingly willful forgetting of tragedy and disaster was yet another pattern that emerged from Jack's research and in his discussions with local townsfolk, like some mad form of collective amnesia, as Crawford had said.

Here and there, throughout the spring of 1897, were strange reports of missing pets and animals maimed throughout northwestern Michigan. A few lines on a missing bird dog in Osceola County with a reward offered upon its safe return. A sad tale of a little girl's pet cat Felix who never made it home one May evening near Manton. Just outside of Cadillac, a chicken coop had been terrorized in the night by an unknown assailant, producing a macabre scene of messy gore that shocked the poor farmer who discovered it. Must have been a coyote or maybe a wolf, he had said, a hollow, fearful expression spreading across his face at the memory.

There were more, and they seemed to accelerate as the spring turned into summer. Many, but not all, of the incidents occurred near the Manistee River and its watershed and in the small country towns in the vicinity. Places like Wellston, Mesick, Yuma, Manton, and a handful of others; small towns that no one outside of them even knew existed.

One story that caught Jack's eye was a report about a farmer found dead near the tiny village of Buckley, north of the Manistee in Wexford County. Buckley, not incorporated until 1907, was a village of no more than 250 people in 1897. However, it was a railway town located along the Manistee and North-Eastern Railroad, making Buckley a center for fruit growing and other agricultural pursuits. Timber was also important to Buckley's economy, as it was throughout Northern Michigan.

From the *Cadillac Evening News,* June 2, 1897 (page 2):

BUCKLEY FARMER FOUND DEAD

According to a report from Wexford County Sherriff Jim Crawford, a local Buckley man, Curtis Brown, aged forty-six, was found dead near his home Wednesday. Brown's body was discovered slumped over his plow in the east field of his property near Buckley in Wexford County at approximately 1:30 P.M. Wednesday afternoon. An autopsy revealed that Brown died of sudden cardiac arrest. "It is my professional opinion that Curtis Brown's heart simply stopped beating suddenly," explained pathologist Dr. Isaac Lindstrom, who is working with Wexford County officials and the local coroner's office on the case. When asked if there were any additional details to report or evidence of foul play, Sherriff Crawford responded, "Not that we can discuss at this time. The only peculiarity noticed by our investigators was the presence of large dog tracks all around the plow and body in the field. I can assure you that our best men are working tirelessly on the case." Brown is survived by his wife Betty, son Robert, and daughter Julia. Funeral arrangements are being made by the Village of Buckley Funeral Home on Main Street.

Jack peeled his eyes away from the microfilm viewing screen, the flesh on his arms and neck prickling, a dull, flat ringing in his ears. He was breathing heavily as he contemplated the story he had just read. The tracks were the common denominator in so many of the stories... that, and the eyes. Those fucking eyes.

Why didn't anyone follow up on the tracks? he thought, feeling a mixture of anger and hopelessness.

Jack scrolled through the newspaper reports for the year 1897, discovering more and more pieces of the puzzle, fleshing out the pattern. Sitting there in that dusty swivel chair before the hulking microfilm reader, the rain pelting the roof and windows of the Traverse Area District Library, he felt like things were really starting to come together.

And it scared the hell out of him.

Jack reached the end of the microfilm reel for the year 1897. He checked his cellphone and found it was half-past noon. Jack was getting hungry, but he was far hungrier to continue on with his research, the inescapable, growing obsession, the unquenchable need to *know* burned within him, coloring his thoughts like a dark, impenetrable shadow.

He unboxed the microfilm of the *Traverse City Record Eagle* for the year 1907 and loaded it onto the spindle and under the rollers, pulling up the first image. His eyes were getting increasingly bloodshot from staring at the viewing screen as the seemingly endless pages whirred by, the black, block text sharply contrasting with the ghostly, illuminated background.

For a moment, he wondered if he was going mad. What if he was the Dogman? The thought crossed his mind and made him giggle dementedly, out loud at first, until he stifled it with his hand. But he continued his mad giggling on the inside at the idea that he was the Dogman. After a few feverish moments, he regained his composure and buried that thought, clenching his teeth and squinting at the screen in front of him. He threw himself recklessly into his task, his burden, his obsession.

Just like ten years before in 1897, the early months of 1907 were relatively quiet and uneventful. But things got more interesting when spring came to Northern Michigan that fateful year.

One story especially piqued Jack's curiosity, which by now was burning him up from the inside out. The story was from the second week of July, tucked away in the middle of the third page as if the newspaper was embarrassed by it or perhaps purposefully trying to hide *(deny)* it. Jack leaned in as he read, his teeth still clenched, hypnotized by the dull glow of the viewing screen.

From the *Traverse City Record Eagle,* July 10, 1907 (page 3):

WIDOW ROBERTS ADMITTED TO NORTHERN MICHIGAN ASYLUM

According to sources close to the family, Henrietta Roberts, widow of Dr. Samuel Roberts of Cadillac, was forcibly sent to the Northern Michigan Asylum in Traverse City by wagon on Tuesday. According to a statement by her son, Matthew Roberts, "Mother has not been well since father passed earlier this year. We believe the sudden, tragic circumstances of his death directly precipitated the breakdown of our dear mother's mental health. Sadly, mother is not well and can no longer care for herself and may in fact, be a danger to herself. Therefore, after many painstaking days and nights of deliberation, the family has decided to admit her to the Northern Michigan Asylum immediately. We feel that this difficult decision is in the best interest of both mother and the rest of the Roberts family. We humbly ask for your prayers and support throughout this very difficult time. Thank you, and God bless."

Recently there have been several troubling reports regarding Widow Roberts, aged sixty-seven, calling her mental health into question. According to multiple sources, she frequently claimed that dogs were circling her house at night. In Widow Roberts's highly agitated state, it was difficult to ascertain whether she was referring to dreams or reality. In any case, she stated on multiple occasions that these dogs were no ordinary dogs, but rather dogs that "walked like men and screamed," according to one report.

"It's a real shame," said a family acquaintance who wished to remain anonymous. "Henrietta never showed no signs of losing her marbles until earlier this year, after Dr. Roberts was killed. Now she's crazier than a bedbug. Just like that! When the family came with the doctors to take her away she was ranting and raving to beat the band about dogs and men, her dead husband, and something about *eyes.* She said she'd been seeing these awful orange eyes for months, looking in on her. She said they burned like fire; that they wouldn't leave her alone. She was clearly deranged. It was a real sad, pitiful sight."

Luckily for herself and her community, Widow Roberts is now in the care of the trained mental healthcare professionals and staff at the Northern Michigan Asylum in Traverse City, where she is no longer a threat to herself or others. Widow Roberts is not currently seeing visitors, but condolences may be sent care of Matthew Roberts of Cadillac.

The wheels in Jack's head were turning. He was sweating, and his breath came in deep, heavy drags, his chest heaving, his mouth slightly ajar, his eyes wide.

Dogs and men, the screams, the eyes! *The eyes that burned like fire!*

His thoughts were running away with him now. The words and the images they evoked in his head were coalescing, swirling in and out of his consciousness, dark phantoms emerging from the shadowy recesses of his mind, solidifying and reinforcing the ghastly pattern that was already taking shape.

And Dr. Roberts! The "sudden, tragic circumstances of his death" earlier in the year? he thought breathlessly. *How did I miss that?*

Feverishly he began rewinding the microfilm, searching

for the "sudden, tragic circumstances" of Dr. Samuel Roberts's death. It didn't take him long to find what he was looking for: a front-page story reported in late February.

———

From the *Traverse City Record Eagle,* February 26, 1907 (page 1):

———

DR. SAMUEL ROBERTS OF CADILLAC, DEAD, AGED SIXTY-EIGHT
Community Mourns

Dr. Samuel Roberts, MD, well-respected physician and beloved husband and father of three, was found dead on his property outside of Cadillac Sunday evening, according to a report by Missaukee County Sherriff Deputy Timothy Clements. Apparently, Dr. Roberts had gone out cross-country skiing that afternoon, and when he hadn't returned after several hours, his wife called the local police to report her husband missing. After a brief search, the body of Dr. Roberts was discovered two and a half miles northeast of his home, just off the trail, at the end of a draw on his property. The body was badly mangled in what Sherriff Deputy Clements called a "freak accident."

According to a statement prepared by the Missaukee County Sherriff's Department, "Dr. Clements appears to have been the victim of an animal attack. The body exhibited severe lacerations and puncture wounds from both teeth and claws, and large canine—or perhaps feline—tracks were found in the snow at the scene. An autopsy was performed, concluding that Dr. Clements died of hypovolemic shock, shock due to blood loss.

———

Jack's heart raced. He kept looking at the screen in disbelief, reading and rereading the story, then pulling his eyes away and staring blankly at the wall to his left, his eyebrows furrowed, mouth agape, a stupefied expression on his face as he mulled over the details in his head, trying to make sense of what he was reading.

THIS! he thought excitedly. *Now THIS is* really *something! This is some hard, circumstantial evidence that—*

"Jack?" a voice echoed from behind him.

Jack jumped in his seat as he whirled his head around so hard that later his neck was sore.

He breathed a shuddering sigh of relief, slumping back down in his chair as he realized it was just Nancy.

"Jesus," he panted. "You scared the hell out of me."

"A bit jumpy, are we?" Nancy asked in a concerned, slightly amused voice, one eyebrow raised. "I just wanted to make sure everything's going okay, that's all," she said.

"Yeah, sorry," Jack sighed, rubbing the back of his head. He yawned. "I guess I've been sitting in front of this thing for too long. Maybe I'll take a break and go grab a cup of coffee and a bite to eat or something."

Nancy nodded. "Seems like you could use a break… But if I were you, I'd stick to decaf." She chuckled.

Jack smiled, a bit embarrassed.

"Can I leave my stuff here and come back in an hour or so?"

"Yeah, that's fine, but the archive closes at five o'clock, just so you know."

"Okay, thanks very much, Nancy." Jack smiled, looking up at her with genuine gratitude. "You've been a big help."

Nancy smiled and shrugged again, cocking her head ever so slightly to one side.

"Don't mention it."

Jack wheeled the swivel chair away from the desk and stood up, stretching his back and legs with a sigh that was more like a groan. He checked his cellphone again. It was about half-past one. He decided to go grab a cup of coffee and a bite to eat as he realized he was starving. Jack remembered the coffee shop around the corner and decided to stretch his legs and try to process the shocking information he had just uncovered.

His brain buzzed like a bees' nest as he strode out of the Traverse Area District Library into the overcast, dull gray of the afternoon.

The Busy Bean was a quaint little coffee shop six blocks down Woodmere Avenue from the library. Jack walked down the sidewalk, his hands stuffed in his pockets, a misty drizzle that could hardly be called rain hanging in the air. It was hot and humid.

Jack had a lot on his mind. It was flying at about Mach 6 as he weighed the evidence he had just seen, trying out combinations of ideas, testing insights and hypotheses, piecing together theories. A picture was starting to develop in his head, the outlines of a pattern coming into focus. He felt like a paleontologist carefully unearthing a fossil. It was exciting, yet he was also frightened and anxious about what he was uncovering, what it would look like, and what he was revealing, unleashing.

Bells hung on the door of the Busy Bean, attached to it with what appeared to be a silky purple scarf. They jangled as Jack opened the door and stepped inside and walked into a wall of refreshingly cool airconditioned air hit him as he entered. The strains of soft jazz music and the aroma of freshly ground coffee beans filled the little shop. He strolled over to the counter and got in line behind a heavyset elderly woman paying for her coffee and donut. She turned and waddled away, taking a seat at one of the tables in the back.

Jack stepped up to the counter. There was no one in line behind him. He glanced up at the barista, a young man named Dave with kind eyes and a nose ring. He had pastel pink hair under a black baseball cap, and his arms were sleeved in colorful tattoos.

"Take your time." He smiled, rinsing a small stainless-steel milk frothing pitcher.

"Thanks."

The countertop was a beautiful polished dark wood with a glossy finish that made it sheen and sparkle. Jack could see his reflection in it. *No glowing amber eyes this time, though,* he thought, looking one more time just to be sure.

There was a bakery display case built into the hardwood counter with all sorts of baked goods and other treats: donuts, croissants, cakes, cookies, muffins, cinnamon rolls, and more. They looked good, but suddenly Jack realized he was hungry and needed more than just a Danish if he was going to have the energy to continue at the library for two or three more hours. In the refrigerated lower section of the display case Jack saw what he was looking for: bagels, sandwiches, salads, the more substantial fare the Busy Bean had to offer.

"I'll take a turkey sandwich," he said, turning his attention to the blackboard on the wall behind the barista. "And a large latte with an extra shot of espresso, please."

"You got it," the barista said, getting to work on the latte. "For here or to go?"

"For here, please. Oh, and you better throw in one of those chocolate chip cookies." Jack smiled.

"Sure thing."

Jack paid the barista and left him a nice tip. He took his coffee and food and found a secluded round table in the corner of the Busy Bean to drink his coffee. It tasted good, and he immediately felt rejuvenated from the caffeine. He sat there in silence, eating his turkey sandwich and sipping his latte, staring at the tabletop but not really seeing it. His mind was improvising along with the jazz music coming out of the speakers, riffing on the various themes he had come to associate with what he was calling *the pattern:* the Dogman; the cycle; the seventh year; the eyes; the deafening half-human, half-canine screams or howls; the bipedalism. All pieces of a terrifying puzzle of great import, the solving of which was fast becoming the dominant theme in Jack's life—his obsession. But it wasn't just his obsession, was it? His father had also apparently been obsessed with uncovering the truth about this creature. But it didn't end there either. The stories and accounts his dad had collected revealed a long history, a deeper connection between his family, his community, and this beast, this Dogman. What was that all about? Why was—

The bells tinkled sharply as the door of the Busy Bean swung open, pulling Jack up out of the mental rabbit hole he had fallen into. A nice-looking young couple came in with a small girl of about three in tow. They smiled at Jack sitting there in the corner, hunched over his sandwich, and walked up to the counter. The little girl reminded Jack of Mel, and he winced as a sudden pang of guilt struck him. He hadn't been the most attentive and caring father of late, not since the obsession had started. He was distant and oftentimes moody, although he had good days and bad. As he thought about this, he remembered how his father had off days too growing up, days when he was sullen and detached like he was thinking deeply about some urgent issue or problem.

The young couple with the little girl had picked up their order and walked toward the door. The little girl waved at Jack as they left, and he smiled and waved back. He finished his cookie and downed the last of his latte. Jack cleaned his table and threw away the garbage before nodding to the barista on his way out.

"Thanks for comin in. See ya next time," Dave, the pink-haired barista, chimed.

Jack left the Busy Bean and headed back to the Traverse Area District Library to continue his research, his quest, his crusade... his obsession.

It was 2:15 P.M. Jack was back in the old wooden swivel chair behind the corner desk at the library, face to face with the colossal microfilm reader. He unboxed the next spool of microfilm he had requested: the *Cadillac Evening News* for the year 1917. Then, feeling reenergized from his lunch and latte, he hungrily loaded the reel onto the spindle and under the rollers and pulled up the first image. The old machine hummed and wheezed, the viewing screen coming alive with its alluring glow.

It was the same pattern as the previous seventh years, a bell curve: a slow start that picked up speed as spring began and kicked into high gear once summer hit.

It was getting late, almost four o'clock, and the archives closed at five, but Jack thought he had enough time to get through one more spool of microfilm, this one for the year 1927. So he repeated what was fast becoming part of his ritual, his obsession, and unboxed and loaded the reel onto the spindle, threading it under the rollers. He pulled up the first image as the machine made its familiar purring sounds, and the viewing screen lit up like an old-style box television.

Same pattern as before: a real slow burner. The first thing that really grabbed his attention was yet another missing-persons story, a genre that was becoming all-too-familiar.

The family of the missing man, an insurance salesman from Manistee named Dick Harper, reported that he had gone missing in early August. Apparently, Harper had traveled to Cadillac on business and never made it home, another familiar theme emerging from Jack's research. Harper had left his home in Manistee on August 4 in his black Ford Model T Tudor sedan. It was an easy drive, one that he had made many times over the years, basically a fifty-mile straight shot east along M-55. In those days, it would've taken around two hours to get there, maybe three, depending on the weather and road conditions.

Harper's wife and brother had called the local sheriff's office when he didn't return home that night. They called again the next evening when there was still no sign of him, no telegraph, no phone call, no nothing. Everyone was mystified by the whole situation. Early on it was only his wife Lynn who had a dreadful feeling that she'd never see her husband again—a feeling she couldn't shake, a feeling which turned out to be prophetic. She never did see her husband again; well, at least not alive.

Over the next few weeks in August, an occasional report came in, updates were printed on the second and third pages of the *Traverse City Record Eagle.* It was no longer front-page news, apparently, and Jack surmised that the local Michiganders had gotten so used to such things happening during seventh years that they unconsciously buried them, easily forgot about them, pushed them down and away and went on with their lives. This was the most pervasive aspect of the pattern that Jack was uncovering, and perhaps the most pernicious: the forgetting, the willful turning away from disaster and tragedy. He saw it everywhere he looked in the newspapers from each and every seventh year.

On August 19, there was a report that Harper's car had been found abandoned ten or twenty miles east of a small town called Wellston. The Model T was parked way back on a secluded two-track road off M-55 near the trailhead of a popular hiking trail along the Manistee River. When Harper's family heard this news, they feared the worst. While Harper had been known to hike that trail on occasion, the circumstances were certainly strange, and they suspected foul play, as did the police. Although there was no sign of a struggle or forced entry, no damage to the automobile, the police suspected it was a robbery of some kind gone terribly wrong.

After that report in mid-August there was nothing for several months—nothing except one pitiful interview with Harper's wife in which she begged her fellow citizens not to give up hope and to continue the search for her missing husband. Although she offered a hefty reward, especially for that time, for any information about her husband or his whereabouts, her pleas apparently fell on deaf ears. They made no impact on a people who had already buried the story, along with so many others, and who didn't appreciate the pangs of unconscious fear and guilt it raised in them, like fog rising on a warm, sticky morning. The newspaper itself also buried the poor woman's story, placing it indiscreetly at the bottom of the fifth page out of seven, next to a story about a hotdog-eating contest.

The big break in the story came in late October. A local man named Nick Emery was out fishing on the Manistee River, not five miles from where Harper's abandoned car had been found. The fish weren't biting that day, and it was starting to get chilly out, so he had decided to give it one more try before packing it in and heading home. It was around six o'clock on the evening of October 30 when Emery cast his line out for one final shot.

Suddenly a wide grin spread over Emery's face as he thought he had a bite. His rod twitched in his hands and he jerked it up, trying to set his hook in whatever it was that was biting.

But alas it wasn't meant to be. Emery's hopes were dashed as he realized his line was just caught on some brush and driftwood in a little eddy on the near side of the river.

Emery jerked and jiggled his rod until it sprang free, bouncing up out of the water as he reeled it in with a clicking buzz. As the end of his line drew closer, he realized that he actually *had* caught something, but it was no fish.

Emery gasped in horror as he realized what it was: speared on the end of his fishing hook was a waterlogged human eyeball, white, filmy, and puffy. It was looking right at Emery when he instinctively flung his pole to the ground in fear and disgust. He screamed there on the bank of the Manistee River and then gagged and vomited on his shoes.

The police came and hauled the mutilated body of Dick Harper out of the river. The corpse, or what was left of it anyway, had been lodged between some thick branches and brush in the eddy on the west side of the river. The left arm was missing below the elbow, the right hand had been reduced to just a thumb and pinky, the right foot was gone, and the torso and left leg were badly chewed and decomposed, like a tree stump gnawed away by beavers. Harper's throat had been torn open, a gaping, wrinkled wound that had turned white and swollen as it soaked in the river. The tattered remains of his finest black suit clung dripping to what was left of his body. Harper's mouth was open wide, his tongue lolling out, in a final scream of fear and panic that had been frozen on his bloated face forever by rigor mortis. One eye socket was empty, its pearl plucked out by the hapless fisherman Nick Emery. The other eye was wide, a look of cloudy terror on it that matched the horrid scream on the corpse's face.

The police filed it as a homicide—yet another Northern Michigan murder that would go unsolved.

Nick Emery collected the cash reward that was offered for information about the disappearance of Dick Harper. Well, he only took half of it out of sympathy for the widow and the dead. In any case, he spent it on a new rod and reel, booze, and a new pair of shoes.

But he never fished the Manistee River again.

───────

Jack finished going through the 1927 papers at a feverish pace, shaking and spent. He had been scribbling furiously in his wire-bound notebook, taking notes and putting things together. Jack's research had hashed out the pattern, the bell curve of violent, frightening incidents that occurred each calendar year ending in a seven: starting out gradually in the spring, then exploding in intensity and frequency throughout the summer, and then finally tapering off as the fall turned to winter. Jack printed copies at ten cents a page of the most compelling articles, which he would later add to his father's collection of evidence in the old trunk in the barn loft. He could feel the obsession growing in him like a living organism—a virus, a tumor, a parasite—feeding on him, slowly consuming him and filling his soul with dread.

He packed up his things, dropped off the boxed microfilm reels at Nancy the archivist's desk, and left the Traverse Area District Library. He had a lot to think about on his drive home to LeRoy.

CHAPTER 10

Friday, September 1, 2017
LeRoy, Michigan

Classes at Ferris State had started back up on Monday, August 28, so the fall semester was off and running. Jack always likened the beginning of a semester to the beginning of a rollercoaster ride: things started out okay enough, but you were a little anxious and knew that the pace would pick up and that there'd be a big frightening drop before it was all over. But once you were on the ride, strapped into one of the cars, you couldn't get off until it was all over.

Jack was sipping coffee in his campus office, working on a lecture for his anthropology of religion course. They were covering E. E. Evans-Pritchard's classic *Witchcraft, Oracles and Magic among the Azande.* In the book, the author famously posits that witchcraft is both rational and logical, a system that explains unfortunate events, such as sickness, suffering, and death, and functions to alleviate stress and anxiety in the face of uncertainty and the inexplicable.

It was about four-thirty P.M., and Jack was wrapping

things up. He saved his PowerPoint, closed the book he was referencing, and tossed back the last sip of lukewarm coffee in his Bulldogs mug.

His cell phone rang.

Jack fumbled for it in his pocket, fished it out, and glanced at the screen. Usually, it was tricky telemarketing calls that always seemed to come from your own area code. But this time, it wasn't.

It was Jack's older brother Brad.

He swiped across the screen to take the call.

"Hey, Brad, what's up?"

"Hey, buddy, how are you?"

"I'm fine. Just finishing up a few things on campus. The semester started back up again this week."

"Nice," Brad said. "Look, I hate to ask, but I was wondering if you could do me a big favor? Please, Little Brother?" Brad sounded like a little kid begging his parents for dessert.

"Well, that depends on what it is, Big Brother."

"It's kind of a long story, but I got caught up in Grand Rapids and—"

"Everything okay?" Jack interjected, a hint of concern in his voice.

"Yeah, yeah, no worries, I just had to run down here this afternoon to pick up some stuff for my next contract. They're running late getting my order ready, that's all."

"Oh, gotcha."

"But see I got a call from the Thompsons last night. They said the power went out over at their new place, you know the one I just finished up for them out in Rose Lake Forest?"

"Yeah, sure."

"So anyway, they checked the fuse box, and that was all good, so they called the Sheriff's Department to report it, and the Sheriff's Department said they didn't have any other reports of outages in their area. So then Bill Thompson called up Consumers Energy, and *they* said there's nothing wrong on their end. Must be a hardware issue, they said. So Bill goes outside to check the breaker and the cables feeding it. He says one of them was severed; says it looks like something chewed right through it."

A cold shiver ran down Jack's spine.

"So I don't know if there's some rogue beaver chewing electrical cables up in Rose Lake Forest or what," Brad chuckled on the other end.

"Probably not a beaver..." Jack said. *Maybe a monster, though—a Dogman.* He pushed the thought out of his head.

"Anyway, I was hoping you might run by there for me on your way home and check it out. If that cable's beyond repair —and it sounds like it is—then I'll need to pick up a new one, and I might as well do that in town while I'm here anyway. Two birds, one stone, ya know?"

A deep amorphous dread settled in the pit of Jack's stomach. But he had decided months ago he would not live his life in fear of this thing, no matter what it was.

There was silence on the line.

"So... whaddya say, Brother?"

Sitting at his desk, Jack closed his eyes, rubbed them with both hands, and took a deep breath.

"Sure, Brad, no worries. I was just finishing up here anyway."

"Great!" Brad nearly shouted, relieved.

"I'll head out in a few minutes and give you a call back once I assess the damage."

"You're the best, Little Brother! I owe you a big wet kiss."

Jack smiled indulgently. "Yeah, I think I'll pass."

They both chuckled, and Jack hung up the phone.

Jack locked his computer, grabbed his messenger bag, and locked the office door behind him on his way out. He hit the stairs with that vague uncomfortable fear still percolating in his belly. It was hot and humid, breezy and overcast; a storm was coming. Jack crossed the parking lot to his Blazer. The wind rustled the big leathery green leaves on the trees lining the campus sidewalk.

He unlocked the Blazer and slid in, dumping his messenger bag in the seat next to him. He fired the engine, backed out of his parking spot, and left campus, headed for 131 North toward home.

It was about a half-hour drive from the Ferris State campus to home. Jack was anxious; his mind racing. He turned on the radio to take his mind off the task at hand. 98.1 WGFN-FM The Bear was playing "When the Levee Breaks," Led Zeppelin's dark, slithery, hypnotic reworking of Kansas Joe McCoy and Memphis Minnie's 1929 country blues classic about the turmoil caused by the Great Mississippi Flood of 1927. Jack sang along, doing his best Robert Plant impression, tapping his fingers on the steering wheel.

Seven more miles till the LeRoy exit, he thought. *I'm sure this is nothing. I'll go there, check it out, it'll be fine, no problem. Probably just a raccoon or a possum or something chewing on the cables.*

As he comforted himself, Jack pushed away the true thought that kept trying to surface in his mind: he had never known a raccoon or a possum that had a penchant for chewing electrical cables.

At the LeRoy exit, he flicked on his turn signal and pulled off the highway. His heart rate picked up a bit as the reality of the situation set in. Jack took a deep breath and bit his lower lip in grim determination. His hands tightened on the steering wheel. Each foot, each yard, each mile drew him closer to what might be a head-on collision with his worst fear. It felt as though the creature was calling to him, beckoning him, taunting him, *daring* him. He wondered if this is how his father felt ten years ago, and his grandfather and great-grandfather before that, and on and on back through time, across the generations. He wondered if the Dogman was the reason his father had left in the first place. The thought hit him like a cannonball to the stomach.

Jack looked at his reflection in the rear-view mirror. It was the face of someone he didn't recognize; a shadow, a ghost, someone from the distant past, someone with a secret. And for one unbearable, frightening moment, he saw an amber glow in his eyes, the all-consuming fire, and he realized they were *its* eyes, the eyes of the beast.

His breath caught in his throat, and he shook his head to break the hypnotic spell. His palms were sticky on the steering wheel and there was a thin gloss of sweat on his brow.

After a few minutes, Jack turned right onto 16 Mile Road. His heart pounded in his chest as he cruised along the undulating road. His turn signal came on again, and he turned right into Rose Lake Forest.

Then the beautiful new Thompson house was in front of him.

The garage door was closed, and nothing looked suspicious at first glance. Jack got out of his Blazer, cautiously made his way up the driveway, and peered into the garage through a small circular window. There were two cars parked in there and no sign of anything unusual.

Jack sighed. *Why am I working myself up about this? It's probably nothing, and I'm sure everything's fine. Quit being paranoid.*

He followed the concrete walkway around to the front porch and mounted the stairs.

His heart stopped as he saw that the front door was slightly open. He stopped dead in his tracks, and his eyes widened as his heart started pumping again, each beat echoing ominously in his head.

What the fuck? he thought. *Why the fuck is that door open?* He had no answers for a few dreadful moments, then his rational mind quickly began throwing out logical explanations for the door being open. *Come on, there are lots of reasons why that door might be cracked, aside from the old classic that a werewolf opened it. It's an entertaining idea, but pretty unlikely, wouldn't you say? Maybe they went for a walk and forgot to close it all the way. Maybe it still smells like paint and sawdust in there, and they cracked the door to air it out a bit. Maybe Bill Thompson is checking the cable around back right now and just left it open. Maybe...*

Jack remembered how to walk again and approached the door cautiously. He reached for the handle and pulled the door open halfway. He poked his head around the door and looked inside.

"Bill? Annie?" he called, a slight tremble in his voice. *"Bill?"* This time it was louder, more forceful. *"Annie?"*

Nothing.

No movement, no sound, except the gentle breeze outside caressing the leaves on the trees like conspirators whispering dark secrets.

Jack opened the door a bit more, and, like a ghost, he glided slowly into the house. He scanned the living room: a book lay opened on the coffee table next to a mug of tea still half-full.

"BILL?" he called again, louder still. No response, just the monotonous ticking of a mantel clock.

Jack continued through the living room into the open dining room and kitchen. He turned to his right, sweating, his breath coming in shallow gasps, and looked into the kitchen. A red plastic bowl with snowmen on it lay on the linoleum floor like a dead bug, a cascade of spilled potato chips scattered around it. His heart was beating up into his throat like it was trying to escape through his mouth.

He turned around and faced the dining room. On the carpet next to the dining table, a magazine lay open, as if it had been tossed or dropped in a hurry.

That's when he noticed the sliding glass door was open, wide enough for an adult to squeeze through. He stood there for a moment like a statue, his mouth suddenly dry and smooth.

"Annie? Bill?" he called again, still staring at the open sliding door. This time his voice was softer, less confident, scared.

He turned to his left and tiptoed through the dining room, slithering down the hall like a paranoid jumpy rabbit. He poked his head in the bathroom: nothing. He proceeded down the hallway. Each step seemed like a mile.

Jack peered into the room on his left. It was an office with a bookcase filled with books, a desk with a computer perched on it, a rolling office chair. But no sign of life. He continued on to the next room on his left at the end of the hall. It was a bedroom, maybe a guest room: a twin bed, a dresser, a bookshelf, a desk, a chair. Nothing out of the ordinary.

Jack turned and faced the final unchecked room across the hall from where he now stood. It was another bedroom, Bill and Annie's room. He poked his head in.

"Bill? Annie?" he called into the deafening silence.

He drew a sharp breath when he saw there was someone —or something—lying in bed. The covers were drawn up, but there was clearly someone under them.

"Bill?" he called, moving toward the bed.

Whatever was in there was completely covered with the navy-blue comforter. Jack reached his hand out slowly, his skin crawling, and gingerly pulled the comforter back.

The first thing he noticed was the blood. Dark red, almost black, blood soaked the pillow and sheets. He gasped and let out a thin croak. There was someone in there, all right, but he couldn't tell who. The body was headless, just empty shoulders and the tattered stump of a neck, torn-up purple-black flesh enveloping raw meat and tendons and the white of a severed spinal cord.

Jack screamed, a short guttural burst of primal fear.

He threw the comforter down like it was infested with snakes, his hands shaking, and backed away from the bed and its grisly inhabitant. As he moved away, something toppled off the bed and landed on the floor with a dull thud. It rolled over and came to rest at Jack's feet.

It was a head.

Jack screamed again as he stared down into the lifeless gaping blue eyes of Annie Thompson, a cloudy gray film cast over them, her blood-speckled face twisted into a final scream of terror.

Jack reeled and backed away, screaming until he was hoarse and breathless. He bolted for the bedroom door and hit the hallway at a run, his breath coming in shuddery gasps, his mouth opening and closing in a futile attempt to formulate a meaningful utterance. At that moment, Jack was incapable of speech, incapable of comprehending the horror he had just witnessed.

Then he found himself again in the dining room. He glanced quickly to his left, shaking uncontrollably, his heart pounding. Through the open sliding glass door, he noticed something he hadn't before. Blood. There were splotches of it on the patio just outside the door.

Jack felt like a man possessed as he floated to the sliding glass door, unconscious of the movement of his legs and feet, incapable of looking away, of turning and bolting for the door and safety, as any sane person would.

He reached out a shaky hand, a sickly feeling of déjà vu washing over him, and slid the door open a bit wider so he could get out. He was on the steps leading down to the concrete slab that was the Thompson's back patio. To the right stood a brand-new Weber gas grill, still shiny and clearly unused. The blood spatter was focused in front of Jack, who had descended the steps to the patio, and off to the left. He looked closer and noticed a print in one of the bloodstains: it was that of a large canine. He followed the blood trail with his eyes, which came to rest on the legs of a wicker dining table with four chairs around it.

Someone sat at the table.

It was Bill Thompson.

And he was dead.

His throat had been neatly cut. Actually, it looked more like his head had nearly been ripped off. A yawning purple wound stared back at Jack as if it was smiling, daring him to blink or scream. Bill's shirtfront was covered in blood, as was the tabletop and the half-drunk bottle of Budweiser standing on it. Blood dripped from the gaping neck wound down Bill's arms and off his fingertips onto the patio, pooling at his feet. His head had rolled back on his neck in an unnatural way so that the back of his skull was nearly touching his upper back between his shoulder blades. His wide eyes stared up at the overcast sky with a blank indifferent look, and his mouth hung open, his tongue sticking out of the corner of his mouth like a deer carcass hanging in a butcher's meat locker.

Jack stood there, gaping at the ghastly scene in front of him. He was unable to scream. Suddenly he felt like he was unable to breathe. His breath was coming in short gasps, and he feared he might hyperventilate.

He wheeled around, his jaw clenched, and shot back to the sliding glass door. He mounted the stairs in one high-stepping stride and was back in the dining room, his chest heaving, a layer of cold sweat covering his body. He looked at the front door, and his face turned a ghastly shade of gray as he noticed that it was wide open now. Then he heard a noise coming from down the hall, back toward the bedrooms.

He froze.

For a moment, he felt as if he was unable to move, like his feet were attached to the floor by some black magic like some demonic energy was calling to him, beckoning him, and he was unable to resist its infernal allure. He listened but heard nothing save the constant ticking of the mantel clock in the living room.

There it was again, that noise. There was something back there lurking in one of the rooms, stirring.

Jack fled the house.

He sat in his SUV with the doors locked, fumbling in his jeans pocket for his car keys. His heart was pounding harder than he had ever imagined it could. He feared it might burst out of his mouth at any minute, like projectile vomit, and land on the dashboard with a wet thud. His eyes were glued to the open front door of the Thompson house. Then he had his keys in his hand. He thrust them into the ignition.

A shadow was suddenly visible on the carpet through the frame of the Thompson's open front door. It was tall, and it was growing by the second, creeping closer.

Jack turned the key in the ignition. The engine spluttered and wheezed but didn't turn over.

FUCK! Jack's mind screamed in fear and desperation.

The approaching shadow now nearly filled the doorway.

Jack tried the engine again.

This time it came to life with a satisfying *VROOM.*

The car was in reverse in a millisecond, burning rubber down the driveway. The tires squealed as Jack whipped the steering wheel to the left. Shifting into drive, Jack nailed the accelerator and sped away from the grisly scene, the massacre in Rose Lake Forest he had just witnessed.

He did not look back.

Jack Allen had just seen something so terrible he couldn't comprehend it. Yet he couldn't shake the gory images of the tattered bodies of Bill and Annie Thompson. Every time he closed his eyes, he saw them, saw their glazed dead eyes, saw the final scream etched forever on Annie's face and the look of complete calm on Bill's face as he sat there dead in his patio chair with his throat torn out.

Jack flew down 16 Mile Road, headed for the Osceola County Sheriff's Office in Reed City. He didn't know where else to go, and he sure as hell wasn't going to stick around and face whatever the fuck that had been in the doorway and end up dead like Bill and Annie. And all the rest of them.

"No," he suddenly said out loud, squeezing the wheel so hard his knuckles turned white. *I know what that fucking thing was. It's no mystery. It was a fucking Dogman! That's what it was, and I'm gonna call it like it is from now on. No more pretending this all isn't happening, or these killings aren't connected. No more pretending that it's some psycho man who's behind it, either. It's no man. Well, it's part man. It's the Dogman, that's for sure, but just what the fuck is a Dogman?*

Jack grabbed his cell phone and called 911.

"911, what's your emergency?"

"There's been a break-in and a—" Jack paused, choking on the words. "A murder. Out at the new Thompson place. 1216 Rose Lake Forest Road in LeRoy. Both of them… Bill and Annie… they're both—" Jack swallowed hard, fighting back the urge to cry. "Dead."

"This is a double homicide situation, sir?"

"I'm not sure. All I know is they're both dead. Could've been an animal attack."

"Are you currently at the scene, sir?"

"No, I couldn't stay. I was… scared. I'm on my way to the Sheriff's Department in Reed City to talk to Sheriff Dearborn about it."

"We'll send someone out to the house right away."

Jack gave the emergency dispatcher his contact information and hung up.

The sky was darkening, and Jack heard the low rumble of thunder in the distance. It started to sprinkle. By the time he had driven through LeRoy and was approaching the highway, the rain was coming down steadily, his windshield wipers swishing back and forth rhythmically like a pendulum.

Next, he dialed the Osceola County Sheriff's Office.

"Osceola County Sheriff's Office, how can I help you?" a pleasant voice said on the other end.

"I need to speak to Sheriff Dearborn, please."

"I'm afraid he's in a meeting at the moment. Can I take a message?"

"Tell him Jack Allen is heading to his office and needs to speak with him immediately. It's a matter of great concern."

"I will, Mr. Allen. Sheriff Dearborn has an opening in his schedule and should be available in a half hour. I'll mark you down."

"Thank you." Jack hung up the phone.

He called his brother Brad next.

"Jack! What's the damage, Little Brother?"

"It's bad, Brad… really bad."

"Oh shit, it's worse than just a damaged cable, isn't it? What'd, the breaker blow?"

"They're dead, Brad."

"*What?* You mean the cables? Oh, that's not—"

"They're *DEAD!*" Jack almost screamed, slamming his fist on the steering wheel. "Bill, Annie, they're both fucking dead. I found them. Torn to pieces—by the Dogman."

There was an audible gasp on the other end. "The *Dogman?* What's that, like a werewolf or something? Jack, Bro, take it easy, you've been through a lot. This has been traumatic, for sure, but let's not jump to conclusions. You can't just go around telling people that a werewolf ki—"

"DOGMAN!" Jack growled. "I'm gonna start calling it like it is, and I'm gonna tell Sheriff Dearborn what's going on. I saw a print, Brad, a huge canine print. It's real, Brad. It's fucking real, and it's killing people." A tense silence. "I saw a shadow too, Brad. In the house. It was *there.* I could have ended up dead just like Bill and Annie."

"Jesus," Brad exhaled, shaking his head in amazement. "Jack, I believe you. You know I do. You're my brother, for God's sake." He paused. "But you can't go burstin into Sheriff Dearborn's office raving like a madman about some Dogman! You just can't, Jack. Think about it, man. You don't want to end up in the looney bin. Folks round here can't handle that. They'd go lookin for a scapegoat. I don't want you to end up that way, Brother."

Jack's resolve was beginning to break. "Maybe you're right."

"Just wait a while and think it over. Let things settle down a bit. Don't jump to conclusions. Why don't we get together and talk it over, come up with a plan?"

"Yeah, maybe you're right," Jack sighed, rain drizzling across his windshield as the wipers kept up their happy dance. "Okay, I won't mention it. I'll think of something else to say to Dearborn. But this is real, Brad, as crazy as it fucking sounds, and maybe we're the only ones who can do something about it—who can put a stop to it. We need to get together and figure out a plan and fast."

Brad agreed. He said he'd stop by the farm later when he got back from Grand Rapids. They said their goodbyes, and Jack hung up the phone.

Jack was getting close to the Reed City exit now. He had one more call to make, the most important one, to his wife. As he called Claire's cell number, he was suddenly seized by a fear that had somehow evaded him until that moment. What if the Dogman is still on the loose and shows up at the farm? A hot bolt of fear shot through his body as Claire picked up the phone.

"Hey, dear," she said.

"Babe, where are you? Are you at home?"

"Yeah… what's up?" Now she sounded alarmed, which was not Jack's intention. In fact, it was the opposite: he *didn't* want Claire to be scared or suspicious, which is why he decided not to tell her about what happened over at the Thompson place until he was home and could do it in person.

"Oh, nothing too serious, babe. Sorry, I didn't mean to scare you. It's just, there's been another animal attack, so I wanted to make sure you and Mel were okay. Can you keep the doors locked tight for me?"

"Yeah, sure, Jack. Where are you?"

"Oh, I'm finishing up some things at the office," he lied. "Sorry, I'm running late. Beginning of the semester paperwork. I'll be home in an hour or so. You and Mel eat if you get hungry and don't feel like waiting for me for supper."

"Okay. Drive safe."

"Will do. Love you."

"Love you too."

Jack hung up the phone just as he was approaching the Reed City exit. He got off the highway, turned east, and continued for a few miles, turning into the Osceola County Sheriff's Office as the rain poured down from the gray sky.

The levee had broken wide open.

PART III

RECKONING

CHAPTER 11
FALL: SEPTEMBER 2017

Friday, September 1, 2017
Leroy, Michigan

As Jack walked up to the door of the Osceola County Sheriff's Department in the rain, he suddenly realized how shaken he was. Fuck that, he was horrified and traumatized. He began to tremble and drew in a sharp shuddery breath. Tears welled up inside him and he squeezed his eyes shut, trying desperately to hold off the emotional storm that was brewing. He stopped and put a steadying hand on the bricks beside the door of the Sheriff's Department. Jack breathed in and out deeply, trying to calm his shattered nerves. After a few minutes, he collected himself and walked through the door.

An officer sat at the front desk and nodded when Jack came in.

"Jack Allen here to see Sheriff Dearborn."

"Have a seat," the young officer said. "He should be ready for you in a few minutes."

"Thanks," Jack plopped down heavily in one of the chairs that lined the wall opposite the long reception desk.

"Coffee?"

"No, thanks," Jack replied with a thin, forced smile. *I'm jittery enough as is,* he thought.

A couple minutes later, the office door to Jack's left swung open, and Sheriff John Dearborn lumbered out. He was a good-natured man, heavy-set, fair, and honest. By nature, he was a gentle soul, quick to smile, but you didn't want to get on his bad side. Luckily Jack and his family had a long, pleasant history with the Dearborn family, but he had heard that Sheriff Dearborn had a nasty temper when pushed.

"Jack Allen!" he said, reaching out a hand. Jack took it, and Dearborn pumped it vigorously. "How are ya, my boy? How's your mother doing?"

"Fine, Sheriff, she's doing just fine. Me, on the other hand, I'm not doing so well."

A cloud passed over Dearborn's face. "What's going on, Jack?" he asked, his head cocking to one side.

"We better talk in your office, Sheriff."

"Have a seat," Dearborn said, pointing with his lips to a chair in front of his desk. He closed the door behind them.

Jack sat and folded his hands together under his chin, looking grave.

"Well, Jack, you look like you just saw a ghost."

"Not a ghost." *A fucking Dogman,* he thought. "You better send an officer or two over to the new Thompson place in Leroy. Over in Rose Lake Forest. Bill and Annie are dead."

Dearborn's eyes widened. "Dead? How?"

"I'm not sure," Jack lied. "Looks like another animal attack." He sighed. "Either that or there's some psycho out there slitting people's throats and cutting off heads." His voice faltered as he spoke, the images of those lifeless bodies swimming up into his consciousness again, overpowering him.

"What?" Dearborn was stunned. "How do you know? Does anyone else know?"

"I know because I saw them," Jack said measuredly. "Brad called me at work this afternoon, about five o'clock, asked me if I could run over there to check on something. Said he'd had a call the night before from Bill Thompson saying the power had gone out. The cable had been chewed clean through by something." Jack had a sinking feeling in his stomach. His mouth was dry.

"Yeah, Burns took a call from Bill last night. Told me about it this mornin."

"Brad's in town today getting supplies, and so he asked me to check it out and report back so he could pick up anything else he might need to fix it. He had just finished up their place for them, you know." Dearborn nodded, a severe look in his eyes, a mix of concern and confusion. "So I went over there; got there a little after five. The front door was open. I called for them several times. No answer. I went in and looked around. Didn't see anything too out of the ordinary except a bowl of chips spilled on the floor. Then I noticed the back sliding door was open too. I went down the hall calling for them. Still no answer." Jack stopped, drew in a deep breath, and put his hand over his eyes, massaging his temples before he continued. "Then I found Annie dead in her bed."

He looked up at Sheriff Dearborn.

"Jesus fuckin Christ." Dearborn looked like he'd been hit by a train.

"That's not all… I ran out of there, but then I saw blood on the back patio." *And a huge paw print in the blood like a rubber stamp, like a fucking calling card from hell,* he thought. "I walked out back… and found Bill dead, slumped back in a patio chair." Jack sighed. This time he didn't look up.

Sheriff Dearborn's expression was one of utter disbelief.

"What the fuck..." he stammered, trailing off. "Did you call 911?"

"Yes."

"Jack, my boy," Dearborn said, shaking his head. "You left the scene of a crime—unless'n it turns out to be an animal again. Either way, that's *not good.* We've got two dead bodies on our hands. It looks suspicious."

"I know how it looks," Jack muttered.

"You're puttin me in a bad spot here, Jack."

"I know, I know."

"Why the hell'd you leave the scene and come all the way down here to talk to me anyway?"

"Well," Jack said, thinking on his feet. "First of all, I was damned scared. But I *was* gonna stick around and wait for the authorities, but then I heard something rustling around in their house." Dearborn looked at Jack, eyes wide, mouth open, hanging on his every word. "Whatever it was that killed 'em was *still in the house,* and well, I guess I didn't feel like waiting around to shake its hand... or paw." That last bit slipped out, but luckily for Jack, it didn't seem to register or stick with Sheriff Dearborn, who was still sitting there in stunned silence, mouth agape.

"Jesus fuckin Christ," he said again, shaking his head.

"So, to answer your second question, I came here to see you because I didn't know where the hell else to go and because you're the goddamn sheriff around here and because I want to see an end to these damn killings, these damn animal attacks."

This was all true. Jack *did* come to Reed City to see Sheriff Dearborn because he didn't know what else to do, and he *did* want to see an end to the killings; and they *were* the result of animal attacks—of some kind or another, depending on how you look at it and depending on whether or not this thing is flesh and blood or some kind of supernatural phantom. Whatever it is, it *did* pull Bill Thompson's throat out and sever Annie Thompson's head, so Jack tended to think it was a physical being, at least on some level.

Suddenly Jack felt emboldened. "Does the seventh year mean anything to you, Sheriff?"

"Huh?" There was a puzzled look in Dearborn's eyes, but somewhere, way back there in the black depths, Jack thought he saw a momentary flash of recognition.

"What about the cycle?" Jack said.

Another confused look from Sheriff Dearborn. Suddenly it dawned on him, and his face brightened. "Oh, you mean the global warmin!" Dearborn was glad to have made the connection. "Err, sorry, climate change, whatever goddamned thing they're callin it nowadays."

"Climate change didn't kill Dave Beckett."

A sudden palpable tension filled the room. Dearborn squeezed his eyes shut and visibly shuddered. In his mind's eye, he went back to the scene of the killing, seeing his reflection again in the ghastly gelatinous mirror of Dave Beckett's congealed blood pooled in his opened stomach cavity.

"A lotta weird things happening around here lately," Jack said, easing the tension.

"Yeah, we've all noticed," Dearborn drawled. "Maybe it *is* the global warmin, the climate change, whatever it is. Been extremes all year long—cold winter without much snow and summer's been hotter'n hell! Lots of rain too. It's got the animals all stirred up. The people too, if'n ya ask me."

Jack was bemused, despite his traumatized state. He had known John Dearborn and his family for many years, generations even, and Jack knew they weren't the sort of folk to speak of climate change, not in a million years actually. It was then that Jack realized just how desperate Sheriff Dearborn must be to solve the mysterious happenings plaguing Northern Michigan that year. It suddenly made Jack nervous, thinking back to what his brother had said on the phone about scapegoats.

As if he had read his mind, at that moment, Dearborn squinted suspiciously under his furry eyebrows at Jack. "Well, Jack," he began. "I've known you and your family a long time. A real long time. I trust you, and I don't see any reason to suspect you in any of this—at this point anyway." He nodded and wagged his finger at Jack. "But if'n my detectives come up with anything at the crime scene that's fishy and points to you, all bets are off. Nothing personal. Hope you understand."

"I do, Sheriff, of course."

"You seem pretty shaken up, and for good reason, so I'm gonna let ya go home to Claire now. But I'll be needin to question ya officially about this later. Monday mornin, let's say, assuming there's no surprises at the scene. And I'll need a statement from ya on this too."

"Absolutely, Sheriff. Anything I can do to help. Thank you."

Sheriff Dearborn stood up and offered his hand. Jack rose from his chair, and the two men shook hands, their eyes locked in a solemn gaze.

"Try to get some rest, son. You've been through a lot today."

"Thank you, sir." Jack's voice cracked a bit.

"And say hi to your mother for me."

Jack barely made it to his car before he broke down.

He sobbed all the way home, wiping his eyes with the back of his hand and reliving what had happened that day, unable to shake the images of the bloody corpses of Bill and

Annie Thompson. His tears fell like the rain outside, neither of which would let up, and left streaks on his cheeks, his shoulders heaving up and down with the pregnant weight of the emotions welled up inside him. The levee had broken, oh yes. The flood was upon him, overwhelming him. He was submerged under water, under the weight of it all, drowning, thrashing to stay afloat.

As he wept, Jack realized he hadn't cried since his father left ten years before. This realization sent him into new fits of tearful sorrow.

The moment Jack walked through the door around six-thirty P.M., Claire could see that something was terribly wrong. A look of confused concern mingled with fear spread across her face as Jack locked and bolted the door and closed and locked all the windows on the screened-in porch. Finally, he took his shoes off and came into the kitchen.

"Daddy!" Melanie said. She sat at the dinner table. "Look what Mommy gave me for dessert Daddy," she said, displaying a plastic cup of chocolate milk with both hands. She had a prominent chocolate-milk mustache on her upper lip.

"Is that..." he paused for effect. "CHOCOLATE MILK?! *No way!*"

"Yes, Daddy, it is! Good guess!" She took a loud careful slurp. "It's yummy."

Jack went to her and hugged her with a fierceness he hadn't anticipated. He kissed her on the top of her head, and the smell of her hair brought on a new wave of emotion. He squeezed his eyes shut and could taste salty tears in the back of his throat.

He went to Claire next as she searched his eyes pleadingly. He hugged her tight.

"Jack?" she said, her voice so full of care and concern it

almost made him break down again. But after his car ride home, it seemed he had no more tears left to cry. "What is it?"

He broke off the embrace, and she searched his eyes again, holding both of his shoulders lovingly.

"I'll tell you later, once Mel's down," he said, pointing with a sideways nod at their daughter sitting at the table finishing her dessert.

He hugged her again and buried his face in her neck as she stroked his hair, her chin resting on his head. They fit well together, like a ball in a socket.

"Let me get you something to eat," she said.

Although he wasn't in the least bit hungry, Jack sat down at the kitchen table next to Melanie and looked at her. Then Claire put a plate of food down in front of him: a baked chicken leg and thigh, some mashed potatoes, and a mess of cooked vegetables. She pulled a cold beer out of the fridge, opened it, and set it in front of him. He smiled up at her, and she smiled back, patting him on his shoulders. In that moment, Jack loved her so exquisitely it was painful. Claire carried him—she was everything. He silently thanked God for her.

While Mel told her daddy about her day, Jack picked at his food distractedly. He had no appetite for the solids that evening, but the beer tasted better, cold and fizzy. Jack drank one down, and Claire brought him another. He looked pale and sweaty.

"So theeeennnn," Melanie said, drawing the last word out for dramatic effect. "We watched *Hercules,* and I had pretzels and raisins, and Mommy let me watch *the entire movie."* Her eyes widened as she looked at Jack. He smiled.

"I love you."

"I love you, too, Daddy."

Jack insisted on putting Melanie down for bed that night. He did so like a man savoring his last day before going away to war, drawing each moment out as long as he possibly could and then wringing it out to make sure he didn't waste a single drop. After three stories (usually they only read one or two), he tucked his little girl in; hugged her tight, tight, tight; and kissed her on the lips, then the cheek, then the forehead where it meets her hairline, savoring each one. As he backed away toward the door, he had to again fight off the urge to cry.

"Goodnight, my sweetheart."

"Goodnight, Daddy. I love you."

"I love you too, Mel. So, so much. Sleep tight. See you in the morning. Goodnight."

He blew her a kiss, and she blew one back to him. He waved to her as he gently pulled the door closed. Jack stood outside his daughter's door and breathed deeply for a few minutes before descending the stairs back down to the living room.

Claire sat on the couch waiting for him.

"Jack, what's going on?" She looked concerned, scared.

Jack sat down on the couch next to her and told her everything that had happened to him since he left work that afternoon—well, almost everything. He didn't get into all the gory details because he didn't want to scare and upset Claire any more than she already was. When he got to the end of his story, tears streamed down Claire's face, and she looked at her husband with a look of deep compassion mixed with sadness, uncertainty, and fear. They held hands as Jack spoke, but now they embraced, a hard, full embrace, each leaning on the other for support and succor. They needed to combine their strength to face this new atrocity.

"God, Jack, what's going on around here lately?" she said

in short gasps, practically crying, thinking of Dave and Barbara Beckett.

"I'm not sure, babe," he soothed, holding her. It wasn't exactly a lie. She was shaking. "As long as we have each other, we'll make it through, I promise."

"So Sheriff Dearborn thinks it's another animal attack?"

"Yeah, that's what he said."

It broke Jack's heart not to tell her more, but he had his reasons to keep his ideas and convictions about the Dogman to himself—for now anyway. For one thing, he didn't want to scare her or—even worse—Melanie. For another, he didn't think she'd believe him and think him crazy. And finally, Jack didn't want to broach the topic of the Dogman until he'd had a chance to discuss it with Brad and the cousins. They needed a comprehensive plan, a unified front if they were going to put a stop to all this.

"And do you believe that?" Claire looked up at him.

"Huh?" Jack mumbled, lost in his own thoughts. He shook his head as if to clear it.

"Do you think it's some rogue animal that's doing all this? Maybe a bear that's acquired a taste for blood or something, I don't know... A cougar with rabies?" Her brows drew together, trying to make sense of things.

"I don't really know what I think right now," Jack said, wincing on the inside because he wasn't being totally honest with her. "I mean..." he sighed. "What else could it be?"

Jack and Claire talked for a while longer and made a plan to keep all the doors and windows locked for the time being until things calmed down. Jack said he would cancel his office hours for a few weeks and work from home more. They also agreed to limit their time outdoors, especially in the woods and at night. As a last resort, he reminded Claire of the shotgun he kept locked in a case under their bed. An extra key was in his nightstand drawer.

Jack told her to try not to worry about it. What happened to the Thompsons was a heartbreaking accident, a once-in-a-lifetime tragedy, and the chances of anything like that happening again in their lifetimes was slim. As he said this, he thought about the seventh-year cycle and all that he knew about Dogman attacks and killings. Not telling Claire what he knew felt like a heavy weight on his chest that pushed a lump up into his throat, but he reassured himself that it was for the best—for now anyway.

"But are *you* doing okay?" she had asked, her eyes red and puffy.

He sighed. "Yeah, I think I'm okay. Brad's coming over here tonight to talk it over, so that'll be good. And thank God I have you on my team."

He hugged her tight and kissed her forehead. Claire poured herself a glass of wine and turned on the television, trying to take her mind off things. Jack opened another beer and sat on the couch next to his wife for a half-hour longer.

Then Brad pulled up in his truck.

Jack went out to the screened-in porch to meet his brother, who looked visibly shaken as he entered the farmhouse. They hugged and patted each other on the back, neither said a word. Brad's eyes were red when he pulled away, and tracks of tears were visible on Jack's cheeks, even though he thought it impossible that he had anything left to cry. He was dried up inside.

Brad said hello to Claire, and they hugged. No one had much to say; they just comforted each other with loving gestures rather than words.

Jack and Brad went out to the porch to talk.

"How about a beer?" Brad said, sitting down at the picnic table on the screened-in porch.

"I think I need something a little stronger than that," Jack said. "Bourbon?"

Brad nodded, and Jack went to the kitchen, returning with two glasses filled with ice and a bottle of Jack Daniels. He poured a shot or two in each and handed one to Brad. They raised their glasses, looking solemnly into each other's eyes. Jack sighed, then they each took a deep gulp.

So it began.

Brad sat in disbelief, listening to the details again, as they both downed several drinks. As unhealthy as it was, at that moment, the bourbon helped them cope with the trauma they were experiencing. Jack told his brother about all the strange things that had happened that year, especially since the summer began—*everything*.

Jack even started to get into the strange connections between their family and the Dogman, his strange feelings of relation to or oneness with the creature that he didn't quite understand and couldn't quite express. There was some mad connection there; he was sure of it but couldn't put his finger on it. As the bourbon flowed, he started to wonder aloud about the nature of the beast, the liquor dissolving away any doubt he had about its existence or the reality of it. Was there just one, or were they legion? Jack felt that there were multiple Dogmen, like some demonic species born to kill. Was it a creature of flesh and blood, or was it a spirit being? Or was it somehow both? These thoughts coursed through Jack's head, surging like high-voltage electricity, and came directly out of his mouth, more or less unedited.

As Brad listened, bourbon in hand, he grew increasingly terrified—not just of what his brother told him, but also because he realized he could no longer deny it. And the implications of that realization or admission were enormous and far-reaching and unequivocally horrifying.

Eventually, he had to call it off. Jack had just covered the details of his meeting with Sheriff Dearborn, and Brad knew they needed a plan. They needed to come together with the boys, the six cousins, and figure out what the fuck they were going to do about this. And they needed to act quickly.

They needed a story to tell so they could keep the cops and everyone else at bay and pursue a course of action that might actually make a difference. Believing blindly that animals stirred up by climate change were responsible for the killings that year in Northern Michigan was not going to stop the killings. But maybe, just maybe, the six of them could figure out a way together to slow it down, or perhaps even kill the Dogman... if that was even possible.

Right then and there, Brad sent out an urgent text message to all of them—Jack, Brad, Pat, Russ, Jay, and Rick—calling for an emergency meeting. There was a family crisis, and everyone needed to be represented, to be present if there was any hope to overcome it. More details would come at the meeting, which would be Saturday or Sunday, depending on everyone's schedules. They would meet in the barn, just like when they were kids.

Even though it was late, all four responded within a half hour.

Pat, the eldest of the six, responded first, writing: *I'm in. When?* Next was Rick: *Me too, of course. This is fucked up. What's going on? I can make it either day.* Brad responded then, writing: *How about tomorrow at four o'clock?* Pat and Rick both responded in the affirmative. Then a message from Jay came through: *Definitely. I'm with you guys.* Finally, last but not least, Russ responded: *I'll see you there, Bros.*

The fateful meeting of the Allen cousins was set in motion early in September. They didn't realize it then, but there was nothing they could do to stop it now, to break the momentum, to undo the chain of events they had set in motion. They were now on an immovable collision course with their own history and their deepest, darkest fears embodied in the shape of a horrible demon monster, the Dogman.

It had to be stopped, once and for all.

The Allens had just started the ball rolling.

All they could do now was sit back and wait for fate to run its course.

Jack and Claire hardly slept that night. Brad went home to Nellie at their cabin on Rose Lake. Jack fell into a thin sleep, eventually dropping down deeper into a horrible dream about blood, death, and dogs that walked like men and screamed. He woke up with a start, the image of the beast's face clear in his mind, a thin layer of cold sweat covering his body and soaking the sheets.

The cousins arrived the next day, starting to roll in around 3:45. The day had been somber and tense at the Allen farm, but Jack and Claire did their best to keep their apprehensions from Mel, who thankfully seemed oblivious to what was going on. For Jack, four o'clock couldn't come soon enough. He was ready to get things off his chest and start something. He told Claire the boys were coming over to discuss the animal attacks, which was true; he didn't tell her anything about the Dogman—not yet anyway.

Pat and his wife Pam arrived first, along with their two little girls, Jackie and Nancy. Pat and Pam lived in the suburbs of Grand Rapids, about an hour's drive from LeRoy. When they turned into the driveway in their Chevrolet Suburban, Melanie literally squealed with joy. She was *very* excited to see them and couldn't stop talking about it all day. They piled out of the Suburban, and Mel ran up to the girls full of excitement. They busied themselves playing with Mel's play kitchen and water table on the front patio, laughing without a care in the world in that magical way only children can. The contrast between their carefree behavior and Jack's anxious, stifling fears could not have been starker.

Pat and Jack embraced, as did Pam and Claire. Then they switched, each hugging the other. A few quiet words of greeting and encouragement were spoken, but everyone was subdued.

As they greeted each other, Russ and his wife Elizabeth arrived. They parked down by the old pear tree just northwest of the house and came up and joined the others on the patio, repeating the same greeting rituals.

Next to arrive was Rick in his green Jeep Cherokee. He and his wife Mary had a three-month-old baby girl, and she stayed back home in Grand Rapids with the little one. Then came Rick's older brother Jay. He and his wife Beverly had also just had a new arrival, so Bev and their baby girl stayed home in Grand Rapids. Rick and Jay's father Clark lived in LeRoy in a nice cabin on Rose Lake, two doors down from Brad and Nellie, so Rick and Jay stayed with their dad and stepmother when they came up north.

Finally, Brad came rolling up in his Chevy Silverado just past five o'clock, nursing a hangover and smoking a Winston. He cocked his head and grinned at everyone through squinty bloodshot eyes. He had a way of lightening the mood, even in dire times such as these.

Now the six were together, the fellowship was sealed. Each of them felt something strange they couldn't explain once they were all together on that cement patio in front of the old farmhouse where they had spent so much of their childhood. It felt like the beginning of something, for sure; something frightening but also something *right,* something preordained, something that was meant to be. They all felt it then. It was undeniable, scary, powerful. It made them giggle a little, but mostly it gave them a reverent feeling that made them all fall silent, nervously shuffling their feet and looking at the ground. The gang was back together and for an urgent reason. A spell had been cast; a bond had been mysteriously forged then that overlay the close bond that already existed between the six Allen cousins. It was strong, sacred. The time for action was upon them and the only direction to go was forward, onward. No looking back now.

Pam, Claire, and Elizabeth went inside the three girls in tow. They were going to make dinner for the crew while the girls played with Mel's Barbies and read books.

The six cousins descended the gravel driveway to the old red barn in devout silence, a thousand long-buried memories flashing through their heads, wondering what the future might hold.

They stood and sat around the barn, some with their hands stuffed in their pockets, others smoking cigarettes, some looking Jack straight in the face, others gazing down at the straw-strewn barn floor. Jack had filled a cooler with beers, and they each cracked one open. All of them listened intently as Jack told his tale. Occasionally one of the cousins interjected or asked a clarifying question or just sighed or gasped in terror and disbelief, but for the most part, they just let Jack speak. And speak he did, laying out all the spine-chilling details of what had happened that seventh year, along with all that he had learned about seventh years of the past, of the beast, the cycle, the family connection, all of it.

When he had finished, they all stood in stunned silence for a few minutes, shaking their heads and forming words with their mouths that they couldn't voice. It was Russ who finally broke the silence.

"Okay..." Russ found his voice, but his train of thought veered off the tracks once he opened his mouth. "God, this is all so fucking unbelievable... and yet I *believe* it. I *know* it's true. I know it's true because I've *seen* it. I've seen it too!" His eyes were wide. It was cathartic for him to come out and say it, and when he did, a stunned Jack noticed a look of relief on the others' faces.

And there was something else—*recognition.*

"The one that really stuck with me was when I was out hunting in 2007," Russ began. "But if I think back, there have been other strange things that have happened to me in the woods over the years. I guess I just dismissed them because I convinced myself that it wasn't possible; you know, like how you forget about a bad dream when you wake up or something. Anyway, in 2007 I was out hunting on Uncle Rob's property on the other side of the road. It was bow season, and I musta been twenty-three at the time. I remember it was close to Halloween, which is probably why I buried it and convinced myself it wasn't real. I figured I had just spooked myself out; gotten too into the Halloween spirit or something." Russ flashed an embarrassed smile. "So I'm up in this tree stand overlooking the field by the crackleberry swamp. It's about quarter to five, and dusk is setting in. It had been a normal night—I hadn't seen much; the birds were chirping away. All of a sudden, the birds stop chirping, and everything gets dead quiet and still. There's not a damn thing moving out there. So I look down into the clearing in front of me and see two does and a buck walk out, real skittish-like. I get my bow up, arrow notched, and then I notice this really foul smell, like a musky, earthy scent, like rot and decay, and it's *strong*. Really strong. So I'm looking around, and I see this thing come walking out from the swamp," he looked down at his arms, which had turned to gooseflesh, the hair on them sticking straight up. He held his arm out to the others. "See? It still gives me goosebumps just thinking about it. Anyway, the sight of this thing freezes my heart. I'm gasping. I feel like I'm having a heart attack. I'd never seen anything like it. At least I thought I hadn't. But after hearing your story Jack I'm beginning to put some things together and wondering if maybe I have seen it before. But not as clearly as that day in October."

"What'd it look like?" Brad asked, puffing on a cigarette with a shaky hand. Somehow it seemed like he already knew the answer.

"It was big but slim... tall. Like six feet tall, at least. And it was standing on two legs, up on its hind legs. It had dark brown fur, but it wasn't a bear. No, it was more canine, like some kind of mutant dog or wolf or something. Its back was sort of hunched over, and it had upright pointed ears. It was sort of stalking those deer, I guess, walking up to them, quiet as death, and they didn't know it was there. And that *smell!* God, it was awful. Thick, pungent. I was trying not to gag." Russ shook his head in disgust at the olfactory memory. "Then those deer they spooked all of a sudden, and this thing just *sprang* after em. I'd never seen anything like it. It was so fast and agile, *and on two legs!* So it chases them through the clearing, and it eventually drops down onto all fours and was bounding after those deer like hell, chasing em off into the woods. Then it was gone, and I just sat up there in the tree stand shaking and scratching my head." He shrugged. "I waited for a while cuz I was scared, tell you the truth, but I eventually climbed down and made it back to my truck. But that was a scary walk, let me tell ya."

Russ sighed then sipped at his beer. No one said a word. Just as Jack was about to say something, Jay stepped forward. He looked over at his younger brother Rick and the two of them locked eyes for a moment, sharing an uneasy look. Then Rick sighed and nodded slowly.

"So we had a similar experience," Jay began. "Actually, like you, Russ, now that I think of it, I've probably had a few, but this is the one that sticks out to me." He drained the last of his beer and went over to the cooler and fished out another one, cracking it open with his lighter. "This happened when Rick and I were going for a trail ride on the golf cart back in 1997, during the summer, maybe July. We were out on the Back Forty, just passed Cherry Ridge. It was late in the afternoon, still light out. Hot. Humid. I remember the blackflies buzzing all around us. Same kind of thing you just described, Russ. All of a sudden, there's this awful smell. I joked with Rick and said he needed to change his diet." He chuckled uneasily, looking over at his brother.

"Then Rick pats me on the shoulder, and he's pointing over to the south, toward the cedar swamp. His face was pale as a sheet. So my heart starts pumpin, and I look over toward where he's pointin. Maybe fifty, sixty yards back where the swamp begins, just off the trail, I see this dark shape, this figure, standing next to a tree. I guess later I convinced myself it was a man—but it was no man. I guess even later I convinced myself—*we* convinced ourselves," he motioned toward Rick, "that it never happened, that we imagined it…" Jay trailed off and looked up into the rafters. "It was just like you said, Russ. Big, tall, dark fur, hunched over, pointy ears. Scary as hell." Jay was silent for a minute as the rest of them shook their heads, not knowing what to say.

"I looked back, but it was gone," Rick said, leaning up against a workbench. "We were so young, we figured no one would believe us. We were scared that night, but I think by the time we ate lunch the next day we had already convinced ourselves it couldn't have been real. Musta been a shadow, our eyes playin tricks on us, ya know?" His lips were drawn so tightly together they were white. "Can I bum a cig, Brad?"

Brad pulled a Winston out of his pack and tossed it to Rick, followed by a red BIC lighter. Rick fired up the cigarette and took a long drag, exhaling the smoke out of his mouth. He tossed the lighter back to Brad.

Jay and Rick's story reminded Jack of what he had seen out in the deep cedar swamp near the marshes that time they were playing the Game. He told them about it, keeping it brief so the others could talk too.

Pat shared a story about an experience he'd had down at the barn one night in 1997. He was at the farmhouse with Grandma and Grandpa. It was later, maybe ten P.M., and it was October, so it was already pretty dark. Grandpa asked him to run down to the barn and turn the light off. Said he forgot to turn it off that evening, and while he was down there, could he lock it up too?

"And I was older then, seventeen, I think, but you know how the barn is at night, especially when we were younger."

"It's scary as fuck," Brad chimed in, and everyone nodded in agreement.

"Yeah, so it's pitch black out, and I'm walking down to the barn, tellin myself there's nothin to be scared of, humming a little tune to myself just to make some noise, ya know? To give me some extra courage or somethin. So I get down there, and the barn doors are open. I'm working fast so I can get outta there as quick as possible. I step into the barn, move over to the left, and flick the light switch. The barn goes black, and now the only light is coming from the floodlights on the windmill and from the farmhouse. I'm working real fast now. I step back out of the barn and pull the barn doors closed, latch it up, and pull the padlock down through the loop." Pat stops and exhales loudly. He mashes a cigarette in the ashtray on the workbench. "That's when I saw it. No, I guess I heard it first. I heard this rustling along the east side of the barn, you know where there's all that overgrowth and raspberry bushes and shit." They all nodded. "So I look over there as I spin around and start running up the hill toward the farm. My heart's racing, and I'm freaked the fuck out. I see this shadow there, in the overgrown space between the hill and the barn. Pointy ears. I guess I thought it was a wolf, but it had these fucking *eyes!* These glowing orange-yellow eyes, like fire."

Their eyes widened when he mentioned the eyes, and it felt like a surge of electricity shot through them. They glanced at one another with a shared look of solemn fear and *recognition.*

"These amber eyes just glowing in the reflection of the floodlights." Pat lit another cigarette and was silent for a moment, reliving that frightful night and overwhelmed by the experience. When he mentioned the eyes, the others gasped. "Well, I made it back up to the farm and got inside. I slammed the door and locked it behind me. I didn't sleep a wink that night and had trouble sleeping the whole rest of the week. I was already freaked out by the barn at night, but after that I wouldn't go near it for months. But then eventually, I guess I convinced myself that I was crazy, overreacting, that it was probably a stray dog, maybe a coyote or a wolf."

"I've seen the eyes too," Jack said solemnly.

"Me too," Russ muttered, nodding.

"So have I," Rick said, taking a swig of his beer.

Then there was a tense silence for a minute or two.

"What about you, Brad? Have you ever seen it?" Pat asked, finishing his cigarette.

Brad looked at them uncomfortably.

"I saw it last week."

"What?!" they all exclaimed.

Then Brad did something no one expected him to do—he burst into tears.

Jack and Pat went to him and put their arms around his shoulders, comforting him. He wiped hot tears from his cheeks and sniffed, regaining his composure. Jack handed him a beer.

"I saw it last week, out in Rose Lake Forest, when I was working on the Thompson house," he croaked. "I was workin late, and I saw this tall, dark figure out at the edge of the woods, not a hundred yards from the Thompson's back patio. And those damned glowing eyes! I saw em!" He drew a shuddery breath. "I got the hell outta there and fast. I figured I was just workin too hard, and my mind was playin tricks on me with the shadows at dusk or something. Just like you guys, I just couldn't believe what I was seeing. Couldn't accept it." He looked over at his brother Jack, tears welling up in his eyes. "What if I got Bill and Annie killed? It's my fault!" he cried. "And I sent you over there and put you in harm's way too! You could've died!" He broke down then, his shoulders heaving up and down with the emotion, his head buried in his hands, the tears falling freely.

The other five cousins surrounded him in a circle and put their arms around him, hugging and reassuring him until he calmed down.

"It wasn't your fault, Brad," Jack mumbled. "Don't think that way. You didn't kill Bill and Annie."

Everyone nodded and murmured their assent.

"You didn't kill em," Jack said, his voice sharp and icy. "The Dogman did."

After the Allen cousins shared their stories, Russ spoke up again.

"Okay, so we all believe in this thing, as crazy as that sounds. We all know it's *real*. Fuck, I can't believe I'm saying this out loud. It sounds so fucking nuts. But is it real, like physical, like a flesh and blood creature that you can touch? Or is it some kinda spirit, like a ghost or something?"

Murmurs and thoughtful looks spread around the circle of six like a bad cold.

"I thought about that," Jack said, a pensive look in his eyes. "And I'm not sure." Suddenly he remembered something, something from his research on similar creatures in Native American mythology in the Great Lakes region. The thought came bursting up from his subconscious like a volcanic eruption, and he made a mental note to follow up on it. Maybe there was a clue there, or, even better, an answer.

"It has to be physical on some level if it can kill people like it does, right?" Jay said, scratching his head.

"Yeah," Brad agreed.

"Yeah, I think so," Jack said. "It's got to be physical in some sense, but where it comes from each seventh year and where it goes back to—and how it *does* that—I'm not so sure about. I think there must be some kind of spiritual element to it, but I also think it has to be a creature of flesh and blood."

"Which means…" Rick said, looking up at the others with a steely glare. "We can kill it."

The six of them nodded and looked around at each other nervously.

"Another question is how many of them are there," Jack began. "Is it just one monolithic Dogman, or are there more of them, like a species of Dogmen?" He shivered at the thought.

"Jesus," Pat muttered, shaking his head.

"There must be more than just one of them, right?" Russ said. It was a statement more than a question. "Otherwise, how could all these sightings and killings be happening all over Northern Michigan *at the same time?*"

"Yeah," Rick nodded, a look of dawning realization on his face. "And also, how could it keep showing up every seventh year if there was only one?"

"Yeah," Jay said. "If it's physical and not—or at least not *entirely*—a supernatural being, then there has to be more than one of them. *DogMEN.*"

He said it as if he were testing the words out loud to see if they made sense, sending them out into the ether for the first time like a bird released from a cage. These words opened Pandora's box and made it all too real to the six Allen cousins huddled together in the barn that day in September. Hearing the plural form spoken aloud sent shivers through all of them and gave a name to their deepest fears.

"Tell us more about what you called the 'cycle,' Jack," Brad said, breaking the uneasy silence.

"Okay, so I heard about this first from Crawford. That old guy I spoke to outside Travelers, must have been back in July," Jack began. "Then I found some things in Dad's old trunk in the loft that confirmed it and followed up on it with some of my own research."

"So what is it again? The 'cycle'?" Russ asked.

"Basically, the Dogman—Dog*men*—only come around during calendar years that end in a seven. It's crazy, I know. It's on a ten-year cycle, so if you think back—1987, 1997, 2007, and now 2017—you'll realize that those were the years when all these things happened. It's like clockwork. Think back, all of you. Can you ever remember a time when you saw something like it during any other year besides a seventh year?"

He looked around at the others. They were squinting, brows furrowed. Some of them looked up into the rafters. Jay was counting on one hand, a puzzled look on his face. After a few moments, they all shook their heads and looked back at Jack.

"See? Weird, isn't it? Well, my research confirms this pattern—this cycle—too. All the strange attacks I read about in the papers, all the interview accounts, they all happened on a seventh year. And this goes way back, into the 1800s at least, probably further. I couldn't believe it myself at first, so I looked into crime statistics in the region too, and they clearly confirm the cycle. Why no one's ever noticed this or made it public, I have no clue. Folks around these parts have a way of forgetting—"

"More like ignoring," Russ interjected.

"Yeah, they look the other way," Pat added. "Like they don't wanna see it even when it's staring them in the face. How could a place that's so beautiful have such an ugly secret?"

"Right." Jack nodded. "So I found that the unsolved murder, death, and missing-persons rates in the area *skyrocket* every seventh year." The others' faces drew in and went pale. "During every calendar year that ends in a seven, the numbers in Northern Michigan are higher per capita than the rest of the state's rates combined." He let that sink in for a moment, pausing for dramatic effect. "And that doesn't even include the unusual deaths that end up being attributed to rogue animal attacks and things like that. Actually, I read about this one that happened at the end of May near Manton. Hansen was her name, I think. They said it was a car accident, that she had been maimed in the accident but managed to crawl a good hundred yards or so from the wreck, ended up torn to shreds in the ditch."

"I read about that one too," Brad nodded somberly.

"Seems to me like that coulda been the work of our boy."

They were all quiet, nodding, eyes on the floor.

"So that's the cycle," Jack concluded. "And I guess what I'm saying is this is the time to fear. This is the seventh year, *right now*. And it explains a helluva lot."

Again, an uneasy silence descended upon the barn. Again, it was Russ who broke it.

"Jesus fucking Christ," he sighed, rubbing his eyes. "Well, it seems to me this all brings up two important questions: first, what are you gonna say to Dearborn when he questions you on Monday?; and second, what the hell can we do about all this?"

The six of them stood in a circle as they came up with the plan. They didn't do so intentionally; it just happened that way, but it seemed fitting. Arms were on shoulders, heads together, like a huddled football team. They felt closer than they had in years.

They decided they would play dumb with Sheriff Dearborn and everyone else for the time being until they could put the plan into action. They could tell their wives and partners if they felt obligated to, but most of them felt that would complicate things unnecessarily at this point. They could come clean later. Besides, they didn't want to scare people if they didn't have to, and a string of random animal attacks was scary enough without the addition of some demonic Dogman creature straight out of a horror movie.

It was decided that Jack would give nothing else away when he was questioned by the Sheriff, nothing more than he had already said when he went to see him in Reed City the day before. Jack would reiterate that the animal attacks this year have been mighty strange, but that surely they're nothing more than that. A bear, maybe a cougar or a wolf, but no mention of the Dogman. Essentially Jack would play the same game they'd all been playing up until that fateful meeting in the barn: rationalize away anything out of the ordinary and ascribe everything to something more reasonable and logical, like rogue animal attacks. They knew it would work because it had worked on them already and had been working in Northern Michigan for well over a hundred years. Give them a reasonable explanation, they're practically begging for one, and they'll forget and move on and never look back. It would work.

"Does he have anything on you?" Russ had asked. "Did you do anything or touch anything at the scene?"

"No," Jack had responded, an intense look in his eyes. "I didn't touch the bodies at all, none of my blood's there, no murder weapon, nothing. My prints will be on the doors, but that's about it, and anyway, that confirms my story." Just then, a thought came to him. "Also, the bloody paw print I saw on the back patio more than likely washed away in the rain yesterday, so that's one less thing to explain. I'll just keep to the animal attack story, no mention of the Dogman, and it'll work. The Dearborns are old family friends, for one thing, but also..." he paused. "I'm innocent. I didn't kill Bill and Annie—" He choked on those last words and drew in a sharp, shuddering breath. Brad squeezed his shoulder, and Rick patted him on the back.

"It'll work," Pat said.

Everyone nodded.

"Okay, so that's the plan for dealing with Dearborn, but what about a plan for dealing with the Dogman?" Jay asked, looking around the circle of six.

"I need to do a bit more research, but I think I know where to look," Jack said. Thoughts flew through his head now at a feverish pace.

"I think we need to get some visual evidence of this thing," Rick said. "We should set up some game cameras around the property."

"Yeah, that's good," Pat said, wagging his finger at Rick.

"We definitely need to keep some guns around," Russ said. "Assuming this thing can be shot and killed with bullets..." he trailed off.

"Yeah, that's a good question," Jay said.

They all thought about it for a moment, and then Jack interjected.

"I'm not sure if this thing *can* be hurt by regular bullets, but in some of the accounts, I read it was spooked and scared off by gunfire. So there's that." He shrugged. "It's probably worth having a few guns at the ready, just in case. Shotguns and rifles for sure, maybe a sidearm too. I hope to figure out a way to kill this fucker once and for all, but I'll have to do some digging. It could take time. A few weeks, maybe even a month or two."

"Shit," Pat said. "Well, we'll just have to buy you some time while you figure it out then. We'll carry guns, especially when we're out in the woods. We'll try to get this thing on film, one way or another, get eyes on it. Maybe try to track it, too. Learn its habits, where it comes and goes, where it sleeps, what it eats, besides people of course," he grinned. "And then when Jack figures out how to kill it, we go in, and fucking kill this thing and put an end to it once and for all." Pat's jaw clenched, and his eyes were like slate.

"We're in this together, boys," Brad said, nodding.

There was silence for a minute while everyone digested and internalized the plan.

"And we stay out of the woods, especially at night, unless we're in a group," Rick added with an air of finality.

They all nodded, glancing around at one another.

Then something strange happened. Without a word, they instinctively linked hands, standing there together in a circle. The energy between them was palpable. It was powerful, and a bit frightening—a true synergy in which the whole was greater than the sum of its parts. When the six Allen cousins spontaneously joined hands that day in the barn, it was pure magic.

It was fate.

It was sealed.

Brad lit a Winston and took a drag from it.

"Gimme a puff of that," Jack said, eyeing the cigarette.

Brad handed it to him, and he took a drag. Then Russ

reached for it, took it, and hit it. It went around the circle that way, each cousin taking a puff. When it made it back around to Brad, he snuffed it out on the barn floor with his boot. No more words were spoken, but their minds were made as one.

There was no turning back now.

Saturday, September 2, 2017
Leroy, Michigan

The six Allen cousins set to work immediately.

After dinner, they descended to the barn and began preparations. They gathered ammunition, knives, axes, hatchets, flashlights, headlamps, and other useful gear, stockpiling it on the workbench in the rectangular shop room at the northwest corner of the barn, directly below the loft. The guns were kept under lock and key in a safe in the house.

"My dad has two game cameras we can use," Jay said, rejoining the group in the center of the barn. "They're over at the cabin. I can get them tonight and bring em tomorrow morning. Then we can all go out together and install them in the woods."

"Sounds good." Pat nodded.

With all the supplies they could muster at the moment stashed away in the shop, they were ready to execute their plan the next morning. It was just past eight o'clock, and the sun would be setting soon. Russ and Pat had a place across the street that everyone called the "little house" where they stayed when they were up north in LeRoy. Jay and Rick stayed with their dad and stepmother at their cabin on Rose Lake, not far from Brad's place.

With a mix of trepidation and excitement, they shook hands, hugged, and went their separate ways for the night. Hollow eyes looked searchingly into pale faces; few words were spoken. They were eager and impatient to begin, to set things in motion, for better or for worse, even though the gravity of it all was palpable and weighed heavily on each of them. They knew that once they initiated the sequence, they wouldn't be able to control the series of events as they unfolded, the enigmatic outcomes that the future held for them. They all had a sense that they were players in something larger than any of them, a sense that fate, destiny, was spurring them on toward a final confrontation with evil incarnate, this demonic spirit being or whatever it was, this *Dogman.*

Jack couldn't sleep that night. Frustrated, he rolled over and looked at the clock on the bedside table. It was just after midnight. Rather than keep Claire up with his incessant tossing and turning, Jack slipped out of bed and padded through the living room, stopping at a bookcase. In their discussions in the barn, Jack had a pang of insight when they were debating about the nature of the beast: was it flesh and blood, a physical creature, or was it purely spiritual in nature? He had remembered something he had read, a collection of myths and legends of the Ottawa, and it was this book he pulled off the shelf now.

The Ottawa are a Native American group who live primarily in the Eastern Woodlands and Great Lakes regions. Michigan's northern Lower Peninsula was their home historically and still is for many today. They are Anishinaabe people, speaking an Algonquian language, and related to the Ojibwe or Chippewa and Potawatomi. The Ojibwe, Ottawa, and Potawatomi collectively comprise the Council of Three Fires, a long-standing Anishinaabe alliance that met at Michilimackinac to discuss important economic, military, and political issues that impacted each tribe.

Jack vaguely remembered something from his research about an Ottawa legend about a creature similar to a werewolf or Dogman, a half-man, half-canine beast that roamed the Northwoods of Michigan in an endless search for prey. He thought it was worth following up on, and maybe, just maybe, it would give them some insight, some answers, some ideas about how to combat this hellish creature.

With the book in hand, Jack slumped down in his easy chair and cracked open the musty hardcover tome. Ever since he was a little boy, that distinctive old book smell always filled Jack with delight and a sense of mystery like he was heading off on an adventure into the unknown. He flipped to the table of contents and scanned the myths listed there.

Here it is! he thought.

He turned to the section titled "Canines in Ottawa Mythology" and began to read. He was pleased with himself for being able to find it so easily, almost as if there was someone or something guiding him, some outside force that was playing a role in all this.

Outside the farmhouse at that very moment, hidden in the shadow of the rusty old windmill not more than thirty feet from the house, stood a tall, muscular figure, barely visible in the ghostly radiance of the waxing gibbous moon. As Jack unwittingly read his book in his easy chair, the figure waited, a horrid leer on its face, its amber eyes glowing like the eyes of a ghastly jack-o-lantern.

The desk lamp to Jack's right shed a warm halo of light on the pages of the book, which was proving to be very useful.

The Ottawa people believed that the wolf was a close relative of humans, that humans in fact, descended from wolves and, like canines, used to be covered in fur. Like humans, wolves and wild dogs are social creatures, cooperative, dedicated to their packs. For many of the Algonquian-speaking tribes, wolves (and canines more generally) symbolized hunting and warfare—predation. They were the ultimate predators and hence models for young hunters and warriors.

Wolves could also be harbingers of misfortune, sickness, and death. In the mythology and oral traditions of the Ottawa and closely related tribes, the Wolf is the brother of the Trickster and becomes ruler of the underworld, the land of the dead. Among the Algonquian speakers of the Great Lakes region, wolves were often associated with witchcraft. Witches or sorcerers are usually men, powerful shapeshifters who don the clothing or physical form of the wolf to carry out their nefarious nocturnal deeds. In any case, the wolf is seen as a medicine animal, an animal of great mysterious power.

Jack came to the end of the section and set the book down on his knee, stunned. He blinked and opened his mouth as if to say something and then closed it again slowly, his eyebrows coming together, deep in thought.

Well, if that doesn't sound like the Dogman, I don't know what does, he thought. *A* predator... *that's ultimately what the Dogman is: a demonic predator that will never stop hunting, killing, feeding, consuming. It will never stop in its endless pursuit of new prey because that's its very essence! There is no logic or reason to it. It simply* is.

And what about these shapeshifting sorcerers? Could that be the answer? Are the Dogmen really just evil Ottawa sorcerers who come out to prey on the innocent every ten years? But why? It just doesn't make any sense. What are they doing during all the years that don't end in a seven?

And what about the Wolf being the ruler of the underworld? The land of the dead. Spooky, but I don't see a connection. Maybe I will eventually, but it's not clear to me yet.

Just then, Jack had an idea. As a cultural anthropologist, Jack studied Native American culture and history, specifically mythology and religious belief and ritual. Since taking the job at Ferris State, he had focused on the indigenous peoples of Michigan, often spending time doing fieldwork in native communities throughout the state. As he sat there in his easy chair, the book of myths and legends resting comfortably on his knee, he suddenly realized what he had to do: he had to talk to some elders about this and see what they knew about it. They could help him find the answers he was seeking. And Jack knew the perfect person. His name was Frank Comings, an Ottawa elder and medicine man, seventy years old or so, and a good friend of Jack's. Jack could pay him a visit this week and ask him for help. He might be the only person who would truly understand what was happening and, most importantly, he might have some answers… or at least some insights.

Jack bookmarked the page, stood up, and returned the book to its place on the bookshelf. Claire always made fun of how reverently he treated his books like they were some sacred religious relic. In fact, he never opened a book too wide for fear of damaging its spine, another devoutly-observed custom that made Claire cackle with teasing laughter.

Jack decided he would get a drink of water and then get back to bed. Now that he had accomplished something and had a plan to meet his friend Frank he thought he'd have better luck getting to sleep.

He padded barefoot around the living room and into the kitchen, where there were large picture windows facing the north and east. He glanced out the east window into the night and saw the old windmill standing there rusty and bent like a decrepit old man. He opened the cupboard above the Formica countertop and took down an old plastic Denver Broncos cup with John Elway's number seven jersey on it and filled the cup with water from the sink. The water was cool and refreshing as it hit his lips, with just a hint of that tinny flavor that the water at the farm always had. He drank deeply and swallowed. The glass was in his right hand when he turned his head and happened to glance out the north picture window, looking out onto the screened-in porch.

He froze.

Jack's heart stopped and his eyes widened in terror. The Broncos cup fell from his hand, landing on the kitchen floor with a wet thud that sent water sloshing all over.

Standing just outside the screen door, looking in on him, eerily illuminated by the moon, was the creature.

The *Dogman.*

Its eyes glowed with a hypnotic amber radiance that beckoned to Jack. As he stared at it, unable to move or breathe, its mouth opened slowly, deliberately, as if it was preparing to bite. Its tongue lolled out, glistening with drool, and its gums drew back from its fangs in a menacing, sneering snarl.

Jack was locked helplessly in a death stare with the Dogman. It held his gaze, and those haunting eyes of fire seemed to be speaking to him, showing him something, letting him in on some dark secret.

Suddenly the beast's jaws snapped shut with violent force, and it took a step toward the door. It was nearly touching it with its massive paws.

That was enough to shake Jack out of his hypnotic stupor.

"NO!" he shouted, deep and powerful. *"YOU GET OUTTA HERE! STAY AWAY FROM HERE!"* He slammed his fist on the countertop and took an aggressive stance, puffing out his chest. Every muscle in his body tensed.

The bedroom door swung open, and Claire came running out toward the kitchen.

"You stay back, Claire! Don't come in here!" He was still shouting as he looked over at her, a look of surprised, confused terror on her face. She stopped in the hallway, her hands up, palms out, waving in a conciliatory gesture like she was trying to talk someone down from a ledge.

Jack jerked his head back to the picture window, looking out onto the screen door.

It was gone.

The beast—the Dogman—was gone. Nowhere to be found.

Jack's whole body suddenly went cold except for a warm tingling in the pit of his stomach. He exhaled a shuddery wheeze, his eyes wide, staring at the screen door where the creature had been only moments before.

"Jack?" It was Claire. Her voice was trembling. "Jack, I'm scared. What's going on? Is everything okay?"

Jack thought fast. He decided he couldn't tell her about the Dogman, about what he had just seen, not yet. The time wasn't right. He didn't want to lie to her, but he didn't want to scare her either, and besides, he was scared enough for the both of them anyway. She didn't need to share that burden; she didn't need to know yet; it would just make things worse if he told her now. But he would tell her, and soon. But right now, he had to dummy up, get himself under control, and think of something to say, and fast.

"What...?" he stammered, feigning a confused look. "What am I doing here? Where am I?"

Claire moved toward him, tiptoeing slowly, her hands still up as if to prove to him that she was unarmed.

"Hey, honey," she cooed. "It's okay. Just calm down, babe. I'm here."

Jack shook his head. "God, I must have been sleepwalking or something. I remember having this terrible dream, this fucking nightmare. I…"

He trailed off as she reached him, putting a hand on his shoulder. She drew him in and hugged him, stroking his hair and patting his back gently. She whispered comforting words in his ear. His eyes were fixed intently on the screen door, still keeping an eye out for the creature in case it returned.

"You know I used to have these crazy waking nightmares when I was a kid. My mom called them night terrors. It was like that. This dreadful panic."

"You've been through a lot lately, baby. Let's just calm down and get back in bed. We can talk about it in the morning."

Jack bent down and picked the empty plastic cup off the floor. He wiped the spilled water with a hand towel and hung it over the faucet. Then, Jack followed Claire back to their bedroom, still looking at the screen door. He thought then how it was dumb luck that Melanie hadn't woken up when he shouted, but his biggest concern now was whether or not that thing was still lurking around the house somewhere.

They crawled into bed and held each other. Claire calmed down, and eventually, so did Jack. His quick thinking had dodged a bullet, but the loaded gun might still be out there, waiting in the shadows, grinning.

Jack feigned sleep until he knew that Claire was asleep again, then he kept a silent vigil that night, scrutinizing every sound and every shadow. Around three o'clock, he fell into a thin restless sleep that lasted until six or so. After that, he waited until sunrise, eyes wide awake and puffy.

Jack got out of bed around six A.M., careful not to wake Claire. He padded through the bathroom and down the hall, but instead of continuing on to the kitchen, he opened the door to the basement on his right. The familiar basement smell like old paper grocery bags hit him as he flipped on the basement lights. Jack descended the stairs quickly but quietly, ducking his head to avoid bumping it on the low frame at the bottom.

At the foot of the stairs on the righthand side was a large steel-gray gun safe. Jack went to it and dialed in the combination, swinging the heavy door open. Instantly the familiar smells of cold steel and gun oil and lubricant mingled with the basement smell. A random assortment of rifles and shotguns lived in the gun safe, standing there in formation like disciplined soldiers waiting for their orders. Mostly the guns were his father's and grandfather's hunting gear, family heirlooms like a Luger 9mm semi-automatic pistol carried by a German soldier in World War II that his grandfather had *acquired* and brought back home.

Jack scanned the shelf above the long guns. Finally, he found what he was looking for lying next to the Luger: a clean black Glock G19 9mm compact semi-automatic pistol. Jack reached for it, along with one of the fifteen-shot magazines he kept loaded in the safe. The pistol felt good in his hands, light and comfortable. With a satisfying click, he inserted the clip into the magazine well in the grip and pulled the slide back. It snapped back into place; the weapon was now loaded. He slid it into its holster and concealed it behind his waistband near the small of his back, then closed and locked the gun safe. He headed back upstairs.

Checking first to make sure Claire was still asleep, Jack approached the main white wooden door in the kitchen that gave on the screened-in porch. He poked his head around the door and looked out the picture window: nothing.

He drew the gun from his belt. With a sweaty, shaky hand, he opened the door and stepped out onto the porch. He scanned the porch, which was all windows but didn't see anything on the porch itself or outside. A sheen of sweat was developing on his brow. He crossed the porch and reached for the screen door with his left hand.

All at once, he swung the door open and peered outside, his head swinging on a swivel from side to side as he searched the yard. He wondered if maybe he *had* been dreaming; if maybe he had fallen asleep reading and didn't realize it.

No, fuck that, he thought. *What I saw last night was* real.

Jack searched the perimeter of the farmhouse and found nothing: no tracks, no evidence, nothing left behind, nada. He warily made his way down the gravel driveway to the barn, searching the raspberry bushes and underbrush to the north for any sign of life. But again, there was nothing. Now he stood in front of the barn. The doors were still locked.

There's no way it could've gotten in here.

He unlocked the doors and swung them open, holding the padlock in one hand, his other hovering over the gun secured just above his right buttock. Nothing.

Jack was beginning to think he was in the clear now, and he heaved a shuddering sigh of relief.

He went down the hill on the stone steps to the east of the barn and searched the flat area in front of the barn's lower-level door. Jack looked out across the rye field and down the lane leading into the deeper woods and the swamp. Still nothing.

With a sense of uncertain relief, Jack holstered his pistol, turned, and headed back up to the farmhouse. It was six-forty-five A.M., and he knew that Claire and Melanie would be up soon. He snuck back inside and made his way downstairs, opening the gun safe for the second time that day. He pulled the Glock out from his waistband and took it out of its holster. He pressed the release button with his thumb, and the magazine dropped into his hand with a metallic slicing sound. He returned the Glock to its place beside his grandfather's Luger and set the magazine down next to it. Finally, Jack swung the safe door closed and spun the dial to lock it.

He took the stairs two at a time on his way back up to the kitchen.

Melanie was making noise in her bedroom just after seven. Jack heard Claire stir and yawn. Then he heard her get out of bed and make her way upstairs. The muffled happy voices of his wife and daughter drifted down the stairwell and made him smile. By the time they were both in the kitchen and scooted in at the table, Jack had breakfast ready for them: scrambled eggs, sausage links, and buttered toast. He handed Claire a cup of coffee, leaned down, and snuck a quick peck on the lips. Claire looked up and smiled at him.

"You're in a good mood this morning," she said.

Brad arrived at the farm first that morning, pulling up in his truck just after nine. Claire and Melanie had run into town to get groceries, and Jack sat at the kitchen table, drinking coffee, lost in thought. He stared intensely at the wallpaper, looking through it as he analyzed various details and scenarios in his mind. It made his eye twitch.

When Brad came in through the screen door, Jack nearly jumped out of his skin.

"JESUS, Little Brother!" Brad said as he swept into the kitchen. "What in the hell happened to you? Ya look like you've seen a ghost or something—"

The knowing look Jack shot his way in response made him trail off, as the realization hit him like a wild fastball.

"Christ, what happened?" He sat down at the table, his eyes turning into saucers.

The rest of the boys arrived within the hour. By ten o'clock they were all in the barn, and Jack was telling them about his close encounter with the Dogman during the night. After Jack's recitation, they all stood in stunned silence. It all seemed to be happening so fast. Jay's hand was shaking as he lit a cigarette and took a deep drag from it.

Pat spoke up first. "It's like it *knows*," he said, and every one of them shivered at this ghastly thought. "It's like it somehow knows that *we* know. Like it knows we were talking about it, that we're gunning for it..." He trailed off, staring out across the barn but seeing nothing, a look of blank terror on his face.

"It's possible," Jack said.

Russ said, "Yeah, and now it wants to get us first before we have a chance to get *it*."

"Fuck," Rick sighed, rubbing his eyes with both hands.

"There's something else," Jack said, looking up at them.

He told them about the Ottawa traditions about the wolf, about the connection between canines and men, about the sorcerers stalking their prey at night in the shape of wolves. It sent a shiver down Jack's spine as he told them, the image of the Dogman's face from the night before suddenly coming into his head in vivid detail. He closed his eyes and forced that horrid sight out of his mind. He said he would visit his Ottawa friend that week; that hopefully he would have some answers for them. Dear God, he hoped so. If not... then what?

They stood and sat around the barn in silence for some time, contemplating what this all meant, what unthinkable harm they were putting themselves in the way of. Just yesterday, they had knowingly and deliberately set themselves on a collision course with this unknowable, unspeakable evil, and now it was already literally coming to their doorstep in the night, watching, waiting, challenging them, daring them, taunting them.

They all felt relieved when Brad broke the tense silence. "Well, fuck it, let's get moving. We've got work to do."

Jack looked at him with gratitude in his eyes. The Allen cousins came out of their funk and got to work, focusing on the task at hand.

Jay and Rick had brought the motion-activated game cameras they had borrowed from their dad, along with the cables and mounting equipment needed to get them up and running. They also came with a loaded 20-gauge shotgun in the back of Rick's Jeep. Pat and Russ carried matching Glock 19s their dad had given them before he passed away in 2011. They all liked that model so well that Jack had bought one of his own, which he was now carrying again, tucked against the small of his back inside his waistband. Brad rounded things out with his Marlin 336C Scoped 30-30 lever-action rifle. Together they had plenty of firepower, and they were all good shots. But the uncomfortable question remained: could this thing even be hurt by bullets? Jack would ask his Ottawa friend about it and try to find some answers in his father's trunk, but until then they had no time to waste. Besides, there were six of them, and it was daytime. What could go wrong?

Jay threw an axe, a hatchet, and a ladder in the back of Rick's Jeep just in case, and they all loaded up; Jay, Rick, and Russ in Rick's Jeep and Brad, Pat, and Jack in Brad's Silverado.

They headed out down the trail, single file. Everyone was nervous, but Jack had reassured them that most sightings occurred at night and most attacks were on lone individuals

—rarely did the Dogman attack a group of people in broad daylight.

They had decided to place the first trail cam near Cherry Ridge, pointing southwest toward the cedar swamp. Several sightings had occurred in that area, so they figured it was a good place to start. Jay and Rick set up the game camera while the others kept watch. It took a while longer than planned, but within a half-hour it was installed and recording images to an SD card. Jay was also going to set up an account online so the cameras would send images to a website and an app on his phone. They placed the trail camera high enough in a tall old cherry tree that no Dogman could reach it, assuming they can't climb trees, that is, like their other canine relatives. It suddenly occurred to Jack that they were going on a lot of assumptions, but he kept this pessimistic thought to himself.

With the Cherry Ridge camera installed and rolling, the convoy lumbered down the Back Forty trail, veering to the northeast, and came to a stop in front of the Big Stump deer blind. The drill was the same as before, but this time the work went faster. They placed the game camera high up in a tall birch tree looking out over the field where Jack and his father had seen the creature twenty years before. The camera also had a decent view of the Bogs, the mixed marshland, and the cedar swamp area where Jack had seen that eerie dark figure while playing the Game years ago.

After they installed the final game camera, Jay and Rick climbed down the ladder. Rick's boots hit the ground first, and as he looked up, Jay's ass grazed the top of his forehead and cut a loud fart that had the force of a shotgun blast. Everyone fell about laughing as a disgusted Rick cussed out his brother. Even though they were all grown men now, they couldn't escape that special timeless *je ne sais quoi* inherent in the big brother-little brother relationship.

The game cameras were positioned and sending out data. Phase one of their plan was underway.

They had all gone down to the lake for lunch. Claire and Melanie stayed to swim and then watch a Disney movie with Brad and Nellie. Mel was *VERY* excited about this.

Jack lied and said he had some prep work to do for his classes and headed back to the farm. Now he was up in the barn loft digging through the dark treasures in his father's old trunk. He figured he was in the clear for at least two hours to search for some answers, answers that were sorely needed now that they were actively pursuing this thing.

He was armed with the Glock again, an unfortunate accessory that was fast becoming a necessity.

Deep in the trunk, Jack came across a folder labeled "French Fur Trade Account," scrawled in his father's barely legible hand. He opened the manila folder greedily to find xerox copies of what appeared to be a journal. After closer inspection, Jack discovered that indeed it was a journal of a French-Canadian fur trader named Pierre-Antoine Truteau who was active in the Great Lakes region in the late eighteenth century. This was by far the oldest account Jack had yet seen, and it filled him with a giddy curiosity and drunken excitement. It stoked the fires of the obsession, pouring gasoline on a wildfire that was already blazing out of control.

The fur-trade account of Pierre-Antoine Truteau came from the Michigan State University Archives and Historical Collections in East Lansing. It was translated into English from the original French by a Dr. Garnier of the French and Francophone Studies Program at MSU. Like most of the voyageurs, Truteau was just a young man at the time of his adventures, twenty-eight, to be exact. It was the early fall of 1797 and he had been trading with a band of Ottawa at their village on the Little Manistee River, where the small town of

Irons stands today, just north of Big Bass Lake and about thirty miles by pirogue (Truteau traveled in a birch-bark canoe) inland from the port at Manistee. He had been trading with the band of Chief Brings Plenty for the last week, a band that was friendly toward whites and eager to trade—the word *Ottawa* means "traders," after all. They were some of the finest trappers and hunters of all the Ottawa bands in the Great Lakes region.

In exchange for Truteau's store of fine wool trade blankets, iron kettles, guns, hatchets, knives, needles, awls, beads, and other items of European manufacture, the Ottawa offered beautiful pelts of beaver and otter of the highest quality that gleamed with an oily sheen in the autumn sunlight.

From the journal of Pierre-Antoine Truteau:

October 3, 1797

At the village of Chief Brings Plenty on the banks of the Little Muskegon River

After the trade was completed and both parties were well satisfied, I gifted the fine chief of this band, Chief Brings Plenty, with a new Northwest trade gun I acquired at Michilimackinac, the very same model I carry myself, along with a good supply of powder and balls. My older brother, as the chief insists I call him, was much pleased by this gift, shaking my hand enthusiastically as a token of his appreciation and our sincere friendship.

One of their medicine men said a prayer of thanksgiving for the abundance the kitchi manitou or great mysteries had provided for them and for the good feelings and relationship between us. Once the long prayer ended, we smoked the pipe in solemn communion, and then there was a grand feast. The people came parading out of their homes—barrel-roofed rectangular structures covered with sheets of fir and cedar bark—with dish after dish of wonderful foods: roasted venison, smoked salmon and rainbow trout, corn soup, boiled beans and squash, and fresh wild berries of all kinds in seemingly endless quantities. Everyone was in great spirits as we ate until we were so full we feared we might burst. In fact, some did. I was astounded by the generosity of these fine handsome people, as I always am among the Ottawa, whose hospitality is legendary. After the feast, we talked and laughed and danced gaily before their campfires in the center of the village well into the night.

The next morning, I prepared my peltries for shipment and loaded them onto my pirogue. After many heartfelt goodbyes and promises to return the next spring, I set off along the course of the Little Muskegon River, headed for the port at Manistee.

When I was nearly halfway there, I docked my pirogue on the side of the river at the edge of a pine forest to relieve myself and stretch my weary legs.

As I did so, I suddenly became aware of an odd overpowering odor. It smelled of decayed leaves, a sour, earthy musk like the smell of death itself. I'm not ashamed to admit that it frightened me. Then I heard a sound not far off in the wilderness. I had my trusty flintlock musket at the ready as I followed the noise with my eyes, whose source also seemed to be where the strange odor was emanating from. What I saw there challenged all that I thought I knew of science and reason.

It was a dog, or perhaps a wolf, but it was walking on its two hind legs rather than on all fours. Its eyes were a haunting golden orange that entrapped me in their hypnotic piercing gaze. It was emerging from the edge of the wood, not fifty yards away from where I stood, gaping dumbfounded at this horrible, mysterious creature. Though my terror steadily grew as it approached, I was unable to move, caught like a fly in the web of those ghastly glowing orbs. The odor grew ever thicker as it neared, that ancient stench of death enveloping me and filling me with panic and a bottomless dread.

God help me if it wasn't the loup-garou I had heard about as a boy in France—the man-wolf, the werewolf, the skin-changer—but that was the stuff of folklore; of children's fairy tales!

When the beast was not more than twenty yards away, I suddenly recalled the prayer recited by my Ottawa friends to their spirits and the good feelings we had shared in their village; the pipe we had solemnly smoked in communion and kinship. Somehow these good thoughts shook me from my languid stupor.

I raised my gun and fired at the creature. Then, I dashed back to my pirogue as if the devil himself was pursuing me... and in fact, I believe he was. I boarded my pirogue as fast as possible without capsizing it, steered it into the middle of the river, and rowed as hard and as fast as I could.

After a minute or so, I turned to look back. My heart nearly stopped. The beast was shadowing me along the south bank of the river! It was nearly parallel with my pirogue, and I had a sickly feeling in the pit of my stomach that it was waiting—waiting for me to capsize or tire and slow my pace so it could dismember and consume me. My face turned an ashen gray as I let out a thin scream and doubled my efforts, rowing for five straight minutes at an exorbitant rate, looking straight ahead.

Finally, I found my nerve again and glanced back. My heart sang when I saw nothing, no sign of that monstrous creature, the loup-garou, the man-wolf. I felt like crying then, but I held back and continued on at a strenuous pace, not stopping again until I reached Manistee several hours later.

Ever since that day, I fear the Northwoods, especially at night. Knowing that creature lives—stalking, waiting—haunts my dreams.

Jack finished the account in a white heat, devouring the words. Afterward, he sat back in the wicker chair in the loft, pulled out his cellphone, and called his Ottawa friend Frank Comings. Jack needed some answers, and he needed them fast. His friend greeted him, and they arranged for a visit the next afternoon. Jack would drive up to see him at his home in Manistee after his meeting with Sheriff Dearborn.

With his plans set for the next day Jack cautiously made his way back to the farmhouse, keeping an eye on the woods and his right hand close to the concealed pistol beneath his waistband. He tried to prep a bit for work the next week while he waited for Claire and Mel to get home from the lake, but he found it impossible to focus on anything besides the creature.

Jack met with Sheriff Dearborn at his office in Reed City at nine the next morning. He hated leaving Claire and Melanie at home by themselves, but Brad had agreed to keep an eye on the house, which made him feel slightly better about it. He had canceled his office hours for the week and decided to work from home until things were under control, only going to campus when he had to lecture or for important meetings. Jack was teaching two courses that semester, both of which were Tuesday/Thursday classes, which meant he could be home with Claire and Melanie Mondays, Wednesdays, and Fridays.

His talk with Dearborn went smoothly. He followed the plan to a T, giving a well-crafted statement that gave nothing away about the Dogman and attributed everything to rogue animal attacks. He even espoused Dearborn's own theory about climate change being a contributing factor in all this.

And it worked. Of course, it worked; because the locals

had already forgotten about the grisly massacre at the Thompson place; had already turned their heads away from that tragedy. It fit the pattern, and Jack exploited it. Sheriff Dearborn was supportive and friendly, sympathetic even, knowing that Jack had been through something awful that most civilians never had to experience. And because there was no evidence of foul play, no murder weapon, no suspicious prints, nothing whatsoever linking Jack to the killings, he walked away that morning.

Jack got into his Blazer and pulled out of the Osceola County Sherriff's Department, heading north on US-131. South of Cadillac, he went west on M-55, which basically took him all the way to Manistee.

His friend Frank Comings was an enrolled member of the Little River Band of Ottawa Indians who had a reservation in the southwest corner of Manistee County, right by the shore of Lake Michigan. Frank lived in a small gray-blue HUD home on the reservation, along with about four dogs, depending on the day, most of whom lived under the front porch and barked ferociously at anyone passing by. Jack had visited Frank at his home on numerous occasions, and each time the dogs startled him when he pulled into the driveway and got out of his Blazer. This time was no different, but after some sniffing of hands and butts and soft words, the dogs relaxed and became more agreeable.

Frank was a respected elder and spiritual leader, a medicine man, as the Indians say. He was in his early seventies, slightly rotund, and had long wispy graying hair that was almost white, which he let flow freely. He had warm, welcoming eyes encircled by creases and a ready, knowing smile that endeared him to everyone he knew. His laugh was quick, hearty, genuine, and contagious, and, like his ancestors before him, Frank Comings's generosity was the stuff of legend. Jack had been on the receiving end of that generosity on multiple occasions, and he felt extremely blessed and grateful because of it. Jack and Frank shared a close friendly relationship punctuated by irreverent ribald humor and good-natured teasing and joking. Jack and Frank genuinely loved each other, sharing a mutually beneficial and rewarding father-son relationship.

Jack climbed the porch steps and knocked on the front door.

"It's the anthropologist!" he heard from inside in a tone of mock fright and alarm. "Quick, cover the TV and hide the cellphones!"

"Hardy-har-har," Jack smiled as he let himself in, the familiar and comforting smell of burnt sage filling his nostrils.

"Jackie, my boy!" Frank exclaimed, a wide grin on his face.

"Frank, my friend," Jack said as the two embraced.

"Uh oh," Frank said, squinting. "It must be serious if you're bringing me that." He pointed to the can of Bugler cigarette tobacco Jack was carrying. "Usually you just bring me beer." He laughed, a warm hoarse chuckle.

"Tall boys," Jack said, smiling. Then his smile faded. "I'm sorry, Frank, but it is serious. Really serious. I wish it wasn't. I wish I was just coming here to shoot the shit with you and drink beer and laugh, but there's some dire shit going on that I need to ask you about. I'm hoping you might have some answers."

Jack handed him the can of tobacco. Frank took it without a word, and they shook hands, signifying his consent to listen and help.

"Well then, sit down, Jack."

Sitting on Frank's old couch that smelled a bit like frybread and smoke, Jack told his friend everything he had experienced and knew about the Dogman. Frank listened silently, rarely making eye contact, his hand on his chin, index finger curled into a hook that periodically scratched at his upper lip. Jack finished by telling him about the book of Ottawa traditions he had revisited the night before.

"So," Jack began. "I was wondering if there's anything else you can tell me about this thing; any other traditions you know about it; any way to fight it or stop it—any way to *kill* it."

Their eyes met then, and they shared a look so intense that Jack eventually lost heart and dropped his eyes to the floor.

Frank picked up a large concave abalone shell lying on a tray table next to his armchair. He grabbed a bundle of dried sage from the table and lit it with a lighter he pulled out of his pocket. The sage blazed briefly and then glowed, seeming to breathe as it pulsed with an orange glow. Frank blew on it, coaxing the cleansing smoke out of the bundle. Holding it with one hand, Frank fanned the smoke onto his face and shoulders with the other, a practice known as "smudging" among Native Americans. Sage is used as a banishing agent: its smoke is unpleasant to evil spirits and used to cleanse a space or an individual of negative energy or malevolent forces.

After Frank smudged himself, he blew on the sage again, revivifying it, before holding it out to Jack. Using both hands, Jack fanned the protecting sage smoke into his face, neck, and shoulders—into his very *being*—four times and then fanned one final waft up over his head, running his hands delicately over his hair and the top of his head.

Frank looked at him as he did this, nodding his head in approval.

"Well, Jack," Frank began, tapping the ashes from the sage bundle into the abalone shell and returning it to its place on the tray table. "The Dark One has been with us for a long,

long time. That's what we call it. It was here long before the Ottawa lived and hunted and fished and trapped on this land —hell, it was here long before the Ottawa were the Ottawa as we know them today." Frank stared off into space as he spoke. "So I can say for sure that it's not one of ours, not an Ottawa evil sorcerer out for thrills in the night. It's more ancient than that, and more powerful.

"The Ottawa people have known about the Dark One for as long as anyone can remember. But we don't talk about it, you see, because if you talk about something like that, a spirit, then you're actually *invoking* that spirit. You're inviting it, calling it… *manifesting* it. You understand what I mean?"

Jack nodded.

"Everything you've said is true, Jack. It *is* a monster, and it *is* real. Well, it's more complicated than that, though, isn't it?" Frank looked contemplative, his brows coming together like one big furry white caterpillar. "It *does* have a physical form, a body. But its underlying essence, its soul, its spirit, is much more important if you want to understand what it is."

"*I do!*" Jack leaned forward.

"My people have fought with it, avoided it, and begrudgingly lived with it for generations, hundreds of years. Our only real defense against it is family—kinship— symbolized by the sacred circle. No beginning and no end. That's why we lived in circular villages. We relied on the circle of our relatives to protect us from danger, from the unknown." He paused and took a slow deep breath. "And from evil. Evil like the Dark One. But *its* ways are not *our* ways. It defies all human logic and capacity for understanding. Yet, it *does* have its own logic, its own understanding of things. Ottawa medicine people have tried to understand it for hundreds of years, and I think we know a few things about it by now."

He lit a cigarette and offered one to Jack. Jack looked at

the pack of Marlboro Lights and sighed. He didn't usually smoke, but it seemed appropriate now so he took one with his thumb and index finger. He lit it with the lighter Frank handed to him and took a deep drag.

"The smell, the eyes, the scream, the way it walks on two legs, these are all things we've known about," Frank said, his legs crossed daintily as he smoked, looking off into the distance. "But the most important thing to know about is the *cycle.*"

"*The cycle!*" Jack nearly leaped out of his seat, dropping his cigarette in his excitement. "Oh, fuck," he muttered, picking it up off the rug. "Sorry," he said, brushing the rug with his shoe.

"It's okay," Frank nodded, like an indulgent grownup humoring a clumsy child. Jack felt like that a lot in his role as an anthropologist. "So anyway, our people believe that this thing, the Dark One—the *Dogman,* as you call it—is an ancient evil. A timeless evil, really. But maybe *evil* isn't the right word for it. It just doesn't fit with our human understandings of the universe, ya see? It's operating according to a totally different rulebook. It's playing a game that's completely different from the game we're playing, and if we caught a glimpse of that game, our heads would probably explode. We just wouldn't be able to process it; wouldn't be able to handle it, ya see? It's like the difference in perspective between how an ant sees the world and how a *god* sees the world." His face lit up when he said this. "There's just no comparison! We will never understand this thing, or what motivates it, or why it's so damn *hungry,* why it's always on the prowl, always hunting, always searching for prey. Well, I guess that's just the way of the wolf. It's a killer by its very nature."

"Tell me about the cycle."

"It *feeds,* Jack," Frank said, looking over at him for the first time in several minutes, a frightening otherworldly look in his eyes. "It sleeps for ten years, and then it wakes up, and it *feeds*. It's always hungry when it wakes up, and in order to feed, it has to take on some kind of physical form. And that's really all we know… that's all we *can* know! We're not meant to understand these things, Jack. This thing sleeps, or *hibernates*, like a bear, for ten years—its incubation period, you might say—and then it wakes up, and boy is it hungry. It's like clockwork! You can set your watch by it," Frank tapped his wristwatch as he spoke. "And when it wakes up every ten years it wants to hunt. We don't know why… the Ottawa people, we don't claim to understand it," he tapped himself on the chest with the palm of his hand as he said this. "We're not *meant* to know why, Jack, you see?" He fell silent, brooding, his hands clasped together in a fist supporting his lowered chin.

"I need a drink," Frank said suddenly, pushing himself up out of his armchair.

He shuffled over to the kitchen and took two glasses out of the cupboard. Grabbing a bottle of Evan Williams bourbon from the cupboard above the sink, Frank walked back to the living room and sat down on the couch next to Jack. Frank handed him a glass and poured him a stiff drink, putting a hand on his shoulder. Then he poured himself a drink and plugged the bottle with the cork cap, and set it aside. He raised his glass toward Jack, who also raised his glass. They looked into each other's haunted contemplative eyes. They drank and swallowed, blowing the stinging heat of the bourbon out with a forceful exhalation. Jack shook his head to clear it, smacking his lips.

He was so very glad to have a friend like Frank Comings to talk to about this.

Jack was in the woods. He stood in the very same spot where he had been gunned down (with a *paintball* gun) in cold blood twenty years before while playing the Game with his brother and cousins. He looked out over the Bogs, the soupy green marshland that gradually transitioned into the dark cedar swamp. But it looked *older* somehow, like how Jack imagined it must have looked to the Ottawa in the 1700s and their ancestors hundreds, even thousands of years before.

Maybe this was how it looked to the dinosaurs in prehistoric times, he thought.

He suddenly recalled that time twenty years ago when he had seen a mysterious dark figure peeking out from behind a tree deep in the murkiest part of the swamp. It had been looking at him, watching, waiting. Then it had melted away back into the shadowy swamp-like dew in the morning sunshine. The memory made him shiver, and gooseflesh broke out on his arms.

As he looked out across the swamp, Jack heard a deep rumbling like thunder in the distance combined with a low hissing like bacon sizzling in a frying pan. Scanning the horizon, he saw a bright streak of light in the sky off to the west. It was a comet that had made its way into the earth's atmosphere from the Oort cloud in deep space. It was approaching fast, descending to earth with a fierce, fiery energy and power that was at the same time startling and frightening. As it fell, the low rumbling and buzzing sound intensified, growing into an atomic roar that shook the earth beneath Jack's feet. Somehow it seemed to Jack to be simultaneously deafening and as quiet as a light summer breeze. In any case, it demanded his rapt attention, like it was the most significant thing in the universe, like it was speaking directly to him.

Jack looked on in awestruck wonder, his mouth hanging open like a kid who just saw someone do something *really* bad. The meteor—if that's indeed what it was—struck the earth with great force. The red-hot fireball destroyed everything in its path, sending muck and brown water and smoke up into the air and shaking every tree and shrub for miles—every blade of grass bowing to its alien power and authority. It took out several gnarled trees in its fiery descent, leaving a hot swath of burning destruction in its wake, and lodged itself in the earth in the deepest part of the cedar swamp, the Bogs, leaving a smooth glassy crater the size of an old Volkswagen Beetle.

Then Jack noticed the smell. It was *the* smell—that horrible smell he associated with the creature, that offensive cocktail of rot and age and death that filled your nostrils and made you nauseous and docile. There was also a glow and a low hum emanating from that newly-formed crater deep in the swamp. From that distance, Jack could just barely make it out. It was a golden orange color, like fire, an amber bulb radiating and buzzing within the earth, a freshly-planted seed of evil radiating a terrible mesmerizing energy that was nameless and formless, unknowable, eternal, transcendent, alien... divine.

And then it was gone, consumed by the earth, swallowed whole by the swamp, like that rowboat would be in the very same spot in the early 1900s, like countless shoes and boots would be too, all of them sacrificial victims, ritual offerings to the dark swamp god of the Northwoods.

Jack awoke with a start. He shook his head, confused, disoriented. He was lying on the trail by Cherry Ridge, twenty yards or so from the swamp just off to the south.

What the fuck? What am I doing here?

He touched his face, scrubbing his cheek with the palm of

his hand. It was sticky. He glanced down at his hand, and his eyes widened in surprised dread when he saw that his hand was covered in tacky dark blood. He felt his face again, wiping it. The blood was all over his cheeks and around his mouth. Terror grew and bloomed in him like tulips in the spring.

He looked down and realized he was stark naked, lying there on a bed of ferns just off the trail. He noticed something else too: there was more blood on his body... and *hair,* several random strands of dirty blonde hair, a few clumps of it held together by spongy clotted blood. He knew that hair. That hair was—

Looking to his right, he screamed in abject terror and grief, a primal apelike roar, or perhaps *howl,* that shook the world around him. He broke down in violent tears of dark bottomless anguish, holding his head in hands, his fingernails digging into the flesh of his face.

Lying there on the trail a few feet away from him was the mangled body of his three-year-old daughter Melanie. Her eyes were open but unseeing.

She was dead.

Jack shot up in his bed. He instantly began to sob, cupping his head in his hands. Although he was horrified and disturbed by what he had just seen, his tears were more from relief than anything else, as he realized it had all been a dream, a terrible demonic supercharged nightmare from hell.

He sat there in his bed, the sheet covering him to his waist soaked in sweat, and cried as soundlessly as he could, shaking with emotion but trying not to wake Claire who slept next to him. It all came back to him: his meeting with

Sheriff Dearborn and his trip to Manistee to see Frank Comings the day before; the meteorite in the Bogs.

(The origin of the Dogman?!)

He forcefully blocked out the last part of his dream: waking up naked in the woods near the swamp, covered in blood, but not his own blood—

NO! STOP IT! he thought, squeezing his eyes shut tightly and burying the memory of that grisly sickening dream.

He was home, in his own bed, Claire and Melanie were here, and they were all safe... for now.

CHAPTER 13
FALL: SEPTEMBER 2017

Thursday, September 7, 2017
Leroy, Michigan

Aside from Jack's meeting with Sheriff Dearborn and his visit with Frank Comings on Monday and the strange and horrible dreams he had that night, the first week of September had been uneventful. Jack was no less uneasy, though, and he continued to carry a concealed pistol most of the time if he was outside.

He had gone in to lecture on Tuesday and Thursday but had given lackluster performances each time. His mind was preoccupied, and he was on edge. His students had noticed, but at this point, he didn't really care. Everything by now had taken a backseat to the obsession, making it impossible to focus on anything else. He was obsessed with stopping this thing but also genuinely afraid for his life and that of his family and friends.

Jack had abandoned his evening trail hikes, something that Claire had noticed and asked about. He told her he had too much on his mind and walked away. He still hadn't come clean with her about the full extent of what was going on that year, and it was putting a definite strain on their relationship. Jack wanted to hold her and tell her everything, but he just couldn't, not yet; not until he had finished going through the documents in his father's trunk in the barn loft.

So that's where he was that Thursday evening in early September. It was a dreary rainy day with thunder grumbling in the distance and lightning flashing on the horizon like giant fireflies in the mist. He had rushed home from campus after his classes were finished, catastrophizing on his way home, playing out worst-case scenarios in his head. He was nearly always afraid now that he would come home, the front door would be ajar, and he would find Claire and Melanie—

They had a quiet dinner. Jack was morose, as he often was these days, picking at his pasta and broccoli, barely able to choke anything down. He made a valiant effort for Melanie, though, turning on the cheer when he knew she was watching or when she spoke to him. He didn't want her to know or to sense the tension and unease that was thick in the room. Claire looked at him as he indifferently chewed on a piece of broccoli, and the look on her face nearly broke his heart. It was a look of utter dejection, confusion, perhaps panic. She looked like her heart was slowly breaking, and she had no idea how to make things right again. He saw that she was on the brink of tears. When she excused herself in the middle of their meal and walked away to the bathroom, Jack heard her crying softly, sniffling and shuddering. A part of him died then. He vowed to tell her what was going on as soon as he finished up in the loft that evening.

After dinner, Melanie and Jack did a puzzle on the living room floor while Claire read a book on the couch. But Jack could tell that she wasn't really reading; her eyes were drifting, and it looked like she was having an internal conversation with herself, a panicked debriefing about the state of her marriage and life, both of which seemed to be upside-down at the moment. Jack could see the tears in her eyes that were ready to fall again the moment she was alone. He shuddered and hated himself in that moment.

Jack put Mel down to bed at seven. He came downstairs and found Claire in their bedroom. She was crying, but when Jack knocked softly on the door, she sniffed and wiped her eyes, trying to hide her tears from him.

"Claire, I want to talk to you about something."

She looked up at him with a look of confusion and terror, having no idea what he would say next.

"I know I've been very distant and moody lately... I've been a real piece of shit, and I'm sorry for that. I want you to know that it's not you and that I love you, and I always will."

She drew in a shuddery breath as glistening tears streaked down her cheeks.

"Please be patient with me, babe. Please. I need to figure a few more things out, and then I'll tell you everything—this week I will."

Suddenly a look of dawning realization swept across her face.

"Does this have something to do with the T-Thompsons?"

He sighed and looked down at his feet. "Yes."

He looked into her eyes. There was still confusion and fear there, but it was calmer, less intense. He also saw a new resolve in his wife's eyes that made his heart soar.

God, she's so brave, he thought. *God, I love her so much.*

Now it was Jack who was holding back the tears.

Jack was up in the loft in the barn, sitting in the wicker chair, the rain pinging and pattering off the corrugated-tin roof. His sidearm was resting on the floor beside him like a sleeping tiger ready to pounce at any moment. He had told Claire to stay alert and keep her phone by her at all times, to call or text him immediately if she noticed anything,

anything at all, out of the ordinary. She had not asked any questions; she just nodded, that gritty resolve surfacing in her eyes again. Then he had kissed her.

As he dug through his father's old trunk, he realized that he had examined all of its contents. He systematically went through each stack of papers, paperclipped or stapled or loose, and made a note of each one, just to be sure he hadn't missed anything. He hadn't.

Okay, so now I know everything that Dad knew about this thing, he thought. *Hell, I probably know more than he did when he left—*

Jack noticed a pocket on the underside of the trunk's lid that he hadn't seen before. A tingling sensation swept through his body, like the feeling he sometimes got before he gave an important lecture or presentation in front of a large audience, only more powerful—much more powerful. It was like static electricity was coursing through his veins, like blue sparks were shooting out of his fingertips, similar to the feeling he and Brad and the cousins had when they had spontaneously joined hands in a circle in the barn less than a week before.

Jack licked his lips and reached a hand into the pocket.

He felt something. It was an envelope. He pulled it out, breathing heavily with anticipation, a sheen of sweat glistening on his forehead.

He saw the back of the envelope first. It was sealed. He flipped it around in his hands, glanced at the front of it, and froze, utterly turned to stone. All at once, his stomach went hot, and his hands went cold. His whole body turned to gooseflesh and the hair on his arms and the back of his neck stood at attention like a balloon had been rubbed against it.

The envelope was made out to *him.*

Written in his father's scribbled hand was: *For my son, Jack Allen.*

Jack blinked, his mouth agape; his hands were shaking as he held the mysterious envelope. Then, like a hungry bear with a bee's nest, he tore open the envelope with ravenous fervor.

Saturday, August 26, 2007

Dear Jack,

If you're reading this letter, it means that you've found my trunk. If so, then there are things that you know about, things that you've read or heard or seen, things that I know about too. I wanted to tell you, Jack, I really did, but I was never able to find a way to do it. I hope you can somehow understand.

Your mother was against me getting you involved in all this, and for good reason. She loves you, as I do, and doesn't want this darkness to fill your soul like it has mine.

All I can say is, it's real, Jack. All of it.

I know it sounds absolutely crazy, but it's real, and our family has known about it since our ancestors first settled here in the 1800s. And the fur traders who knew this area, and the Indians before them who lived on this land, they all knew about it too. Who knows how long it's been here?

(The image from his dream of the meteor crashing to the earth vividly filled Jack's head like blinding sunlight; the swamp, the smell, the fiery amber glow, the vibration.)

And other people know about it too, Jack. You might know this already, but many of the older folks around the area know about it. The local people know more than they lead on. They try to forget about it, to block it out and turn away from it. That's been going on for generations. It's like a sickness. No one can admit to themselves what's happening. No one can explain why. No one can stop it. They're scared.

Read the things I've collected here, Jack. Learn them well and prepare yourself. Stay safe. It's a monster, Jack. Some terrible curse on this land. It's part dog and part man, with a smell like sour swamp muck and dead rotten things and eyes that burn with a hypnotic orange glow. Whatever you do, Jack, don't look into those devil eyes! They'll pull you in, as they've done to many fine people over the years. Its scent can overpower you too, lull you into a dazed stupor, and make you easy prey. It's a predator, Jack. That's what it is at base. What it does is feed. It's a predator that hunts and consumes. It feeds on flesh, sure, but also on fear, on our negative energy and emotions... on our souls.

I don't know how to explain or prove it, but I know it's true. It comes around on a ten-year cycle, terrorizing Michigan's Northwoods every calendar year that ends in a seven. I've gone back as far as 1797 in my research, and the pattern is clear as day. The best advice I can give you, Jack, is don't go out at night, especially alone. Lock your doors and keep a gun handy, just in case.

Can it be killed? I don't know, but I'm going to try to kill it myself. Right now. Trinitite, Jack. There's some connection to trinitite, a light green glassy stone that I learned about from my Ojibwe friend Wilmer Slow Bear one day while we were having a smoke break at the mill. His people know about the Dogman too, Jack, although they call it by another name. Wilmer said there's an Ojibwe legend about trinitite being used to wound or even kill the creature.

Last year I gathered some of it myself, out in the deep swamp. There was this spot, this round depression in the ground out there that was lined with the stuff. I felt like I was really on to something, son; like I was close, like I could feel the essence of the creature in that spot somehow. I can't really explain it, but I've melted some of it down into slugs and left a few of them for you in this trunk, should you ever need them.

Jack's dream of the meteorite impact in the swamp

flashed through his head with fiery clarity. With numb shaking hands, Jack fished around in the pocket on the underside of the trunk's lid. Sure enough, he found a small manila envelope containing seven small round slugs of a translucent light green stone. He slipped the envelope into the breast pocket of his shirt, blinking, so full of emotion he was totally devoid of any feeling whatsoever.

I'm setting off on a fool's errand, Jack, and I hope you and Brad and Mom can forgive me. But I have to. It's a duty, an obsession. It's something that I can't ignore, son. It's a part of us, and it always has been. It's in my blood. It's in your blood, too, Jack. But you probably know that by now. Well, I'm leaving now to find it, to hunt the hunter, to root out this evil once and for all. I suspect it comes from the swamp, son. I don't know how and I can't explain it, but it uses the swamps somehow, like tunnels or sewers or a highway or some damn thing, to travel, to get around. I'm going after it, and if I don't come back, well, now you know what happened. Now you know the truth, Jack.

And most importantly, Jack, I want you to know that I love you. I hope and pray that you know that already and that I've been a good father to you, son. I'll always love you, and if I don't make it back from this, I will see you again, Jack. In one way or another, I will see you again, my son.

With undying love and affection,
Your Father

I know, Dad, Jack thought, tears streaming down his face. *I've always known, and I love you, too.*

Jack was in shock. So many thoughts swirled in his fevered head he couldn't keep track of them all; streams came together into creeks into rivers into an endless tumultuous sea, whitecapped waves from the depths of his unconscious, long-forgotten memories, crashed onto the sandy shore of his consciousness with tremendous force, spraying whitewater into the air. He feared he might lose his mind if he couldn't reign it in and get control of himself.

The first thought that surfaced singly, without accompaniment from a cacophony of other competing voices, was this: *the date this letter was written is the very same day my father left us.*

He's another victim of the Dogman! Just one more of the missing persons, the unsolved murders, the disappeared, the lost without a trace. The thought struck him with the force of a battering ram and nearly took his wind. Somehow deep down, he knew it to be true. His conviction was ironclad.

And this mysterious letter from his father, lost in the mail for ten years, confirmed many of the details he himself had discovered over the last few months about the Dogman and its insidious nature. Nevertheless, Jack got the feeling there were still questions to be answered.

I knew Dad wouldn't have just walked out on us like that. I never truly believed it, and it's haunted me for ten years. For ten years, I wondered why; ten years of heartache and confusion and anger and sadness and grief. It never made any sense. He was so good to us. He cared so much for us. He never would've walked out on us.

He was a bit aloof and contemplative at times like he had some dark secret or was lost in thought about something very serious. Maybe that's why some of us were able to believe that he could've left that way. Maybe that's how we were able to rationalize what happened. But this letter explains all of that. It exonerates him, vindicates him from an end that was so grossly out of character it never fit or made sense to any of us who knew him best. Not to me, not to Brad, not to Mom—

Suddenly Jack's lips thinned, and his face went dark and took on a look so steely it could have cut glass.

Mom... he thought, his eyes as dark and smooth as slate. *Mom* knew. *She knew all along. She knew about the Dogman, and she must have known that Dad went after it, which means she knew that he didn't walk out on us! He was killed by the Dogman, another one of the missing, and Mom let us think he left us.* Jack seethed with a wild, uncontrollable rage he had never known before. *He didn't betray us; she did!*

Jack slammed his fist against the wall of the barn. It echoed through the old structure, producing an odd rhythm in unison with the pattering raindrops on the barn roof. His eyes were slits of orange fire, burning with blind fury. He folded the letter and slid it back into the envelope made out to him by the ghost of his father ten years ago. He closed the trunk and latched it, then he reached for his gun, slipping it into the concealed holster inside his waistband. His breathing came shallow and terse.

Jack stood and descended the ladder out of the loft and onto the main floor of the barn. He exited the barn, closed and latched the double doors, and walked to the Blazer without looking back. Jack sped away, heading west on 16 Mile Road. At the stop sign at the intersection of 16 Mile and Mackinaw Trail, he paused briefly to send Claire a text message. It read: *Going to visit Mom at her place in Cadillac. I need to talk to her about something, and it can't wait. Then I can tell you everything. Don't worry about me, and don't wait up for me. Keep the doors locked, and text me if anything happens. I love you.*

Jack's mother, Mary Allen, lived in a bi-level condominium in Cadillac near the movie theater. Since her husband's mysterious disappearance ten years ago, she had become increasingly isolated and eccentric—*paranoid* might be a better word for it. It had put a strain on her relationship with her two sons, Jack and Brad, and on her relationship with their partners and Melanie. Jack and Claire weren't sure they liked having Melanie around her grandma because of her increasingly strange and erratic behavior and ideas.

It was a dark rainy night, rather foreboding. Jack drove fast along U.S. 131 headed north for Cadillac. He made good time and soon pulled up to his mother's driveway. It was just after nine P.M. The curtains were drawn, the blinds down, and no lights were on that Jack could see. He switched off the lights on his SUV and killed the engine.

She better be home, he thought as he stepped out of the Blazer and began walking up the driveway. *Of course she's home! Where the hell else would she be?*

He took the front stairs two at a time and walked calmly across the porch to the front door. He knocked three times, hard enough to be heard but softly enough so as not to unnecessarily frighten his eccentric mother. He listened, but heard nothing. He knocked again, harder this time.

"Mom!" he called, his face close to the crack of the door. "Mom, it's me, Jack! Your son!"

He listened again. After a few moments, he heard something stir in there and the shuffling of feet on the floor approaching the door.

"Jack?" his mother called from behind the door.

"Yeah, Ma, it's me. Open up!"

The door opened cautiously, and there stood Jack's mother, Mary, slightly hunched over in an old blue and white nightgown with a tacky Dutch windmill print.

"Jack?" his mother said, a confused sleepy look on her face. "Jack, what the hell are you doing here at this hour?"

He just looked at her, that fire in his eyes, and somehow she knew. She just *knew.* She knew without him having to say a word.

"I'm sorry, Jack," she said flatly. "How could I have told you? You wouldn't have believed me even if I had."

"Dad didn't just walk out on us, Mom. I knew he wasn't capable of that! How could you lie to us about something like that?!" He was red hot.

"Come in. Sit down."

His fists and teeth clenched, breathing like a man preparing to jump off a cliff, he went inside and sat down on an old maroon couch that had an odd sweet dusty smell. His mother eased into an easy chair next to the couch. They faced each other, squared off for a battle to the death.

"Now I never said *that*," she explained, her hands up, palms out. "Not exactly. I said he was gone, that's all." Tears welled up behind her eyes now, her last defense.

"You told Brad and me that Dad left us!" he screamed. "What the fuck, Mom?! How could you lie to us about that?"

"I didn't lie!" She was getting desperate and emotional now, and she was dangerous when she was like that. "Sure, I didn't tell you kids *everything,* but how could I?! Like I said, you never would've believed me! It's all too crazy." She put her head in her hands and sobbed silently, her shoulders shaking.

"He went off the deep end, Jack. I didn't know what to do." She looked up at him but then averted her gaze again when she saw the steely resolve in his eyes, the rage of betrayal. "It consumed him, Jack. It was all he could think about. He spent all his time researching it. It drove a wedge between us; between all of us. And I had you and Brad to think about!"

Suddenly the parallels between himself and his father became glaringly obvious.

"He wouldn't tell me exactly what he was up to that day when he left, but I knew somehow. I had an inkling that it had something to do with that evil thing... that devil dog."

She shivered and fell silent for a moment, her usually bright eyes foggy with memory and pregnant with emotion. "I asked him not to go, *begged* him, actually. He wouldn't give me a straight answer, but I told him he was putting his family and me on the line. And for what? To quench his thirst for knowledge? To appease his obsession? This thing wasn't worth it, and I told him so. But in the end, he went anyway."

She reached for Jack's hand and held it, stroking the back of his hand with her thumb. She stared at the wall as if she were looking far off into the distance, back in time.

"So I didn't lie to you exactly, Jack. I didn't tell you the whole truth either, though, and for that, I *am* sorry. But he did run off, and he did go away. He was another one of the missing, I guess. Another one who disappeared under strange circumstances. A self-fulfilling prophecy, really. I was gonna tell you, Jack, I promise I was. I was gonna tell you and Brad in time... in *my* time. When the time was right. I just needed to find a way to tell you." She fell silent again, her lips quivering, a tear tracing a glistening line down her cheek. She squeezed her eyes shut tightly and shook her head in hopeless sorrow. "I would've filed a missing-persons report, Jack, but I was afraid of ending up in the nuthouse, you know, at Pine Rest. You know a lot of folks around here who lost loved ones in similar ways ended up that way, in a padded room."

Jack pulled the envelope out of his pocket.

"What do you know about this?" he said, brandishing the envelope with his name on it.

She glanced up at it, a look of cold resolve on her face.

"He wrote to you about it, did he? Told you what he knew?"

Jack nodded, his eyes burning a hole in her.

"Where was it?"

"In a pocket in his old trunk in the barn loft."

She nodded knowingly as the information sunk in. "So *that's* where he kept it all. God, if I'd have known that, I would've burned that damned thing the day he left."

"He didn't leave!" Jack shouted.

"I would've burned it all up, Jack! We're not *meant* to know of such things! And that's really what killed your father! He just couldn't accept that." She quieted for a moment before raising her voice again. "He just *had* to know! He just couldn't accept that there are things that humans aren't meant to understand—healthy mysteries! He challenged that thing! He taunted it in a way by learning too much. Knowing too much. He was obsessed with finding out about it, and it ended up killing him."

Jack was silent, still staring daggers at his mother, holding the envelope in a quaking fist.

"And you're damn right I didn't tell you!" Her tone was now self-righteous, her voice shaking with religious fervor. "How could I?" She stared at him with wild-eyed intensity. "And you know what?" She paused, breathing in deeply, shrinking away from him as if she were suddenly frightened. "Right now, you look just like he did at the end."

Jack gripped the wheel of the SUV with a death grip as he drove back home. He had left his mother, telling her that he loved her but that he didn't know how or when he would ever be able to forgive her for what she had kept from him—for what she had led him to believe and let him go on believing for ten years, even though deep down in his heart he had never truly believed any of it.

She had asked him what he planned to do. He told her he wasn't sure. She begged him not to keep digging, not to go after it like his father had, to just let dead dogs lie. He told her he couldn't promise her anything. That's when she really broke down. The weight and stress and anxiety and grief and anger of all those years came pouring out of her like a woman possessed. She became frantic: screaming, clawing, sobbing, moaning.

"I already lost my husband, Jack!" she had bellowed, her voice hoarse. *"I can't lose my son too, goddamn it!"* She pounded on his chest with quaking fists, like she was trying to resuscitate a dying man, bawling pitifully, the tears streaming down her face. *"Goddamn,"* she had repeated, her voice growing softer so that it was barely a croaking whisper. *"Goddamn it."*

That's when Jack had told her he loved her, but that this betrayal had cut him deeply, all the way down to his soul. He set her down on the couch and made her a cup of tea. Jack stroked her hair and told her she could come stay with them for a while if she wanted to, but that he had to go now. She suddenly looked very old and had that distant foggy look in her eyes again, like she was looking through the wall and back into the hazy mists of the past, the realm of memory. Her mouth opened as if to say something, then closed again. A thought struck Jack then as he looked forlornly at his mother, a heartbroken emptiness filling him up inside: *This is exactly how all those poor folks end up at Pine Rest or the Northern Michigan Asylum. It's not just the missing and the murdered; these people are casualties of the Dogman too.*

By the time Jack got home, it was nearly eleven o'clock at night. Claire had waited up for him. She was scared, pacing around the house, everything locked up tighter than a drum. When Jack came in the door, she ran to him, and they embraced. Claire was trembling in his arms, and for the third or fourth time that day, Jack felt like crying. He resisted the urge, though, maintaining his composure for his badly shaken wife. Jack whispered soothing words in her ear and made her a cup of tea. They sat down on the couch together, holding hands.

Finally, after many long months of tension and sneaking around and recriminations and general unpleasantness, Jack spilled his guts to Claire. He told her everything, from the beginning to the end, holding nothing back. Occasionally sipping her tea, Claire listened intently, her emotions running the gamut like a widow going through the five stages of grief. First was disbelief and denial. Then fear and anger, followed by bargaining. ("Whoa, whoa, whoa, let's not jump to conclusions here! Don't we need more time to be sure about this?") Then there was depression and sadness. Finally, as Jack finished his strange tale of horror and wonder, describing the scene in the barn loft that very night, the envelope addressed to him from his father, and his mother's confession, Claire reached the stage of acceptance and understanding. She was so brave. Jack was thankful in that moment that his wife was such a resilient and courageous person. She was a rock, and Jack needed her now more than ever.

They hugged and cried together, sitting there on the couch in the living room at the farm. The rain had stopped but a whistling howling wind blew in its wake.

"I want to help, Jack."

"NO!" he shouted, grabbing her shoulders with both hands. There was an intense pleading expression on his face. "You and Mel should leave here and fast. Why don't you go and stay with your folks in Rochester Hills for a few weeks? None of the incidents ever occur that far south or in densely populated areas. Why don't you and—"

The look of grim determination on his wife's face made him stop mid-sentence.

"I'm staying," she said softly, holding his eyes with an iron stare. "I'm with you, Jack."

He started to protest, but she cut him off.

"I'm not going anywhere, Jack, at least not right now. You might need me, and I can contribute. I insist on it, actually, and you can't make me go away. I'm your wife, Jack. I go where you go. We fight our battles together."

Despite his fear and reservations, Jack had never loved her more than at that moment. He reached for her and kissed her with a ferocity that only comes in dangerous situations of life and death. Later they would make love with such passion and reckless abandon that they both lost themselves completely in the act of union, becoming one, floating off into space in a shared out-of-body experience that was bizarre and indescribable.

"If things get too crazy around here, we can send Melanie to stay with my parents," Claire said. "And maybe we should even think about doing that now. But unless something happens that changes my mind, I want to stay with you, Jack. We can talk more about it sometime, but I don't wanna leave you alone right now."

"But I'm not alone, babe," Jack said. "There's six of us: me, Brad, and the four cousins."

"I'm staying, Jack," she said quietly but definitively, skewering him with her eyes. "At least for now."

Wolf at the Door

Tuesday, September 26, 2017
LeRoy, Michigan

The weekend had been uneventful. The cousins had come up north on Saturday morning, all except for Jay who had a prior commitment in Grand Rapids that weekend.

Saturday evening at the lake, Jack, Brad, and the cousins studied the new game camera footage on Rick's laptop over at his dad's cabin. There was nothing of any significance to report. They were all a bit disappointed but also relieved. They decided to set out some bait within range of the cameras to see what might materialize. They set out in a two-vehicle convoy Sunday afternoon with a few cheap beef roasts that they got discounted at the Village Market and a couple of old half-frozen venison roasts that had passed their prime from a white chest freezer in the barn. These they skewered on a few strategic pine trees at the edge of the cedar swamp and in a clearing near the Bogs. Lastly, they decided that if there was still nothing when they checked the footage the next weekend, they would move the cameras to a new location.

On Tuesday, Jack left his office at Ferris State. It was twenty minutes after five P.M., and he had just finished teaching his second class of the day at four-forty-five, an introduction to the anthropology of religion. This topic was Jack's bread and butter in terms of his theoretical interests. That day he had lectured and led a class discussion on animism, using ethnographic examples and readings from native North America, particularly the Siouan tribes of the Great Plains and the Algonquian tribes of the Eastern Woodlands and Great Lakes region.

In class, Jack lectured on beliefs about animal spirits in the traditional nineteenth-century hunting cultures of the Lakota—or Western (Teton) Sioux—and the Ojibwe. He also spoke about powerful shamans or medicine men who could transform into animals for various purposes, using the example of the Ottawa sorcerers taking the form of wolves to terrorize their enemies and spread fear and sickness. When he mentioned this, he suddenly tensed up and shuddered but didn't think his students noticed.

The drive home had been stressful, fraught with nightmare scenarios playing out in Jack's head. Finally, he pulled into the driveway at the farm, his mind back in survival mode as he scanned the tree line west of the house, looking for anything strange.

Jack parked the Blazer in its usual nook between the apple and pear trees, opened the glovebox, and pulled out his holstered Glock. He slid it behind his waistband in what was fast becoming a necessary ritual of paranoia. He got out of the SUV and looked up at the patio: everything looked normal.

Jack sighed. He had gotten into the habit of calling Claire as soon as he got on the highway heading home from campus, but for some reason, he had forgotten that Tuesday. Maybe the day's lecture topic had gotten to him—it did bear some striking resemblances to his current situation, after all. Looking around cautiously, Jack walked up to the screen door, unlocked and opened it, and stepped onto the porch.

Claire and Melanie were chatting in the kitchen. Mel was playing with her plastic Disney princess figurines at the kitchen table. At the moment, Belle and Ariel were her favorites, but these things shifted quickly, like blades of grass in a stiff summer wind.

"Daddyyyyy!" she crowed in her sweet singsong voice.

"How's my little miss?" Jack said, sweeping her up in his arms.

They hugged, and she gave him a loud smacking kiss on the lips, the kind they called a "Bugs Bunny kiss."

Mel went on playing with her toys as Jack embraced Claire and kissed her on the cheek.

"How'd it go today?" he asked, looking at her conspiratorially.

She sighed and licked her lips. "Everything was fine," she said softly, so Mel wouldn't hear. "Nothing out of the ordinary."

"Good," Jack said with a sigh of relief, rubbing and patting her on the back and shoulders. "I'm gonna go change. How about pizza for dinner tonight?"

The Allen family ordered pizza from Pibbs that night and enjoyed a low-key dinner, all things considered. Melanie ate all of her carrots so she got a special treat for dessert: a Melanie-sized bowl of chocolate ice cream. She was *delighted* with the situation, smiling ear-to-ear with chocolate smeared all over her face. They sat around in the living room; Mel and Claire colored on the floor while Jack checked his work email on his cellphone.

The phone rang. It was Brad.

"Hey, Bro," Jack said, picking up the phone.

"Jack, what are you up to?"

"Just hanging out after dinner. What's up?"

"I hate to ask, but could you swing by for a few minutes? I need a hand with this new couch I got in town today."

Jack bit his lip and looked down at Claire and Mel coloring on the floor.

"Come on, Brother, pleeeeeease?" Brad pleaded. "It should only take a few minutes. I know it's crazy right now, but I want to get this taken care of."

Jack sighed. "Yeah, alright. But it better be quick."

Jack talked to Claire about it, and she seemed fine with him stepping out for a bit. It was going on seven o'clock, so there were still two hours of light. He promised he'd be back by nightfall, and Claire acquiesced. They had talked extensively about how they would handle things living in the scary-movie reality they were now in, so she knew the drill.

Jack kissed Melanie goodnight and squeezed Claire on his way out the door. He was in the Blazer and on the road in a matter of minutes, heading east on 16 Mile for his brother's cabin on Rose Lake. Jack arrived and let himself in, mentally shooing away some nagging intrusive thoughts that were biting at him like the mosquitoes and blackflies that were just now starting to lose their hold on the Northwoods.

"Brother!" Brad said, reaching out and grasping Jack's hand like they were going to arm wrestle. He pulled him in for an embrace and clapped Jack on the back. "Thanks for coming, man. Sorry about the short notice."

He handed Jack a can of Budweiser. Jack cracked it open and took a long swig. It was cold and refreshing.

"Hi, Nell," Jack said, waving to Brad's live-in girlfriend Nellie, who was sitting in an armchair, knitting something colorful with the TV on.

She looked up and smiled. "Hey, Jack. Thanks for coming."

"No worries," he said, taking another slug from his beer.

"Well, let's get to it," Brad said, clapping his hands together.

The work went fast. They unloaded the new couch, wrapped in a clear plastic tarp, from Brad's Silverado and hauled it into the house. Nell opened the door for them, and they had the spot all cleared and ready for the new couch to just slide right in.

"Another beer?" Brad asked, eyebrows raised, once they finished the job.

Jack pulled out his phone and glanced at the time, then looked out the window at the sun descending on the western horizon.

"I suppose I have time for one more."

Brad grabbed two more Buds from the refrigerator and handed one to Jack. They both cracked them open and then clinked them together.

"Cheers," Jack said, tipping an imaginary hat in Brad's direction.

"Here's to you, Little Brother," Brad said, taking a healthy gulp. "Thanks again for your help."

They drank their beers in silence for a moment, and then Jack spoke up.

"There's something I need to talk to you about, but it'll have to wait. Maybe you can stop by to chat one night this week? I can't leave the girls home by themselves for long right now with everything going on."

"Yeah, of course," Brad said, nodding. "Is it serious?"

Jack nodded.

"Does it have to do with You-Know-Who?" His voice dropped a couple of decibels when he said this, and he glanced over at Nell sitting on their new couch, making sure she wasn't listening. Brad hadn't told her yet about the extent of the Dogman situation. Like Jack had been with Claire, Brad struggled with how to tell her about something so unbelievably crazy and frightening.

Jack nodded again, his lips pursed and thin.

"Yeah, I can stop by tomorrow night, no problem," Brad said.

"Maybe we could all have dinner or something," Jack added. "I'll ask Claire about it."

"Yeah, sure."

Just then, Jack got a text message. The alert sound made him jump, and he reached into his jeans pocket, fumbling around for his phone. Suddenly he was worried, and the intrusive thoughts from earlier came back with a vengeance, filling his head with dark ideas and images.

It was from Claire. His heart leaped in his chest.

Then it calmed down, and he was left with that panicky breathless feeling you get after a close call on the road.

Can you stop at the store and get a gallon of milk and some bread on the way home? Thanks, luv.) the message read.

Relieved, Jack finished his beer and tossed it in Brad's recycling bin under the kitchen sink.

"You headin out?" Brad asked. He was now sitting next to Nell on the new couch, watching a crime drama on their widescreen TV.

"Yup, gotta run," Jack replied. He shook hands with both of them. "Let's just plan on dinner tomorrow night at our place, okay?" They nodded. "I'll text you if I hear otherwise."

Jack swung into the Dighton Store on his way home. Since 1887 the Dighton Store had been a one-stop-shop for folks in the area. Between Marion and Tustin from east to west and Center Lake and Rose Lake from north to south, the Dighton Store carried just about anything you could ever possibly need and many things you surely would never need.

Jack and the Allen family had patronized the Dighton Store for generations, stopping in for an ice cream cone or a movie rental or a twelve pack of beer or a bottle of bourbon or some beef jerky or fishing line or plastic beach toys or a few other essentials.

He grabbed a gallon of milk and a loaf of wheat bread. At the register, he added an Almond Joy to his order for Claire. Claire loved Almond Joys. He paid in cash, thanked the cashier (a nice heavy older woman named June whom he'd known for years), and was on his way.

He turned right off of 16 Mile, pulling into the farmhouse driveway, and parked between the pear and apple trees. It was still light out, but the hint of dusk was in the air. He killed the engine and reached into the glovebox, slipping his pistol inside his waistband. On a whim, he pulled his cellphone out of his pocket and checked the time: it was 8:15 P.M.

That's when he noticed he had a missed text message.

The text was from Claire, and it had come at 8:04 P.M., while Jack was at the store. His heart froze, and all the air left his lungs at once.

It read simply: *HELP.*

His head swung around, and he drew his gun at the same time. He practically leaped out of the Blazer, his eyes glued to the north side of the farmhouse, his Glock held firmly in both hands in a shooting stance, the barrel pointed at the ground. Jack shuffled up to the patio.

The screen door was closed, but the screen had been slashed along the bottom. It swayed there in the delicate fall breeze like a sheet hanging from a clothesline. His heart sank as adrenaline pumped through his body in great waves.

He took one step onto the patio and glanced down at the cement beneath him. His heart raced as he saw massive black dog tracks approaching the screen door, like menacing rubber stamps imprinted in thick swamp muck.

"Jesus Christ." He clutched at his mouth, his hand a gnarled claw of terror and worry, and said a silent feverish prayer. He wanted to rush in, gun drawn, screaming for his wife and daughter. But he knew he couldn't do that; that would be foolish, playing into the beast's hand. He had to survive himself and secure the house if he hoped to save his family.

He approached the door, tiptoeing around those ghastly paw prints. Peeking through the slashed screen, gun drawn, he saw nothing on the screened-in porch except more of the black muddy tracks leading into the farmhouse. He shuddered and closed his eyes for a split second.

The white wooden door that gave on the farm was yawning wide open on its tarnished hinges. There was a crack in the wood between where the doorknob had been and the deadbolt several inches above it. The doorknob lay on the floor amongst splintered debris. The doorframe too was cracked on the inside, raw yellow lumber exposed where the bolt had been ripped through its mooring with frightening force. Deep jagged scratches were etched into the door, leaving dreadful veins of exposed raw wood.

Jack approached the entryway, shaking with nerves and raw emotion. The scene in the kitchen was enough to send a deep shudder through his body: a stemless wine glass lay shattered on the floor near the refrigerator, a puddle of pink wine the size of a pancake pooling around the broken glass. A half-full bottle of rosé lay on its side against the refrigerator door like a fallen soldier. A magazine usually found on the table had been thrown to the floor, and bags of chips and pretzels from the countertop were torn open and littered the floor, flung violently around the room helter-skelter.

Jack's mouth fell open in dread when he saw splotches of

dark red blood on the rug, some of them in the shape of human footprints, which made their way around the sink and into the living room.

The mucky dog tracks led in both directions from the kitchen: toward the bathroom and Jack and Claire's bedroom and toward the living room. Jack stopped and listened silently for a moment: he heard nothing.

It's probably hiding somewhere waiting to tear my guts out, he thought.

He decided to investigate the living room first. As he warily made his way to the wooden swinging doors that gave onto the living room, he saw that one of them was torn off the wall, hanging on by a single hinge.

Jack had his gun raised to eye-level in the combat pose his father had taught him years ago. With one quick fluid movement, he stepped into the living room, scanning the room down the barrel of his pistol.

There was nothing. Just more muddy canine tracks and a wake of destruction: an overturned coffee table; more books and magazines torn up and flung around the room; a long gash across the face of the sofa and some of its fluffy white stuffing bulged out of it like intestines from a disemboweled corpse.

The swinging doors that led upstairs were open, which made Jack shudder and tense up. He could feel the sweat, damp on his forehead and under his arms. But he decided he had to secure the main floor before going up there, so he continued around to the swinging doors that gave on their bedroom.

He burst through the entry with his gun at the ready. Jack's head was on a swivel as he scanned the room.

That's when it fell on him.

He emitted a deafening scream of rage and terror, reeling around as it hit him on the neck and shoulders.

It was the broom they kept leaned up against the wall in the corner of the room, knocked down when Jack burst through the doors. He sighed in relief and wiped the sweat from his brow, shaking his head.

There was nothing in their bedroom either—just more of the massive dog prints and destruction. The bathroom was clear too, and Jack swung around the hallway full circle into the kitchen.

Where the fuck are they? Jack thought.

An insane frenzied panic filled his entire being.

The main floor secured, Jack checked the heavy door to the basement: there were no signs of forced entry or distress there, so he decided to check the basement last. He headed back around to the open swinging doors that lead upstairs.

Jack paused at the foot of the stairs, listening intently, looking up the dusty, empty stairwell that always smelled faintly of mothballs. He heard and saw nothing, aside from the sickening black paw prints that climbed the stairs all the way to the top. Jack began to ascend the old stairs. They creaked and moaned like a steel drum under Jack's weight, his Glock aimed straight out in front of him. There was a bookcase at the top of the stairs and two open doors on either side of it. Jack's eyes flitted from one side to the other, his gun alternating between each potential angle of attack. The last of the fading light of twilight slanted in through the second-floor windows, illuminating the dust floating in the stairwell.

This was a dangerous situation for Jack, one of many, but perhaps the most dangerous since he had entered the farmhouse. He couldn't possibly cover both sides simultaneously, and if he picked the wrong side, he would be eviscerated by a seven-foot werewolf creature from hell.

Jack bit his lower lip with grim determination and sprang onto the second-floor landing, bursting into his home office on the left. He flung his gun around, scanning the room as fast as he could, saw nothing, and reeled around to face the open doorway into his daughter's bedroom. There was nothing in his immediate line of sight. He cautiously approached Mel's room, breathing heavily. He pointed the gun in first, then leaned into the room, his eyes darting here and there.

No Dogman. No blood.

Just more of the tracks. The bed was disheveled, and one of his daughter's pillows had been torn apart like a ragdoll. Jack clenched his teeth in a blind rage, his muscles tensed.

This motherfucker, he seethed. *I'm going to find this thing. I'm going to find it, and I'm going to kill it.*

After going through the upstairs and finding nothing, Jack dashed back down the stairs. He looped around and went back through the living room into the kitchen. Jack circled past the kitchen table and came to a stop in front of the heavy wooden door leading to the basement. He gripped the doorknob and twisted it open.

The door creaked open, and he looked down the stairs. The light was on down there and—

A shadow moved at the base of the stairwell. He aimed the Glock and nearly fired, the gun held tensely in both hands. His left eye had automatically shut as he drew a bead on the shadow and prepared to squeeze the trigger.

He lowered the gun slightly, realizing with a shaky sigh that it was just the shadow cast by a tree in the yard outside the downstairs window.

That's when he noticed there were no gigantic dog tracks printed in black swamp muck on the tan shag carpet of the stairs. He shook his head in confusion and pointed the gun straight up in the air.

"*CLAIRE! MELANIE!*" he shouted. His voice reverberated in the stairwell and throughout the farmhouse.

Suddenly there was a scratch at the bathroom window, a sound that chilled Jack's blood, which felt like it was slowing down and thickening in his veins.

He dashed down the hallway to the bathroom about fifteen feet away. Jack burst into the room like a battering ram and pointed the Glock at the window where the noise had emanated from. His finger began to squeeze the trigger.

It was another false alarm, this time a branch from a bush tousled by the autumn breeze, scraping against the bathroom window like nails on a chalkboard.

Jack relaxed a bit, whirled back around, and returned to his position at the head of the stairs leading to the basement. He descended the stairs quickly, gun at the ready.

The basement at the farm had always creeped Jack out, ever since he was a boy. It was just so old and decrepit in its way, like an open invitation to ghosts and ghouls and spooky stuff of all varieties. The stairwell opened into the main room, an old musty space with a cement floor, a table with a few chairs, an ancient wooden floor chest that Jack and his brother and cousins had always joked—more like *feared*—contained a body, and an old non-functioning wood stove. Aside from that, the room was full of random junk: boxes of odds and ends that should have been tossed decades ago, some expendable antiques, dishes, you name it. Jack and Claire inherited the room this way and had just never gotten around to cleaning it up.

There was nothing in this main room when Jack reached the bottom of the stairs. It was dark outside now, but someone—or some*thing*—had turned on the light. Jack swung around to the left and went into the creepiest part of an already creepy basement. This was the furnace room, so named for the ancient gas furnace that bumped and churned on the sandy dirt floor. This was also the darkest part of the basement, illuminated by only three bare lightbulbs in each of the three main rooms. Jack wasn't sure what to think as he pulled the drawstring attached to the first lightbulb. It snapped on, bathing the room in a soft incandescent glow. The next room Jack investigated was a pantry, basically a closet with homemade shelves. It was where the Allens had stored canned goods, potatoes and other root vegetables, and jars of preserves and fruit for generations. Jack's shoes crunched on the dirt floor as he pulled the drawstring to switch the lightbulb on in the pantry.

Nothing.

Finally, Jack made his way to the northwest corner of the basement, another old junk room full of all sorts of nameless oddities collected and hoarded over many years by Jack's parents and grandparents. There were old picture frames and photo albums, boxes of Christmas lights and decorations, and, creepiest of all, a complete deer carcass that had been stuffed by a taxidermist friend of Jack's grandpa in the 1960s. It stood on all fours facing the furnace. One of its golden-orange marble eyes was missing, while the other stared dreadfully at whoever was unlucky enough to be servicing the old furnace or grabbing a can of green beans. Jack and his brother and cousins always thought their grandfather had arranged it just so because he got a kick out of giving the grandkids a good scare. In any case, again, Jack saw nothing out of the ordinary in this room either. He took one final look into that spooky amber marble eye and turned on his heels, turning off the lights on his way out of the furnace room.

The last room in the basement was the mud room, which housed the washing machine and drier, a big plastic sink, and an ancient refrigerator that resembled a spaceship from a bad 1950s science-fiction movie.

Again, there was nothing there.

Then Jack drew in a sharp breath as he noticed that the

door leading from the mud room to the garage was open wide, as if it had been opened in a hurry and left ajar. He moved toward it and leaned through the doorway, pistol pointing into the open space of the garage. The garage door was open, and the car was gone, which Jack had somehow failed to notice when he pulled into the driveway. Looking at the dirt floor of the old garage, Jack saw scuffs, maybe some shoe prints, leading to where the car had been parked. He felt a sudden shimmer of hope, as there were no signs of the dreadful paw prints anywhere.

Where the hell are they?

Instinctively, he reached down and felt for his cellphone in the front pocket of his jeans. It wasn't there. He realized he had left it in the Blazer after reading the horrifying and succinct message from his wife. Pistol in hand, Jack ran out through the open garage door and circled around the farmhouse toward the northwest and up to the parked Blazer between the pear and apple trees. In his haste, he had left the driver's side door open, the dome lights were on, and his cellphone was lying on the floormat under the steering wheel where he had dropped it after reading his wife's frightful message less than forty-five minutes ago.

Keeping one wary eye on the patches of pine to the north and west, Jack keyed in the PIN on his cellphone. He had a missed call and a missed text message, both from Claire.

Bright fireworks of relief and joy exploded in his head, sending rippling waves of hope through his body.

Oh dear God thank you thank you thank you oh God oh Christ THANK YOU!

The text read: *We're at Leslie's. Please call NOW!*

Jack pulled up the missed call and tapped the phone icon. Claire picked up on the first ring.

"Jack!" He could tell immediately by the tone of her voice that she was hysterical with fright and worry but that she

was keeping it together for Melanie. "Jack, where are you?! Don't go inside, Jack! It's there! It's *there!*" As she spoke, her voice dropped to a choked, panicked whisper.

"Baby, it's okay, just calm down," Jack blurted, realizing that only two minutes ago, he was too panicked to speak himself. "I'm outside the house right now. It's gone, I just checked. It's gone, baby, I promise."

She uttered a shaky wheezing sigh that sounded more like a moan of primal fear. "Oh God, Jack it was awful. It was so terrible Jack it wa—"

"You're okay now, baby. Just try to calm down," he interjected. "I'm coming to get you right now. Just stay close to Les and take care of Mel, okay?"

There was silence on the other end.

"Okay?" Jack repeated, trying and failing to sound calm. "Claire? Claire?"

Then she was back. "Uh-huh. Yeah, I hear you, Jack. I will. Hurry. Please."

"I will. I love you. Don't go anywhere."

Jack hung up the phone and slid into the Blazer. He fired up the engine and tore up the ground getting out of there. He flew down 16 Mile, heading for Leslie Patterson's house just south of LeRoy off of Mackinaw Trail, the adrenaline still pumping like crazy, but full of relief and happiness, indescribably grateful that his wife and daughter were safe—for the moment.

There were tearful shaky hugs and kisses when Jack arrived, although everyone tried to play it cool around Melanie so as not to freak her out more than she already was. Leslie, bless her heart, had already set up a guestroom for Mel, and Jack and Claire put her down to bed soon after he arrived, explaining that they were going to stay at Leslie's for a special fun sleepover that night. That excited and pleased Melanie, but they could tell she was anxious and thrown off by the evening's events, even though they had shielded her from the worst of it.

Claire and Jack sat together on the couch in Leslie's living room. Claire wrapped herself in a throw blanket and sipped from a cup of tea spiked with bourbon, her hands trembling as she brought the cup to her lips, her eyes wide and staring off blankly into space. As soon as he got there, Jack systematically locked all the doors and windows and drew down the blinds.

Jack held Claire's quaking hands in his, periodically stroking her hair and back, as Leslie fixed them all a stiff drink to calm their frazzled nerves. Jack took a big swallow of bourbon, wincing and pushing out air through pursed lips as he felt the liquor run its course and warm his insides.

Then Claire told them what had happened.

It had been just before eight P.M. Melanie slept upstairs in her bedroom, while Claire read a novel on the couch in the living room, sipping a glass of rosé. She got up to get a refill, making her way into the kitchen. It started almost exactly like Jack's experience earlier that month: Claire opened the refrigerator door and reached down for the bottle of rosé. She noticed an odd smell like death and decay and swamp filth. She straightened up and closed the fridge door. Glancing to the right, she saw it standing there through the small oval window in the door: a seven-foot canine beast covered in dark fur with a long snout, lips raised in a leering grin that made Claire's face go a ghostly white; shiny black gums loaded with long razor-sharp teeth; glowing amber eyes that stared vacantly, expressionless but inexpressibly menacing. It stood on two legs on the patio just outside the screen door. As Claire stared back at it, frozen with terror and a horrid irresistible fascination, the creature cocked its head to one side, like a dog who just heard something interesting.

It took one lurching step closer to the screen door and put a massive claw-tipped paw on the screen.

Claire dropped the bottle of rosé. It toppled to the floor with a loud bang, rolling forward into the fridge door, wine sloshing around inside it. Her glass fell to the floor and exploded into a million pieces, leaving a pool of wine and jagged shards of glass.

The Dogman raised its sinewy arm—its hunched back and shoulder muscles bulging under matted fur—and slashed through the screen with such force it shook the entire porch and front of the old farmhouse.

This broke the spell that bewitched Claire. She screamed in horror, more like a prolonged, hoarse moan, and wheeled around, taking three steps before her feet were under her. She winced as her heel came down on a shard of her broken wine glass, opening a gash in the bottom of her foot. She bashed her hip into the edge of the countertop, crying out in pain, as she scampered from the kitchen, leaving a trail of bloody footprints behind her.

She took four leaping strides across the living room to the bottom of the stairs. She pounded up the stairs two at a time, screaming Melanie's name. When she reached the top of the stairs, she heard the pounding begin: the creature smashed its massive paws into the door, shaking the old farmhouse to its very foundations with each deafening blow. It dug its scalpel-like claws into the wood and slashed deep trenches through it like a child playing in the sand.

Claire ran to Melanie, who looked up at her mother with wide frightful eyes.

"Come on, Melanie, we have to go. *NOW!*"

Claire collected Melanie in her arms and went down the stairs as fast as she could. Her mind raced like a stockcar at Daytona. She was trapped—that was the first thought that went through her head. But if she could get to the basement, she might be able to get them out through the garage. Carrying Melanie in her arms (*oh dear God her arms were getting tired!*), Claire ran to the swivel doors that gave on the kitchen. Shielding Mel's eyes with the crook of her arm, she pushed one of the doors open with her elbow and looked into the kitchen toward the front door.

The Dogman stood just on the other side of the door, its fiery eyes peering in through the small oval window built into the door. Her mouth dropped open in horror as it grinned at her again and caught her in its mesmerizing golden-orange gaze. Suddenly the beast grunted and forcefully exhaled out of its nostrils, producing a heart-shaped splotch of condensation on the door window.

Claire screamed and whirled around, sprinting across the living room. She tore through the bedroom as the pounding began again in earnest. Claire heard a sickening cracking sound as the door and its frame began to give under the violent force of the beast's blows. She flew through the bathroom and into the hallway on the other side of the front door, tears streaming down her face as she struggled to keep Mel in her aching arms, which began to cramp.

Another deafening blast followed by the groaning and cracking of wood. The wood was starting to splinter as the power of the blows forced the deadbolt in its casing through the doorframe.

Claire screamed, and Melanie let out a pitiful whimper and started to cry. With one hand clinging to Mel, Claire reached with the other and fumbled with the slippery porcelain knob on the door leading to the basement.

Another shattering bash on the front door, mere feet behind Claire's back, followed by the crack of splintering wood.

She managed to get the door open, hit the stairs to the basement, and slammed the door shut behind her. She nearly fell down the stairs in her rush to get away from the horrifying wolf at the door. As she reached the bottom of the stairs, she heard the front door crash open, slamming against its hinges and banging into the wall.

It was inside now.

It was inside their fucking house! Oh, Jesus Christ, oh, dear God, help us!

Still holding onto Melanie by some miracle (or by the magical superhuman strength brought to you by adrenaline), Claire ran through the mud room in the basement and ripped open the door to the garage. She opened the Camry's passenger door and plopped Melanie in the seat, fumbling to secure the seatbelt on her. She slammed the door and circled around the front end of the car, jumping in behind the wheel.

Her heart sank as she realized she didn't have the keys.

Leaping up, her mind surprisingly limber and calm in that insane moment, she remembered they kept a spare set hanging on a nail inside the frame of the garage door. She put her hands on it and pulled the key ring off the nail. A moment later, she was in the driver's seat with the keys in the ignition. The engine burst into life, and her heart leaped with joy. She opened the garage-door.

Without thinking, Claire put the car in reverse and floored it, cutting the wheel so they banked left, leaving a streak of burned rubber on the gravel in their wake. She threw it in gear, and they barreled ahead, hardly stopping to look for traffic before peeling out onto 16 Mile Road.

"Jesus Christ," Leslie muttered after Claire had spun her tale. "What the fuck? I just can't believe it, and yet... somehow, I know it's true. It's *real.*" She stared off into space just as Claire had earlier.

Then her face suddenly changed, twisting into a grimace of horror.

"Katie's dog!" she gasped. "The Williams's dog, Lyra! Could it be?" She looked to Jack for confirmation, but he just stared ahead gravely, still holding Claire's hand.

Then her face contorted, taking on a ghastly pale hue as the blood drained out of it. "Dave Beckett? Bill and Annie?" she mumbled, her face a mask of white stone, her eyes beginning to glisten. "The... the *Thompsons.*" It was no more than a whisper, and as it left her lips, like a butterfly flitting off a leaf, her hand came slowly to her face and cupped her mouth in shock. She was trembling, and a lone tear descended her cheek as the muscles in her face began to twitch with emotion.

Leslie looked to Jack again for support and validation. Claire was trembling again, the well-worn tracks on her smooth cheeks from earlier in the evening renewed with fresh tears. Jack just looked back at Leslie and nodded.

Because he didn't know what else to do at that moment, Jack told Leslie a slightly truncated version of everything he knew about the Dogman. As Jack shared the horrifying story in vivid detail, she went through the same stages that Claire had—and that all grieving people are said to go through: denial, anger, bargaining, depression, and finally a stolid acceptance. Then, after he had explained things as best as he could, Jack shared some advice with Leslie: beware of the swamp-muck smell, that overwhelming odor of rot and decay—of death itself—that he had come to associate with the Dogman; if you see the creature, don't look into its eyes and get lost in them—they have a bewitching power that can stupefy unsuspecting victims; keep your doors and windows locked and secured; stay in a group if you go out into the woods; and, most importantly, don't go out at night. As Jack shared this advice with Leslie, he couldn't help but wonder if it would even stop the beast. After all, Jack and Claire had been very careful, and still they both had dangerous close encounters with the Dogman that nearly resulted in their deaths. But it was all he could do for now.

The foursome spent a frightened, sleepless night at Leslie's house. Jack and Claire decided she and Melanie would leave for her parents' house in Rochester Hills the next morning and stay for a few weeks until things hopefully calmed down. Jack had been secretly formulating a plan that he needed to go through with his brother and cousins, and he hoped it might end the Dogman's reign of terror prematurely. Leslie called her boyfriend, Matt, and asked him to stay with her for the foreseeable future while things played out.

In the morning, once daylight had cracked the darkness and the sun was fully up over the eastern horizon, Jack returned to the farmhouse in the Blazer. His Glock in hand, he went through the house, reliving the harrowing experience of the night before: the black paw prints, the shattered doorframe, the bloody footprints on the floor, the violent destruction, all of it. He quickly packed a bag for Claire and Melanie: just the essentials, mainly clothes, and toiletries. They could stop at a store on the way to Detroit if they needed to.

As Jack packed the bag, he looked over his shoulder every few seconds, listening intently for any noise that was out of the ordinary. He was paranoid after all that had happened to him and his family over the last few months, and rightfully so.

He slung the stuffed duffel bag over his shoulder and left the bedroom, walking through the living room to grab Claire a couple of her favorite novels to hopefully take her mind off of things. Jack jammed four paperbacks in the bag and zipped it shut. He continued around toward the kitchen, and as he did so, he stopped dead in his tracks, drawing in a sharp shuddery breath.

Somehow he hadn't noticed it the day before, but the Allen family pictures that hung on the wall beside the doorway to the kitchen had been completely decimated: photos of himself and Claire and Melanie, his parents, Brad, the cousins, and aunts and uncles, along with older photographs of his grandparents and great-grandparents, some going back to the 1800s—all of them smashed and shattered and torn to shreds; a sacred Allen shrine utterly desecrated by the demonic beast that haunted the Northwoods.

As Jack stared at this unpardonable violation, his fear turned to anger, a burning fiery rage that welled up inside of him and threatened to burst out at any moment.

And then it did.

As Jack stood there seething at the destruction of his family's history in photographs, his fists and teeth clenched in rage, he suddenly erupted with a deafening roar—a terrible primal scream that almost sounded like a howl. The house shook with the violent outburst, and as Jack stood there, his chest heaving up and down, he caught a glimpse of his eyes in a jagged shard of glass left in a frame on the wall.

For the second time in as many months, Jack saw the glowing golden-orange eyes of the beast looking back at him.

In the Doghouse

Friday, September 29, 2017
LeRoy, Michigan

Claire and Melanie made it safely to Claire's parents' house in Rochester Hills, about a three-hour drive southeast of LeRoy on I-75. Jack felt a great sense of relief about this, but also a growing sense of urgency, an obsessive need for *revenge*. The Dogman had violated everything Jack held sacred, his very sense of order and reason, even the sanctity of his home and the safety of his family. He was nearly certain it had murdered his own father. It had terrorized Northern Michigan for too long, and Jack was determined to stop it, even if he died trying. It had become personal.

Jack called Brad and texted his cousins, arranging a meeting for that weekend in the barn. He left the farmhouse as it was so they could all see what had happened. Then he would have it professionally cleaned and stay there, focusing his entire life and being on one goal: destroying the ancient evil that lurked in the Northwoods darkness and took the form of the Dogman.

It was the last Friday in September. Brad pulled into the driveway at the farm, and Jack came out to the patio to greet him. They clasped hands, but neither said a word. Brad eyed the slashed screen door with a fearful wide-eyed expression. Jack motioned to him, and they approached the farmhouse.

Jack gave Brad the entire frightful tour, narrating the story of what had happened as they went through the house. Aside from a few gasps, Brad was silent as they walked through the destruction left behind by the Dogman. When they finished at the shrine of desecrated family photos, Brad was breathing heavily, clearly upset and scared. Few words were spoken.

As the afternoon turned to evening, the four cousins trickled in over the course of an hour. Each, in turn, got his own tour of the farm; each, in turn, reacted in horror, shock, and amazement. Underlying these emotions was also anger, but none were as hot as Jack, who still seethed over the breach of order, the destruction and chaos brought to his door—and even *into his home*—by the Dogman.

They were all armed now, and together they descended the gravel driveway to the barn.

An awkward silence filled the old barn at first. Then Rick pulled his laptop out of a backpack he was carrying.

"You all have to see this," he said.

Jack flipped the laptop open and set it down on an old green card table. The computer came to life with an eerie white glow, and Rick pulled up a video file from one of the game cameras, the one overlooking the Bogs, the dank cedar swamp in the center of the Allen property.

The six cousins huddled around the screen, the incandescent white glow illuminating their faces like an open refrigerator in the dark. On the right side of the screen was the rye field; on the left was the Bogs. The time stamp on the bottom left-hand corner of the screen read 09-28-2017–9:16 P.M. It was nearly dusk.

"This was last night," Rick said, looking up at them warily. "Just wait for it."

Suddenly they all gasped and jumped as if they had heard a gunshot.

"*Holy shit!*" Russ exclaimed.

"*Oh. My. God,*" Jay muttered, his mouth hanging open.

Before their eyes, in real-time, they saw a dark shape emerge from the swamp—literally *emerge*: it rose up out of the swamp muck as if it were walking up a flight of stairs that ascended out of squelchy black quicksand. The tension in the room was palpable; you could feel it in the air, almost like you could reach out and touch it, taste it, smell it. Thick wet clots of swamp sludge dribbled off the figure and plopped onto the ground, leaving dark splotches that wriggled like Jell-O. By the time the creature was ten feet past the edge of the Bogs from which it had emerged, lumbering on two muscular hindlegs, it was clear who it was: it was the Dogman.

"What the fuck?!" Pat exclaimed, slamming his fist down on the card table. "What the fuck was that? How did it do that?"

"Yeah, what the fuck did we just see there?" Brad stammered, a blank, lost look on his face.

"Yeah…" Russ trailed off, nodding and looking off into space. "And how the hell are we supposed to fight something like that?"

"I might have an idea," Jack said.

Jack filled the cousins in on a number of things. He had

already told Brad the truth about their father, and now he explained this painful part of the story to his cousins, who sat and listened in raptured silence. This shocking revelation hit hard and close to home, considering this was a man they had all known and loved and grown up with. On a positive note, it seemed to solidify their resolve, sparking that anger in all of them that was consuming Jack like wildfire.

Jack told them about his father's letter, written to him on the day he "left" ten years ago. He told them what his father had said about the swamps, how the creature somehow uses them as a kind of supernatural highway system. After watching the unnerving game-cam footage, this hypothesis seemed feasible.

"Maybe it can just materialize like that out of any swamp in Northern Michigan!" Rick said.

Pat said, "That would explain how it can show up in so many different places."

The others nodded.

After they mulled this over for a while, Jack began to explain the reference in his father's letter to trinitite, the melt glass left behind by a nuclear blast or a meteorite impact. He told them how his father had gathered some of it from a crater deep in the swamp.

Suddenly a series of connected thoughts struck Jack. Jack recalled the strange vision of the meteor falling to earth that was swallowed whole by the hungry swamp; the noxious smell of rot and death, and the pulsing amber fire emanating from it like a demonic crystal ball. His breathing was reduced to ragged gasps as his synapses fired wildly, putting the pieces together at a feverish pace.

He told them about his dream or vision of the meteorite impact in the swamp, of the possibility that the trinitite was created by the molten fireball when it landed all those years ago. *Was it hundreds of years ago? Thousands? Millions?*

"It's like the meteor contained the spirit—the *essence*—of the Dogman. Like it transported this evil extraterrestrial organism to earth in ancient times, this skin-changer that takes the form of a terrifying half-man, half-dog beast, preying on our darkest human fears. Straight out of our worst nightmares." Jack said, a shudder creeping into his voice. "It sounds crazy, I know, but maybe the meteor *is* the Dogman. Maybe the *swamp* is the Dogman, like they share an essence or something." He shrugged.

Brad and the cousins looked on, chilled to the bone, dead silent, deep in thought.

Jack plowed ahead, visibly excited. He was on a roll. "And the trinitite was created at the exact moment the meteor—the *Dogman*—impacted the earth. It's like the earth's rejection of this malevolent predatory entity. Maybe it's like the yin to its yang, an antidote to its evil—like its kryptonite." He looked expectantly at the others.

A long anxious pause filled the space.

Then Russ said, "Maybe," drawing attention to the giant elephant of uncertainty in the room.

In any case, this revelation provided a possible answer to the question of how—or if—this devil beast could be fought and killed. It was their best shot.

Armed with this new information, they decided to go on the offensive, to take the fight home to where the Dogman lives and comes from. They were going into the doghouse, into its wretched lair.

The six Allen cousins were going into the swamp.

Either they would kill the creature and end its centuries-old reign of terror, its suffocating grip on Northern Michigan, or they would be killed themselves, six more casualties left to rot in the muck, victims sacrificed to the dark swamp god of the Northwoods.

302 | DAVID C POSTHUMUS

Saturday, September 30, was a day of planning and preparation for the showdown with the Dogman. They spent several hours in the barn and the farmhouse getting supplies together: checking guns, stockpiling ammunition, laying out knives and medical supplies. Each man had his own gear he would hump, consisting of at least a firearm of some kind, a knife, a canteen, and a satchel or backpack for food and other essential supplies. Most of them laid out camouflage fatigues and boots or shoes like Plains Indian warriors going into battle in their finest regalia, singing their death songs, ready to meet their fate. The parallels between what they were doing in that moment and the Game they had played as kids were apparent to all of them. There was a palpable tension in the air but also a sense of grim determination born months ago in the barn when the six Allen cousins had joined hands in a circle and sealed the mysterious pact between them. Perhaps it was a pact foretold centuries ago. Few words were spoken that day; few words were needed.

After a restless night, the day of reckoning arrived.

It was a beautiful fall day: sunny, with a pleasurable chill on a delicate breeze, the temperature forecast to reach the mid-60s by midday. The leaves on the trees were just beginning to turn; soon they'd transform into brilliant fiery tones of orange and red and yellow as they passed through the timeless cycle of the seasons—of decay and death followed by phoenix-like rebirth.

Jack awoke from a shallow sleep and glanced at the clock on his bedside table. It was just after seven A.M.

It was time.

He got out of bed and took a quick shower before making coffee and getting breakfast started. He was cooking a big meal for everyone so they could fill up before heading out into the woods—into the swamp. He wanted it to be special because, and he couldn't really consciously admit this to himself, they all knew this could be their last meal.

Jack sipped black coffee as the cozy kitchen at the farm came to life with the sounds and smells of cooking breakfast. He made a mountain of scrambled eggs, sausage links, bacon, hash browns, wheat toast with butter and jam, and pancakes with maple syrup. The timing was perfect: the first of the gang arrived just as he was flipping the pancakes and taking the toast out of the toaster. By eight, everyone was there, dishing up breakfast in the kitchen and eating together at the picnic table on the screened-in porch. Despite their nerves, they really packed it in, each man having at least two helpings of the delicious breakfast smorgasbord. It was a solemn occasion in many ways, but there was some conversation and heartfelt smiles, even some laughter between bites of toast with scrambled eggs piled on top. They were all resigned to the future course of events they had set in motion; determined to execute what they had set out to do; to protect their lands, homes, and families as their forebears had done before them.

They were going to destroy the Dogman or die trying.

They drank coffee and sipped orange juice as an uneasy silence descended among them after breakfast. Each man had his own thoughts and fears to contend with; each man psyching himself up for the coming storm in his own way.

Without a word, Jack stood, brought his dishes into the kitchen, and walked down the hallway to his room. He undressed and then methodically put on his camouflage pants and OD green t-shirt, slipped into his camo army coat, and laced up his hiking boots. This ritual was repeated by each of the cousins, some of them in the farmhouse, some of them in the barn. By ten to nine, they gathered on the concrete patio in front of the farm, ready to set out on their most-dangerous quest.

What happened next was strange but fitting.

Brad, who normally wasn't very religious at all, asked them to join hands, creating that sacred circle of six again. He recited a long solemn prayer for protection and good luck, naming each of the cousins and their loved ones. It happened organically, and as Brad finished his spontaneous prayer, they all felt that inexplicable energy build and flow through them again, that static electricity that had surged through them months before in the barn when they had first spoken openly about the Dogman. They interpreted it as a good omen, a sign that made them all smile and nod, giving them a feeling of confidence and assurance, like a validation of what they were setting out to do. The six Allen cousins stood there, hand-in-hand in a circle of power, absorbing that energy—that synergy—that flowed between them and was bigger and more powerful than any of them individually.

The moment passed as quickly as it came, like a beautiful delicate bird alighting on a tree branch for a brief moment before taking wing and flying off into the sky.

The ritual completed, the six Allen cousins filled their canteens and descended the driveway to the barn where their arms and supplies were laid out neatly in piles, one for each cousin. They checked magazines, and cocked weapons. Jack carried his Glock as well as his grandfather's old muzzle-loading shotgun that would fire the trinitite slugs his father had left him. Brad carried his Marlin 30-30, while Pat and Russ carried Glocks on their belts. Russ also had a semi-automatic .22 rifle. Rick carried the 20-gauge and a pistol, while Jay carried a Russian-made AK-47. They hoped all this firepower would buy them some time and give them some space from the creature, long enough anyway for Jack to get a shot off with the shotgun.

If the trinitite could even kill the creature, that is.

They were locked and loaded, packed and ready. They reverently passed a bottle of bug spray around, each cousin taking a solemn moment to apply it to their bodies, like holy water baptizing a baby, like smudging with cleansing sage at Frank Comings's place. They all looked at each other one last time in the safety and ordered familiarity of the barn, nodding and sighing, wide eyes determined yet anxious.

Then they set out into the woods, into the unknown, the realm of chaos, of wild nature.

———

They started out together, heading down the trail west of the farmhouse. First, they passed the apple and pear trees, then the rows of tall, straight jack pines. Soon they stood before the ancient sugar maple, that giant symbolic gateway between the familiar safety and order of civilized humanity and the chaos and destruction of untamed nature and animality. The immensity and uncertainty of what they were doing, the frightening reality of it all, suddenly struck Jack with great force. He nearly lost his breath.

Well, this is it, he thought. *No turning back now.*

Jack peeled his eyes away from the majestic old maple and looked around at the others. They, too, stared reverently up at the tree, and Jack got the unshakable feeling that they were thinking the same things he was; that they recognized the significance of this tree and what their passage beyond it meant.

When they looked at each other, they shared that same look of wide-eyed anxious determination on their faces, like they were haunted by some ghost or monster—and indeed they were. As they all stood looking at each other, standing on the threshold between mankind and wild nature, between order and chaos, between reason and instinct, hot blood rose to the surface in each of them, bubbling and boiling with an ancestral call that was undeniable. It was in their very blood to do this, to take this creature on, to fight. Their fathers and grandfathers had done so before them, and now it was their turn. Each generation had a solemn duty to fight, to try to understand the creature and its ways, and to put an end to its reign of terror and violence.

Suddenly the chill fall breeze whipped up, blowing their hair back and cooling their faces, which were still red and hot from the blood stirring deep inside them.

It was Russ who broke the silence. "Let's move out, boys," he said, his teeth clenched, a look of fierce resolve on his face.

They crossed the threshold, walking along the trail in two single-file columns of three, brothers standing next to brothers. In the short space between the old maple sentry and the Sahara sandplain to the west, a distance of not more than a hundred yards, the cousins noticed the chill on the breeze growing colder. In fact, the temperature seemed to be dropping rapidly, the wind picking up and whipping the tall grass, ferns, and leaf-covered branches on either side of the trail.

Each cousin was responsible for covering their specific area: Russ and Pat oversaw the front of the column, Rick and Jay covered the column's center and flanks, and Jack and Brad covered the rear so nothing could sneak up on them unawares from behind. They were determined not to be outmaneuvered by the Dogman, although they still had unanswered questions about its nature, two important ones being: (1) Is it fully flesh and blood, or is it pure spirit? And (2) Can it just appear out of nowhere at any place and time or does it have to emerge from the swamp, as they had witnessed on the game-camera footage?

The Allen cousins continued their trek, heading north on the trail where it becomes sandy, their boots digging into the soft earth like they were wading through water. They passed the great white pine and continued on toward the north, heading for the stone bridge and the deeper woods beyond it. A dense tangle of various species of pine, oak, and maple loomed far off to the east, while the landscape toward the west was more open: a field of tall grasses interspersed with purple wildflowers swaying in the increasingly cool autumn wind.

The plan was to penetrate the Bogs through the field in the center of the Allen property and trudge through the marshes deep into the heart of the dark cedar swamp, where the meteorite had landed. It was there, where the rowboat had been swallowed whole over a century ago, that the creature emerged from the dank black swamp in the game-cam footage.

It was also the spot where Jack had seen the menacing figure step out from behind a cedar tree and then disappear twenty years ago when they were playing the Game.

Jack shivered at the memory, holding the butt of the shotgun in his left hand, the barrel resting in the crook of his elbow. It was loaded with a trinitite slug, and six more of the slugs rattled in Jack's left hip pocket. His right hand was free, and he found it frequently drawn to the grip of his holstered Glock.

The hope was to facilitate some kind of conflict with the creature: maybe they'd be able to flush it out like a partridge and get a shot at it out in the open; maybe they'd have to wait there, hunkered down in the Bogs for hours, lure it into a false sense of security, and hope that it would emerge; or maybe it wouldn't show at all, in which case they were prepared—they had packed several headlamps and powerful flashlights with extra batteries—to stay into the night, apparently the most active time for the beast. In any case, it was a loose plan based more on feeling and intuition than anything else; it had come to them collectively in one of those strange moments of synergy and synchronicity that they all felt but couldn't explain. Jack had an unwavering certainty, an unshakable confidence, that their plan would work, that it was the right plan of action, that it was somehow meant to be. What success might look like, he wasn't so sure. What failure would be… he shuddered at the thought.

They descended the slight dip down toward the stone bridge, the Crick flowing silently beneath it. Their boots clicked with a hollow sound as they marched across the bridge, the darkness of the deep woods descending all around them, engulfing them like an ominous black curtain. Suddenly they were filled with an overwhelming choking sense of dread. They all felt it, looking around at each other nervously, their eyes saying more than words ever could.

This time it was Brad who gave them heart. "Just focus on your assignments, guys," he said. "I think it's trying to fuck with us, to scare us. Just keep your mind on what we're here to do and focus on your assignment."

They all felt better after hearing this, and that heavy sense of doom and dread faded ever so slightly. To their astonishment and relief, the darkness and density of the woods seemed to brighten and loosen in some strange mad way.

They trudged on, entering the deep woods, tangled growth and trees on either side coming together above them in a tunnel-like canopy. The wind continued to blow, swirling harder and harder, and the temperature continued to plummet. They could see their breath now, and above the canopy of trees, the first snowflakes began to fall, dancing on the breeze, something that was quite odd for early October, even in Northern Michigan.

The Allen cousins marched along the dark trail heading north past the stone bridge. The stiff autumn wind blew the trees and ferns this way and that, whistling eerily like demonic children. The snow that had begun to fall was just beginning to penetrate the dense canopy of trees and land on the trail, where it evaporated quickly.

In this part of the woods, there was a sea of ferns three or four feet high on the left side of the trail; farther back, thicker woods took over and eventually transitioned into a murky cedar swamp. On the right side of the trail were more dense woods that eventually became a soupy marshland as the Crick wound and slithered through it like an anaconda. This was prime Dogman country with plenty of thick trees and massive old stumps to hide behind. It could easily find cover and ambush them at any moment, slipping in and out of the woods and swamps like a a ghost. All the cousins could intuitively sense this, the precarious predicament they were in, and just how vulnerable their position really was. But they were all in, and there was no turning back now.

They neared Old Uncle Rob's deer blind at the apex of the trail on the left side where it forks, one fork leading to the northwest and Cherry Ridge, the other leading up and around to the northeast, passing the Bogs off to the right and eventually coming to the Big Stump.

That was when Jay let out a surprised choking wheeze that was immediately followed by a short, low scream, almost more of a desperate moan. They all spun around and looked at him, then frantically scanned their assigned areas.

"There's something out there," Jay whispered, his eyes as big as saucers. "About thirty yards back off the trail." He pointed with the barrel of his AK-47 to a thick clump of pines intermixed with oaks and maples.

They all looked, straining their eyes, but no one saw anything. Whatever Jay had seen back there in the deep woods was either gone or had taken cover.

They stood there, squinting into the white pine and mixed hardwood forest when suddenly the smell hit them.

It was overwhelming, filling their nostrils and seeming to seep into their minds and souls, driving them mad; a thick black swamp stench, like the musk of a wild otherworldly animal mixed with the reek of decaying organic material—like the essence of all the death throughout all of history boiled down and concentrated into one noxious scent. The toxic stench nearly overpowered them. Brad and Jay started shaking their heads and clawing at their noses, trying to plug their nostrils with the backs of their hands. They all were coughing and gagging, spitting and drooling on the dirt trail and dry grasses alongside it. Some of them started to lose their focus, their consciousness, drifting off into a sluggish stupor that would metastasize once those flickering fiery eyes began to bore into them, burning them with their hypnotic glare.

But luckily, Jack had experienced these effects, even dreamed of them, and had some idea of their seductive power.

"*Keep moving!*" he shouted, burying his nose in the crook of his arm. "Keep moving and try not to think about the smell! Don't focus on it! That's one of the ways it can get you!"

Jack had prepped them all on the bewitching danger of the Dogman's odor and eyes, but in the heat and panic of battle, sometimes these important lessons are forgotten.

"Remember about the eyes, too," he said. "Don't look into the eyes!"

They started moving again, the column holding up, and the smell began to dissipate. At the same time, the unusual

October blizzard that came on so suddenly picked up in intensity, swirling and blowing cold wind and snow all around them. The melting crystalline snowflakes made everything wet and squelchy. The wind howled among the treetops like an angry spirit in mourning.

Reaching Uncle Rob's blind, they took the right fork and veered up and around an especially sandy and rocky part of the trail, ascending a gentle curving slope.

That's when Brad screamed.

A good-sized rotten jack pine tree with orange needles cracked and swayed toward the column. It could have easily crushed them like bugs or at least broken several bones, hobbling them there near the Dogman's den like flies caught in a spider's web.

"Look out!" Brad yelled, pointing at the tree.

Brad turned and tackled Jack. They hit the muddy ground hard and rolled away as fast as they could. The pine tree came crashing down with great force and speed, jagged broken ends of branches jutting out like a medieval morning-star club adorned with menacing spikes. Rick saw it and leaped out of the way, agile as a mountain lion, dropping his shotgun in the dirt and tucking into a roll when he landed. Russ and Pat at the head of the column were not in immediate danger; they turned and stepped aside, mouths agape, eyes wide. Pat reached for Jay, who was the last to notice the dead pine tree barreling to the earth... but he was too late.

Jay dropped his assault rifle and leaped headfirst, trying desperately to get out of the pine's deadly path. But a splintered branch glistening with pinesap caught his right leg, skewering his calf. He screamed an awful, gut-wrenching howl of pain and panic, lying face down on the side of the trail. He reached down and touched the bloody puncture wound in his leg, a look of shocked dread on his face.

Rick and Pat ran over to him as he screamed and writhed on the ground in agony. The branch had passed clean through his leg, embedding itself at least a foot into the ground. Jay was literally staked to the earth.

Brad, a determined grimace on his face, pulled a hatchet off his belt and started hacking away at the branch where it attached to the tree trunk. Rick and Pat were each holding one of Jay's hands. He was shaking like a leaf, grimacing, trying not to scream. Jack held the branch as best he could so it wouldn't move and tear Jay's leg when Brad connected with his hatchet. After a brutal and tense minute, Brad severed the branch.

"Pull it out," Jay croaked, his face pale, his hands and leg bloody.

They stared at him in disbelief, not because it wasn't the right thing to do, but because of his quick resolve and bravery in the moment.

"Are you sure?" Jack stammered.

"Yes! Pull it out, goddamn it!"

Brad dropped the hatchet and knelt by Jay's savaged calf. Jack held the leg at the knee and ankle while Rick and Pat continued to hold Jay's hands. Brad gripped the branch; as he did, Jay winced and gasped.

"Do it!" Rick cried.

Slowly at first, Brad extracted the pine branch, as if he was pulling out a massive gory sliver. Jay screamed and fought against his constraints, kicking his free leg violently. Continuing with steady and smooth movements, Brad successfully extracted the branch, which was about two inches in diameter. The yawning gash left by the puncture wound bled profusely. Jay lay there on his back sweating and breathing heavily, his face the color of cottage cheese as Rick cleaned, dressed, and bandaged the wound.

It could have been worse. Much worse. It was just a flesh

wound, although it had nicked some muscle. It bled like a sieve, but they were able to control and eventually stop the bleeding. But if it had broken Jay's leg, their mission might have been over right then and there. Or worse, they might have been attacked by the creature while Jay was immobilized.

They sat in silence as Rick and Pat tended to Jay. The only noise was the brisk wind singing as it swirled amongst the trees, dropping wispy snowflakes on the soft earth. Some of the snowflakes landed on the bloody ground near Jay's injured leg and evaporated there in the warm stickiness. Jack stared off into space, his teeth clenched in rage, his finger tapping against the grip of his pistol. He looked over at the dead pine tree that had fallen so unexpectedly. His blood went cold as he saw the color of the dead pine needles still clinging to the tree.

They were the same golden-orange hue as the Dogman's mesmeric eyes.

"Fuck that, I'm not going back," Jay said after Rick wondered aloud whether his brother should turn back and go to the hospital.

"I'm not turning back. Not now. This thing… we're all in it together. You know that, Rick." He winced as he sat up, Rick and Pat each holding one of his arms. "You *all* know that. There's somethin happenin here that's bigger than all of us, and you need me. We all need to be together for this to work. I just know it. I'm not gonna be the one to ruin that, bad leg or not."

They all nodded, but some looked to Rick for confirmation. Rick wavered but then nodded along with the rest of them.

"Help me up," Jay grunted.

Pat and Rick held him under the arms and hoisted him up as he groaned and got his good leg under him. He stood there on one leg, his brother and cousin still helping to support his weight. Jay grimaced as he straightened out his wounded right leg, biting his lower lip. He cautiously put some weight on it, his right hip lowering slightly. He winced and drew in a sharp breath as a fresh dot of blood expanded on his bandage. But that was it. The bleeding was quickly under control again, and he could put some weight on the leg. He'd be able to walk, albeit with a limp and maybe an occasional rest on one of the other cousins.

Brad handed Jay his rifle, who slung it over his shoulder.

"Let's move out," Jay said.

The Allen cousins continued their quest, Jay fighting through the pain, limping on his injured right leg. Rick was right there next to him, ready to be his crutch when he needed one.

They continued up the trail toward the open field overlooking the Bogs where they had placed one of the game cameras. Despite the uncharacteristic cold and stiff breeze, they were sweating, especially Jay, who was still getting used to hobbling on his bad leg.

The trail was sandy and gravelly, rising uphill on a gentle slope, winding up and over to the east, then back again toward the west before straightening out again toward the north. At the top of the hill, the trail opened up onto a wide tall grass field with a massive old cherry tree in the center of it. Farther north across the field, you could see the Big Stump deer blind where the field ended, swallowed up by the thicker woods around it. Jack and his father had seen the creature emerge from behind that cherry tree when they were deer hunting at the Big Stump in 1997 when Jack was just twelve years old. The cousins had strategically placed one of the game cameras high up in that very same tree, which had captured the footage of the Dogman emerging from the deep swamp like a phantom materializing out of the shadows.

The column moved deliberately to the old cherry tree in the open field, its branches and leaves swaying in the crisp, biting wind. That tree must have been at least two hundred years old, but compared to the Dogman, it was a newcomer to these parts, a spring chicken.

They set up a temporary base at the base of the tree. The cousins stood around it, some sitting down for a brief respite and taking swigs off their canteens. They checked and rechecked their weapons and made sure their spare magazines were loaded and within easy reach. Jack double-checked the shotgun loaded with the trinitite slug; it was ready for action. Some of them solemnly smoked cigarettes. Russ dug into his OD green satchel and produced a pint of Fireball whiskey. He took a healthy pull from it and passed it around, and each cousin took a nip.

The wind howled around them, seeming to pick up in intensity as they drew nearer to the Dogman's den. The temperature dropped as well, and there were flurries of snow billowing and eddying. To the east of the cherry tree, across the trail they came in on, the tallgrass field continued before dropping down into the marshes and swamp known as the Bogs. This was where Jack had seen the figure emerge from behind the tree twenty years ago, but also where he had seen the meteor descending to earth in a fiery orange ball, landing dead center in the swamp and emitting that portentous stench and glowing there, embedded in the wet muck, like the amber eyes of the Dogman itself.

The Bogs was their main target, that old cedar swamp that had so much dark history. There had been many sightings and strange happenings there before, far back into the past and as recent as only a few days ago. They were all convinced through some deep magical certainty that the Dogman originated from that place.

The Allen cousins stood huddled around the old cherry tree with the game camera perched high up in it. From their elevated central position, they kept an eye on the land around them, but everyone felt and somehow *knew* that the real fight would take place in the mysterious Bogs—in the creature's home territory.

They readied themselves for the final attack, the offensive assault on the beast. Russ passed the pint of Fireball around again, and they all partook, nodding at each other as the tension built, swallowing the cinnamon fire with a wince and a sharp exhaled breath. The cold wind bellowed all around them.

The time had come.

They stood and assumed their two-column formation and began the march down toward the edge of the foreboding Bogs.

With bated breath, the six Allen cousins left the trail near the giant cherry tree and scuffed along through the tall grass field. The knee-high buckskin-colored grasses and purple wildflowers swayed in the stiff cold breeze and crunched under their boots. Delicate snowflakes landed and quickly dissolved around them. Dust rose and swirled as the column descended the slope through the field to the edge of the marshland that led deeper into the dark cedar swamp.

At the bottom of the slope, they stopped and looked out over the wet green marshes. Tall marsh grasses and tag alders grew in clumps out of the black, moist soil. They stopped at the edge of the marsh and looked at one another, soldiers heading into a horrific battle to the death with an unfathomable nonhuman evil. Jack shivered as Russ took the first fateful step into the marsh, his black combat boot splashing as it sunk down into the mucky soil. At this time of the year, the ground was wet and muddy, but there was no standing water, except in a few deep spots.

With eyes peeled and heads on swivels, they moved in formation into the murky wasteland. They stepped carefully in the muck between the clumps of marsh grass. They knew from experience that you could easily twist an ankle if you landed wrong on the thick clumps of the stuff, and they weren't taking any chances. Rick helped Jay as he limped along, wincing, and sometimes Brad provided support from behind. But Jay's stride was beginning to look more normal. Maybe the pain was subsiding, or maybe it was the adrenaline, but in any case, by the time they were twenty feet into the marshes, he was walking fine, and there was no fresh blood on his bandages.

They noticed nothing unusual as they trudged through the soupy marshes, except that the wind continued to pick up and the temperature continued to drop. They could see their breath intermingled with the swirling snowflakes all around them. The marsh grasses and shrubs swayed together hypnotically as if they were one living organism. Pat pulled a compass out of his hip pocket and studied it. Looking back at the others, he pointed toward the southeast. They all nodded and slogged along. The plan was to go as deep into the swamp as possible, to drive into the darkest, greenest, murkiest part of the swamp and trigger some kind of confrontation with the creature. The plan was to antagonize the beast.

The line between the marshes and the beginning of the swamp is blurred, a shrub swamp taking over in the transitional zone before the real cedar swamp begins.

Suddenly they were in this transitional zone, where tag alders and other wetland shrubs dominated. Jack looked up and saw four enormous turkey vultures circling lazily overhead, their black wing feathers tipped with white. Seeing the red-headed vultures sent a shiver through Jack, and he thought about pointing them out to the others but thought better of it.

Suddenly Rick jumped and swung his shotgun around. They all froze, their hearts beating out a deafening cadence in their chests.

A large garter snake slithered away from him. He exhaled as his shoulders went lax.

"Fuckin snake," he panted.

They continued on. The dark canopy of the cedar swamp loomed ominously ahead, approaching fast. Brad lit a Winston and smoked it like it was his last... and maybe it would be.

They marched toward the darkest green shrubs and trees until they came to the edge of the cedar swamp, dominated by northern white-cedar. This was where Jack had seen the figure and the meteorite impact. This was where they had chosen to make their stand.

The swamp was a mix of cedar, spruce, and hemlock that formed a dense canopy and shut out most of the sunlight. The trees were tangled like spiders' webs, some leaning into one another, others bent and fallen, all intermingled with vines and ferns and other shrubs. The land undulated more here, and the soil was black and spongy, covered with a layer of dead pine needles and moss. Fallen trees lay rotting on the ground, presenting obstacles for unsuspecting travelers—not that anyone came back here very often. The deeper reaches of the Bogs were mysterious, dark, and, in a word, spooky.

They were far off the trail now but could still see the tallgrass field they came from and the huge old cherry tree standing in the middle of it. Once they entered into the cedar swamp, there was no turning back, and visibility would be extremely limited.

Then their boots broke the threshold, and they were in the swamp.

They had to duck under and weave around leafless—or needleless—branches to get under the canopy and into the deeper part of the swamp. It was darker there, and Jack felt the light, delicate pull of spider webs and cobwebs as he walked between a hemlock and a cedar tree. He brushed the webs from his face and noticed a few of the others doing the same.

Russ got his boot stuck, tripped, and nearly fell on his face, but Pat grabbed his shoulder and was able to steady him. Rick stepped up on a massive cedar trunk laying on the ground, and it disintegrated beneath his foot, rotten to the core. He nearly lost his balance and fell but was able to regain his composure. Jay caught his wounded calf on a sharp spruce branch that seemed to be reaching out for him. He uttered a low grimacing scream, his face contorting in agony. Fresh blood spread on his bandages like a red Kool-Aid spill on a paper towel. But he kept walking; they all did, trudging up and down the mossy rises and dips, penetrating deeper and deeper toward the thickest, greenest, dankest part of the swamp.

After ten minutes of following behind Russ and Pat, pressing deeper and deeper into the dark foreboding swamp, they broke out in gooseflesh. They were sweating, and not just because they were exerting themselves—they were scared.

"We should be in the middle of it by now," Jay said, a sharp note of alarm in his voice.

They stopped, looking at one another, eyes wide and fearful.

"Well, there's no way we're lost," Pat said, pulling out his compass. "I was keeping track of what direction we came in from."

He looked down at his compass.

Suddenly his eyes bulged, and his eyebrows raised in surprise and terror.

"What?" shouted Russ, grabbing his brother's arm. *"What's the matter?"*

Without a word, Pat showed him the compass.

"Holy fuck," Russ said.

Jack moved up to the front of the column and looked at the compass's face. His heart dropped down into his stomach. The needle spun in lazy circles.

"What the FUCK?!" shouted Pat, flinging the compass into his satchel.

"Hold on, hold on," Rick spoke up, pulling his cellphone out of his pocket. "I have a compass app on my phone."

After a few moments, Rick's cool confidence drooped and sagged into a scared, long face. "No signal," he said. "Doesn't make any sense, though. I always get signal out here." He frowned, then his expression turned frightened and desperate. "What the fuck's going on here?"

"Alright, alright," Jack said, his hands up, palms out. "Let's just calm down and stop and think for a minute."

"Let's try to get back to where we came in and reboot this operation," Russ said.

They all agreed and started to make their way back the way they had come. Rick was the best navigator and had the best inner compass, so they let him lead the way. Without realizing it, they dropped out of their two-columns-of-three formation.

It didn't take long for them to realize they were lost. The first pangs of panic began to set in, largely unconscious and unnoticed at first. They felt like they were going in circles, and indeed they were. In their hasty drive to get to the center of the swamp they had failed to mark their path in any way. Relying solely on their compasses, they hadn't even noticed any landmarks or unique trees or other land formations as they made their way into the swamp. The swamp was like a horrible soggy maze, and some otherworldly evil was controlling it, rigging the game against them. They became disoriented, each tree and path looking like all the others. The panic welled up in their stomachs and into their throats like bile.

"Fuck," Rick said in a shaky voice. "It all looks the same, and I can't find any point of reference. I'm all turned around."

"If we can find the Crick, we can follow it out of here," Jay suggested.

They all nodded, looking around at one another with quick darting glances, their frightened eyes flitting about like paranoid hummingbirds.

That's when Jack noticed the smell. It was that overpowering swampy death smell that took your breath away. It filled their nostrils, making their heads and stomachs swoon. The fear grew unchecked in each of them as that foul stench thickened in the dark swamp all around them.

Jack's face twisted in disgust, and he covered his nose and mouth with his hand, taking a few blind steps backward.

He stepped on something. It cracked beneath his boot, a dry snapping sound. He looked down.

There, on the black bed of the swamp under a misshapen cedar tree, was a headless skeleton, its bones glaringly white amidst the brown and green hues of the swamp. Upon closer inspection, Jack recognized with mounting horror the tattered remnants of a red and black checked flannel jacket clinging to the remains, relatively well-preserved in the wet spongy soil. An initial wave of shock and horror shuddered through his body. Scanning the skeleton's midsection and legs with his eyes, Jack saw something that made him scream in terror.

The corpse was wearing his father's brown leather Caterpillar Work Boots.

The veins in Jack's neck bulged as he gasped for breath and screamed again, a dry desperate shriek like the sound of a cornered animal.

They all looked over at him, their eyes wide with fright and panic. It had seeped into them like a slow-acting poison the moment they realized things weren't as they seemed, when the compasses wouldn't work, and the realization that they might be lost in the deepest part of the swamp sunk in. Then there was the nauseating death smell. But the panic went into overdrive when they heard Jack's horrible desperate screams.

Jack was pointing down at his father's skeleton lying there headless on the spongy earth. He was shaking like a leaf, his eyes filled with pure horror, panting and stammering, trying to speak but unable to do so. Brad looked down and saw the remains. He saw the remnants of the flannel jacket and the CAT boots and put things together quickly.

Brad shrieked in utter terror and took off at a dead sprint, leaving the rest of the Allen cousins standing there in the swamp in a state of absolute panic and dread.

"Oh fuck, Brad!" shouted Russ, taking off after him.

"Russ!" It was Pat screaming now. "Russ! Don't go after him! Come back!"

But Russ was gone, vanished into the green darkness of the swamp in pursuit of his cousin Brad.

"Oh *fuck!*" Pat screamed, his fists clenched, a high-pitched desperation and panic in his voice.

Jack was still shaking, quivering uncontrollably as he stared at the decapitated remains of his father. Rick had come over and put an arm around him.

"Is it…?" he trailed off.

"Yeah," Jack breathed, shuddering violently. "It's him. It's my dad." He paused, a blank haunted look on his face. "It's my *FUCKING DAD!*" He screamed the last two words and burst into tears, sobbing into his cupped hands, his shoulders heaving up and down.

Rick pulled him into an embrace. "It's okay," he said, holding his cousin, his friend. "It'll be okay." He held Jack's head against his shoulder as Jack sobbed. "Jack, we need you right now. We need you to keep it together and help us. You're the one, Jack. You know more about this thing than any of us." He pat Jack on the back. The soothing tone in Rick's voice had a mesmerizing effect on Jack. It pulled him out of the deep dark place he had fallen into after stepping on the bones of his father.

Jack drew a deep, shuddering breath. He sniffled and put an arm around Rick's back, and that was when Rick knew he would be okay. Jack pulled his wet face away from Rick's shoulder and hitched in a few more breaths, wiping the tears from his eyes and cheeks. He stood there in front of the four remaining cousins, tottering on his feet like a drunken sailor.

But his eyes were sharp again. He exhaled, with just the hint of a shudder.

"Let's keep moving," Jack said.

They decided to follow Brad and Russ's trail like they were tracking a deer. Rick and Jay were especially good at this, and so they moved through the deep swamp in search of their missing comrades. They were scared and panicking, but they did their best to keep those counterproductive emotions down. Their very lives depended on it.

The smell of the Dogman was still in the air, waxing and waning like the moon, which multiplied their anxieties.

"Brad!" Pat shouted, his hands together over his mouth forming a makeshift megaphone. He waited for a moment. "Russ!"

No response.

"The tracks are pretty clear up until this point," Jay said, grimacing and reaching for his punctured leg as he knelt down to examine the ground. "You can see the tracks from Brad's CATS here." Suddenly the image of his father's boots attached to skeleton legs flashed in Jack's mind. "And Russ's boot tracks are here." Jay drew a line in the air with his finger just above the ground. "But after that, I lose them." He looked over at his brother Rick, shrugging his shoulders.

"Yeah, I can't see where they went from here either," Rick said.

The air thickened. Sounds dampened and slowly faded, as if they were all in some mad collective hallucination. All that remained was an omnipresent ringing in their ears. The stench of the beast overpowered them, that musky ancient mind-numbing smell of rot and death. Pat and Jay were bowled over by it. Rick held onto a tree and slid down its trunk, breaking off thin branches as he descended into madness. Jack went limp, frozen, a man possessed. The shotgun loaded with trinitite slipped from his fingers.

Jack found himself staring into globular amber eyes that cut and tore at him, eating away at his soul. He was in trouble, mesmerized by the evil force of the beast, which had suddenly appeared, hovering no more than thirty yards from them, peering out from behind a tree. It was the same tree, in fact, from behind which the Dogman had first laid its dreadful eyes on Jack twenty years before. It had come back to claim its prey, and now that Jack was caught in its hypnotic gaze, he belonged to the creature. His smart twenty-first century defenses were shattered and laid bare in the face of the ancient, timeless death and evil that was the Dogman.

The beast exploded with an eardrum-shattering roar that shook the swamp from the tops of the trees to the spongy black earth. Rick whimpered, and Pat and Jay covered their ears. Jack couldn't tear his gaze away from the beast; the golden-orange eyes burning like candles in the swampy green darkness, calling to him, beckoning him.

Suddenly Jack's eyes grew wider still. They looked empty like he was hypnotized. He stood and began to walk toward the creature looming next to a cedar tree thirty yards away, drawn to those glowing amber eyes like a junkie staggering toward a fix. He was thirty yards away. Now twenty-five. Now twenty. Rick, Pat, and Jay were sickened by the overwhelming stench of the creature, but they hadn't looked into its eyes, as Jack had. Rick vomited on the ground, strewn with dead pine needles. Pat and Jay were on the verge of madness.

Jack stumbled toward the creature, locked in its mesmeric gaze. It beckoned to him, inviting him, calling him home. "Join me," it purred in Jack's head, those eyes bearing down on him. "Join *us*. You are one of us, Jack. I am you, and you are me. We are *one*."

It was fifteen yards away.

Now ten.

Soon, Jack stood a mere five yards away from the massive Dogman. The beast's snout yawned open, foamy drool dripping from it before it snapped shut menacingly.

At that moment, Russ burst through the trees east of the creature.

"Jack!" he screamed, coming right between Jack and the Dogman. "Jack! Snap out of it! Get outta here!"

326 | DAVID C POSTHUMUS

That was all he could say. But it was enough. Jack came to and was there again, aware, present. The spell was broken.

That meant Jack was fully aware and lucid when he saw the Dogman eviscerate his cousin and best friend, Russ.

The beast fell upon Russ with unbridled fury, an evil rage that made all of Jack's strength leave him instantly. Jack fell to his knees as he witnessed the Dogman literally cut Russ in half. Its massive paws, tipped with scalpel-sharp claws, hit Russ with such shearing force that the top half of his body went flying ten or fifteen feet, leaving his torso and legs standing there like half of a department-store mannequin.

The bloody stump toppled to the earth moments later, and Jack again came face-to-face with the snarling popping jaws of the Dogman, standing at least seven feet tall, its fiery amber eyes fixed again on Jack.

Jack screamed and took a few stumbling steps backward. His bladder let go, spilling hot urine down his left thigh, dripping down to his boot.

After witnessing the dismemberment of his cousin at the claws and paws of the Dogman, Jack let out a guttural cry of mourning mixed with rage. But Russ had shocked him out of his hypnotic state, and now he shielded his eyes from those glowing amber orbs, harbingers of death, and did his best to plug his nose against the awful smell.

Jack turned and took three loping strides, finding cover behind a crooked elm tree. The wind ripped through the trees and shrubs with violent, thunderous force. It blew Jack's wispy hair back on his forehead. He knelt on one knee and stole a quick glance back at the creature, avoiding those demonic eyes. It still stood where it had cut Russ down moments before, its muscular body heaving with each rasping breath, its shoulders and hunched back cocked forward in a menacing attack position.

"Jack!" Pat called. Pat hunkered down fifteen feet away

behind a cedar tree, numb after witnessing the killing of his brother but running purely on adrenaline.

Jack swung his head around just in time to see Pat toss the muzzle-loading shotgun over to him. He was too shaken to take the shot himself. Miraculously, given the circumstances, Jack caught it. He swung it around, running more on instinct now than conscious thought or reason. Remembering the lessons his father had taught him, he drew a bead on the creature, his left eye squeezed shut as his right looked down the barrel at the hairy beast, not forty feet away. Jack's entire body shook. He breathed deeply and began to squeeze the trigger with his entire fist, as his father and grandfather had taught him.

At the last possible moment, the Dogman lumbered forward and slightly to the left.

The shot rang out.

The acrid smell of gun smoke filled Jack's nostrils, momentarily masking the horrible ancient death scent of the beast. The shotgun kicked back into Jack's shoulder, and his ears were ringing. For a few moments, he was in a dazed dreamlike stupor. When Jack's focus returned, the ringing still waxed and waned in his ears.

His heart sank. He must've missed the creature. It stalked toward him, taking long, deliberate strides on its rippling hindlegs, its face and snout contorted in a ghastly sneer. It was thirty feet away and gaining fast, gnashing its impossibly sharp teeth.

Jack hitched in his breath, his heart thudding madly in his chest. He had never been so scared in his life, yet somehow he was able to dig down and find some calm. First, he reached into his green satchel and pulled out a pre-measured pellet of gunpowder, dropping it into the barrel. Next, he reached into his hip pocket, his hand shaking, and pulled out another chunk of trinitite. Fumbling to get it into the barrel, he dropped it on the moist bed of black earth and pine needles.

Jack cursed under his breath, biting his lower lip hard until he tasted blood. He stole a glance up and saw the Dogman closing in, now only twenty feet away.

He pulled another slug out of his pocket and got it into the barrel. Reaching again into his satchel, he extracted one of the patches he had readied beforehand, along with some lubricated wadding. He pulled the ramrod out from below the shotgun's barrel and carefully pushed the powder pellet, trinitite slug, patch, and wad down into the barrel, being careful to seat the slug securely on the powder charge. Jack felt as though someone—or something—guided his hands and movements.

Jack looked up again. The growling hulking figure of the Dogman was ten feet away from him. The noxious smell was thick in the air; Jack could *feel* it on his skin.

I'll never get this shot off in time, Jack thought as he loaded a percussion cap, seating it on the shotgun's nipple. He cocked the weapon.

Just then, a shot rang out.

Then another.

The beast paused and looked around, confused and startled. Jay and Pat, ducked down behind trees fifty feet away and fired at the beast from close range. Pat quickly emptied the magazine of his Glock, hitting the beast several times. But aside from startling it and buying Jack some precious time, it seemed that bullets had little effect on the Dogman. Jay unloaded with his AK-47, spitting at least twenty rounds at the creature. It looked over at Jay, huddled down in a kneeling shooting stance, and caught him in its hypnotic gaze. The AK-47 fell from Jay's hands, landing lifeless and impotent on the ground with a muffled thud.

Jack brought the shotgun up and took aim. The Dogman was ten feet away, still focused on Jay.

Jack's left eye closed, and he drew a bead on the creature.

"Eat this, you son of a bitch," he whispered as he began to squeeze the trigger.

Suddenly Brad came bounding out of the dense woods to the east.

"You killed my dad, you motherfucker!" he screamed, lowering his head and shoulders. He blasted into the Dogman like Lawrence Taylor sacking an unsuspecting quarterback.

But the Dogman barely moved. It budged a few inches, maybe, then swatted Brad away with a gigantic paw. Brad's head snapped to the side, and he sailed through the air like a rag doll. A bloody gash opened across his shoulder, revealing the white bone of his shoulder blade. Brad's flight ended abruptly when he smashed into a bushy blue spruce and slid down its pokey trunk, hitting the ground like a ton of bricks with a guttural moan.

Looking down the barrel of the shotgun at the Dogman hulking ten feet away, its fur matted and bloody, Jack exhaled slowly and squeezed off a shot.

The shotgun exploded, filling the air again with that acrid smell of gun smoke that tugged at your nostrils. The bark of the gun had momentarily disoriented him again. When he came around, he first noticed the *sound:* it was a ghastly high mewling sound, like a demonic alien creature straight from Hell. He covered his ears and bowed his head, his chin nearly touching his chest. His ears rang and he squeezed his eyes shut, balled up on the ground like a scared child.

"Jack!" It was Pat who brought him out of this childlike state. "Jack! Look!"

Jack trembled, his hands still covering his ears against that horrific squealing. But he looked up when Pat called to

330 I DAVID C POSTHUMUS

him. His eyes first landed on his brother Brad, lying in a heap at the base of the spruce tree like a sack of potatoes. He wasn't moving, and Jack feared he was dead, just like Russ.

"Jack! It's getting away! Look, damnit!"

The mewling sound was more distant now, less intense. He followed the sound with his eyes. He saw the Dogman scurrying away from them. It was limping, doubled over and clutching at its chest. As it lumbered away from them, it made another sound aside from that wretched squealing: it seemed to be crying or yelping.

Jack knew he hit the beast and did some damage. He stood and felt all the shaky panic and fear leave him. He knew what they had to do now.

He drew the Glock from its holster behind his waistband.

"Come on!" he shouted to Pat, Rick, and Jay, motioning to them with his pistol.

They came together then and surged forward, their collective will and energy pushing them onward toward the completion of their mission. As they closed the distance, they began shooting at the beast, peppering it with rounds and tearing up the ground, shrubs, and trees around it. The wounded Dogman screamed, a high-pitched ear-shattering mewl that made them all cover their ears, wincing at the terrible otherworldly sound. Then they charged it again, pumping it with gunfire and driving it back farther and farther into the darkest, murkiest part of the swamp.

Working together, the four of them uniting like a single organism and concentrating their focus and energy on a single purpose, a single goal, they forced the creature back, beyond where Jack had seen it twenty years ago when they were playing the Game. They kept up their pursuit, firing ceaselessly at the beast with reckless zeal until they forced it to the spot at the very heart of the dark cedar swamp. The spot rumored to be like quicksand where the rowboat had been swallowed whole back in the early 1900s never to be seen again; the location of the meteorite impact hundreds or thousands of years ago.

The Dogman stopped and stood there for a moment on that very spot and glared back at his attackers. The hunter had become the hunted, the predator the prey. Its glowing amber eyes still shone with a ghastly hue and cut into them, but its power over them was weakened, diluted by its wounds and the collective force of the Allen cousins' grim determination.

Then something miraculous happened.

On a day when many dreadful, horrifying, and astonishing things happened, this stood out as perhaps the greatest of all.

The Dogman began to sink into the muck.

As it sank into the black squelchy earth, as if it were being pulled down by some terrible monstrous force into a pool of thick bubbling lava, the Dogman emitted a scream of rage and pain. But there was also something else in that wail.

The creature's scream was one of surprise, perhaps even betrayal.

They all heard it, and it made them shiver and break out in gooseflesh, the hair standing up straight on the backs of their necks and arms. The creature thrashed and flailed, trying to break free and stay above ground. Its grunts and growls of exertion and rage turned again to shrieks of pain and fear. The cousins were relieved when those final yelps of rage and betrayal were drowned out by the squelching suction sound of the black swamp.

And then the Dogman was no more—it was eaten, swallowed whole.

It became a sacrifice to the ancient swamp god of the Northwoods, just like the Allen family's rowboat over a hundred years before. The harsh wind suddenly died, the offensive odor evaporated as quickly as the breeze, and the temperature rose. Jack and the cousins swore they heard a sound then, a gurgling, chuckling, swallowing sound deep in the core of the swamp.

Then there was silence.

CHAPTER 16

Monday, October 2, 2017
LeRoy, Michigan

They took Jay and Brad to the Cadillac Hospital that Sunday night, where they were treated for their injuries. Jay's puncture wound required no more than a few stitches. He was lucky that it wasn't any deeper into his thigh muscle and that no bones were broken. Brad's injuries were more severe, but again, he was extremely lucky, like fucking lottery-winner lucky. His shoulder was dislocated, and there were simple fractures in his left humerus and clavicle, none of which required surgery, and he walked out of the hospital with his left arm and shoulder in a sling.

"What in the hell happened to you boys?" the old doctor, Dr. Kelly, had asked them as she shuffled into their examination room.

Jack, Rick, and Pat explained awkwardly that they had a close encounter with a black bear sow out in the woods. Each of them cut in, filling in the story for the other whenever it got too thin, like kids explaining to their parents why the lamp got broken in the living room. They had the story worked out ahead of time, but the doctor's suspicious gaze made them trip and stumble on their words.

"Yeah, well, the reason the mother bear charged us was because we accidentally stumbled upon two cubs bumbling around near the swamp," Rick explained, his eyebrows raised.

"Yeah," Jack and Pat nodded.

The old doctor looked at them with a cynical expression on her face. "Well, what were you boys doing back in the swamp in the first place?"

Silence.

"Uhhh," Jack stammered.

"We were... uhhh..." Pat fumbled with his words. Although he was as empty as a hole in the ground after losing his brother, he still managed to come through for them. "We were out scouting for good spots for a new tree stand!"

"Yeah!" Rick agreed, a little too enthusiastically.

"Yeah, we're big hunters, you know," Jack nodded.

Dr. Kelly looked down her crinkled nose at them for a moment. "Well, you boys lucked out," she said. They all breathed a silent sigh of relief. "You're lucky all five of you are still alive. Black bear attacks like that usually end up a lot worse."

Then they told her about Russ.

"We've never seen anything like it," Rick said, choking up. He wasn't lying about that, but he was lying about the culprit being a bear. What else could they do? Tell the good doctor that a werewolf cut their brother and cousin in half? Pat had to leave the room as his emotions overpowered him.

They had carried and dragged Russ's remains out of the swamp and up to the tallgrass field, placing them reverently beneath the old cherry tree where they had passed around his pint of Fireball. Understandably, Pat couldn't watch the proceedings or participate. Jack and Rick were the ones who carried Russ in two pieces back to their base camp, sobbing and buckling under the emotion of what had happened to their best friend.

Jack and Rick laid him under the cherry tree and covered him with their jackets. Kneeling down and touching Russ's hair, Jack said a silent prayer, tears streaming down his cheeks. He brushed a deerfly off of Russ's pale, cold face and covered it with the jacket. Then he pulled the pint of Fireball out of Russ's satchel, opened it, and took a deep pull from it. He winced as he swallowed the fiery spirit, then he passed the bottle around again in a moving tribute to their fallen comrade. Each cousin took a drink and mourned for Russ in his own way, which is how he would've wanted it.

Then they called 911. Because it wasn't an emergency, they didn't send an ambulance; instead, they sent Sheriff Dearborn. It took a half-hour for him to get there. Jack went to meet him at the farm to lead him to the scene. He walked back along the trails, over the stone bridge, passing the white pine and the massive maple tree, crossing the threshold between the wilds of the Northwoods and the civilized, ordered human world. He tried to reflect on everything that had transpired that day, but his grief was too sharp, too fresh, too heavy. He knew they had won some victory, no doubt, but at what cost? His cousin, his best friend, was dead. Russ had always been more like a brother to Jack than anything else, and now he was gone forever. Russ had saved his life, no doubt, sacrificing himself to save Jack.

Sheriff Dearborn arrived in his squad car just after two P.M. Jack slid into the passenger seat full of emotion. It was written all over his face. They had their story worked out, and Jack explained to Dearborn what had happened as they crawled along the trails back to the old cherry tree in the center of the tallgrass field. Dearborn listened with a grim

336 DAVID C POSTHUMUS

expression on his face. At first, Jack was worried he wouldn't believe them, but after the Beckett and Thompson killings and all that had happened in the region throughout the year, after that fleeting look of recognition, Jack had seen in Dearborn's eyes that day in his office coupled with Dearborn's clear desire to wrap these kinds of cases up, brush them under the rug, and attribute them to anything natural. After all that Dearborn was more than willing to accept Jack's yarn and move on. It was, after all, the major symptom of the forgetting disease so prevalent among the locals. And besides, would Dearborn even have believed him if he had told him the truth? Jack thought not.

Sheriff Dearborn nodded to each of the Allen cousins when he arrived on the scene. He removed his campaign hat out of respect for the dead and knelt down to examine the body. When his examination was finished, he went to his squad car and popped the trunk, retrieving a black body bag. The thin plastic swished as he unzipped the bag. Hearing that sound, so final, Pat broke down in a shuddering fit, hitching in breaths as tears streamed down his face. Jay put an arm over his shoulder, nodding. Pat reached up and gripped Jay's hand on his shoulder, then he walked away from the somber group to get some air.

Jack helped Sheriff Dearborn load Russ's remains into the body bag, then Dearborn zipped it up.

Jack and Rick wept. Pat stood off in the field a hundred yards away like a lost child, looking blankly up at the sky. Jay leaned against the cherry tree staring at the ground, his face wet with tears. Each taking a side, Jack and Dearborn carried the body bag to the squad car and loaded it into the backseat. Then Dearborn shook all of their hands and said his condolences, his hat off again. A silence filled the air so thick you could reach out and touch it. It was as if the entire Northwoods participated in a spontaneous collective moment of silence to honor the dead. Then Dearborn drove off, ferrying the mortal remains of their cousin and friend Russ to the Patterson Funeral Home in Cadillac.

Jack Allen sat on the old swing chair on the patio at the farm, the very same place, in fact, where his father had sat twenty years ago after they had seen the creature emerge from behind the massive cherry tree while they were out deer hunting at the Big Stump. Like his father before him, Jack caught himself peering down the trail toward the pines, expecting to see a dark blood-thirsty figure stalking toward him with glowing orange eyes like the headlights of a hearse coming to drag him to his grave. He couldn't help himself, even though he knew the terror was over. He could *feel* it in his bones.

Thinking about that old cherry tree brought back a wave of memories and emotions: older memories of his father, of childhood and growing up in the Northwoods; newer painful memories of discovering his father's remains in the deep swamp, of the horrific death of his cousin Russ. Jack shuddered as the emotions welled up inside him. He wiped fresh tears from his eyes with his fingertips.

Jack and Brad decided to leave their father's remains where they lay, a symbol of his enduring bravery, a sentinel left behind to guard against the possible reemergence of the ancient evil that had terrorized Northern Michigan for so many generations.

"That's how he would've wanted it," they had both concluded, nodding as the tears streamed down their faces in glistening streaks. They knew it was the right thing to do.

The familiar crunch of gravel behind him announced that the Camry had pulled into the driveway. Jack was waiting for his wife Claire and daughter Melanie, who were coming home after their short stay with Claire's parents in Rochester Hills. He smiled, his lower lip quivering, as he fought off a powerful urge to weep.

Swallowing the lump in his throat, Jack stood as Claire parked the car in the nook between the apple and pear trees. She got out and unbuckled Melanie, who sang happily in her car seat, "Let's Go Fly a Kite." As soon as Mel's sneakers hit the dirt, she was off and running up the driveway toward Jack, her eyes bright and innocent, arms outstretched, an enormous smile on her sweet face. Jack scooped her up, and they embraced. He spun her around in his arms as he kissed her and buried his face in her hair and neck. She giggled.

"That tickles, Daddy!"

"I love you so much, my sweet, sweet girl."

Then Claire was with them, and they all locked into an epic family hug, cleansing themselves of the horrific events of the past year like a mighty spring flood after a dark winter. Holding Mel with one arm, Jack hugged Claire tightly with the other, kissing her cheeks, mouth, eyes, and hair.

"Jack," Claire cried.

"It's okay now, Babe. Everything's gonna be okay."

They were all crying now except for Mel, who was busy giving Jack a detailed play-by-play of everything she had done at Grandma and Grandpa's house. Jack felt happier than he ever had before.

Although they didn't know it at the time, there was another Allen on the way, a boy, the first to be born in a thousand years free of the dreadful specter of Michigan's Dogman looming over its head like a bloody stain, a dark and deadly storm cloud. Now the storm had passed, the skies were clear, and the future was bright.

They went inside and began the rest of their lives

together with a shared sense of joy, gratitude, and hope for the future.

Monday, October 2, dawned warm and sunny. All the locals at the LeRoy Village Market and Mr. Pibbs talked about how strange that early October blizzard had been the day before. Later that night, the regulars at Travelers and Mineral Springs also marveled at it. But somehow, they all felt better, like some weight had been lifted from their shoulders, like the storm had somehow cleansed the land and cleared space for something new and fresh. They couldn't quite explain it, but then they had always been a people of few words. They were, after all, folks who moved on, put their heads down, forged ahead, and went on with their lives, as they always had been. As they always would be. As they still are to this day.

But 2027 would come eventually. And what would happen then? Jack and the rest of the Allens couldn't help but wonder. All Jack knew is that after they drove the Dogman back into the swamp, back to its lair where it was swallowed whole by the wet black earth, the attacks and disappearances stopped.

At least for that seventh year.

David C. Posthumus began his writing career at age six, when his grandfather read one of his first-grade publications and affectionately labeled him "Ernie (Hemingway) Jr." Posthumus is a voracious reader of many genres, fiction and nonfiction, and an avid horror fan and fiction writer. He has published extensively in the fields of anthropology and Native American studies, including one published book (*All My Relatives: Exploring Lakota Ontology, Belief, and Ritual*, University of Nebraska Press, 2018), one book forthcoming (*Lakota: Culture, History, and Modernities*, University of Oklahoma Press, 2022), as well as several journal articles, book chapters, and reviews. Aside from having the perfect surname for horror, Posthumus loves dogs and the Great Outdoors, and is a musician and lifelong music lover.

If you enjoyed *The Legend of the Dogman,* please consider leaving a review on Amazon or Goodreads. Reviews help out the author and the press.

If you go to www.timberghostpress.com you can sign up for our newsletter so you can stay up-to-date on all our upcoming titles, plus you'll get informed of new horror flash fiction and poetry featured on our site monthly.

Take care and thanks for reading *The Legend of the Dogman* by David C. Posthumus.

-Timber Ghost Press